DATA CAPTURE

What Reviewers Say About
Jesse J. Thoma's Work

Seneca Falls

"Loneliness and survival are the two themes dominating Seneca King's life in Thoma's emotionally raw contemporary lesbian romance. Thoma bluntly and uncompromisingly portrays Seneca's struggles with chronic pain, emotional trauma, and uncertainty."
—*Publishers Weekly*

"This was another extraordinary book that I could not put down. Magnificent!"—*Rainbow Book Reviews*

Pedal to the Metal

Sassy and sexy meet adventurous and slightly nerdy in Thoma's much-anticipated sequel to *The Chase*. Tongue-in-cheek wit keeps the fast-moving action from going off the rails, all balanced by richly nuanced interpersonal relationships and sweet, realistic romance."
—*Publisher's Weekly*

"[*Pedal to the Metal*] has a wonderful cast of characters including the two primary women from the first book in subsidiary roles and some classy good guys versus bad guys action. ...The people, the predicaments, the multi-level layers of both the storyline and the couples populating the Rhode Island landscapes once again had me glued to the pages chapter after chapter. This book works so well on so many levels and is a wonderful complement to the opening book of this series that I truly hope the author will add several additional books to the series. Mystery, action, passion, and family linked together create one amazing reading experience. Scintillating!"
—*Rainbow Book Reviews*

By the Author

The Chase

Seneca Falls

Pedal to the Metal

Data Capture

DATA CAPTURE

by

Jesse J. Thoma

2018

DATA CAPTURE

ISBN 13: 978-1-62639-985-3

This Trade Paperback Original Is Published By
Bold Strokes Books, Inc.
P.O. Box 249
Valley Falls, NY 12185

First Edition: January 2018

Credits
Editors: Victoria Villasenor and Cindy Cresap
Production Design: Susan Ramundo
Cover Design By Sheri (graphicartist2020@hotmail.com)

Acknowledgments

I am grateful to the wonderful team at Bold Strokes who are so supportive of us authors, especially Rad and Sandy, but everyone who touched this manuscript made it better, and I am thankful. I would like to take a few moments to profusely praise my editor, Victoria Villasenor, for her wisdom, patience, knowledge, and skill. No matter the track changes blood bath after a first draft, I know my manuscript will always come out better and stronger for her editing, and I am lucky to have her in my corner.

I am also incredibly grateful to the readers who have contacted me and asked for more adventures from Holt and company. I love these characters and hope you enjoy their next chapter.

Finally, to my wife, thank you for putting up with my weird writing schedule and being more supportive than I have a right to ask. We are writing a pretty great love story.

Dedication

To my whole world, Alexis, Goose, and Bird

CHAPTER ONE

L ola Walker hurdled a log at a full sprint and didn't break stride when she landed on the other side. She slowed her pace when a branch whipped her in the face and made her eyes water. She cursed and wiped away the sting before setting off at a sprint again in pursuit of the man she'd been chasing through the woods for the past twenty minutes. She'd take her city living any day over the bugs, rocks, branches, and arboreal hiding places out here.

The guy she was chasing was a high value bail jumper they'd been chasing from Rhode Island heading west, one of three out here in the woods in bumblefuck Michigan. She'd arrived with Holt, Dubs, and a plan, but as often happened, things went a little sideways. But one of these clowns was connected to the car theft ring they'd taken down a little over a year ago, and she *needed* to catch him. It wasn't Lola's fondest set of memories; between her spectacularly embarrassing public breakup and Dubs getting shot, things could have gone better. *Don't forget you didn't notice the bad guy lurking a few feet away for months at a time.*

She wasn't interested in leaving loose ends from that period in her life, which was why she was careening through the woods now in a Bounty Hunter 5K.

She stumbled as the ground sloped downward steeply under her feet. *Why do people come out here for fun?*

Lola half jogged, half skidded down the hill. She couldn't see the man she was pursuing until she reached the bottom. He hadn't descended with as much grace.

"You in one piece?" Lola asked, looking down at him.

"My neck ain't broke. So I guess that counts," the man said. "Ankle's bad."

He was sprawled on the ground and didn't look like he was going anywhere anytime soon. Lola was worried she was going to have to carry him back to the rendezvous point. She handcuffed him, alerted Holt via her comms unit nestled in her ear that she had her man, and had begun explaining what his life was going to look like for the next few days, when two gunshots cracked loudly in the distance, disturbing her overly nature-filled morning in the woods.

"That better not have been a gunshot," Max said through the comms. She sounded worried.

"Pretty Girl, please. I'm just out for an early morning jog. Doing a little bird watching. I think you heard species Pistolasis," Dubs said. She sounded out of breath, like she was running hard.

"Angry fucking bird," Max said.

Another shot rang out, and Lola scanned the trees to see if she could spot movement, but everything was still around her.

"You had better be hole free when I get to you," Holt said through the comms.

"Oh, hi, boss. Good news, I caught up to my guy. Sort of wishing I'd let you or Lola handle the armed asshat. Having been shot before, I'm very motivated to never repeat the experience," she said. "If I could communicate that to my avian friend here…"

"Where are you?" Lola asked. She slipped a GPS tracker on her capture and sprayed him with tagging nanocrystals, then re-cuffed him to a short branch on the log. Even if he slipped away while she was gone, they would find him again. She looked at the man on the ground. "I'm sending a friend of mine to collect you. It'll be less pleasant for you if he has to chase you a second time. Understand?"

He nodded and settled against the log. Lola didn't know if he would stay put, but she needed to get to Dubs. Moose and Jose were with them in Michigan and were now on cleanup duty. Moose had not appreciated being second team on this capture, but they never sent everyone into the field at once. Too many things could go wrong, especially so far from home. He and Jose were perimeter cover and their backup. They were also the cavalry if they needed them.

Lord help me if I ever need Jose to ride in to save my ass.

"You lost her? Holt, I thought you brought her with you for training?"

"Good morning, Isabelle," Dubs said. "This seems to be live ammunition training. I've always liked pass-fail tests best."

"Good morning, Dubs. Please be careful, honey. This isn't my favorite part of what you all do," Isabelle said.

"Concentrate on where you are and not getting shot," Holt said forcefully. "Lola and I are on our way. Can you find cover? Get to higher ground?"

"I'm in the woods. Just like I have been since we got up here. I'm a reformed thief, not a cartographer. I don't see any caves and I can't run up a tree."

Max came on. "Babe, she's going to need more than that. You're in the Upper Peninsula of Michigan. Woods and water aren't very specific. Help them get to you."

Lola thought Max sounded scared now. That wasn't good. Max never sounded scared, except for the time Dubs actually had gotten shot a year ago. Everyone had been scared then.

"Look, I have no idea where I am. Don't you have me tracked or something? I'm sort of too good to let get away. You should probably microchip me so I can be returned to owner when lost."

Dubs's breathing and tone had a new quality to it. Lola recognized it as the beginnings of panic. Things were going downhill quickly.

"GPS isn't working all that well out there. I don't have a good location on you. I didn't expect you to wander off on me," Max said.

"No fancy Dubs retrieval app that just sucks her right back to you when you miss her?" Lola asked. She needed them to start thinking about something other than Dubs getting shot. She kept moving in the direction she hoped the gunshots had come from, but she was running blind.

"I haven't finished it yet," Max said. "And Isabelle won't let me redirect a satellite to look for her."

"I think the U.S. military would notice."

"They'd never know it was me," Max said. "I'd come save your ass myself, but I'm stuck here in Rhode Island behind my computer. And now no one is even letting me use that to help."

"Well, now I'm picturing you in all your Batman baddassery and I've almost run into a tree. And Isabelle's right; they would totally know it was you. Who else would be scouring the woods looking for a barely reformed ex-con?" Dubs asked. "Besides, I don't think they allow conjugal visits in whatever black site they would dump you in and it would take me a couple of weeks to spring you."

"Fine. I could've used a Russian one."

"Jesus, World War III over Dubs," Holt said. "Any markers you can give me yet, Dubs?"

Lola could hear the evidence of Holt's sprint to get to Dubs. It sounded through the comms like she was running through cellophane. Given that Lola was dodging rocks, flinging branches out of her way, and crashing through bushes, all at a full sprint, she could picture Holt doing the same. She just hoped she was running in the right direction. She'd judged the gunshots as coming from her left and set off in that direction, but Dubs and her skip were also running, so they could be anywhere.

"Excuse me," Dubs said. "I'm totally worth it. The Russians would start it themselves if they'd had the pleasure. But I'm not sure even I could get you out of the gulag, Pretty Girl. And there's just trees and more trees, boss."

"Your ego does know some bounds. Amazing," Max said softly. "No prisons for me. No bullets for you."

"Deal," Dubs said. "Some good news, though. No gunshots for these last few acres, and I don't see my new friend right up my ass, which means I'm much harder to shoot. That and I wore waterproof mascara. I wasn't expecting a marathon, but I came prepared. See, H, I'm paying attention to those things you've been teaching me."

"When have you been giving Dubs makeup advice, boss?" Lola asked.

"I don't remember that lesson," Holt said. "If he's not right behind you, this is the time to hide. Find a bush, or a big tree, a little dip in the ground you can curl up in, anywhere you can disappear from view. If you aren't moving, you're easier for us to find."

"GPS is back online for two of you," Max said. "I've got Lola and Dubs. Lola, you're close. Can you pick up the pace? You're heading right for her."

Lola's quads and lungs burned, but she pushed harder. No way was Dubs dying out here in the woods today.

"Maybe I should duck behind a tree and confront this guy. We could get what we came for. We do need this capture, right?"

"No!" Lola and everyone else on the comms said.

"Sorry, I'm not you, Pretty Girl. Or you other two superhumans, who can run, and jump, and punch to the end of time, and I gotta tell you, I don't see a single thing I can hide behind without looking like a bad cartoon character. I gotta work with the formidable skills I got. Besides, you all remember what Dubs stands for, right? Wonder Woman? I'm bulletproof. Don't take too long, Lola. I'll be waiting."

"Dubs, what the fuck are you doing? You are *not* bulletproof. Neither was Wonder Woman, you idiot, that's Supergirl. Don't use inaccurate comic book references as justification to get your ass shot again," Holt said.

Lola wondered if Dubs screwed up the comic book reference just to get a rise out of Holt. Dubs did that sometimes when she was scared.

"How about you don't get shot again?" Max suggested.

"I'm not going to die on you, Pretty Girl," Dubs said, her breathing slowing. "Holt, Lola, I can see my guy about fifty feet behind me. He's headed my way with his gun on me, but he's not shooting."

"Max, what's my updated position now that Dubs is stationary?" Lola asked.

She'd been running at maximum velocity for a long time and she was tiring. Her words came out haltingly.

"It looks like you're about quarter mile from her. Still headed directly for her," Max said.

"I'll be there in ninety seconds, Dubs. Don't die on me before—"

Lola stopped as the ground in front of her disappeared. The drop-off was less than ten feet, but a stream gurgled along below. She couldn't tell how deep it was and didn't want to slow down to find safe passage across it. Several branches from a large tree hung out over the stream and were low enough for her to reach.

She said a little prayer, backed up a good distance, and charged at the drop-off. Without breaking stride, she leapt for the farthest branch she thought she could reach comfortably and get a grip on when she landed. Her momentum almost carried her too far, but she released from the branch and landed with an unpleasant thud on the other bank. *Why wasn't anyone around to see that?*

She took off again toward Dubs. "H, where are you?" Lola asked. "I'm almost to her."

"I'll meet you there," Holt said.

"How was your night, boys? Sleep well?" Dubs asked.

Dubs's voice in her ear broke through Lola's single-minded focus. She sounded for all the world like she was back at the office with her feet up, shooting the shit.

"Seem to recall you were the one wrapped in Holt's arms this morning when I woke up," Moose replied casually.

Lola had wondered about the scene they'd walked in on that morning, but wasn't stupid enough to comment on it at the time.

"Excuse me now?" Max said.

Lola was glad Max didn't sound scared anymore. If she wasn't scared, she was focused. Lola thought she heard Isabelle chuckling. Isabelle didn't usually listen in during their captures, which meant she was scared too.

Another voice joined the conversation, but not through her earpiece. He was asking Dubs if she was alone. She realized it must be the man who had been chasing her. If he was close enough for her to hear him talking to her, he was too close to miss if he decided to start shooting. She pushed her body harder.

"Just me. And you. *Only* me and you," Dubs said.

"I was dreaming about Isabelle," Holt finally chimed in. She was practically growling, though it was obvious she was breathing hard from running to get to Dubs.

"You Holt Lasher?" the man asked. "Was Holt with you when you chased me and my boys out of camp this morning?"

"Never heard of him," Dubs said. "And I didn't chase you out of anywhere, big guy. I was out for a walk and you started chasing me."

"He's a she. And I need to talk to her. Are you her?"

"Do I look like someone that would walk around with the moniker Holt? Do you think that suits? Whoever this chick is, she'd be damn lucky to look like me, but the name doesn't fit."

"How am I supposed to know what Holt Lasher looks like?" the man asked.

"You're the one looking for her," Dubs said.

"Based on the naked pictures you sent earlier, you look nothing like Holt," Isabelle said.

Lola held back a laugh. Maybe she shouldn't rush getting to Dubs. Holt was going to kill her when she got there anyway, if Dubs was sending sexts to Isabelle.

"You snuck off earlier so you could send Isabelle naked pictures?" Holt asked.

The man was speaking again. "I was hired to deliver my message and be on my way. If she was with you in the camp, I'd have delivered it right then. But now, you're unfortunately in the way. Too bad, cause you're kinda hot."

"Dubs, stall this guy. If he's got a message for me, I want to talk to him."

"Whoa, whoa, whoa. Let's slow this down, boss. Don't want anyone getting hurt. I was out for a walk, stumbled into your camp, you got all skittery and started shooting at me. I'm not an idiot. I ran. But now that we're chatting, who is Holt Lasher? What's the message? And why did you think you'd just happen to run into her out here?"

"None of your damn business."

"None of my business? That's insulting. I was enjoying a beautiful morning in the woods. Then you pulled your tiny little pistol outta your pants and started waving it around. That's really not my thing."

Lola could picture Dubs's face and her "not impressed" expression. She hoped this guy didn't shoot her for insulting his dick.

"Fucking bitch."

"Hey, buddy, I'm talking about your gun. Little sensitive? Whatever you got going on, that's not my thing either."

"I've got no problems."

"Of course not. Why don't we keep everything all tucked in though, since there's nothing for you to measure against anyway? Except your little pistol. I'd hate for you to shoot your dick off just to prove something to me. But there's really no need to point it at me, either."

"Dubs," Max said, her voice holding a clear warning. "Stop baiting him into killing you."

"We're becoming friends. I can tell. But I'm feeling a little exposed. Naked, even. How about partially naked, given that you've got your little pistol, but all I'm packin' is my smile," Dubs said.

"Jesus, Dubs, you sent them to me," Max said. "I asked Isabelle to check my phone because I was busy with something."

"You've got a weird way of making friends," the man said.

"See, like I said, friends. So maybe we can keep all your equipment put away for now, since I'm clearly not the person you were looking for. Good boy. Isn't it better without the gun waggling around in my face? You aren't the first person to insult my social skills, but I'm not holding it against you. I'm also not going to hold it against you that you just threatened to kill me. I don't think you meant it. We're friends now, remember? You even told me about your pistol problems."

"Do you ever stop talking?" the man asked.

"No," Dubs said as Max, Isabelle, Holt, Jose, and Moose answered simultaneously over the comms.

"You've piqued my curiosity. Why do you want to talk to Holt Lasher?"

"That's between me and her," he said. "Sorry, but I'm done talking to you, and I think you were one of the ones who stormed my camp. Morning stroll, my ass. If I kill you, maybe Holt will get my message after all."

"Oh, fuck it. I'm done playing nicely with you," Dubs said.

Lola figured that was her cue to get her ass to Dubs because she was about to do something stupid. Good thing she was about thirty seconds away.

"Here's the thing, Mason. I'm a bond enforcement agent and I work for Holt. You're right. I targeted your camp. So if you want to talk to her, it's my business. I also take it really fucking personal when someone shoots at me, and I happen to know that Holt's on her way here. So is my good friend Lola, who is built like the expansion pack of Holt. But I'm reasonable, so I'll give you a choice. I can tell her that you're already disarmed and of no threat to me since you didn't actually shoot me, or I can leave out that bit of information since you tried and you can get your ass kicked. It's up to you. I really, really enjoy the shit-storm when someone threatens one of Holt's pack, but you probably won't."

"Fuck you," Mason said.

"I was really hoping you'd say that," Dubs said.

Lola saw Dubs and Mason about twenty feet ahead of her in a small clearing. Mason had his gun six inches from Dubs's chest. Lola's vision tunneled in on the gun trained on someone she loved. She felt fury blossom from her chest and spark through every pore.

A branch cracked loudly when Lola stepped on it, and for a second, she thought Mason had fired. Dubs must have thought the same thing because she looked down at her chest and raised her hand, maybe looking for a wound or steadying a runaway heartbeat.

Lola crossed the distance to Mason in six strides. As she approached, he swung the gun toward her. She could see he was preparing to fire, but she didn't care. She was just relieved to have the muzzle safely away from Dubs.

She lunged for his arm and flung it skyward, sending his shot blasting into the treetops behind them, showering the ground with leafy confetti. She hadn't gotten a good grip on his arm when she deflected the shot, and he scampered away. She was sure he thought it was a safe distance to regroup and take aim. He clearly didn't expect her to keep coming at him. As Holt always said, possessing a firearm gave a false sense of security and invincibility.

Mason backpedaled away from Lola at a good pace, but wasn't looking where he was going. He smacked into a tree and dropped to one knee. When he stood again, he seemed to remember he had the gun and raised it. Lola saw his hands were shaking, though, making the gun wobble wildly. She kept moving forward, although more cautiously than she had been.

When it looked like Mason was about to fire again, she prepared her charge. She went for his gun hand again. As she slammed into his arm, again forcing his shot wild, Holt flew out of the shrubs nearby and executed a near perfect tackle. She drove her shoulders into his chest. They flew through the air and landed four feet away, Holt on top. The gun flew from his hand on impact and slid a few feet away and lay harmlessly in the dirt.

"Dude, I've been on the bottom of that pile. It's not fun. I did try to warn you," Dubs said.

She pulled a pair of handcuffs from Lola's back pocket and handed them to Holt, who was explaining Mason's rights and next steps. She had her knee planted firmly in his back.

Holt looked down at Mason. "I hear you want to talk to me? Who hired you? How did you know I'd be coming after you?"

"Get off me," Mason said.

Holt let up the pressure on his back and pulled him into a sitting position.

"Talk."

"I never show up for court. When I teamed up with the other two, everyone knew I'd get you on my ass. We all got the same message. Whoever got to you first got to deliver. It's from Kevin Garvey."

Lola heard a gasp through the comms.

"Never heard of him," Holt said.

Holt didn't react. Lola didn't know if she was being "work Holt" or if she had turned off her earpiece. Lola was pretty sure the gasp was Isabelle and Holt never ignored Isabelle. She glanced at Dubs, who was staring at Holt speculatively.

"Uh, boss," Lola said.

Holt continued to stay focused on Mason. "Not now."

"Turn on your comm, boss," Dubs said.

Clearly, Dubs had heard it too. Lola hadn't thought Holt would have her comms off. Maybe her earpiece had gotten turned off or fallen out when she tackled Mason.

Holt flicked at her ear and activated her earpiece.

"He knows you," Mason said. "And he wants to talk. He's offering a lot of money to anyone who gets a message to you. If you don't talk to him, he said he's going to pay a visit to his relatives, starting with his daughters. Then he'll move on to his grandkids." He shrugged. "That's it. He said you'd find a way to get in touch."

"And why would I care ab—"

"Holt, baby. Kevin Garvey. That's my father," Isabelle said. "My father's threatening our family."

Falling in love with Isabelle had mellowed Holt, cooled her temper, but Lola knew it was always lurking. The Hulk was angry now.

Holt nodded toward Dubs and pointed to Mason before she walked a short distance away. She looked like she was laser focused on a tree in front of her, but Lola knew her attention was back in Providence, with her family. She was radiating so much energy, Lola was surprised a few trees hadn't come down around her. Dodging gunshots from Mason hadn't provided the same adrenaline rush of watching Holt's eruption of rage. It was like standing next to pure kinetic energy knowing you were about to get hit with the wave from the explosion. It would knock you on your ass, but it also meant something powerful had just happened. She wanted to be along for the ride.

"Isabelle, get George and go home. Call Ellen and have her and her family meet you at our house. Max, get Tuna and whoever else isn't working a high priority case. Secure my house. There's a nest of baby bunnies in the side yard. They don't twitch a whisker without you knowing, understood?"

"Seems like overkill, love," Isabelle said. "He wants to talk to you, right? I'm sure we'll be fine until you get back. He's a jerk, but I don't think he'd really hurt us." Isabelle didn't sound all that confident.

"He raised his hand to you. He's already hurt you, and he's offered money to these assholes in order to get a message to us. That's all I need to know. Humor me," Holt said. She sounded a little desperate. "I'm twelve hundred miles away."

"Okay," Isabelle said. "Anything you need. But I'm not the scared teenager I was back then. He wouldn't be able to knock me around anymore. And he would never lay a hand on George. All the same, get home soon."

"Max, get us a route out of these woods. Jose, Moose, meet at the rally point. You'll be taking possession of Mason, my guy back at their campsite, and Lola's skip. Dubs, we're going to need a way home. Think you can handle that?"

"Jesus, boss, I love it when you talk dirty to me."

Lola moved closer to Holt. She'd learned everything she knew from Holt, they were as close as family, and right now it looked like she could use a friend. Holt looked less angry than frantic. Not being able to get to Isabelle was probably eating her up. Lola understood. They were both women of action who didn't sit well in the quiet times, but when those busy times put loved ones in danger, the quiet started to look damn good. Whatever menace was coming at them now, she'd stand with Holt, and Heaven help anyone who threatened Holt's pack.

CHAPTER TWO

I swear, H, if you don't get your ass back across the street, we're not going anywhere."

"Dubs, just get me a fucking ride and point it toward Providence," Holt said. She was trying to keep her temper under wraps, but Isabelle was in trouble and she was too far away. Whatever bullshit Dubs was playing at, Holt wasn't in the mood.

"I will. As soon as you move back across the street."

So far, Lola hadn't said a word; she'd just stood watching Holt and Dubs spar. Now she came over and spoke quietly to Holt. "Whatever you're about to threaten her with, you might want to reconsider. I know you're scared. But even you haven't been hit in the head too many times to see she's trying to protect you."

Holt considered. Most of her crew had worked with her for so long they were like a second skin. Anyone new she trained in a very specific way. Dubs had been a wildcard from the moment she walked onto the scene, and she was nowhere near trained yet.

"Will you get me the damn car if I threaten to fire you?" Holt asked.

"Not where you're currently standing," Dubs said.

"Threaten to fire Max?"

"She'd understand."

"You're protecting me?" Holt glanced at Lola and saw her grin.

"Finally, the truth trickled through that thick head of yours," Dubs said. "Kindly move your ass out of sight of these cameras and we can be on our way."

"Lola gets to stay for the fun?" Holt said, grumbling as she moved across the street. Dubs still surprised her, which was nice and a little unnerving.

"I'd only be in the way," Lola said. "I'm coming with you."

Stealing a car wasn't Holt's first choice, but they were in the middle of nowhere. It was after dark and long past closing time for anywhere that could've rented or sold them a car. This was the only dealership within a reasonable distance, and according to the handwritten sign taped to the window, the owner was out of town for a long weekend. Moose and Jose were driving to Detroit to process their prisoners, not quite trusting the size of the local police force here with such high value captures. So she was having Dubs commandeer them a ride.

They only had to wait a couple of minutes before Dubs pulled up next to them in a flashy sports car and pushed open the passenger door. Lola glared at Dubs before cramming herself into the backseat of the slick two-door coupe. Holt felt bad for Lola. She was over six feet tall, and it didn't look like a comfortable ride in the back, but Holt wasn't about to trade. She wasn't much shorter. Being the boss had some perks. The only one who could comfortably fit was Dubs, and Holt knew prying her out of the driver's seat right now would take an act of God.

"Subtle car."

"It is. There was a Jaguar F-type back there. Do you know how hard it was for me to leave that beauty behind? But this car will blend in. Besides, I thought you wanted to get home fast. This is fast. Now, a few rules. I drive, obviously. I control the radio. Lola has the worst taste in music so she doesn't even get veto power. Isabelle's gonna need you in tip-top shape, so take a nap or something. You two should also probably do something about those cuts on your arms and face. Did you even look where you were running out there? If the Queen asks, Moose and Jose were in charge of keeping you looking pretty. I had nothing to do with it."

Holt stifled a laugh. The thought of Isabelle hearing Dubs refer to her as "the Queen" was too much. She was *her* queen, but she didn't know if Isabelle would appreciate the rest of the crew giving her a royal title. "Does Isabelle know you call her that?"

"Does it matter? It's what she is, right?"

Holt couldn't argue. She'd had this conversation with Isabelle. If her crew was forced to choose sides, she wasn't sure she would have anyone standing in her corner anymore. It was something she was thankful for. It meant everyone who worked for her, her extended family, watched over Isabelle and their son, George, as if they were flesh and blood.

"Does that make me the king?" Holt asked.

"Nah," Dubs said.

"Why not? I'm the boss, right? Isn't the king the boss?" Holt asked. She thought she understood patriarchy.

"You're so adorable, H," Dubs said.

Dubs hit the highway onramp and accelerated rapidly. They were flying toward home. Holt felt calmer than she had since she'd confronted Mason and learned there was a threat to Isabelle.

"Aren't you going to do anything to defend me?" Holt asked Lola. She could use a little backup.

"That last pothole shoved my kneecap into my eardrum," Lola said. "I've got bigger problems than explaining to you exactly how fast your crew would drop your ass at one word from your lady."

Holt nodded. Just as she suspected.

"And turn her down a crank or two," Lola said. "Pretzel's not a shape I can pull off."

Holt looked at Dubs. She was always vibrating with energy, but it was pouring off her now. She remembered Max telling her how keyed up Dubs got after stealing cars back when they were working on their first case together, busting a massive car theft ring.

"You drive for now," Holt said. "Put whatever you want on the radio. I'm going to check in with Max." She keyed her earpiece and waited for Max to pick up. Before she did, Dubs paired her phone with the car stereo, and bass heavy pop music came through the speakers at such a volume that Holt felt her heartbeat synchronize to the bass line.

"That you, boss?" Max said in her ear.

Holt switched off the radio. Dubs protested loudly. "Yeah. We're headed back. Half of Michigan is charting our progress via sonic boom."

"Look," Max said. "She doesn't get to steal cars anymore, but the high she gets from it hasn't gone away. Unless you're going to have sex with her—"

"I'm not."

"Damn right," Max said possessively, "you gotta let her burn it off with music or she'll be breaking the sound barrier for real. It's not louder than the gym. Everyone's tucked in here. Isabelle and George are asleep. Everyone's safe, H. I got you."

"Thanks, Max. CB, thirty."

Dubs looked at Holt when she hung up. "Can I turn my music back on? And is everyone all right?"

"I thought you drove extra carefully right after you stole a car," Holt said, leaning her head back and closing her eyes. "Right now you're twenty miles over the speed limit."

"And your music is terrible and loud enough to be heard from space," Lola said.

"Please, I know you love crappy pop music, so don't start. And we need to get home. It's worth the risk. This car won't be reported for a couple of days, if it gets reported at all. And I'm riding with Holt Lasher, Captain America, Superman, Captain Marvel, you know, disgusting levels of upstanding goodness. I'm safe. If we get pulled over, just show your decoder ring, or flex, or something."

"And yet you wouldn't let me be seen on camera stealing a car."

"Well, I served my time. I'm mostly reformed. I'm practically a good guy now," Dubs said.

"It's the 'practically' that makes me nervous," Holt said. She didn't seem particularly nervous at all.

"You going to yap through my adrenaline rush and kill this for me, or let me wind down, H? I barely get this kind of rush anymore since you forced me into retirement."

Holt shook her head and laughed. She didn't quite remember forcing Dubs to give up stealing cars, but she wasn't going to argue right now. She leaned over and turned the music back on.

Twenty-seven minutes later, Holt woke from her doze when the music went silent.

"Max will be calling, boss," Dubs said as way of explanation.

"Come down from your high?"

"Can think of some better ways," Dubs said. "But yes."

"Max gave me a heads-up about that," Holt said. "And a pretty clear hands-off message."

"Like she has any reason to worry," Dubs said, looking incredulous.

"Don't think you could handle me?" Holt nodded knowingly.

"Excuse me?" Dubs said, choking a little as she did.

Holt heard Lola groan in the backseat. She could almost feel the eye roll.

"How was this the best option for me to get home?" Lola asked.

"Oh, I could handle you, boss. You don't scare me," Dubs said. She'd clearly found her footing again.

"You know who scares me? Isabelle. Pretty sure neither one of us could handle her if she went super-jealous-crazy."

"Truth. Although I'm not sure I want to be on the receiving end of angry Max, either."

The phone rang exactly thirty minutes after Holt had disconnected with Max. She answered and put the call on speaker.

"Boss, we've got a problem."

"Is my family okay?" Panic knotted Holt's stomach. She pictured Isabelle and George injured or worse and could barely resist the overwhelming urge to fling Dubs from the driver's seat and take over herself.

"Yes. Shit, sorry, H. Not that kind of problem. Everyone is safe."

"Jesus. Lead with that next time. Continue." Holt knew her voice was a little shaky, but she was so relieved, she didn't care.

"Right. So, the problem is in your email."

"Do I even want to know what you're doing in my email?" Holt asked. It felt like she was asking why Max had been pawing through her underwear drawer.

"My job."

"Of course." Holt wasn't sure how Max scrolling through her email was at all part of her job description, but she let her continue.

"You know she could read the president's email if she wanted to, right?" Dubs said. "It's better to just give her the passwords to everything, then there's no challenge and she gets bored and moves on."

"Please, who says the president's emails are challenging or not boring?"

"Max, my email?" Holt said. She tried to refocus the conversation. She really hoped Max was kidding and hadn't been hacking government emails.

"Not boring at all. Well, not the one demanding one hundred thousand dollars in exchange for Isabelle's father and containing a proof of life video."

"Hold up," Lola said. "This is the same guy who supposedly paid that clown in the woods to get in touch with Holt so they could go to hot yoga and grab a coffee? Now someone kidnapped him and wants us to pay them for the pleasure of his safe return?"

"If we take everything at face value, then yes, apparently," Max said.

"And if I don't pay?" Holt asked. She didn't like being this popular, didn't like the timing of the two events, and really didn't like that Isabelle's father had popped back into her life.

"Then your new pen pal starts corresponding with Isabelle and is less polite. If she doesn't want to talk, then Ellen is next."

"Is there a timeframe?" Holt asked.

"If there is, they declined to share," Max said. "That's weird, right?"

"Yes," Lola said. "Very. Describe the video."

"There's a guy who says he's Kevin Garvey tied to a chair. It looks like he's in a warehouse or abandoned building of some sort. Commercial, not residential. He's holding a newspaper with today's date on it."

"What's his condition?" Lola asked.

"Unkempt and tired, but more or less unharmed. I can't quite figure the timing of when he would have been snatched."

"Can't have been long since he hired Mason and the others to get a message to Holt," Dubs said.

"Fuck." Holt needed time to think, but right now her judgment was clouded by anger. She prided herself on remaining calm under almost any circumstance, but when it came to Isabelle, and now her son, emotions clouded her thinking in ways they never had. She and Isabelle had been together long enough that she knew to let the feelings crest. Her clear thinking would return enough for her to protect those that meant the most to her quickly if she just let herself feel the anger and fear so she could move beyond it.

"How much does this guy mean to Isabelle?" Dubs asked.

"I'm here," Isabelle said, joining the call. "Max filled me in on this new wrinkle. To answer your question, Dubs, he doesn't mean a damn thing to me. I haven't had any contact with him in years. He doesn't know anything about my life, or I didn't think he did. Ellen never told him he had grandkids, and neither did I. He's not a nice man and was never a father to me."

"I wouldn't have put it so nicely," Holt said. "Whatever decision we make will be for Isabelle and our family's safety, not her father's."

Holt thought about the man who had beaten Isabelle, breaking bones and terrorizing her as a child. She didn't care where he was or what his kidnappers were doing to him. In fact, part of her hoped he was suffering. But whoever had sent the email had threatened her family. Just as Mason's original message had. That had to be taken seriously, whatever quarter it was coming from. She could see multiple paths available to her, but this wasn't the time or place to make a final decision. She had a team she trusted and relied on. She needed them now.

"We'll be back as soon as we can. The minute we walk in the door, I want a full team meeting. Max, bring everyone to the office with you. You know Isabelle doesn't allow business in the house. Babe, if you're fine with George still going to daycare and then Amy's, that's fine with me, but someone stays with them all day. Before I get there, find who sent that email and find her father. We need to end this quickly."

"On it, boss." Max disconnected.

"All right, Dubs. Get us home. Sounds like our ladies need us and we have work to do. You said you grabbed us a fast car. Put it to good use."

Holt looked to the backseat and held Lola's gaze. Lola looked the way Holt felt, determined, angry, impatient, but calm. They had hours of driving ahead of them. There was no point burning out emotionally before they got back. She nodded to her and closed her eyes. She was tired after the chase earlier and the adrenaline spikes from rescuing Dubs. Isabelle was safe at the moment, and right now the best thing she could do to help her was show up at home ready to get to work. Sleep claimed her quickly.

CHAPTER THREE

D r. Quinn Golden looked up from her computer for the first time in hours and wondered if she'd be able to get herself to the door when she needed to get to class. She'd completely surrounded herself with unsteady stacks, perilous piles, and one leaning tower of articles. She'd effectively hemmed herself in by her night's work, and looking back at her computer, she wasn't sure what she had to show for it. Somehow this grant wasn't coming together and it was frustrating her no end. She'd been working on it for weeks. She'd helped on other grants before, but that was when she was in grad school, and they weren't *her* grants.

Most postdocs didn't write their own grants until their second year, but she wasn't most postdocs. She'd always done things on her own schedule. So here she was, barely out of graduate school, trying to write a grant she had no enthusiasm for. She thought about the research she'd spent all night reading. It was the same kind of research she did, and that might be the problem. She reread the program announcement she was answering with this grant application.

Nothing about this feels exciting. Research accomplishments and advancements don't mean anything if I'm starting out my career building my own scientific straightjacket.

She'd made significant breakthroughs using data from first her undergraduate, graduate, and now postdoc mentors in ways they hadn't, but now she wasn't sure she was all that interested in the field of study where she had the most name recognition. But science was concerned with the past, for all the talk of forward thinking and hopes for innovation and discovery. Money only went to those with a track record in a field. If she wanted to make a change, it was going to take a lot of convincing that she was worth the risk. And she would have to know what she wanted to do if it wasn't her current research program. *No wonder I haven't gotten anything done.* She rubbed her face and ran her hands through her hair. She needed to get a haircut; it had grown out and was becoming a little too "crazy scientist." She didn't need to give her colleagues one more reason to talk about her behind her back. Competition was fierce among the postdocs, and although some had made friends, she wasn't part of the in crowd. She knew it was due to the successes she'd had, but the last few months had been exhausting, trying to prove that she was a good person, as well as a good scientist, and worthy of their friendship. It was tiresome and lonely.

"You okay, Dr. Golden?" Jessica, the department secretary, and a very good friend, poked her head into Quinn's office.

"I'm fine, Jessica. Wait…what time is it? And I told you, call me Quinn, even at work." It didn't matter how many times she reminded her, when they were at work, Jessica referred to her formally.

"It's seven fifteen. You aren't late for class yet. There's coffee in the lounge."

Quinn could've kissed her. Jessica was always the first staff member in the building and had caught her sleeping in her office more than once. She seemed to go out of her way to keep Quinn caffeinated, which she appreciated.

"Write any papers last night? Finish that grant? Upload a new TED talk I won't understand? If you're going to sleep here every night working, tell me you're being productive."

"Don't play that 'simple-minded secretary' thing with me. It might work with some of the others around here, but I'm not buying it for a minute. We're friends, remember? And I don't sleep here every night." Quinn's argument didn't hold much fire. She barely remembered she had an apartment.

"Of course we're friends. That's why there's always coffee going when you remember you don't actually live here. And why when you realize you're better than this place, you'll also realize you need a good secretary and your best buddy to come with you. I'm the only one not trying to get something from you, or kill you in your sleep."

Quinn laughed. "I thought you said you didn't want anything from me? Besides, I could end up anywhere in the world. Why would you follow me?"

"I like you. There are worse people to work for, and I want out of here."

Suddenly, Quinn entertained the idea that Jessica was flirting with her. They had a good friendship, but that didn't mean Jessica couldn't want more. Quinn was so bad at picking up on the cues that she had no idea if she was reading the situation correctly. She was good at her job and that was about it. There was a reason her longest relationship was with her student loan servicer.

Jessica didn't seem to have nearly as much trouble at reading her.

"Whoa, Dr. Golden. Should I be insulted that the idea of my flirting with you is causing you that much panic, or flattered that I could cause that much turmoil? I'm not looking for anything from you but what I said. No ulterior motives. If you do spring me from this place, that means there's a whole new dating pool of ladies just waiting for me. Besides, I'm a bit out of my league with you."

"I'm sorry," Quinn said. "It's already been an eventful morning and I haven't even been to class yet. But don't sell yourself short. I might not be the woman for you, but I somehow doubt there's a league you couldn't play in." Quinn envied her. She was always so sure of herself. "Still not looking for the love of your life?"

"Did you not just hear me?" Jessica asked. "Whole new city full of women to get to know? I plan on finding out how many of them can be the love of my night."

"Romantic," Quinn said. She wasn't judging her, just amazed at her confidence and ability to understand what she wanted. She had that with her work, mostly, but was a little more hopeless in her personal life. She'd dated, but hadn't found anyone that kept her attention long enough to distract her from whatever research she was doing at the time.

"I've never gotten any complaints," Jessica said. "I'm not even going to ask you, since you and that couch in your office seem to have exclusive dating privileges. You should let me take you out sometime, help you meet someone."

"Don't look like I could manage on my own?" Quinn asked, amused.

"No offense," Jessica said. She had the decency to look a little sheepish.

"None taken. If your fantasy escape plan ever comes true, I'll take you up on it. Deal?" They'd had this conversation before.

"Sure thing," Jessica said. "Your coffee will have to be to-go now. Don't want to keep the hooligans waiting."

"We were hooligans just a few years ago," Quinn said. The undergraduates she taught were challenging, but she enjoyed her time with them.

"You have a year and a half on me and can round up to thirty. You're ancient."

"Oh, is that how it works? I seem to recall a rather important birthday coming up in a few weeks. Important rounding implications. I'll be sure to let the chair know it needs to be widely celebrated."

Jessica's eyes got large. "You wouldn't."

"I might."

"But your coffee."

"Shit, you're right. I would do just about anything for coffee."

"Perfect, I have you right where I want you." Jessica raised her arms triumphantly.

Quinn looked at Jessica skeptically.

"Still not flirting," Jessica said, holding up her hands defensively. "Just perfecting my skills for our big move and all the ladies waiting for me."

"The only place I'm moving at the moment," Quinn said, "is to class."

Jessica hustled to the coffee machine and came back with a to-go mug and followed her out the door. "Have a good class, Dr. Golden."

"My name's Quinn." She hurried out the door. She knew half her class would roll in late, but she always arrived on time and prepared. Teaching didn't come easily to her, but she took it seriously. Research was her true love, but she'd fallen in love in a classroom because of a teacher who had clearly loved science. Every day she reminded herself that all she had to do was stand up there and explain to the hooligans, as Jessica called them, the many virtues of science. It practically sold itself.

Yeah, right, simple as that. Must be why you're so damn nervous for every class.

CHAPTER FOUR

L ola had sat in hundreds of briefings, staff meetings, and planning sessions, but she never tired of them. The work they did was, at times, solo, relying on individual instincts, skill, and ability, but they were a team. She liked that and the comfort that came from Holt's steady leadership. *I wonder what kind of leader I'd be if I had a team under me?*

"Anytime you're ready, Max," Holt said.

Holt sounded annoyed.

"Uh, right. Just a sec, boss. Dubs, move over."

Lola knew Dubs and Max had missed each other, but Dubs was in Max's lap, which wasn't standard for these meetings. Only Isabelle was allowed to sit on any lap she chose.

"Lola," Holt said. She inclined her head toward the couple.

Lola stood and scooped Dubs off Max's lap, one arm under each of Dubs's arms. She dumped her in the empty chair next to Max and returned to her own seat. She tried to hide her amusement at Dubs's surprised flailing and outraged expression.

"What the hell?" Dubs asked. "Isabelle's on your lap, H."

"What's your point?" Holt's voice was much too calm.

"Long car ride, you two?" Isabelle asked sweetly, effectively and abruptly defusing the tension threatening to envelop the meeting.

"She has terrible taste in music," Holt said, almost smiling.

"And she's a damn control freak," Dubs shot back.

"And I was held hostage by this crap the entire trip back from Michigan. In the backseat of a toy car. Everyone's got a beef."

"Anyone want to hear about missing persons and blackmail now that we're done with the pity party?" Max asked.

"Yes, please, Max, let's hear what you've got. You know how much I enjoy hearing about people threatening me," Isabelle said.

"No one is going to get near you," Holt said, wrapping her arms tighter around Isabelle's waist.

Lola loved the way they loved each other. She'd known Holt most of her life and had never seen her happier. Isabelle had provided something for Holt that Lola desperately wanted—stability, support, unconditional love, acceptance, and peace. She was thankful every day that they'd agreed to adopt George and that they were both part of her life. She couldn't have given him a quarter of the life he had now.

Since her last girlfriend, Tiffany, had left her in a spectacularly humiliating way, she'd finally realized what lousy instincts she had with women. She was pretty sure Holt and most of the people in her life had been trying to tell her that subtly over the years, but she hadn't been interested in their opinions. Falling so incredibly short in that department was enough for her to finally get it through her head. She had terrible taste and instincts. She was done with women.

If only her uncertainty in that aspect of her life hadn't started to bleed over into her professional life as well. The entire episode with Tiffany had rocked her confidence, not just personally. With Holt's family in danger it was a bad time to be getting a case of the yips. *I just need something to get me back on track. Prove to everyone I can handle my business.*

Lola turned her attention back to the task at hand. Moose and Jose were still making their way back from Michigan, and Holt's cousin Danny was working his real job as a Providence cop. The rest of the crew was out and about hunting down leads and bringing in bad guys who had declined their invitations to court. Max started the briefing for the small group that was there.

"Everyone up to speed on the extortion money demand in Holt's email?"

Everyone nodded.

"At a later date, we need to have a talk about you and your access to my email account," Holt said to Max.

Lola shuddered to think of the access Max had to any of their electronic lives if she was so inclined. She had nothing to hide, but she didn't like the idea of someone being able to snoop around in her life anytime she wanted. If just felt weird.

"You have a very boring electronic life, H," Max said as if that made it okay for her to have accessed her email. "The highlights were really that cookie recipe Amy sent. Tuna made them—they're delicious—and Isabelle's question about paint. I've got two follow-ups. Why did Amy think you were going to bake, and why were you two so quick to dismiss Subtle Touch and Phantom Mist for the dining room? They were a tad neutral sure, but I think the colors could really work in there. They weren't as bold as Salty Tears or Lauren's Surprise, but—"

"Max?"

"Yes?"

"Extortion. Proof of life videos, please."

Lola thought this was a perfect example of the new and improved Holt 2.0. The old Holt, pre-Isabelle would have torn Max into very tiny pieces with the precision of a human shredder. Holt 2.0 looked disgruntled, not deadly.

"Fine. I've contacted the police and they already have an open missing persons case. Apparently, your father." Max looked at Isabelle.

"His name is Kevin Garvey. He threatened me and my sister, and now he's been stupid enough to get himself kidnapped, although the result is the same for us. That's his only relationship to me," Isabelle said. Her tone left no room for misunderstanding or argument. Holt wasn't the only one who commanded the troops around here.

"Yes, ma'am," Max said. "Pertinent details then. Kevin Garvey is married and his wife filed a missing persons report. They don't seem to have any leads. They were surprised by my call. I've been spending a lot of time with the video we got, but so far I've got nothing useful to report. I'll keep working."

"What have we heard from Moose? He's had plenty of time to get information from Mason," Holt said. "Anything more about why Garvey wanted to talk to me? Was he really the one who hired Mason? Anything he can provide to prove that?"

"Moose checked in a couple of hours ago. He and Jose collected all three of the boys you left in the woods for them. As you might expect, Mason's not feeling incredibly cooperative. We don't have much leverage on him. We're taking him back to jail, and he knows it."

"I'll call the district attorney handling his case in Detroit," Holt said. "I don't know that there's anything to be done, but it's worth a shot. I won't compromise a case to get information from Mason, but maybe he has other information that would be useful to them. I want to know how Garvey passed the message on, how he got in touch."

"Do we know anything about the people who sent the video?" Lola asked.

"Not yet. I've got a program running trying to trace the origin of the email. Whoever sent it covered their tracks pretty well."

As if on cue, Max's computer beeped and her face lit up. Max was evidently chasing an email through the Internets, whatever that meant. Lola pictured a dog chasing a squirrel around the cemetery near the office, but she suspected it was a bit more complicated.

"Gotcha," Max said triumphantly. "College of LA. The email originated from the CLA servers."

"What would someone at CLA want with Kevin Garvey, or any of us?" Isabelle asked. "He never attended college or ever had any particular interest in it as far as I know. Last I heard he was living in Arizona."

"He worked in the maintenance department," Max said, looking intently at her computer screen. "Guess he relocated."

"So what do we do about the extortion threat?" Dubs asked, for once looking serious. "Since I used to be a thief and you all found me in prison, I don't believe these guys will just take the money and go away."

"The extortion threat is a concern, but at the moment it's just that, a threat. They don't have anything of ours. Maybe they're overplaying their hand thinking Kevin Garvey means more to Isabelle and Ellen than he does, or maybe they think we're unprepared to protect our own. I'm not sure, and I don't like being unsure. I think we report the threat and the attempted extortion and officially let the authorities handle this."

"And unofficially?" Lola asked. She could tell Holt was formulating a plan and was fairly confident she knew what it was. If she was right, she had to convince Holt she was the right one for the job.

"I'm not a fan of people thinking they hold leverage over me. And I really hate not having enough information to know what the fuck is going on. I want to know who these people are and how to get them out of our lives."

"Sounds like you're going to Los Angeles," Isabelle said. She didn't look or sound happy. She wrapped her arms around Holt's neck in what looked like an unconscious gesture of comfort seeking.

Holt wrapped her arms around Isabelle's waist and pulled her closer. "No, sweetheart, I'm not going anywhere. I want information, but I need to know you and George and Ellen's brood are safe. My place is by your side. What good is paying a whole crew if I can't send them across the country whenever I feel like it?"

"Maybe I sound like an imbecile," Dubs said, "but how is trotting off to LA going to help us?"

"We can look for Kevin Garvey ourselves, for one," Holt said.

"Can't work a kidnapping from across the country," Lola said. "Not easily. And it's easier to be a pain in the ass with the local cops in person. Although I'm sure you would have no problems either way."

"And LA is where Garvey lives. It's where his life is. This guy wanted to talk to me, and now someone supposedly snatched him and *they* want to talk to me. The people who know why are out there. Max can do amazing things with a laptop, but sometimes you need boots and eyes on the ground," Holt said.

This was what Lola had been waiting for. For months now, she'd been looking for an opportunity to get her life back on firm footing, and this job felt like the way to do it. She was tired of feeling unmoored. In LA, by herself, with only work to worry about, she'd finally have that chance. And without Holt to bail her out if she screwed up, she would have no choice but to come through.

"I'm volunteering," Lola said. "I'll find Garvey and your pen pals."

"No," Holt said. "Moose will be back in a day, two at the most. I'll send him when he gets back."

Lola's stomach churned. Her heart sank. *Holt doesn't trust me on this. She doesn't trust me when it's Isabelle on the line.* She had to prove her wrong.

"That's forty-eight hours of wasted time, H. I can be there six hours from whatever flight Max can find for me. I'll stand in the cargo hold if it means finding who's threatening Isabelle and Ellen faster. Moose will be tired when he gets back, especially if he's been fighting off Jose for a week. I'm fresh. I won't fail you. Or Isabelle."

Holt looked surprised. She started to speak, but Isabelle put her hand on her shoulder and stopped her. Isabelle whispered something in her ear that Lola couldn't make out. Holt nodded, kissed Isabelle on the cheek, and finally made eye contact with Lola.

"My choice of Moose wasn't a reflection of my thoughts about you. It wasn't about you failing me. I don't think you ever have. Get on a plane as soon as you can. Moose will join you in California, but only as backup in case you need it. There are some cold leads on other cases he can follow up on the West Coast while you're searching. I'd prefer if you had someone relatively close in case you need him."

"I don't need a babysitter, H," Lola said.

"Moose was going to get one too," Holt said. "I was going to send Dubs." Dubs's eyes lit up, and Holt held up her hand to stop her. "You weren't going to be allowed inside a car the entire time you were there."

"You're no fun, boss."

"Lola," Holt said, looking at her seriously, "this is ghost surveillance only. You find Garvey if you can. See what you can find out about our extortionists, but don't compromise yourself. Moose will be close, but don't put yourself at risk. The states aren't spaced like they are on the East Coast. California is huge. I have no idea how many Rhode Islands will fit in it, but you will essentially be without a parachute for long stretches of time. I'm sending him with you because it makes me feel better to have him in the same state, but I don't know how close he'll actually be, and he'll be working his own cases while you work yours. You know how nervous that makes me. Keep a low profile and be safe."

"I always am," Lola said. That wasn't true, especially lately, but Holt didn't need to know that. She turned to Max who hadn't looked up from her computer since Holt gave the go-ahead for Lola to head west. "So, when do I leave, kid?"

"You're booked on a flight tonight. You'll land in LA around one a.m. I got you a long-term sublet apartment close to CLA. It's furnished so you don't need to worry about bringing anything with you. And you're the newest hire in the CLA maintenance department, custodial staff. Hope you're good with a mop. And graveyard shift."

"That was…efficient," Lola said. Max could make her computer do things Lola didn't think possible. Email was still a little magical to her. "Did you get me transportation?"

"I've got a Ducati Scrambler Sixty2 with your name on it waiting at the airport."

"They're trying to market that bike to hipsters, Max," Lola said. She was horrified.

"So put on your skinny jeans and ironic T-shirt and suck it up. That bike handles well in cities. It's also reasonably affordable. You are a custodian, after all. Now get out of here and pack. You have a flight to catch. Didn't you hear Holt?" Max tried to shoo her away.

"Anything else before I go, H?" Lola asked, not willing to be dismissed by Max.

"Be careful. Keep your comms with you and check in with the Wonder Twins daily. If you need me, call day or night. Moose is your immediate backup, but if you're in trouble, I'm your first call, got it?"

Lola smiled. Holt had always been overly protective of those she loved, but especially of her. "Got it."

She felt a thrill that had been absent lately. She was finally getting an opportunity to set things right, to get back on course. It didn't hurt that the job was so far from everything she knew. Right now, a little distance was welcome. Maybe it would help her get her head on straight before she came back after this got sorted out and settled back onto the team under Holt. *God, I hope so.*

CHAPTER FIVE

Okay, buddy, you're going to go easy on me, right? Mama's in the other room, but I really don't want to have to call in backup." Holt looked down at her son before scooping him up and flying him over to the changing table in his room.

George squealed with delight as he soared over his toy-strewn floor and landed on his back on the changer. As soon as his back hit the soft fabric, however, he was a man in motion. Arms, legs, and torso shifted in equal and opposite directions, and it was all Holt could do to keep him on the table, much less get the diaper changed.

"I thought we agreed you were going to go easy on me," she said. Although Isabelle made this look easy, and she could call for her help and they would be done in a third of the time, she wasn't willing to give up and take the coward's way out. Just because George seemed to reserve his strength, willfulness, and excess urine for her, didn't mean she couldn't handle it, most of the time. *Isabelle hasn't ever been peed on.* Holt needed to change her clothes regularly. It had become their thing. She didn't remember her godson, Superman, ever being this single-mindedly wiggly, although the peeing they shared. *Boys.*

She handed George his favorite book, and the distraction was enough to get the diaper off and a new one in place. She was sweating by the time his feet hit the floor, and he took off for the kitchen where he could hear Mama singing along to something on the radio. Despite it being completely meaningless to his chance of lifetime success, Holt was proud that he had been an early walker. He was just over a year old now and was close to running, where many of his age matched peers were still cruising along furniture, waiting to take their first wobbly steps.

Holt followed George, inordinately pleased he was leading her to Isabelle. She'd thought her life was complete before she'd splash-landed in Isabelle's pool and circumstances had forced them to face down one of Isabelle's deranged clients together. But Isabelle, and now George, had shown her what true fulfillment was. If only people would stop threatening those she loved.

"Holt, sweetie, I thought we agreed, only Carol Danvers lives here. Captain Marvel stays at the office."

Holt realized she must have the look that Isabelle called her "work face."

"I was just thinking about how much I love you and George."

"That look wasn't the one you have when you tell me you love me," Isabelle said. "I trust you with my life. You'll keep us safe. What were you really thinking about?"

Holt leaned against the counter, and Isabelle slipped into her arms and kissed her. Isabelle felt so good, and as Holt always did when Isabelle was close, she felt the tension she was carrying melt away.

"It should probably bother me that you can read my mind," Holt said. "But I kind of like it."

"Me too," Isabelle said. She turned her attention to George, not leaving Holt's arms. "Just a little quieter please, buddy." He'd been punctuating each of their sweet sentiments with a loud, jarring whap of his wooden spoon against a metal mixing bowl. He was sitting on the floor in the kitchen surrounded by measuring spoons and cups, two mixing bowls, three wooden spoons, and a whisk.

"Looks like I'm off the hook for making dinner tonight," Holt said. "What's on the menu, bud?" Reluctantly, Holt let Isabelle go and knelt down to collect a runaway whisk and return it to him.

"Oh, that reminds me. Amy and Superman are joining us tonight. Tuna's been escorting Ellen and the kids around all day, so I figured we should invite him to stay too."

Holt laughed at the day Tuna was probably having. "Is Ellen pretending she's a celebrity in town with her security detail and dragging him to every store in the state?"

"Probably," Isabelle said. She was laughing now too. "She's taking this well. It's a good thing she married the most patient and understanding man alive. Having her fawn and drool over you is one thing, but Tuna is a walking Greek god and very much single."

"She doesn't fawn all over me," Holt said.

Isabelle shot her a look that told her not to argue anymore.

"Amy's also mad at you. Fair warning."

"What could I have possibly done since I saw her last?" Holt couldn't think of anything worthy of her ire. Not anything that was worth Amy going to Isabelle and not calling and yelling directly at her.

"I guess Superman won't stop demanding a brother. She blames you."

Holt couldn't help the smile and full heart when she thought of her godson. She'd been there the day he had been placed with Amy as a foster child and stood next to her in court when he legally became Amy's son. He was only a couple of years older than George, and the two boys loved each other. She wanted them to be close, and watching their relationship grow was one of the great joys in her life.

"He has George. He's over there with them so much, he's practically like a brother. I don't know what we'd do without Amy helping us out so much."

"That's what I told her. She said he was very clear. He wants an 'all the time, overnight brother,' not a 'sometimes brother like George.' Amy said she's adding this to your list of things to handle. Out of curiosity, what are the others?"

Holt counted them down on her fingers. "The sex talk, why he can't play football, buying a jock strap, tattoos, and now, apparently, baby brothers."

"That's a good list," Isabelle said. "You can cover both boys, although I don't know if we should rule out baby brothers in the future."

"Really?" Holt liked the sound of that. They'd never talked about it, but she could see having a whole army of kids with Isabelle. "Are Max and Dubs coming to family dinner tonight too?"

Holt started meal prep since George wasn't likely to be any real help. She pulled what she needed from the fridge and juggled olive oil, spices, and the other ingredients on her way to the stove.

"Probably, but you know how easily they get distracted. With each other, with work, computers, cars. I'll remind Max," Isabelle said. She saved an onion from rolling off the counter and gave Holt's ass an affectionate pat as she moved across the kitchen to get a cutting board from the drying rack.

"They're good kids. It's going to feel weird not having Moose, Jose, or Lola here though. I hope I made the right decision sending her across the country on her own." George pulled on her pant leg and lifted his arms, grunting. She scooped him up and showed him what she was doing, pointing out the types of food and cooking utensils.

"She needed to go. I don't know why, but something's going on with her. She hasn't been the same since Tiffany. I don't know if the trip is a good thing, but I think forcing her to stay would have been worse."

Holt agreed. She'd noticed Lola's strange behavior too, including her overeagerness in the field and taking every case she could get her hands on. It was like she was just learning the ropes again, or trying to prove something. She'd also been less present with the group, disengaged. Holt hadn't been able to get her to talk. They'd been friends for years, but for the first time since Lola's brother died, Lola had clammed up. Holt thought about George, Lola's late brother and her son's namesake. He had been one of her best friends, and her own grief still felt like an unhealed wound that could reopen at any time. She could only imagine what it was like for Lola.

"After George the First died, it took Lola forever to talk to me, or anyone, about what she was feeling, thinking, anything. She's kind of like that now. She'll come around, I hope. Maybe Jose's had more luck. They're pretty close. I'll talk to him when he gets back."

"You think she's going to listen to you and stick with surveillance only?" Isabelle looked concerned.

"Why wouldn't she?" Holt was surprised by Isabelle's question. Lola knew the rules of the crew, and they'd come up with the plan as a team. Surely Lola wouldn't do anything to jeopardize her safety.

"I don't know. She just had a funny look on her face when you tried to send Moose in her place today. Sort of desperate. And you said yourself, she's been clammed up and not talking to you. I'm worried about her. It was Tiffany's new guy who almost killed Dubs. I don't know if she blames herself for not figuring that out…"

Isabelle didn't finish her thought. She didn't need to. Holt knew what she was thinking. She should have been thinking the same thing herself. She ran her hand through her hair. *Damn it. Why haven't I been checking on her more? If she's been carrying that weight and I let her down...Damn it.*

"Hey, babe," Isabelle said, stroking her back, helping her reel in her emotions. "I'm just speculating. No proof. She got cheated on, dumped, and embarrassed in front of her family. That alone is enough to explain why she's been a little distant."

"Yeah, but if she does blame herself, she's going to try and make up for it. And I should have seen it coming." Holt wasn't willing to let herself off the hook.

"Well, you do now," Isabelle said. "And we aren't supposed to be talking about work at home."

"You started it," Holt said. "And how did you become better at my job than I am?"

"Oh, I'm certainly not. I do *not* look good in ass-kicking boots." Isabelle whispered "ass" since George was still in Holt's arms.

"You look good in anything," Holt said. She took her time looking her up and down to make her point.

"Stop it," Isabelle said with a grin that would have sent them racing to the bedroom before George, and if they weren't about to have a house full of people.

The doorbell rang, signaling the arrival of their first guests for family dinner. Holt knew it was probably Amy. She usually got there first so Superman and George could play.

"Guess I'm going to have to break the news to Superman," Holt said. "Amy will probably enjoy watching me stumble through this one."

"You'll survive, tough guy," Isabelle said. "And, sweetheart, Lola will be okay. You'll make sure of it. Tonight let's enjoy family dinner. No more work talk."

Holt hoped so. Isabelle was right. Now that Holt was alerted to the possibility that Lola was carrying an extra burden, she would be more aware of her actions. But she was out on a limb three thousand miles away. *Damn it.*

CHAPTER SIX

Quinn pinched the bridge of her nose and looked around her office, hoping to find some patience hiding somewhere among the stacks of books and papers. Her office hours started in five minutes and midterm grades had posted that morning. She wasn't worried about her graduate students, but she had two sections of an undergraduate psychology course. They complained about everything. At least a few of them, and they were the ones who would likely be visiting her in, she looked at the clock, three and a half minutes.

Turns out she didn't even have that long. Two of her students knocked and came in before she could answer. Why did they always have to travel in pairs? They sat in the chairs in front of her desk and started arguing their case immediately.

"Quinn," the first one said. "How could you even for a second put that grade up there? I know you'll work it out, but I've been freaking out all afternoon."

"Dr. Golden," Quinn said.

"What?"

"My name," Quinn said calmly. "Is Dr. Golden."

"Uh, Dr. *Quinn* Golden, right?" the woman said.

"Correct," Quinn said.

We're off to a fantastic start.

The woman and her friend looked confused, maybe a little less confident, but they seemed to get the point and respected her desire to be addressed formally. Her graduate students called her by her first name, but the undergraduates didn't. Not when she could enforce it.

They already had enough trouble adjusting to the differences between high school and college, and despite her age, she wasn't their BFF, there to coddle them and make their lives easy. She was Dr. Quinn Golden, who not long ago had been in their shoes and had worked her ass off to get where she was. They could do the same.

"So my grade," the woman said.

"Did I make a mistake in the grading?" Quinn asked. She tried to look sympathetic.

"Well, not exactly. But it's still not fair."

"I'm not sure I follow."

"I am not a C-plus student. You have to fix it." The woman's voice rose.

"If the grading was correct, then there's nothing I can do right now. I know it's frustrating, especially after you study hard for an exam." Quinn was giving her way more credit than she suspected she deserved. "But it's only the midterm. This isn't insurmountable."

"I don't understand. I came in to talk to you, just like you said we should if we have a problem. You're really not going to do anything about my grade?" The woman looked stunned.

"I'm really not," Quinn said. "That's *your* job over the next few weeks. But I'm here to help you as much as you need."

The two women left without another word. Quinn heard her student mutter to her friend on the way out. It sounded like "stupid fucking bitch," but she wasn't sure. The rest of her office hours were a variation on the same theme. Only one student actually wanted to discuss the exam and see where she'd made mistakes. The rest wanted to complain about how unfair it all was.

Jessica stuck her head in once the last student had finally left.

"The hooligans were rough on you today," she said.

Quinn didn't answer; she just put her forehead down on her desk in defeat. She was a researcher. That was what she loved. Teaching wasn't her strongest skill and she knew it. She didn't mind it most of the time, but it was times like the last two hours when she remembered the beautiful, glorious, fantastic nature of her research. Data didn't talk back.

"Good thing I'm taking you out tonight. Cheer you right up," Jessica said.

"Excuse me?" Quinn said. She looked up quickly and tried to judge Jessica's expression. The offer didn't sound terrible.

"Well, I'm not taking you out, out. Just out with my non-judgmental, non-whiny, awesome friends. You've met a few of them before, but now we're all going to hang out. It's Friday night, you're young and hot, and if I don't drag you out of here, that's where you'll sleep." Jessica pointed to the couch across from Quinn's desk. "I'll pick you up at eight."

She probably wasn't wrong. "Fine," Quinn said. She really did need to get out more, and she wasn't really in the mood to work. Not after an afternoon with the hooligans. She finished work and headed home to relax and shower before heading out with Jessica, something she found she was looking forward to.

Just after ten, Quinn followed Jessica and her friends into the club they'd chosen for the evening. Jessica's friends were as advertised, and dinner had been full of laughter. Most of the jokes had seemed to come at Jessica's expense, but she didn't seem to mind. Best of all, no one seemed to care what Quinn did for a living outside of what was initial polite small talk. The most intense line of questioning had revolved around whether she was joining in their quest to get drunk and find hot women for the night.

They found a table and Quinn and Jessica elbowed their way through the crowd to the bar.

"You know," Jessica said, shouting over the music, "you never answered if you were joining in our fun for the evening. But if you're not, you probably shouldn't have worn that dress in here. Jesus."

"What are you talking about?" Quinn asked.

"Hey, why don't you try to look at the woman already hanging all over you. You've got plenty to keep you busy," Jessica said, physically pushing the face of a woman nearby away from Quinn.

"And here I thought you weren't flirting with me in my office," Quinn said. She was amused at Jessica's protection even if it was over the top.

"I wasn't," Jessica said. "Still not. Doesn't mean I want you to get mauled. Unless it's by special invitation."

"So you're playing bodyguard? Isn't that going to get in the way of your quest?"

"I can multitask."

"Okay, so let me understand. I've picked up an overprotective bodyguard because you think I can't be trusted, or everyone else can't, because of what I'm wearing? You know that doesn't sound very good, right?" Jessica was starting to take her self-appointed protection detail a bit too far.

"Not when you put it like that. I meant it as a compliment," Jessica said.

Jessica looked a little chagrined, so Quinn tried to soften her reproach. "Oh, I know. To be clear, if I find someone else to chaperone me, will you go and continue your quest?" Quinn wasn't exactly eager to ditch Jessica, but she also didn't need an escort around the club. She wanted to have fun tonight, and she wouldn't if Jessica was worried about her the whole time.

"Who'd you have in mind?" Jessica looked excited at the thought of Quinn joining in their fun.

Quinn wasn't about to tell her that wasn't exactly what she'd been implying. She searched around and caught sight of a woman at the end of the bar.

"Her." She pointed. She'd chosen her at random, but now that she looked at her, her breath caught. She was in profile, but she was gorgeous. She was wearing dark skinny jeans and a black tank top. Her arms were muscled in a way Quinn hadn't ever seen on a woman, but nothing about her looked masculine. She had long dark hair pulled back in a ponytail that cascaded down her back. Quinn could tell she was tall, even though she was sitting, but it wasn't her physical size that was taking up space across the bar. She just oozed a presence that radiated around her. When she picked up her glass and brought the drink, something amber on the rocks, to her lips, Quinn held her breath.

"I don't think..." Jessica started. Before she could finish, the woman turned and looked at them. She caught Quinn's eye and slowly raised her glass in salute before turning back to the bar.

"Yes," Quinn said. "Her." Before Jessica could object further, or Quinn could think about the fact that she usually sucked at picking up women, Quinn patted Jessica on the cheek and slipped past her. She moved through the crowd until she was standing next to the stranger at the bar.

"Anyone sitting here?" she asked. It was difficult to hear over the loud music, but they were far enough away from the DJ and speaker that it was just manageable.

The woman looked up and studied her. Her gaze was intense and it warmed Quinn's face.

"No," she finally said, "I've been saving it for you."

Quinn laughed at the audacious comment. "Oh really? And how long have you been here saving my seat, Ms…?"

"Lola. A couple hours. You should thank me. It's been a tough job."

Lola was smiling too. Quinn liked her smile. Her eyes sparkled and her entire face relaxed and lit up when she did.

"I'm Quinn. And since I just got here an hour ago, I'm calling bullshit on your seat saving, but thank you all the same for keeping it for me now. Can I buy you a drink?"

"Ouch," Lola said. "You LA girls are rough." She nodded her assent at Quinn's offer and flagged the bartender.

"Not from around here?" The thought was disappointing. Quinn didn't know why it mattered if Lola was only here for a quick vacation stop. It's not like she would see her again after tonight. She also didn't intend on seeing her after leaving the club. *Enjoy the moment.*

"Just flew in on Wednesday," Lola said.

"You just got here, somehow made it to one of the hottest clubs in the city, but are sitting at the bar alone?" Quinn was confused. Women who looked like Lola didn't stay alone at clubs unless they wanted to.

"I told you, I was saving the seat for you."

"So you've said."

Before either of them could say anything else, Jessica's friends surged out of the crowd and stumbled into Quinn.

"Come dance with us, Quinny," one of them said. They noticed Lola.

"Who's your new friend? Definitely bring her too."

"Do you dance?" Quinn asked Lola, already being pulled to the dance floor.

"I do," Lola said.

Quinn liked the half smile playing on Lola's face. She was clearly amused at Quinn's losing battle to remain at the bar.

"Join me?" Lola wasn't giving off the receptive and open vibes, and Quinn really didn't want to lose the small connection they had. She was beautiful and intriguing and just aloof enough that Quinn, in her slightly tipsy state, wanted more.

"I'll meet you out there," Lola said.

"I hope so," Quinn said before giving in and being sucked back onto the dance floor. She figured Lola had just blown her off and that was the end of their time together. She realized too late she should have tried to get her number.

After twenty minutes of dancing, Quinn figured Lola wasn't going to join her. She'd gotten separated from Jessica's friends, but had enjoyed dancing with the women around her. Despite Jessica's warning, no one had seemed overwhelmed with the urge to get inappropriately handsy.

As the thought crossed her mind, a hand wrapped around her waist from behind, pulling her tightly to a solid body. A drink materialized on the other side of her. She took it, enjoying the attention. For someone who kept insisting she wasn't flirting with her, Jessica was pretty good at flirting. If Jessica wasn't careful, Quinn would start enjoying it, if for no other reason than it was nice to be looked after. She turned around in Jessica's arms to tell her that. When she did, she nearly crashed into Lola's chin. Now that she was standing, Quinn realized she was about six inches taller than her own five feet seven inches. She had to step back half a step to see Lola's face. That meant that Lola's arms were wrapped around her back, instead of loosely at her sides. She'd be lying if she said she didn't like the way it felt. A lot.

"You're not Jessica," Quinn said lamely.

"Are you disappointed? Should I go?" Lola asked. She leaned in close to Quinn, her breath tickling her neck as she spoke.

Quinn felt as if Lola's breath tripped a switch that caused a chain reaction across her skin. She was pleasantly on fire.

"You did ask me to dance."

Quinn shook her head, suddenly aware they were standing the middle of the dance floor, the only two not dancing. She felt awkward.

She'd been dancing without a problem, but now, encircled in Lola's arms, she didn't quite remember what to do.

Lola seemed to pick up on her uncertainty. She took Quinn's hand and led her a few feet away, as if a change of scenery would solve the problem.

When they stopped, Lola leaned in close again. "Dance with me?"

Quinn nodded again. She took a sip of her drink, found a place to put it down, and took a step away from Lola. She crooked her finger and gave a small smirk, indicating she should follow. She started moving her hips in time with the music and waited for Lola to move with her.

Maybe it was because she was half a drink past buzzed, or maybe it was the assumptions she'd made about Lola by the cocky way she filled up space at the bar, but Quinn soon became frustrated on the dance floor. Lola was a very good dancer and wasn't passive, but she was being too damn respectful, chivalrous even. Quinn felt like they were at a middle school square dance. She'd waited as long as she was willing for Lola to make a move, and she was done waiting.

When the next song started, she moved into Lola's personal space and ground her hips against her lightly. She ran her hands through Lola's hair, mostly just to get her attention. Judging by the look on Lola's face, it seemed to have done the trick. "Are you scared of me?"

"Not especially," Lola said.

"Then do you want to explain why you're dancing three feet away from me?"

For a split second, Quinn thought she saw uncertainty in Lola's eyes, but she didn't have a chance to explore it further before it was gone. Lola wrapped her arms around Quinn, forcing their bodies even more tightly together. Quinn groaned as Lola's thigh found its way between hers. Lola moved her hands down Quinn's back to her ass, moving them both in time to the music, keeping a steady, tantalizing pressure.

"Is this your way of saying be careful what I wish for?" Quinn said. She bit down lightly on Lola's ear.

"No," Lola said.

She leaned in to Quinn's teasing and Quinn barely stifled a groan.

"It's my way of telling you how sexy you are."

"Oh." It could have been a practiced line, but if it was, it was delivered with such earnestness, it took Quinn's breath away.

Lola leaned down and kissed along her jawline, her lips brushing so lightly it took Quinn a moment to realize what she was doing. Once she did, it was all she could feel. Lola's lips were soft and gentle, but there was nothing gentle about the way Quinn's heart pounded at the attention.

She spun in Lola's arms and ground her ass into Lola with the music, tilting her head to the side, giving Lola better access to her neck. When Lola took full advantage, Quinn leaned back into her, reaching an arm up behind her, curling her hand behind Lola's head, tangling her fingers in Lola's hair.

Seeming to enjoy the new position, Lola threaded one hand tightly around Quinn's waist, holding her in place. She let her other hand wander down Quinn's side, past her hip, and down her thigh. It felt like Lola was touching her everywhere. She felt more drunk from the feel of Lola's caress than from anything she'd consumed from the bar. *God, she feels good.*

While they danced, Lola's hands continued to wander, and she occasionally traced light kisses on Quinn's jaw or neck. Quinn was almost desperate for her to kiss her, but again, she didn't make the first move, or any move beyond what Quinn had initiated.

When Quinn first laid eyes on Lola, all dark sex appeal and confident bravado, she would have pegged her as the brash, forward type. She didn't expect Lola to be quite so…"polite" wasn't the right word. Cautious? Restrained? Whatever it was, it was making Quinn crazy. She wasn't usually the aggressor, but Lola was forcing her hand. It was as if Lola needed her to make the first move every time. If Quinn was being honest, it was pretty hot being in control of this powerful woman. She liked showing Lola where and how much she wanted to be touched.

Quinn spun around in Lola's arms so she was facing her again and laced her arms around her neck. She felt Lola pull her tight and thrilled at the way their bodies fit together despite the difference in height. The sudden reappearance of Lola's thigh between her legs made her gasp. Quinn pulled roughly on the back of Lola's head, dragging her down for the kiss she'd wanted since they first started dancing.

Lola's lips were a whisper away when Lola's thigh, still between Quinn's leg, began vibrating. Quinn jumped back in surprise. Lola's eyes snapped open and she yanked the phone out of her pocket, clearly annoyed, but not before pulling Quinn in close.

She looked at the caller ID and murmured in Quinn's ear, "I really have to take this. Come with me?"

"I'm not having sex with you in the bathroom," Quinn said.

When Lola laughed, her eyes danced and lit up her entire face. "You're safe with me," she said. "But I have to take this call."

She pulled Quinn off the dance floor and toward the back of the club, in the direction of the bathrooms. They stopped just outside the doors, tucked in a corner of the long hallway. Lola leaned against the wall, pulled Quinn close to her, and answered the call.

"Max, you had better be on fire, or Dubs has you tied up in a compromising position in the conference room and you're scared Holt is gonna be the one to find you tomorrow. Everything else could've waited until tomorrow."

Quinn had been more interested in resuming the exploration of Lola's body she'd begun on the dance floor, maybe even finding a way to steal a kiss while she was otherwise occupied, but now she was intrigued by the phone conversation. Max and Holt could be men or women, but from the sound of the other person on the phone, she was guessing Max was a woman. She had no idea what a "dubs" was.

Lola saw her watching and shrugged an apology. "I'm busy, Max. All of this can wait. I don't start until tomorrow. Now, I'm going to put Quinn on the phone and you're going to apologize to her for interrupting our dance."

Before Quinn could protest, Lola handed her the phone. She put it to her ear and started to say "hello." Max was still talking to Lola.

"Lola, who's Quinn? And since when do you dance? Lola? Lola?"

"Um, hello?" Quinn said.

While Quinn was distracted by the phone, Lola pulled her closer and traced the neckline of her shirt first with gentle kisses, then with her tongue. When she got to just below her ear, she bit down lightly.

Quinn's senses were so overwhelmed with the pleasure of Lola's touch she wasn't sure she was still holding the phone until Max's voice cut through.

"Hi. You must be Quinn. Lola said, I'm supposed to apologize to you."

Quinn didn't know what to say, and didn't really want to stay on the phone. She had more important places to focus her attention. "Apology accepted." She knew she sounded a little breathless. She thought a small moan might have escaped.

Max might have been laughing. "Okay, well that's my cue to end this call. Nice chatting with you. Quinn, be careful with her."

The warning didn't feel like a threat, or Max trying to steer her away from a bad experience. If anything, it sounded like a plea. She didn't have the capacity to think about it any further.

The call ended and Quinn shoved the phone in Lola's back pants pocket letting her hands wander over Lola's ass.

"Sorry 'bout that," Lola said.

She resumed kissing along Quinn's jawline.

"Make it up to me." Quinn tilted her head, exposing her neck to Lola's exploration.

Lola stilled and pulled slowly away from Quinn, or as far away as she could since she was still pressed against the wall. She spread her legs slightly and lowered her arms so they hung by her sides, palms out. "Anything you want."

Quinn felt like Lola had just touched a match to her center and started a raging inferno. She fisted her hands in Lola's hair roughly and pressed her lips to Lola's. The kiss wasn't gentle and Lola returned it hungrily. Quinn didn't know if they kissed for a second or a lifetime. All she could feel was Lola.

It took much longer than it should have for Quinn to realize they were no longer alone in their cutout. It wasn't until Jessica spoke that she really became aware of her presence.

"There you are, Quinn. I've been look—get your hands off her."

Quinn felt Lola try to pull away, but since Quinn still had her pushed up against the wall, she didn't have anywhere to go. Quinn was slow to give up the kiss. Jessica had no claim to her and didn't get to direct her actions. Lola wasn't doing anything Quinn didn't want. Badly.

Apparently, Jessica didn't see it that way. She grabbed Quinn by the shoulder and tried to pull her away from Lola.

Quinn felt Lola's posture change. She still looked relaxed, but she didn't *feel* relaxed. She felt like a panther ready to strike. Quinn couldn't help it. She found this overt display of pent up power even more of a turn-on than the submissive role Lola had been playing all night.

"I said, get your hands off her," Jessica said, more forcefully this time.

Quinn moved closer to Lola, into her embrace, and placed a gentle kiss on her pulse point. Lola wrapped her arms around Quinn protectively.

For a moment, Quinn considered letting Lola deal with Jessica so they could resume kissing. Knight in shining armor wasn't working for Quinn at all. Especially since she didn't need rescuing and Jessica had interrupted the hottest kiss she'd ever had. But Jessica seemed a little drunk, and she was her friend, even if she was acting like an ass and she didn't know Lola or what she would do if all that power were released.

"Her hands were invited, Jessica," Quinn said.

"And I don't believe yours were," Lola said, her voice menacing, a clear warning.

Jessica jumped back. Lola looked like she wanted to smile, but she refrained. Quinn wanted to kiss her again.

"I warned you what would happen," Jessica said.

She's not going to give this one up. "That I would have a woman pinned up against the wall by the end of the night, kissing her, and in total control of the situation?" Quinn said. "Pretty sure you didn't mention that."

Jessica looked like she was seeing them for the first time. Quinn guessed it wasn't exactly the positioning she was imagining in her mind's eye.

"I haven't been mistreating your friend," Lola said. She looked to Quinn. "Has anything happened that you didn't want?"

"You know it hasn't," Quinn said. She kissed Lola again. "But this did kind of kill our buzz, didn't it?" Quinn glared at Jessica.

"Someone as beautiful as you is a walking buzz," Lola said. "But it's late, and your attack Chihuahua is good to make sure you get home safe. Are you safe with her?" When Quinn nodded, Lola pulled her close again and kissed her deeply. "Thank you for a great night."

Before Quinn could argue, or Jessica could object to the insult, Lola was gone.

Quinn whipped around, ready to eviscerate Jessica. She didn't need to. She already looked appropriately hangdog.

"Are you going to be speaking to me on Monday?"

"That depends," Quinn said. "Are you still going to be acting like a nineteen fifties misogynistic asshat?"

"I'm really sorry," Jessica said. "It's not an excuse, but I invited you out, and I guess I got a little carried away making sure you had a good time. My friends have been giving me shit about how hot you are and why I didn't bring you out with us sooner, and I was worried they were going to be jerks to you. Looks like I'm the only jerk here. Who was that woman, by the way? She was…I don't even know. Words fail me."

Quinn didn't want to forgive Jessica just yet, but it was hard when faced with her obvious guilt. And who wanted to be mad at Jessica when she could be thinking about the last few hours she'd spent with Lola?

"Her name is Lola. That's about all I know about her, except she made even my toenails tingle when she kissed me."

"Did you get the human vibrator's number?"

"No," Quinn said, not letting on how disappointed she was. "I think she's only in town for a short time anyway." Quinn was suddenly tired and not interested in standing and chatting in the back hall of the club with Jessica. "Let's get out of here."

CHAPTER SEVEN

L ola stared down at the keyboard and back up at the screen in front of her, willing the computer to magically do what she was silently asking. It seemed to work when Max did it. Max's step-by-step instructions through her earpiece might as well have been in Swahili. She wished she'd paid more attention one of the hundred or so times Max had tried to teach her a few things about technology.

She'd just finished her graveyard shift at her new custodial job at the College of LA. It was the end of her first week. The sun had risen about an hour before and the campus was waking up, but Lola didn't know if she should be eating breakfast or dinner. The flipping of night and day, and subsequent sleep disruption, was hard to adjust to, but other than that, she was settling in. *If you count finding and kissing the hottest woman on the planet "settling in."* Too bad her overly protective friend had shown up. Or maybe it was a good thing. Lola was left with only good memories of the night with the woman at the club before things went sideways, like they always seemed to whenever Lola and women crossed paths.

She hadn't asked about Kevin Garvey yet, but she would soon. Locating him seemed a far easier task than tackling the technological monstrosity in front of her now. Max and Holt wanted her to log in with her newly assigned CLA credentials and access her email. Max had sent her pictures of George to open that had been altered in some way that she didn't understand. Once she opened them Max would be able to access the CLA servers. Or that's what she understood of the conversation. If only Lola could log in to the damn computer before the students started wandering in for the day.

"Do you see the box where it says username?" Max asked. "That's where you put in the username they gave you. Under that should be password. I'll read it out to you when you're ready."

"I hate these things," Lola said.

"Excuse me. You can't be in here."

Lola jumped. She was facing the door, but hadn't seen or heard the woman walk in. She'd been too focused on the computer. She quickly rewound the past minute, trying to remember if it was obvious she was talking to Max.

"I'm sorry. I was just trying to log on to the computer. I'm new." She kept it simple. And truthful.

"This is a private computer lab I use for my research. There are—Oh."

The woman came fully inside and Lola was rendered speechless by her previous dance partner, Quinn. She looked, if possible, even more beautiful now. Her strawberry blond hair was in disarray as if she'd just woken up, and her black pencil skirt and untucked green silk shirt were wrinkled as if slept in. She looked put together and comfortable enough in her clothes that Lola figured she was every bit as professional and brilliant as she looked. But the slightly rumpled appearance made her seem approachable and real. It was an appealing combination. Lola thought back to their dance and felt heat explode in her belly and work its way down until every nerve was at attention.

"Hello again." Lola stood, very aware of her custodian coveralls showing all the signs of her night's labor.

"Guess we skipped over the part where we work together," Quinn said. "I like the parts we didn't skip better."

Lola knew this was the part where social propriety dictated she should respond instead of standing there like an idiot, staring and grinning. But how was she supposed to do that, exactly? She'd guessed at the club that Quinn was way out of her league, and now the proof was right in front of her, and yet…Too bad she'd sworn off women after Tiffany, especially women who might be involved in a case. Quinn worked at CLA, making her off limits. Quinn short-circuited just about every system. *Say something, you moron. And stop thinking about kissing her.*

"I don't think we're exactly coworkers," Lola said. She indicated her janitorial supplies parked outside the door and then motioned to Quinn and her professional attire.

"You work here, don't you?" Quinn asked. "Or should I be calling security?" She was clearly teasing and not the least bit concerned with Lola's custodial credentials.

"Your floors, toilets, and wastebaskets have been lovingly tended all night. I'm sorry to be using your computers. I was trying to check my email. I can find another place on campus before I head home."

Max practically exploded with protests in her ear. Lola was a little worried Quinn would hear her, but she felt pretty confident she knew what she was doing.

"You can use the computer in my office. These computers have a lot of crazy research software on them. No one is allowed to do anything except what I tell them when they use them. They're a little extreme for email checking."

"I got that you like to be in control," Lola said. She thought she saw Quinn blush before she motioned for Lola to follow and hurried off down the hall. Lola was tempted to cut her earpiece connection to Max so she could spend some time truly alone with Quinn, but she needed Max to give her the username and password. Besides, spending time alone with women had always gotten her in trouble in the past. The fact that she'd been thinking about Quinn since they'd danced was almost a guarantee she was a murderer or in the habit of stealing the batteries from paraplegics' television remotes.

Lola followed Quinn into a suite of offices she'd cleaned earlier. As they entered, Quinn's friend from the club jumped up from behind one of the desks.

"Little Chihuahua," Lola said with as much cheer as she could muster. She wasn't all that thrilled to see the woman. "Are you Quinn's guard dog?"

The woman ignored her and looked to Quinn quizzically.

"This is Jessica Serrano. I don't think you two were ever introduced. Jessica, this is Lola…I don't actually know your last name."

Max suddenly made her presence known again chirping about not revealing her true identity since she was undercover. *No shit.*

"Badger," Lola said.

"Like the animal?" Jessica said. "And you make fun of me?"

"Yes, like the animal. Also means to harass or annoy," Lola said under her breath.

"Very funny," Max said.

"Since we're sharing," Lola said, looking pointedly at Quinn.

"Golden," Quinn said, appearing shy.

"Yes, you are." Lola liked that her comment seemed to fluster Quinn just a little bit.

Quinn helped Lola log on to her office computer. When Lola had been cleaning in this office suite earlier, Quinn's office door had been closed with a "do not disturb" sign, though at the time she'd had no idea who the office belonged to. Lola wondered how many nights Quinn slept on the couch that was nearly surrounded by books. She could picture Quinn stretched out there, her hair falling around her face like a halo. Did she not have anywhere else to go at night? No one waiting for her?

Lola discreetly took in Quinn's high cheekbones and flawless skin. Her green silk tank top hugged her breasts and shadowed her torso so alluringly Lola wanted to run her hands down her sides, the way she had when they'd danced. If Lola was waiting at home for Quinn, she wouldn't be okay with her sleeping on this couch even once.

She shook her head to clear those thoughts. *What the hell?* Quinn was hot, yes. That was a clearly established fact. It didn't mean Lola needed to go planning a life with her. She was in LA to prove she could do her job and not lose her head. Whatever she was doing right now wasn't a great start.

"You should be all set," Quinn said. "I've got class in fifteen minutes, but you can take as long as you need."

"Oh, I just wanted to check my email. I got some new pictures of my nephew. Just the ticket after a long night of work." Lola was looking forward to the pictures of George. She missed the little guy.

"Ooh. Can I see them? How old is he? What's his name?"

Lola grinned at Quinn's enthusiasm. "Of course. He's just over a year. His name is George." Lola almost added "the second" but stopped herself. She loved that Holt and Isabelle had named their son after her brother, who'd been killed many years ago now, but it hadn't yet stopped hurting when she heard someone talk about little George, or turned around when someone called his name and she saw it wasn't her brother. But now she had an adorable walking, almost talking, namesake to lessen the pain associated with the loss.

With Max's help through the comms, Lola pulled up the pictures of George from her email. There were three of them. As soon as they opened, Lola got confirmation from Max that her program was blasting off, or initializing, or deploying, or whatever it was that secret programs hidden in pictures did. As soon as she got the all clear, Lola subtly scratched her ear and turned off the comms. She didn't want Max to be part of her time with Quinn any longer, potential criminal mastermind or not.

"I can see why you wanted to see these as soon as you could. He looks just like you," Quinn said. "He would make my day too. Is he your brother's or sister's son?"

Lola's heart ached for a moment. Her brother should be married with kids right now. "Sister," Lola said. Holt was her family. Isabelle too, and they were as close as sisters could be. Quinn was right; George did look like her. Luckily, a few physical characteristics were about all she shared with George's biological father. He was cooling his heels in prison for multiple counts of grand theft auto, racketeering, and attempted murder for trying to kill Tiffany while she was pregnant with George, though he'd shot Dubs instead. Hopefully, being a shitty human being wasn't an inheritable trait.

"He's wonderful," Quinn said. "You can stay as long as you like, but I have to get to class."

"May I walk with you?" Lola asked impulsively. She was tired, and thinking about both Georges made her melancholy. Quinn seemed to be a balm for her battered soul. She didn't care at the moment why that was.

Quinn's eyes lit up at Lola's offer. That was almost enough for Lola to back out. She didn't want anyone to look at her like that. *Or maybe I do.* But she certainly wasn't interested in anyone that might be involved in her case. Quinn worked at CLA and that's where the email came from. *She could be a suspect.* Lola almost rolled her eyes thinking about the likelihood of Quinn being the mastermind behind a kidnapping.

"You sure you aren't too tired?" Quinn asked.

Lola must have looked as confused as she felt, being ripped from her wandering thoughts.

"You worked all night. My class is across campus. Not that you look like that would be particularly strenuous for you."

Lola was pretty sure Quinn was flirting. She felt like flexing but contained herself. "Lead the way."

"Give me five minutes," Quinn said. She grabbed a change of clothes hidden behind her office door and disappeared.

Lola closed out of her email program, congratulating herself that she remembered how, and wandered back into the common area. She'd barely emerged from Quinn's office when Jessica was on her.

"She's amazing, you know. Brilliant, driven, dedicated, loyal. If you're just here to find a quick fuck, go sniff around somewhere else. She's way out of your league."

"But she's in yours?" Lola asked. She wasn't really annoyed at Jessica's protectiveness, but she was curious.

"Hell no," Jessica said. "Even if I was interested, I wouldn't stand a chance. Doesn't mean I like the look of you."

"Hey, man, I got a couple good licks in on that garbage can before it dumped this awesome smelling muck on me. Besides, coveralls and whatever the hell this is," Lola indicated an unidentifiable slimy stain just above her knee, "makes for quite a compelling look. Don't judge."

Jessica looked like she was trying not to smile.

Lola didn't let her think too long. She understood overly protective friends; she occasionally was one herself. "I have no intention of, how did you put it, going for a quick fuck with Quinn. If that's all I was after, last week would have been a much better time for that, Little Chihuahua."

"Why didn't you? You guys were all over each other." Jessica's tiny hackles had come down a few levels.

"Wasn't my intention and wasn't my call. I wasn't leading the interaction that night. I thought we made that clear to you the first time you played overprotective guard dog and nipped at my ankles."

"So you're telling me you only look like you know your way around every dark alley of this city and spend your days pumping iron in a prison yard?" Jessica asked.

At least she looked a little less sure of herself.

"Jesus, should I thank you or growl and watch you wet your pants?" Lola asked. If Jessica only knew who she really was. Although the part about knowing her way around dark alleys wasn't far off, but not for the reasons she thought. "I'm going to change so I can walk Quinn to class."

"Don't forget to carry her books," Jessica called after her, but there was no malice in her tone this time.

"Truce, Little Chihuahua," Lola said. She held up her hands in submission. "Looks can be deceiving. I come in peace."

Chapter Eight

Lola hadn't meant to sneak into Quinn's lecture, and once she did, she certainly hadn't meant to stay, but here she was, trying to blend in with a bunch of college kids making their way out of class so she could make an unseen exit. She hunched her shoulders to try to make herself shorter, but she was still way taller than most of them. After escaping undetected, she headed toward her motorcycle and thought about the fifty-minute lecture. Even though she hadn't graduated high school, she'd always loved being in the classroom. She'd had dreams of college, but her life fell apart before that could happen.

Now, her brain felt like her muscles did after time in the weight room, tired, challenged, expanded. She liked the feeling. She keyed her comms as she neared her bike. Despite having been up all night, she had work to do.

"Finally, you call me," Dubs said. "I've been dying since you got all bent out of shape at Max. You don't call, you don't write, you don't send pictures of your new squeeze."

Lola ignored Dubs's teasing. "What do you know about neuroscience?"

"Neuroscience?" Dubs asked, sounding incredulous. "Does this have anything to do with our case?"

"Sure, sort of." Lola regretted asking.

"I'm reasonably conversant in mechanical and software engineering and physics, you know, the things I need to make cars stop and go at my command. And of course I can talk about cars until your ears fall off. I'm starting to love hearing all about computer guts and brains, but neuroscience has nothing to do with stealing things or getting my lady worked up. So, I guess I can't help you. Why do you ask?" Dubs's voice was overly sweet and sugary. She was fishing for information, but doing it so obviously, it made Lola laugh.

"I sat in on a lecture today at CLA and it was interesting. Maybe I'll add a couple neuroscience books to my library reading list."

"You know, most people only read textbooks because they have to. Your library list is like a torture chamber's greatest hits. What do you do when you want to punish yourself? You know what, don't answer that. I don't want to know. We should keep the mystery in our relationship."

"What do I do for punishment?" Lola asked. "Isn't it obvious? I call you."

Dubs didn't even pretend to be offended. "This new interest in neuroscience wouldn't have anything to do with a new lady would it? Hot for teacher?"

"I'm not worked up over a lady," Lola said.

"Uh-huh," Dubs said. "So what's your Professor Hotty's name? Max already told me, but I want to hear it from you. She always leaves out the good stuff. No one just happens to sit in on a college lecture to stimulate their neurosciences."

"I called for work purposes," Lola said.

"Sure, sure, we've got plenty of time for that," Dubs said. "I'm working on my information extraction skills at the moment. Holt's been giving me a few pointers. For instance, right now, I know you're evading and I should keep pressing for the information I need."

"Quinn Golden," Lola said. "But she's not my anything. I just sat in on her class." Lola ignored the replay of how beautiful Quinn looked this morning, rumpled from sleep, or how she'd felt in her arms while they danced, or what it felt like to kiss her. *Jesus, women are nothing but trouble.*

"Quinn Golden," Dubs said. "Isn't Quinn the name of the woman you made Max talk to the other night when you were out dancing?"

Lola was spared further interrogation when someone back at the office interrupted Dubs with some business Lola couldn't make out. It didn't take long before she was back.

"Isabelle wants to know if your Quinn Golden is actually Dr. Quinn Golden, the hotshot neuroscientist who is apparently doing something to change the world, or build a better tomorrow, or something clichéd like that."

"Probably," Lola said. "How many Dr. Quinn Goldens can there be in the world?" She wasn't interested in dating again anytime soon, and even if she was, she already knew Quinn was far out of her league. But it sounded like they weren't even playing the same game, on the same planet. It was a little discouraging.

"Damn," Dubs said. "You better start reading a whole lot more textbooks. And journal articles, and technical manuals, and sit in on a few more college classes, girl. Max could get you a real impressive college degree if you want one."

"Dubs."

"I know, I know. You good guys are opposed to that kind of tinkering."

"You wear a white hat now too, you know." Lola couldn't think of anyone with a better heart than Dubs.

"And sometimes it's so stifling. Can we get to work?" Dubs asked.

"Finally," Lola said. "That's why I called."

"What took you so long then? Yammering my ear off about lady problems. What do you need?"

"Name and address of Kevin Garvey's wife and any other known associates. Also, any new leads I don't know about? How is that computer thingy coming along? Has Max had time to trace the email?"

"Whoa. One thing at a time. You want the addresses texted to your phone? These are just for surveillance, right? Like H said?" Dubs sounded suspicious.

"Of course. Except his wife. I want to talk to her. She might be able to give more information on where he might be. I doubt she's a threat and I'll be careful. Anything new to report?"

"Nothing yet," Dubs said. "Who knew even Max has a limit on the magic she can work? She's been mumbling at her computer since you got that program up and running. I'll let you know when we have more."

"Thanks, Dubs." Lola was about to sign off when Dubs spoke again.

"And, Lola, be careful. Moose is on the ground in California, but it's a big state. Don't do anything stupid."

"With you chirping in my ear?" Lola said. "How could I even think it? I'll be safe. Just get me those addresses and take care of everyone else."

A few minutes after disconnecting with Dubs, her phone buzzed. She read Kevin Garvey's address, kicked her bike to life, and hoped his wife was home.

Twenty minutes later, when Lola knocked on the door, a petite woman with neat curly brown hair and suspicious brown eyes opened the door. She was dressed in business casual attire and looked like she was probably home on her lunch break.

"Are you Mrs. Garvey?" Lola asked.

"I'm married to Kevin Garvey," the woman said, "if that's what you're asking."

"Do you have a few minutes? I have a couple of questions related to his disappearance."

"Look, the police were by here already. They said they'd be in touch. I call and check in every day or so. I don't know what else you want me to say."

"I'm not with the police, ma'am," Lola said. "I have a private interest in finding your husband."

Lola knew immediately she'd struck a nerve, apparently, a particularly unpleasant, nasty one. While before the woman seemed wary but accepting, now she was anything but. Her eyes flashed with fury and something else Lola struggled to place, maybe terror, or loathing. She didn't have time to evaluate more before she was warding off a two-handed, slap-happy physical assault designed more for emotional outlet than damage infliction.

"So that's what it's come to, huh? Those low-life bookies are sending women to try and get information from me? And what, are you supposed to appeal to me woman to woman? And if that doesn't work, break my kneecaps just like the others threatened to do? I don't know anything. For the last time, I don't know anything."

Once she was all out of gas, Lola led the weeping woman back in the house and got her settled on the couch.

"Can I get you a glass of water?" Lola asked. When she received no response, she sat on the couch too, forgoing beverages in case the assault resumed and her time to build trust was short. "My name is Lola. I'm not going to hurt you. I don't work for anyone that means you harm. It's important you understand that. I understand you don't trust me. How about I tell you a little bit about why I'm looking for your husband? Then you can decide whether to throw me out?"

The woman nodded. Of course, Lola already knew a great deal about this woman, but she wanted to give her the opportunity to share what she wanted in her own time. Right now, she was their only lead on Kevin Garvey, and any information she had was important.

"I work for someone your husband wanted to talk to very badly before he disappeared. He went to a lot of trouble to try to contact her, and he wasn't very polite about how he asked."

"Do you work for Holt Lasher?"

Lola's stomach flew into her throat and she had to work very hard to keep her expression neutral. She wasn't sure she was completely successful.

Kevin's wife must have read her expression. "It's just that he was obsessed with that name right before he disappeared. He kept telling me all our problems would go away as soon as he found Holt Lasher. Kept saying she wouldn't turn her back on family and he would make her understand. I know he has daughters, but I'd never heard that name before. I thought his daughters were named Eleanor and Adele or something like that."

Despite the seriousness of the situation, Lola found it funny that another person mistakenly called Isabelle "Adele." She'd thought Holt's mother did that just to annoy Isabelle.

"I do work for Holt Lasher," Lola said. There was no point in lying about that. She wanted this woman to trust her. To help her. "And I really need to find Kevin. I think that Holt, and those she cares about, are in danger until he's found."

"From Kevin?"

"I don't know. Probably not. But first he wanted to talk to Holt, and now the people who took him do. I don't like that coincidence. I want to talk to Kevin to get any information he has and find out why he wanted to talk to Holt. You said bookies are after Kevin, and now you. Do you think it's related to that?"

"You said people who took him. The police think he ran off. I've never believed that, but they don't listen to me. Do you have evidence that I'm right?"

Lola weighed her options. *Nothing like walking the high wire without a net.* This was what she'd asked for though, the chance to prove herself. "He didn't run off and we do have evidence of that. If you recall my saying that your husband wasn't asking very politely to get in touch with my boss, well, the folks who are providing his current accommodation are even less so."

"What do you mean by that?"

"We don't have any indication that Kevin has been harmed, if that's what you're asking," Lola said. She wasn't sure if she was reading the situation correctly, but Kevin's wife seemed more agitated and stressed than worried. "But the threats against Holt and her family were more aggressive."

She seemed to accept that Lola wasn't going to provide more substance. "Have you given the information to the police?"

"Of course," Lola said.

"And is your goal to find my husband?"

"My goal is to keep Holt and her family safe," Lola said. "And I believe that involves finding your husband. We still don't know why he wanted to talk to her. I would very much like to find out."

"You said you mean me no harm, but you didn't say anything about Kevin. Don't be offended by this, but you don't look like a big talker. You look like more of a silencer. What happens when you find him? Are you going to kill him?"

Lola almost laughed, the question caught her so off guard. She'd forgotten that she wasn't operating in New England where the name Holt Lasher was all the business card she needed. No one would assume she was a hired hit woman. But Kevin's wife was looking at her so seriously and with such suspicion, it was easy to see how serious the question was.

"No, ma'am, that's not how we work. Couldn't be further from the truth, actually."

"I looked up Ms. Lasher. I know all about her. What I don't know with any certainty is that you work for her."

"It's not great for business to put our roster on a website," Lola said. She wondered what exactly this woman had found about Holt online that led her to believe she knew all about her. She doubted it was even a fraction of the truth of the real woman. "But I do have a business card."

"I could spend a little time on my computer and get a thousand business cards mailed to me in a couple days. Then I could work for Ms. Lasher too."

The woman was careful and smart. Lola liked that, even if it was making her job more difficult.

"If you're going to work for Holt, you should probably stop calling her 'Ms. Lasher.' That drives her nuts. How about you call and ask to speak with Holt? You'll probably get a woman named Max, or if you are exceptionally lucky, Dubs. Either one can find Holt for you." Lola didn't like that idea at all, but it seemed like the best option to build trust. She felt like she should be able to do that without having to pull Holt in as a personal reference.

"I can see my calling your boss would be embarrassing to you."

"I'll get over it. Please call if it will ease your mind."

Mrs. Garvey looked at her thoughtfully. "How about we compromise? You said you passed along the information about Kevin being abducted to the police, correct?"

Lola nodded.

"I'll call over and verify that. If you are telling the truth, I don't see why I shouldn't trust you. It's not like anyone else that's knocked on my door has been all that helpful."

While she waited, Lola tried not to doze on the couch. Her overnight shift was finally catching up to her. Uninvited, thoughts of Quinn sprang to mind. She'd been so commanding and sexy standing at the front of the lecture hall in full professorial glory. She was clearly brilliant and knew more about basic levels of neuroscience than Lola knew about anything. It probably should have been intimidating, but the way she delivered the information and wielded all that knowledge made Lola want to learn more. *Hot for teacher indeed.*

Garvey's wife interrupted her musings. "Seems you were telling the truth. I'm Susan Sandstrom. It was his third marriage. I kept my name, in case you were wondering."

"Nice to meet you, Susan," Lola said, shaking her hand. "No judgment on my part. Do you mind my asking you a few more questions about your husband? I'm also a little worried about your safety after how you greeted me. Do you have somewhere else you can stay?"

"Ask away," Susan said. "I may go stay with my sister for a while. I'm rather fond of my kneecaps."

"You said your husband talked about Holt before he disappeared, so you knew of her. How did you know I worked for her?"

"I guessed," Susan said. "But you look like the type. I told you I looked her up when he kept talking about her. There are pictures of her out there. Not a lot, but a few. She looks like an army tank. So do you. Someone shows up at my door asking the kind of questions about Kevin you were asking? I can draw a straight line."

As Lola had suspected earlier, Susan was sharp. "Fair enough. Your husband has gambling debts?"

"He did. Look, you're going to find out all of this I'm sure, but my husband's a flawed man. But when we met, he cared for me. I was sick. Cancer. He literally nursed me back to health. He's a lot of things, but with me, he's different than a lot of people say. I just want you to remember that when you're out there looking for him. There are a lot of reasons to write him off. Most of the people in his life, rightly in a lot of cases, already have."

"I'm not writing anyone off, Susan. I want to find him." Lola tried to reconcile this description of a caring man with what she knew of the father Isabelle had grown up with. She knew people changed, but it was still hard to come to terms with these two versions of the same man. She hoped the information he had was worth the headache.

"All right, well yes, he did have gambling debts. He was a typical gambler. Casinos, the track. You name it. I guess about nine months ago he met some kids at the college. He's a custodian there. It wasn't long after he met these new kids that all the gambling moved online. Suddenly, he was making money. But he got weird and secretive. And then all of a sudden people started coming around demanding he pay them back or else. I don't know what that was all about. About six weeks ago he started talking about Holt, and how she could solve all of our problems. That she would never turn her back on family and he would just have to make her understand. It freaked me out a little, to be honest. He was obsessed, but he wouldn't say more than that. I don't think she's actually family, though. No family I know about."

"How do you know the kids from the college were involved with gambling online? Did you ever meet them?"

"They came by the house once. Typical college boys. I think there were about five of them, and I overheard them talking about it. Kevin told me one night he found a get-rich-quick fix for all his problems but wouldn't tell me what it was. But he spent all his time on his laptop."

"Do you still have the computer?" Lola tried not to get her hopes up, but she knew Max would want access to anything Kevin Garvey had been spending that much time on.

"No, I don't. The police searched for it, but never found it. You're welcome to look around if you want. He spent most of his time out in the garage."

Lola followed Susan's direction through the house and out to the attached garage. A workbench crammed with tools dominated one wall. Pegboard hung behind the bench from floor to ceiling, allowing tools to hang. Two nudie posters from decades ago, weathered and worn, hung above the bench. A lawnmower, a couple of folding chairs, and a washer and dryer were against another wall. There was no space for a car.

She surveyed everything carefully from the middle of the room. Susan said Kevin spent most of his time out here, so Lola tried to picture what he would spend hours at a time doing. She pulled one of the folding chairs from its perch against the wall, opened it, and sat down. At that level she could see the pegboard under the bench. A section just under the bench about two feet square had been cut out. The original pegboard was back in place now, but Lola could see a handle that allowed the board's removal.

What do we have here?

Lola squeezed under the bench and removed the pegboard. She took a deep breath and reached inside.

Please no spiders.

Her hand connected with something cool and metallic. She pulled it out. It was Kevin's laptop. She flipped on her comms and Max answered.

"I've got a laptop for you," Lola said. "I'm turning it over to the police, but I figure you want to have a look around too."

"Of course I do," Max said. "You still have that thumb drive I gave you?"

"The one you told me never to lose?"

"Yes, that one. Plug it in and turn on the computer," Max said.

"And if there's passwords or security or something?" Lola asked.

"That's why I told you not to ever lose the thumb drive. I'll take care of it."

Lola did as she was told, and before long Max alerted her she had everything she needed from the computer. Lola shut down the laptop and checked that it was the only thing in Kevin's hiding place.

"I found the laptop," Lola said when she found Susan. "You should alert the police. They'll probably want to have a look." She handed the laptop over.

"Anything useful on it?" Susan asked.

"Who said I took a look?" Lola asked.

Susan gave her a look that could best be described as "oh please."

"I don't know yet," Lola said. "We're still decrypting the data." She hoped that was the right term. She'd heard Max use those words strung together in that way before.

"All right," Susan said. "I'll give the police a call. Maybe someone can find something useful."

"One more thing before I leave," Lola said. "Do you mind giving me a list of the casinos and tracks Kevin frequented? And any of the people he liked to gamble with, or any other names you have that might be associated with either his gambling or his disappearance? Even if you gave them to the police."

Lola left with a list of places and names, ready to start her hunt. But first, she needed some sleep. She was physically exhausted, but emotionally riding a bit of a high. Not only had she found a potentially really useful piece of evidence for finding Kevin Garvey and hopefully those holding him, but she'd run into Quinn again. That alone was enough to make today a fifteen on a one to ten scale. *Dubs is right; she stimulates my neurosciences. Not good.*

CHAPTER NINE

"What brought you to my fine city, Lola Badger? Please don't tell me it was my Intro to Neuroscience course."

Quinn wanted to laugh at the look on Lola's face, part embarrassment, part guilt, part kid getting caught with her hand in the cookie jar, but something in Lola's eyes stopped her. There was vulnerability there, shyness maybe.

"Spotted me, huh?" Lola asked. "You're an amazing teacher. I'm learning so much."

"And here I thought you just slipped in to watch me for an hour." Quinn was teasing, but she realized she didn't mind the thought.

"Shame on me for not mentioning how smoking hot it is to watch a woman show off how brilliant she is for an hour. I definitely stayed to watch that," Lola said.

Quinn felt herself blushing. She looked down at her breakfast and made a show of pushing her pancakes around her plate while she willed her cheeks to return to a normal color. Lola had spontaneously invited her to breakfast after one of her shifts ended, and since Quinn didn't have class that morning, and had once again slept at the office, she'd agreed. Since then, it had just become an unspoken thing they did, and Quinn was beginning to look forward to it more than she probably should. There was no pretense to Lola and no underlying agenda. She wasn't competing with her or trying to outmaneuver her for praise or grant dollars. It didn't hurt that she was hot as hell and every time they were together, and quite a few times when they weren't, Quinn couldn't stop thinking of how she kissed.

"So, you didn't answer my question," Quinn said. She was determined not to look at Lola's lips now that she was thinking about kissing her.

"And what question was that?" Lola asked.

Lola slowly brought a bite of omelet to her mouth. Quinn followed the path of the fork. *Shit.*

She pulled her eyes up from Lola's mouth and fell into Lola's gaze instead. Clearly, Lola knew exactly what Quinn had been thinking about as she broke into a large grin before popping the bite of omelet into her mouth and chewing slowly and licking her lips unnecessarily.

"My city, what brought you to my city?" Quinn said.

"Oh, right. I needed a change. The weather sucked back East. Bad breakup. Take your pick."

"Well, that was intriguingly cryptic," Quinn said.

"I didn't mean to be," Lola said. "I really was just looking to do something different. Get out on my own for a little while."

"You must miss George though."

A look of raw, unfiltered pain and sadness flittered across Lola's face before she smiled, and her eyes lit up at the thought of her nephew. Quinn wondered at the source of the pain. What or who had hurt her so deeply? The thought of Lola in that much distress made her more uncomfortable. They didn't know each other well, but there was something about Lola that drew her in.

"I do miss that little guy. Since the day I found out about him, he's been one big adventure."

"What's your sister like? Does she look like you?" Suddenly, Quinn wanted to know everything about Lola. She had a grant waiting for her back at the office that wouldn't write itself, but lingering over omelets and pancakes with Lola was much more appealing.

"God, no. Holt is a walking, talking, Greek god. Captain America is jealous of her. She's got the moral compass to match as well, which is just the tiniest bit annoying to be honest."

Lola said it with a smile, so Quinn knew Lola didn't really resent her sister.

"Holt is the kind of woman that walks into a room and everyone stops and stares at her. She just has a presence that commands a room and fills up the space. Not in a threatening way, but in the kind of way that lets everyone know she's in charge. She used to notice, but she doesn't anymore now that she's found Isabelle." Lola frowned. "Actually, now everyone is staring at Isabelle. Poor Holt. Lost her place at the top."

Quinn stared at Lola. If anyone else had given Quinn that description, she would have thought she was talking about Lola. Sure, she wouldn't have used such masculine descriptors, Lola was much more feminine than Captain America, and she was all goddess, but the rest was spot-on. "It sounds like you and your sister are exactly alike." Quinn reached out and traced her fingers up Lola's forearm. It wasn't a gesture meant to entice so much as reinforce her words.

Lola shook her head. "That's just because you haven't seen Holt in person. She's built and could clear this room with a glance."

"Sweetie," Quinn said. "I could bounce a quarter off your ass, and if you flexed you could send someone to the hospital on the rebound." *That ass is as close to perfect as they get.* "And as for clearing a room, on the night we met, you had two bar stools all to yourself at the most popular club in town."

"Well," Lola said, looking a little flustered, "I was saving one for you."

"So you've said."

Quinn flagged the waitress and paid for their meal. "Walk me back to campus?"

Lola got a text that she read quickly before answering.

"Yes, of course. But we've spent all breakfast talking about me. I've seen your Intro to Neuroscience class, but I have a feeling that's just scratching the surface of what you do. Tell me more. What's on those fancy computers I was about to blow up when you dragged me out of your lab? Or what about what you work on all night, every night in your office? Or what's your family like?"

"You really want to hear about the reason Jessica scolds me every morning and no one in the department likes me? Or about how my family doesn't talk to me because I can't stop thinking about women like you?" Quinn knew she sounded bitter and a bit sad, but she couldn't help it.

"Of course I do," Lola said.

Lola went out of her way to make eye contact even when Quinn tried to avoid it, which Quinn appreciated.

"What is it that keeps your brilliant mind occupied? I see it working even when we're talking." Lola waved away Quinn's apology. "I never feel deprived. There's nothing more invigorating than watching a mind at work. But just as a point of clarification, is it women *like* me, or me specifically, filling your thoughts?"

"I'm sure you'd like to know," Quinn said.

That got a smile from Lola.

Beautiful smile. Definitely you. "As for the rest, I know I'm not always the best company. I've been told as much many times before."

"Well, then you've been keeping the wrong company." Lola scooped Quinn's hand, laced their fingers together, and gave her a reassuring squeeze. It felt nice, really nice. Quinn would have been happy to walk around the rest of the day holding Lola's hand, but apparently, Lola didn't agree. She pulled away quickly. The gesture did seem out of character for Lola who, so far, had let Quinn lead all of their interactions, but as far as Quinn was concerned, Lola could lead away if that's the direction her initiative took her. It turned out Lola wasn't blowing smoke when she asked to know more about what Quinn did. She was curious about everything, asked great questions, and had a better understanding of some of the complexities of Quinn's work than a few of her graduate students.

"Have you been holding out on me, Lola? Are you a professor, or graduate student spying on us for some reason?" Quinn was clearly joking, but she did wonder why Lola was working as a custodian when she should have been in a research lab.

Lola looked so confused Quinn didn't prolong the teasing.

"Some of my graduate students don't understand half of what we were just talking about. I'm the one invigorated by the brilliant mind at work now. Where did you study?" Quinn thought Lola looked embarrassed and uncomfortable. She wondered why.

"You know I've been sitting in on your class," Lola said.

"Lola," Quinn said. "I'm a middling professor at best. I'm a researcher at heart. It's not possible you learned all of this from my class."

"I guess that's true. I've been doing some reading too. Some books and articles. A few you wrote, which are intense and amazing."

Lola's voice was almost a whisper now, and now she wasn't making eye contact despite Quinn's best efforts.

"So you never took any of this in undergrad. You learned all of what we just spent the last couple of hours chatting about from my class and reading on your own?" Lola nodded and Quinn felt like her mind might explode. "Jesus, and I always thought I was a fast learner. So, if this is just something you picked up on the side, what topic captured your heart in school? Can I guess your major? Please don't tell me you were a double major?"

Quinn wanted to know what academic pursuit was worthy of Lola's full attention.

Lola looked horrified.

"Triple major?" Had Quinn underestimated her and been insulting?

"Look, I've got to go," Lola said.

She was out of Quinn's office and loping down the hall before Quinn could react. Quinn replayed their conversation quickly as she hurried after Lola. *Shit. I made a lot of assumptions in that conversation. Not everyone goes to college, you idiot.* In her rush to catch up to Lola, who had a head start and a much longer stride, she didn't notice that Lola had stopped just inside the double doors leading to the campus quad. She would have smacked right into her, and given how rock hard Lola's ass was, probably bounced three or four feet into a heap on the floor if Lola hadn't turned around and caught her in a tight embrace, stopping her momentum.

"Whoa. Where are you going in such a hurry? People are trying to stand here grumpily without being bowled over, you know."

"I'm sorry I upset you," Quinn said. "You just sort of knocked my socks off back there and I made some assumptions."

Lola still looked embarrassed, but she looked at Quinn this time.

"My big cowardly escape plan was thwarted by the rain," Lola said, pointing outside. "I'm not prepared for riding in this weather. I'm too tired to risk it anyway."

"I have a hard time picturing you on a bicycle," Quinn said.

"Then don't try. That's not the kind of bike I was talking about. Mine has much more horsepower."

"Could you get any sexier?" Quinn realized she'd muttered it out loud, and contemplated her own jog back down the hall to escape but settled for clamping her hand over her mouth instead.

"If you feel that way, it makes me happy," Lola said. She gently moved Quinn's hand from her face. "But I have to work hard at it. You just have to walk in a room and no matter what else is happening, you're the most beautiful thing in it."

It took a moment for Quinn to be able to speak. Lola was incredibly sweet and often caught her completely off guard with a sincere declaration of admiration and attraction. "Come on, smooth talker," Quinn said. "I'll drive you home so all your hard earned swag doesn't wash off in the downpour."

CHAPTER TEN

Holt waited impatiently for Lola to answer the phone. Everyone else in the office was busy working. She didn't feel like getting an update from Lola was real work, but it was all she was left with. She'd delegated the rest of the work to everyone else. If she was being honest, she missed Lola and was happy for the chance to talk to her, even if it wasn't real work.

Lola answered.

"Update," Holt said gruffly.

"Good morning, H," Lola said.

She sounded way too cheerful for someone who had been up all night.

"Where are the Wonder Twins? Wait, you're grumpy and taking my report. That means everyone else is busy and you have nothing better to do but talk to me. Sucks being the boss and having a fantastic, capable, well-trained, loyal team."

"And here I was thinking I missed you," Holt said.

"You do miss me," Lola said. "But we can talk business for a while to make you feel better. Has Max found anything from that laptop?"

"I thought you were giving me the update," Holt said. She already felt less grumpy. It was nice to have their connection back, even if it was only over the phone. Lola wasn't just her employee, she was a vital part of Holt's inner circle. It had been difficult operating without her most trusted core fully intact since Lola and Moose had been gone.

"Oh man, you are in a mood. Fine. I've been following up with the gambling contacts I got from Kevin Garvey's wife, but so far there's no sign of him. I've been to a couple of the casinos and I'm hitting tracks this week. I'm sticking to the plan, ghost surveillance only, but that's not getting me a lot. From what his wife said, his interest in you started with those college kids and the thing on the onlines."

"It's called the Internet. Do you do that on purpose to get under Max's skin?"

"I followed up with Quinn about her lab and the computers there, just like Max asked. Why did she need information about Quinn's lab?"

"She found some interesting things on Kevin Garvey's laptop. That led her down a few more interesting paths and, well, I could have her explain it to you in nerdy detail, but you just called the Internet 'the onlines.' How about we leave it at she thinks she figured out what Kevin was mixed up in and why his wife told you he thought he was going to be rich. Isabelle and Max are following the money now. The short version is it looks like he moved his gambling habit online. Max and Isabelle seem to think he was making a lot of money. There are still a lot of unanswered questions that we need answers to. Aside from finding Garvey, I'm hoping you can help on that end as well."

Lola didn't say anything for a few beats. Holt waited her out.

"What does all that have to do with Quinn?"

Holt noted Lola asked about Quinn, not her lab, not Kevin Garvey, not any of the information Holt just gave her. That worried her. She needed to know where Lola's head was, and right now, she had no idea. After the Tiffany debacle, Lola hadn't seemed herself. Holt didn't want her falling for someone else that was bad news, and Lola hadn't always had the best track record of telling just what kind of news was standing in front of her. On top of that, she was three thousand miles away and Holt didn't have any way of protecting her if she got into trouble. She hated not being able to get to her people if they needed her.

"Since you're full of questions and clearly can't wait to get started tracking down all the new information I need you to get for me, sounds like it's probably time for a full briefing."

Holt's prodding had the desired effect.

"Sorry, H. My first questions should have been about the case."

"CB, two minutes. Let me get the rest of the crew and we can Skype you in." Holt hung up, confident she would hear from Lola again in exactly two minutes. She was also glad for the excuse to call everyone together and have something useful to do. Not for the first time she wondered when she'd become superfluous because she'd hired such a talented team.

She headed for Isabelle and Max, who were exactly where she'd left them, hunched over their computers. She nuzzled into Isabelle's neck, letting the comfortable feel and smell remind her of everything that was good in her life. She kissed Isabelle's cheek. "If you two wouldn't mind joining me in the conference room, Lola is calling in for an update."

"Just give me a few minutes, H," Max said. "I've got a couple more things I want to run down."

Isabelle was already up and packing her laptop. She leaned in and whispered in Holt's ear. "You really should give her more than a minute's warning. She's working hard enough already."

"Forty-five seconds, Max," Holt said. She'd been doing this to Max more and more, springing frustrating and nearly impossible situations on her. Max didn't know it, but it was part of her training. Max had started going out in the field from time to time, but physical confrontations weren't the only time Holt needed Max to react without thinking, act on instinct, and be able to remain calm no matter the pressure cooker she faced. Right now, she was still stubbornly determined to look for an easy out or argue her way to a solution.

"H, you've got to be kidding me. I can barely make it across the room in that much time," Max said.

"Thirty-five seconds," Holt said. "If your report isn't on the screen and ready when my phone rings, all your fancy toys go in the drawer for an indeterminate amount of time. Keep arguing if you like."

Max shot across the room, practically sprinting.

"Whoa, did you drop a lit match down her shorts, H?" Dubs asked. "She's not usually a morning person."

"Conference room, Dubs."

"Just between you and me?" Dubs meandered toward the gathering crowd but held back.

Holt looked at her watch. She was going to be late to this meeting because Dubs was walking like a dawdling toddler.

"This tough love training, springing things on Max to force her to perform under pressure, isn't working like you hoped. It's just stressing her out. She thinks you're mad at her. That doesn't motivate her to get better. It would totally work for me of course. I love an excuse to prove your ass wrong. But you've got to try something different for her, otherwise you're just kicking your puppy and I've got to make her feel better at the end of the day. Although to be honest, that's not the worst thing in the world for me personally—"

"Stop, now," Holt said. She didn't need to hear where Dubs was going with the rest of that thought, but she appreciated Dubs looking out for Max. They were sickeningly over-the-top into each other, and drove everyone a little nuts from time to time, but Holt respected how much they loved each other. Plus, she cared about each of them. If Dubs was telling her Max wasn't responding well to her attempts at training, she needed to reevaluate.

Despite the Dubs delay, Holt slid into her chair just as the phone rang. Max beamed Lola onto the big screen.

"Welcome back," Holt said. "Max and Isabelle have been following a money trail they stumbled on when poking around Kevin Garvey's laptop. They can fill you in on what they've found. It might give you some better leads to follow up out there. And as I mentioned, we could use some information that you might be able to gather for us on the ground." Holt hated how Isabelle flinched every time her father's name was brought up during their daily discussions of this case. She hoped they found this guy fast so he could once again be out of their lives. If she had her way, she would pay him a personal visit and make sure he never bothered them again, but she knew it wasn't what Isabelle wanted.

"Briefing first," Lola said. "But then I need the important updates. I've been gone a long time. Isabelle, you have to fill me in on everything George is doing since Holt only says 'he's good.' Dubs, has Max knocked you up yet? How is Jose without Moose? Please tell me Tuna finally stopped calling what's her face? I need the important things."

"Can we get to work, please?" Holt asked, trying to use her best mock serious voice. "I've got people sending me threatening emails. I don't take kindly to that."

"Were you listening? I clearly said work first. But when was the last time you got one of those emails anyway?" Lola asked. She was obviously joking.

"An hour ago," Max said.

"Excuse me?" Holt said. The atmosphere in the room was drained of its lively good cheer. "How many have I gotten since the first?" She didn't know they were still coming in and was furious Max hadn't kept her updated. This was her safety, her family's safety. She didn't realize she'd gotten up, but she was standing next to Isabelle with her hand on her shoulder. She quickly reviewed where George was and would be for the rest of the day. *Safe.*

"This is the only one since the first. It just arrived an hour ago. I updated the LAPD as soon as it came in. I didn't have a chance to add it to my official briefing since you dragged me away from what I was doing, but this one is almost identical to the first. Demands for money, threats to come and talk to Isabelle and her sister. There are two important differences. There's no proof of life video attached here, and this one has a deadline. If you recall, the first one didn't, which we all thought was strange. Forty-eight hours to pay or I guess something bad happens. They don't get into specifics, which is sort of weird."

Holt wasn't sure whether she was annoyed or encouraged at Max's salty attitude. She tamped down her own anger at not being alerted immediately to the new threat. Anger had always fueled her, but Dubs said that wasn't working with Max. Perhaps she needed a different approach. "So these guys are either complete amateurs or they think we'll be more compliant without a proof of life video, any true threat for what happens with non-compliance, or an actual deadline."

"Aren't we supposed to be able to use our imaginations?" Isabelle asked.

"I guess," Holt said. "But the scariest scenario here would be them killing the hostage. In order for that to be so unimaginable an outcome that I would do anything to prevent it, including pay a lot of money, it would have to be someone I cared for deeply. Kevin Garvey isn't someone I care about, although he seemed to think he would be, for some reason. Don't get me wrong, I don't want him to die, but they haven't threatened me with that. The most they've really spelled out is that they might email Isabelle. That pisses me off and makes me want to find them more than I want to find Garvey. The worst-case scenarios I'm picturing are them coming after her. I don't know if that's the conclusion they're hoping I'll jump to, but it's dangerous for them if that's the game they're playing."

"Did you get a briefing from Moose before he headed out here with me? Did Mason give up anything useful?" Lola asked.

"Nothing," Holt said. "He's convinced Garvey hired him. Moose believes him. Whatever the truth is, Moose doesn't think Mason was lying. What else can you tell us, Max?"

"Well," Max said, "like I said, the email came in about an hour ago. Isabelle and I have been working on this laptop data since we got it from Lola, though. And it's been very chatty. Our little friend Kevin sucks at any kind of computer security. His password was password1. Not even a capital letter."

Holt gave Max a warning look.

"Not important. Moving on. We know Kevin is a gambler, but from what his wife said, he's always been a face-to-face kind of guy. Casinos, tracks, that kind of thing. Well, it seems that about a year ago, he got into daily fantasy sports online, football specifically, but he dabbled in the other big sports as well. Does anyone here play daily fantasy football or know what I'm talking about?"

Only Dubs raised her hand, which prompted everyone in the room to look at her like she had three heads.

"What? I stole cars for a living. You think gambling isn't another way to get my rocks off? At least this is mostly legal."

"Are we going to have a problem here?" Holt trusted Dubs to be able to flirt the line between legal and illegal and ask for help if she needed it. She just worried she and Dubs would have different ideas of where that line should be drawn.

"Nah," Dubs said. "Turns out taking rich dudes to the cleaners or picking which freak athlete is going to rush for a gazillion yards one week just isn't much of a thrill. Catching bad guys is much closer to the old buzz. And whenever Max sees fit to handcuff me to her bed."

"Could've done without the last update," Lola said.

"Think we all could have, but we're happy you're happy," Holt said.

Max, who was now impossibly red, raised her hand. Holt waved her on.

"Like I was saying. Daily fantasy sports are big business. Players pick a new fantasy team each day, or week, depending on which sport they're playing, and bet money on their teams. You get points based on how the players you chose perform. There are all different formats to different games, but the long and short of it is, the games are almost impossible for an average Joe to make any money. But Kevin was making money. A lot of it, and had been since he started."

"Wait," Isabelle said. "Why is it so hard to make money? Isn't it like regular fantasy football? My sister's in a league and spends an insane amount of time researching her team before their draft and before every game so she can beat her friends in their fake football league."

"Hey, our league isn't a fake football league," Holt said. "It's a fantasy football league. Fake football makes it sounds like the lingerie bowl or something. How is this online daily thing different from regular fantasy football?"

"Fantasy football and lingerie bowl sound like they should go together," Isabelle said.

"In traditional fantasy football, you join a league and draft your team at the beginning of the season. With the exception of waiver wire additions or trades, you keep the same team the entire football season," Dubs said. "With this daily fantasy, as Max said, you can draft a new team each week and play a bunch of different types of games."

"There's also a lot of money involved," Max said. Max, as always, was typing while she spoke, pulling up images relevant to the case and throwing them onto the screen. "But it's hard to make money in the daily fantasy leagues because of how many people are playing at any given time and because everything is online, computers are involved. Very industrious people have figured out ways to write algorithms to enter thousands of games and maximize the odds of selecting the ideal team each week. Those teams are entered into the big money games, but also smaller ones that earn points to the high stakes games later in the season. The top winners each week are almost exclusively those computer-entered players. There just aren't that many openings for an actual person to pick a perfect team week to week and actually come out on top."

"So the games are rigged?"

"No, that would mean collusion or deliberate action by the owners of the companies who run the games. This is just intelligent people seeing an opportunity to take advantage of a weakness in the system and capitalizing on it."

"Is that what Kevin Garvey was doing? Is that why he was winning?" Holt had a hard time believing he was capable of writing the computer code required given what Max described of his security measures. Surely anyone developing that kind of algorithm wouldn't be dumb enough to leave it vulnerable with such lousy data security.

"I don't think he was, but he was certainly taking part in something similar. He has the algorithms on his computer, and I think that's why he was winning so much money," Max said. "I've been trying to trace the code. Every code writer has unique nuances to their style and writing. It's possible I can figure out who wrote this. I don't think he was the author. There's no other evidence of computer coding on his laptop or Internet history. Aside from the fantasy sites, I would have pegged him as relatively computer illiterate."

"Okay," Lola said. "If this is all aboveboard and he didn't write any of the computer gobbledygook, why are we getting proof of life videos for him?"

"Oh," Isabelle said. "You misunderstand. Just because the computer part is aboveboard, doesn't mean the money part is. Someone has been financing the whole operation, and he's probably been skimming a little off the top for himself."

"Naughty boy," Dubs said.

"So we think they're the ones who snatched him?" Holt asked. It made sense, sort of. Kevin was putting a lot of hope in daughters he had treated like shit for most of their lives and hadn't spoken to in years. First, he tried to contact them directly, through Holt, hoping they would bail him out, and now he must have told his captors about them.

"What are you thinking, H? That's your 'bullshit detector' expression," Lola said.

"It's the simplest explanation, so it's probably the right one," Holt said. "But Kevin would need to massively oversell his relationship with Isabelle and Ellen to make anyone believe they were going to come running with the cash to save his sorry ass. Plus, no one's really put the hard sell on us yet. Aside from a couple of vaguely threatening emails."

Holt hated that Isabelle looked a little queasy. It was the main reason she tried to avoid having her in these meetings, but whether she liked it or not, Isabelle and her financial knowledge had become an invaluable asset to the team. So here they sat, Holt complaining that they hadn't been properly threatened, and Isabelle scared enough already.

"You forget, H, you're rich as Batman," Max said.

"And just as ornery," Lola said.

"Maybe the connection doesn't matter, as long as there's a chance they think you'll pay to keep us safe and him away?" Isabelle asked.

"Like I said, it's the simplest narrative that fits all the facts, so it's the one we should go with for now. It just feels off to me somehow. Sweetheart, have you had any luck following up on where the money has been coming from?" Holt asked. She still didn't like it, but for now, it was the best theory they had. They needed more information.

"Not yet, butter biscuit," Max said.

Holt didn't mind a little laughter at her expense. She liked her team loose. Too much tension meant things were overlooked and people weren't thinking clearly. That led people to freeze up in critical moments and that's when people could get killed. "Anything else before we all get back to work?"

"Yes, actually," Max said. She looked a little unsure of herself after boldly poking the bear. "Kevin Garvey isn't the only one running this algorithm. There are at least three others, but I think it's closer to five. He's been emailing with a group. I think they're students at the college where Lola's working."

"Hey, finally someone remembers me and all my hard work over here," Lola said. "Is this the connection to Quinn's lab that you had me run down?"

"Uh-huh. I helped myself to some of Garvey's emails and it seems that this group meets up at Dr. Golden's lab to actually run the algorithm and enter their teams. I gather the computers there are very powerful."

"Does Quinn know anything about it?" Lola asked.

Holt noticed Lola's intensity had increased. There was something about this new woman that had gotten under Lola's skin. Either she was worried that she was caught in this mess, or she was hoping she wasn't.

"I don't think so," Max said. "They talk a lot about not getting caught. There are a few emails talking about how she works all night and what a pain in the ass that is. Doesn't sound like a coconspirator."

"Still, it's her lab. She might know about it," Lola said. "Why did you ask me about the username and password for her computers?"

"Because one of Garvey's friends gives him a username and password to log in to the lab computers and I wanted to know if it was specific to him. Now, thanks to you, we know that the only username and password those computers will accept is the one Garvey received. The bad news, the one he uses is registered to Dr. Golden."

"So, Quinn could be involved in all of this. You have no way of exonerating her?"

"Look, Lola, I really don't think she is. But I guess technically, no, I don't. I'll keep digging though. I could see if she was logged in to her computer at the same time, but I'm not sure I want to breach her privacy just to make you feel better," Max said. "What's your hang-up with her? She's seems tangentially related to all of this at best."

"It's her lab. If she's involved, I want to know. All you've given me is that we might be tracking some kids who play fake football and a ghost who maybe stole money from someone, somewhere, and now might be mad about it."

"And it wouldn't have anything to do with wanting to know if she's a criminal before taking her for another spin on the dance floor?"

Lola looked ready to explode.

"Enough, both of you," Holt said. "Max, do you have the names of any of the guys Kevin was collaborating with?" It felt good to have tangible leads to follow.

"Sure do."

"Good, send them to Lola. Lola, no more ghost surveillance for these guys. You need to talk to them. But stay in your cover. You're the custodian, so it's not weird to talk to them if you see them in the hall. Worst-case, pay them a visit. We need to find Garvey. The email says we have forty-eight hours."

"You got it, H." Holt wished Lola didn't look quite so enthused. She knew that look. Hopefully, Lola would be careful, because backup wasn't that close if she got in over her head. Moose had checked in when he landed and was hunting one of their cold cases in Santa Barbara. He could get to her in a couple of hours if she needed him. *Unlike me. I'm useless to her.*

"All right, everyone, back to work. Let's find Garvey and catch whoever is threatening us. You know how I feel about threats to my family. That includes all of you. Oh, and, Max, figure out Quinn's role in this so Lola can un-bunch her shorts. Dismissed."

Isabelle was the last to leave the room after lingering for a long hug and an even longer kiss. Time with Isabelle always settled her, deep in her soul. Isabelle had calmed places she hadn't known existed, let alone were in turmoil, and her life was forever better because of her. She would do anything to protect the life they'd built together.

"Will you send Max back to talk to me?" Holt asked before Isabelle left. She snuck one more kiss before she let Isabelle go.

"Be nice to her," Isabelle said.

"Why does everyone keep saying that?" Holt asked. "I'm a very nice person."

"Of course you are," Isabelle said. "You just need to work on your people skills. She's not fragile. She won't break if she fails."

"Wait, what? I thought you said to be nice to her? What are you talking about?"

Isabelle turned around and closed the door behind her. She put her hands on Holt's chest and snuggled into her. Holt wondered if Isabelle knew she found it impossible to think, hear, process, when Isabelle was this close to her.

"I don't pretend to know what all these superhero training games you are putting Max through are designed to do, but I can see you aren't letting her fail. You have to stop protecting her."

"Less than an hour ago Dubs told me I was being too hard on her. You two need to get your stories straight." Isabelle had her hands in the back of Holt's hair, at the nape of her neck, and it was all Holt could do to form a complete sentence.

"I'm sure it feels that way to Max, and looks that way to Dubs. But she's not failing, she's just getting angry at you. And she'll never stay mad at you for long. She loves you too much. So she can't ever fail. Her superpower is interfacing with computers, right?"

"Yes, Cyborg."

"So you have to put her up against computer problems. Not make her run across the office in under a certain amount of time. Play to her strengths, then get out of the way and let her succeed or fail. Don't make her do things she won't have to do."

"And just when did you learn to do all of this so much better than I did?" Holt didn't know if she should be amazed or embarrassed at Isabelle's obvious explanation.

"When I was one step back from whatever is scaring you so much it's blinding you," Isabelle said. "I hope you'll talk to me about whatever that is too. After you sort things out with Max."

"Of course I'm scared. Someone is threatening you," Holt said.

"That usually scares you for a few minutes and then makes you really angry. This feels like something else. Like I said, I'm here to talk when you want to."

"I love you," Holt said.

"Lucky me," Isabelle said.

She left Holt speechless, as she always did coming or going. She thought about what Isabelle said. What was she scared of? For the first time in a long time, a vivid memory of Lola's brother George dying in her arms flashed through her thoughts. It felt like a physical gut punch. She was barely recovered when Max poked her head in.

"You wanted to see me, H?"

"It's come to my attention that you think I'm being a shithead."

"Dubs tell you that? I told her not to say anything." Her shoulders were slumped and she had something very interesting to examine on her shoes.

"Isabelle too. Moose would join in I'm sure, but he's in California. He probably knows though and is just waiting to tell me in person when he gets back. He's polite like that." Holt actually thought that was possible. "Look, the point is, I've been trying to take your training to the next level, but I've got to take the kid gloves off. For both our sakes."

"This has been the kid gloves?" Max looked alarmed.

"Yes. No. Sort of. Isabelle can explain it better. The point is I haven't been doing a very good job choosing tasks to push you and test you. All I've been doing is making you mad at me. I think I've been quite successful at that."

Max nodded. "I've also felt like *you're* mad at *me*. I don't work very well when I feel like that."

"I'm not mad at you." Holt felt awful. She didn't want Max to feel that way. She needed Max working at peak performance, not stressed about how she was going to react to Max's work. "I've never taught anyone like you before. I'm learning too. I know how to teach someone to be good in the field. Your computer stuff is half mystery to me. Isabelle said I was scared to let you fail so I was setting up challenges where you could be mad at me instead. I was protecting you. That's on me. I'm sorry."

"I know I'm not as good as everyone else here out in the field," Max said. "I don't have the life experience you all have. I haven't caught anyone from the FBI's ten most wanted list. I haven't been to prison or been a heroin addict, or been doing this for my whole life, but I take care of my business with the computer stuff."

"That's true," Holt said. "You haven't done any of those things. And I'm grateful for that. But you've been kicked out of your home. You've lived on the streets and survived. Do you know why I spend so much time wandering around the office restless and driving you and everyone else around here crazy?"

"You like that we send Isabelle to calm you down."

"No, although that's a definite perk. I'm really good at tracking people down on the streets. Hunting people, kicking in doors, facing scary situations and not backing down. I can sit in a car for fourteen hours just to talk to someone's cousin's mother's sister's hairdresser to get information we need. But there isn't nearly as much need for an ass kicker because you do so much around here with your fancy computer skills. Well, you and Isabelle with her financial wizardry. You find some of these folks for us before we warm up the coffee in the morning, and then we just have to knock on one door, politely, and scoop them up."

"That's modern times," Max said with a nonchalant shrug.

"It is. And you're also really good at what you do. But up until now, you've always had plenty of time to do what you do. We give you assignments and you can research, poke around, work your magic. There will come a time when you have as little time to solve a problem on the computer as you did in the park with me the day we met Dubs."

"You mean the day you took on two really big dudes and one of them pulled a knife?"

"Exactly. What did you do when you saw them?" Holt asked.

"I think I panicked and then kicked one of them in the shin."

"And that's what I need to do to help you grow. I need to lessen the panic and increase the shin kicking when it comes to your computer work. I don't know how you'll react if you're the only one who can save my life by working some computer something or other, but you have to do it in less than a minute. Or we need vital information but it has to be extracted in under thirty seconds. Do you?"

"No," Max said.

"We both have to figure out how to change that answer. Can you work with me to do that?" Holt asked. It might not be conventional, but this would probably only work with Max's buy-in.

"Yes. I'm in." Max looked like herself again—eager, enthusiastic, happy.

"Good, then get back to work on our Kevin Garvey problem, and I'll figure out how to scare your socks off with a computer problem."

After she left to rejoin Isabelle, who was following the money through cyberspace, Holt found herself, once again, with nothing to do but wait. She thought about George the First again. This time the memory didn't catch her off guard, but it still hurt. It was too late to be scared for Lola's brother. Holt leaned back in her chair and ran her hands through her hair. Isabelle was right. She was scared. For Lola.

She hasn't seemed this lost since right after George died when I let her make decisions I think she still regrets. And I sent her three thousand miles away, alone. But no one's coming after her this time. She's safe. I hope.

CHAPTER ELEVEN

H, I love you, but what the hell are we doing here?" Jose asked.

"Just call Lola. Get her on Facetime. Then I'll explain." Holt saw Jose about to launch into an endless series of questions. "Don't make me regret bringing you. Get her on the phone." She was nervous enough without having to get Jose in line.

"If this is a job, you know I'm not qualified. The last time I was involved in one, I almost got you killed." Jose looked terrified at the memory.

Holt took a deep breath. Her temper was more controlled than it used to be, but Jose still had the access code to the self-control override button. "How many times do I have to tell you? That wasn't your fault. And this isn't a job. Not the way you're thinking. Now, are you going to yap all day or call Lola so you can figure out what this is all about? I promise you're going to like it."

That seemed to motivate him. Lola appeared on his phone, looking as confused as he did when she realized they were crammed in Holt's truck and not in the office.

"What's the emergency? I'm supposed to be at work in a couple hours. Can we take care of this in that time?"

"Lord help me if we can't," Holt said. "You are two of my best friends, along with Moose and Amy, but they would be terrible helping me here. You two are the only ones I trust to help me with this. I tried to do it on my own, and…it didn't go well."

"Just spit it out, H." Lola looked worried.

Jose felt her forehead. Holt swatted his hand away.

"I want to buy an engagement ring for Isabelle." Holt said it in a rush. She felt small beads of sweat form on her forehead. She'd tried to pick a ring out on her own. It seemed like the kind of thing she should be able to do, but the number of options had overwhelmed her.

"Seriously?" Jose said. He was beaming. There was no other word for it.

"About fucking time," Lola said.

"Let me guess, you don't know your ass from a princess cut?" Jose asked.

"Oh and you do?" Holt said. She was embarrassed she couldn't do this without help. How could she not figure out what ring to buy the love of her life? Wasn't this supposed to reflect her commitment, love, and devotion to Isabelle? The physical embodiment of all those things didn't seem like the kind of thing you were supposed to outsource. But walking into the jeweler the first time hadn't been a success. Getting shot in the chest by Isabelle's crazy stalker had gone better. There were literally thousands of combinations, and she lost track of the options after about four. She wasn't too proud to admit she needed help, so she'd called in reinforcements. This was too important to screw up.

Jose and Lola gave her a look she could only describe as "bitch, please."

"You came to the right place. Do you know what kind of stone you want? Cut, color, clarity?" Jose asked.

Holt wasn't sure what exactly was so funny about the look on her face, but Jose and Lola were laughing a little too hard.

"Okay, let's back up. Do you want there to be a stone? If so, what color? Blue, green, red, purple, diamond? More than one?" Lola asked. She seemed to understand they needed to talk to her like she was a preschooler.

"Yes to a stone, diamond. I don't know if there should be more than one. I also like blue."

"Good work, H. Blue are called sapphires, just so you know. You might need to know that when we go inside," Lola said.

"Okay, next. What shape do you like? Square, round, heart, oval, rectangle, teardrop or pear, football. Anything calling out to you?"

"There's a diamond cut called 'football'? How are all engagement rings not in that shape?" Holt asked.

"No, it's called marquise cut. Would you know what shape that was if I had said that?" Jose asked.

"Not a clue," Holt said.

"But you know what shape a football is. I was translating. Same with princess and emerald."

"It seems so simple. You buy a ring, drop to a knee, don't drop the ring, and ask the question. But how is anyone supposed to buy the damn thing on their own?"

"You aren't. You call your friends who know more than you and they save your ass."

"Like always," Holt said.

"You said it," Lola said.

"Okay, I like round, or square. Or maybe rectangle. The other ones seem like they wouldn't fit on her finger very well."

"Almost ready to go in. One last question. Do you like the idea of the band being smooth, or do you like it decorated with either etching or diamonds?" Lola asked.

"Oh, good point. I had forgotten about that," Jose said. "Can we just decide for her? She's gonna screw this up."

"Let her tell us what she thinks and then we'll overrule her in there," Lola said.

"Guys, I'm right here," Holt said. "And I'm the one buying the ring."

"And you want it to be perfect, right?"

"Of course. That's why I called you two. The only thing I took away from my first attempt at this is that I liked bands that had fancy stuff on them. They looked so beautiful and old-fashioned."

"Whoa. Maybe we underestimated her," Jose said.

"All right, let's go get our lady a ring."

"Jose, can you do a first pass? I know you won't let me look at anything until you two narrow down my choices anyway. I have to ask Lola a work question," Holt said.

Jose practically skipped to the store, eager to start shopping.

"You didn't give him your credit card did you?" Lola asked.

"Hell no," Holt said. "He'd bankrupt me."

"Thanks for including me in this. I'm sorry I'm not there in person, but I'm glad I'm still involved. You know I've always got your back."

Holt hadn't known how to broach the subject she wanted to raise with Lola, but that was as good an opening as she was likely to get.

"I know you do," Holt said. "I'm starting to wonder if I've always had yours."

Lola started to argue vehemently, but Holt cut her off.

"Hear me out, then you can yell at me if you want. I've been worried about you lately. Isabelle too. I haven't seen you like this since George the First. Back then I let you drop out of school and come work for me. I should have made you go to college. I don't want you to make another decision you'll regret now, and I'm too far away to protect you. It's driving me a little crazy."

"How long have you been twisting yourself in knots about this?" Lola asked. "First, you didn't *let* me drop out of school. I did that on my own and then you gave me a place to land and probably saved my life. What the hell did we know? We were kids. You made me get my GED. Maybe college will happen for me someday."

Lola didn't need to be in Holt's physical space for her to know that Lola was pacing wherever she was, gesturing wildly with the hand that was off screen.

"You would be licking your wounds if Tiffany had worked you over the way she did me. I'm entitled to that, and there's nothing more going on. Not everyone has Isabelle to go home to. If you think Quinn is the decision I'm going to regret, don't worry about it. There's nothing happening and she's completely amazing."

"You know those two things contradict each other, right?"

"No, they don't," Lola said. "She can be amazing, I can notice, and there can be nothing going on. We're about to pick out your engagement ring together. I'll tell you if there's anything for you to get excited about, worry about, stew about, yell about…you get the idea."

"Fine. I'll mind my own business. After I say one more thing."

Lola rolled her eyes, but Holt could see there was no true annoyance behind the gesture.

"I got a phone call from the director of my foundation today. She's considering retiring. She's had a long career working with at risk youth, setting them on the right path, and is planning her exit strategy. She asked if I knew anyone who would be a good candidate to take over from her if she left in one year, two years, or five years. She's willing to stay to provide an apprenticeship to the right candidate. I thought of you."

"Me?" Lola looked stunned. "Do you not want me working for you anymore?"

"I love having you working with me," Holt said. "But I think you would be amazing with those kids, and I can't think of anyone I would trust more to run the foundation. It's just as hazardous as our current job if you're worried you'll get bored. You'd have to interact with my mother."

Lola groaned.

"Just think about it. If it's something you're interested in, your college degree would be part of the apprenticeship."

"I don't know what to say."

"You don't have to," Holt said. She wasn't offering this out of pity or to assuage her own guilt or fear. Lola would be perfect. She hoped she considered it seriously. "Take all the time you need. Right now, I think we've left Jose in that jewelry store unsupervised long enough. Shall we go get me a ring?"

An hour later, Holt made it home with the most beautiful ring she'd ever laid eyes on burning a hole in her pocket. She never would have found it on her own, but Jose and Lola had sorted through option after option with ease, skipping over the initial offerings that had tripped her up on her first foray. She'd spent a fortune, but what she'd come away with was truly a reflection of all that she felt for Isabelle. She couldn't wait to give it to her. Now all she had to do was find the perfect time.

Isabelle greeted her at the door with a kiss. "I missed you."

"I'll stay away more often if this is the greeting I get when I return," Holt said.

"Better not," Isabelle said. "How was Jose? Is he worried about Lola too? Does he know anything more?"

"What?" She forgot that was the excuse she'd used for meeting Jose this evening. "Oh, yeah, but you know how Jose is. He's hard to pin down. I asked him to check in with her when he gets a chance."

"I know you'll both keep an eye on her," Isabelle said. She ran her hands through Holt's hair and kissed her. She trailed her hand down Holt's cheek, neck, and finally down her chest. When she made it to Holt's belt, she hooked one finger under her belt buckle and tugged gently. "George is down. If you're done being a superhero for the night, wanna give pinning me down a shot?"

Holt scooped Isabelle up and carried her to their bedroom. "I think I'm up to the challenge," Holt said.

Isabelle was already shedding clothes as Holt crossed the threshold to their bedroom. She kicked the door closed and laid Isabelle down on the bed. She let her hand brush her left pant pocket as she discarded her pants. She couldn't imagine loving Isabelle any more than she did. Soon she would give her the physical symbol of that love for the world to see. But for tonight, she would show Isabelle her love another way, and that was just fine with her.

CHAPTER TWELVE

Lola needed to talk to the college kids Max had identified through Kevin Garvey's emails. One of them, conveniently, was enrolled in Quinn's Intro to Neuroscience class that Lola had been unofficially auditing, but the class was large, and these kids all sort of looked the same, despite their attempts to differentiate themselves. Lola didn't want to be late meeting Quinn after class, so she felt extra pressure to find her guy quickly.

She texted Quinn that she'd meet her at the diner and scanned the group of kids again. Max had sent her a picture of her target, but it seemed everyone at CLA was a nondescript sandy blond, hazel-eyed dudebro. Lola had just thought she was going to have to get more aggressive with her approach and pay him a visit in his dorm, when, finally, she spotted him. He wasn't alone, but she could fix that easily enough.

She made her approach as he passed a service entrance to one of the neighboring buildings and jostled him just enough to force him to step into the enclosed space. It wasn't enough contact to alert his friends that anything strange had happened. When they looked for him, he would simply no longer be next to them. He could figure out what to tell them when they caught up later.

"Hello, Brayden. I'd like a word," Lola said. "I'm not going to hurt you." Lola put her hand over his mouth when he looked ready to scream. "Jesus, buddy, I just want to talk. What's got you so jumpy?"

When he looked like he was calmer, she slowly released the pressure on his mouth but didn't fully uncover it. "Are you going to scream?"

He shook his head.

"Good boy. Do you know who I am?" She was asking about her undercover identity. She would be stunned if he knew who she really was.

He nodded. "You're the new janitor in the psychology building."

"And how do you know?" She was curious, although not really surprised.

"I have psych classes so I'm in that building sometimes. I've seen you."

"You've seen me working? Well, now I want to know what you were doing in the building in the middle of the night."

Brayden didn't answer, but his eyes got wide.

"It's okay. You don't have to tell me. I know what the old janitor and you and your buddies were up to at night in the neuropsych research lab. I want in."

"I don't know what you're talking about," Brayden said.

"Of course you do," Lola said. "You've got missing money, a missing janitor, and missing access to the building at night. It's harder for you to get in now, isn't it? I can fix a few of those problems for you. All I want is the same opportunity to make some money the way Kevin did. Only difference, I don't steal off the top."

"Assuming I know what you mean," Brayden said. "And I'm not saying I do, you're Dr. Golden's bitch. Everyone knows that. That's not good for our enterprise. The whole point is keeping her away from what we're doing. She can't know anything about it. Assuming there's anything to know."

"Little boy, I'm nobody's bitch," Lola said. "And if you want to play at being a kingpin, then step up to the plate and make decisions that are good for your whole crew. Time to take the diapers off and take the big boy step of pissing or getting off the pot. Call me when you decide you're ready for it." Lola slipped a piece of paper with her phone number in his pocket. "I'll be hearing from you."

She walked away and didn't look back. She didn't enjoy playing into the stereotype of her appearance to scare people, but in this case, with Holt's family on the line, she was happy to. She wondered how long it would be before she would hear from Brayden. After years of running the streets chasing after messed up young kids, she was a pretty good judge of the look in someone's eyes. Brayden was in over his head and scared of something. Certainly her, but it seemed like something else too. Hopefully, that made him desperate enough to bring her in, sight unseen. A seasoned criminal would never dream of it, but Brayden was far from that.

Brayden was the kind of kid she would get the chance to help if she took Holt up on her offer to eventually take over at the foundation. She knew how much the charity meant to Holt. It was appealing, but right now she had a job to do. She'd think about it more once she sorted out this case and everyone was safe.

She headed to the diner and Quinn. As she walked she thought about Brayden's assertion that she was Quinn's bitch. Seemed like the kind of rumor the Little Chihuahua might have started to get under her skin. She didn't think a few weeks of after class breakfast meant she was Quinn's anything.

Breakfast bitch maybe. You do walk her back to her office even on days you're almost too tired to drive home.

For some reason, right now, Quinn was fine hanging out with a high school dropout custodian. Lola didn't really want to ask her why. And Lola was sticking close to Quinn because she might be involved in the case. She was going to have to come up with another excuse soon, because Max had seemed pretty confident that Quinn wasn't involved and Brayden had all but backed that up. Lola hadn't thought Tiffany was involved in anything either though, and Mr. Malevolent had almost killed Tiffany, unborn George, and Dubs. All because she hadn't kept her guard up when she should have. *But how much has my worry about Quinn being the boogey man pulled my focus from where it should be?*

Lola was so distracted by her brooding self-flagellation that she didn't notice Quinn standing in front of the diner waiting for her. She would have walked right past her, except Quinn stopped her by intertwining their hands and placing a quick kiss on her cheek.

"Hi, sexy. I was worried you were going to stand me up."

"That would be criminal," Lola said. She stiffened a little when Quinn held her hand, but she didn't pull away, not this time. It felt too damn good. "Besides, I'm hungry." She winked when she said it, making sure Quinn knew she was teasing her.

"Well, you do know how to make a girl feel special."

You are to me. Lola just smiled, her doubts about her professionalism still plaguing her.

They settled into their booth and ordered. Quinn looked reluctant but released Lola's hand.

"So, how did I do today? Class felt a little disjointed. I haven't been able to get a good flow to this lecture. I've reworked it over and over, but it still kinda sucks."

"Not as far as I noticed," Lola said. She hadn't ever noticed a lecture that was anything less than brilliant. "But I've got a little bit of the hots for the teacher. You said you don't like teaching. Does that mean you don't want an academic life?"

"I think I said I was a middling professor. That's not the same thing as not liking something. Although I guess I don't love it. I like it fine. I just happen to love being a scientist. But research requires money, and a lot of research institutions are academic in nature, or affiliated with colleges and universities."

"So you have to teach? That doesn't seem fair." Lola didn't understand how the academic world worked, but forcing Quinn to do something she didn't like seemed ridiculous.

"No, I don't have to. Well, right now I do. As a postdoc. But once I'm on my own, if I have my own grant funding, I don't have to. It's just a matter of where I get a job, and how much funding I have. Every researcher is constantly chasing the next grant to keep themselves, and their research staff, funded. If you have a job where teaching is an option, that at least guarantees some salary. Some people buy out of teaching with their grants when they have the money, and when they don't, they teach some more."

"But that's not what you want?" Lola found the world of higher education and research fascinating.

"I'm trying to secure my own grant funding now and get a full-time position so I can leave my postdoc early. I haven't applied to a position that requires lots of hours of teaching, so no, that's not what I want."

"Wait, so you're not going to be in Los Angeles? When are you leaving?" Lola's heart sank. She knew it shouldn't matter. After all, she wouldn't be in Los Angeles past completing this case, but for some reason, it did matter. A lot.

"I don't know," Quinn said. She didn't seem to pick up on Lola's real question. "I've applied to places all over the country. And I've got two grant applications I'm working on. You always ask me what keeps me up all night. Now you know."

"Okay, so now you have to give me the juicy details. What are your grants about and what lucky institutions will be fighting for you?" Lola tried hard not to think about other things that could be keeping Quinn up all night.

"You really want to know all this?" Quinn asked. "You've been up all night, plus you sat through my class. We're supposed to have a quick breakfast and then you go home to sleep."

"And I'll do that. But I really do want to know. This is important to you. So it's important to me. Besides, how am I going to tease Jessica about what horrible city you're going to drag her off to if I don't have insider information?" Lola was jealous of the idea of Jessica going with Quinn to wherever her next job took her. She didn't want to think about why.

"How do you know about that?" Quinn looked horrified.

"The little Chihuahua thinks she can make me jealous by lording it over me that you and she are tight. She told me she'd go with you if you ever left."

"And can she?" Quinn asked. Her voice was low, almost shy, and she didn't make eye contact with Lola.

"Can she what?" Lola asked.

"Make you jealous?"

"Yes," Lola said. She couldn't lie. Quinn's smile, so big and bright and beautiful it lit up the entire diner, was enough to make Lola wish she could have. She wished she could have added "but you're leaving, I'm undercover, and you could be involved in people threatening the people most important to me," but she didn't. Quinn's smile was all she saw.

Lola tried to concentrate on what Quinn was saying, but she was too busy beating herself up for not putting a stop to whatever was going on between them. She shouldn't be leading Quinn on. But when she looked at her across the table, all she saw was Quinn as she was right now, happy and relaxed, and the way she looked when she was lecturing, how brilliant she was, and how she made Lola feel smart too, despite her background. *Some superhero I am. Guess we know what my kryptonite is.*

"...in Providence," Quinn said.

"Did you say Providence?" Lola said, snapping back to what Quinn was saying. She felt butterflies surge in her stomach.

"Yes, that's where one of the jobs is. It's in my top three actually, but it's a long shot. Their research program is outstanding and the position available isn't one I'm really qualified for. I'm only a postdoc and they're looking for a more established researcher. I applied for it on a whim. I figured it couldn't hurt to get my name out there."

"A friend of mine already knew who you were when I mentioned I was having breakfast with you. She gave me the impression your name is already very much out there. I might have asked Google to tell me more as well. I told you I'd read some of your research papers, but I didn't realize you were already kind of a hotshot. Why are you worried about not being qualified? I admit to not really knowing much about how these decisions get made, but wouldn't everyone in the world want you?" Lola felt her cheeks flame at little at the last part.

"I'm flattered, but I think you've overstated my importance. I've just expanded on work done by my research mentors. That's the problem though. I'm not all that interested in the research topics I've built my reputation on. And that sucks because securing funding is all about proving you know what you're doing and that you've successfully done something similar before. I've been really good at what I've done, which is basically a lot of work with fMRI and emotion regulation, to put it simply."

"I know. Your work has been brilliant," Lola said. "From what I can tell, you've moved that field forward in ways no other researchers have in years."

Quinn waved her off. "Like I said, I've been lucky to work with great mentors and have access to data and research subjects that allow me to do interesting work. But I'm not really passionate about it. I don't want to build my independent research career based on any of the work I've done so far. And that's damn scary. Certainly for me, and probably for anyone who wants to take a chance on hiring me. Not to mention the government, who I'm asking to give me a lot of money."

"But you've already shown you're an incredible researcher. Isn't that enough?" Lola didn't quite understand the problem.

"I hope so, but I'm not sure. Maybe since I'm still a postdoc. Research is a funny world. People choose a path and then build incrementally on it their whole careers. Very few have projects on a wide range of topics they're interested in, scattershot all over the map. It's unusual for someone to change course and start a new program of study." Quinn looked worried.

"What is this new program of study that has won your heart and mind?" Lola loved listening to Quinn's mind at work.

"I'm interested in behavioral medicine. I want to find MRI correlates of addiction or Parkinson's disease treatment outcome predictors. In laymen's terms, let's put someone in the scanner and expose them to craving cues and see why some people are better able to remain abstinent from nicotine, or drugs, or alcohol, while others aren't. Or why do some people go through cardiac rehab and maintain their weight loss and exercise and others don't? What clues do their brains hold?" Quinn's excitement and passion were palpable.

"So you want to save the world?" Lola was attracted to Quinn for so many reasons, but none more so than this, listening to her talk, watching her face light up and her eyes sparkle as she explained what she was passionate about. There was nothing sexier.

"No," Quinn said. She looked a little flustered and took a bite of her waffle. "But if I could do a small part to make it a little bit healthier, I'd be happy."

"I know you will," Lola said.

"Have you ever seen a brain light up on a scanner in real time? It's so beautiful. It sparkles with possibility."

"I feel like I'm looking at something similar right now," Lola said. Quinn's eyes were dancing like they always did when she talked about her work. Lola was mesmerized. "Can I see it?"

"A scan?" Quinn asked.

"The way you talk about it. I want to see it. And it's clearly so important to you."

Quinn looked thoughtful. Lola could tell the moment an idea came to her.

"We have a training for a new group of techs on Friday. You can't see any of our research participants because of confidentiality, but you could sit in on the first training. You can see my brain."

"I'd love that," Lola said.

"But it's in the middle of the day. You should be sleeping."

"I'll be there," Lola said. "But only if you agree that I can take you out afterward. Friday is my night off."

"How could I refuse an offer like that?" Quinn asked.

Lola couldn't remember looking forward to anything more.

On her way back to her apartment after she'd walked Quinn to her office, Lola thought about Quinn's research. She believed so strongly in doing work she loved she was willing to start over completely to do it. She also wanted to do work she thought would make a difference in people's lives.

So much for not thinking about Holt's offer until the case is over.

Lola considered the work she did. There was no doubt it made a difference. She'd personally dragged a startling number of very bad people off the streets and put them back in the hands of the criminal justice system. But there were also a lot of people whose interactions with the law were less severe. Was she doing a public service by returning them to court? It wasn't her place to judge. With the growth of Holt's reputation, they had had fewer of the petty criminals and more of the high profile, dangerous captures. It was harder to feel ambiguous about a triple murderer on the loose in your community.

Not for the first time, though, she wondered if there was something more for her than chasing supervillains in the name of justice. What if George the First had had Holt's foundation as an option? What if his killer had?

With morose thoughts filling her head, Lola finally fell asleep after a long night. She'd been asleep less than four hours when her cell phone rang. She considered throwing it across the room, but glanced at the caller ID before sending it flying. The number was blocked.

"Hello," Lola said. She tried to clear the sleep from her voice and her overly tired brain.

"Um, hi. Uh, do you still want in on the game?" The caller didn't identify himself, but Lola could tell it was Brayden. He sounded like he was trying out his best bad boy impression while simultaneously trying not to wet himself.

"I do," she said.

"Good. Meet me in thirty minutes. Don't be late. I'll text you the address." Brayden hung up.

"Little shithead," Lola said to herself as she waited for the text. She dressed quickly and called to check in with whichever of the Wonder Twins was on duty.

Dubs answered. "Aren't you supposed to be getting your beauty sleep? Not that you need it of course. What's up?"

"Just got a call from the college kid I made contact with this morning. He's texting me the address for a meet." Lola felt her phone buzz. "Just came through. Can you have Max trace the phone number? It was blocked on my caller ID." Lola read the address to Dubs. "I need everything you can give me on that address too. I've got thirty minutes to get there according to my new BFF. I'm tempted to keep him waiting, but I don't want to push him. He seems like the kind that's scared of his own shadow. I don't want him to rabbit on me."

"CB twenty," Dubs said. "And, Lola. Be careful."

Exactly thirty minutes later, armed with as much information about the abandoned warehouse as Max could pull up, Lola pulled her bike up to the address Brayden had given her. "It's always got to be abandoned warehouses," Lola said. Her comms were active so Dubs was along for the ride.

"No proper villain would go for anything else. Unless a cave or volcano were available. Maybe an icy mountain fortress. Not many of those in LA though."

"Well, next time I'll have H send me to Siberia. A little variety is good for you, right?"

Lola opened the door cautiously and stepped inside. She wasn't armed. She never was. Like Holt, she could handle herself well in a fight, but that didn't mean she was going to walk blindly into a hail of bullets.

The warehouse was exactly as Max had described, a giant open room with a small office in the back. Not many places for bad guys to hide. Lola slid inside and closed the door quietly. A group of people was gathered on the far side of the room. They all had their backs to her. It looked like the nondescript commercial setting from Kevin Garvey's proof of life video.

"Trusting idiots."

She approached silently. As she got closer she recognized Kevin Garvey. *Fuck.* "Dubs, I think we have a problem. Kevin Garvey is here, and he's not a hostage. I'll keep you posted on what else I see. Get Holt on the line if this goes south."

Lola waited until she was almost directly behind the group before announcing herself. There were five kids including Brayden and Kevin Garvey. All six almost jumped out of their shoes when she spoke.

"Hello, boys. Nice place you got here."

"What the fuck?" one of the college kids said. "How'd you get in here?"

"Well, you left the front door open," Lola said. "And my invitation said don't be late." Lola felt a little bad for this sad pack, especially Brayden. She wondered how many pairs of underwear he'd gone through already today.

"How do you know about our operation?" one of the other college guys asked.

"Shut up, man," said another. "Don't tell her anything. We should shut her up for good."

Lola gave him a look that let him know he was welcome to try. He shrunk back behind one of his buddies.

"She already knew," said Brayden.

"Quiet," said Kevin.

Lola evaluated Kevin Garvey. If she squinted, there was a slight resemblance to Isabelle, but she and Ellen must take after their mother. She tried to reconcile the man standing in front of her with the different descriptions given by Isabelle and his wife. She couldn't make them mesh so she threw both out and focused on Kevin as if he was a complete unknown. In a sense he was, since he was supposed to be a hostage about to die. She glanced around. She was convinced this was the location of the video shoot.

"How *do* you know about our little operation?" Kevin asked. He looked wary, but not overly dangerous. Not yet.

"You can't possibly believe you're the only six on campus who know about it?" Lola said. "People talk. And nobody thinks of the custodian as being a person worthy of keeping their mouth shut around. You of all people should know that." Lola looked pointedly at Kevin. She knew the comment hit home.

"Tell who ratted us out," one of the other guys said.

"Wouldn't even if I could," Lola said. "And not relevant to current events. What is relevant to me is what happened to you?" Lola pointed to Kevin. "Rumor on campus is that you ran out on your wife, that you got whacked by the mob, and that you got kidnapped by some psycho. You look pretty good for a dead kidnapped man. If you got a lady on the side, this is a shitty place to show her a good time."

Kevin looked like he was weighing his options. He deliberated a long time. Lola found it interesting that the college kids deferred to him. He didn't look like he could lead himself out of a bathroom stall, let alone lead whatever the fuck this was.

"You got money to buy into our group?" he finally asked.

"I do," Lola said.

"How much?" Kevin asked.

"How much you require?"

"One hundred grand."

"Whoa," Lola said. She held up her hands. "You've got to be insane. I'm a fucking custodian. I'm looking to make money, not piss away my life savings to you clowns."

Dubs weighed in to the conversation through her earpiece. "That's the amount the extortion email is asking Holt for. You think these guys…"

Lola took a chance. "Hey, you guys in some kind of trouble? I'm not interested in any weird shit. If you need fast money to bail yourselves out and you're trying to get it from me, forget it. I'm out."

She emphasized her point by heading for the door. Brayden was the one to retrieve her. "Hold up. We're not in any kind of trouble. We've got a plan to fix it."

"Well, which is it? You're not in trouble, or you've got a plan to fix it?" Lola raised her voice loud enough that the rest of the group could hear her.

"Get back over here and let's talk business. Don't yell at the kid," Kevin said. "How much will you buy in with?"

"What are the terms? I need more details."

"We have a financial backer. Each week we each use an algorithm these boys created to enter daily fantasy contests. Hundreds, sometimes close to a thousand. Depends on the sport. We each can spend up to one hundred thousand entering, but our profit's close to ten percent daily. We get a cut and the rest goes to our investor."

"Okay, and I need to buy my way in? What if I'm not interested in entering at that kind of level? I don't have that kind of cash," Lola said. She was impressed with the scope of their operation. "Sounds too good to be true. I get paying my own way, but that doesn't explain why I have to give you personally a penny, or why you're chillin' in this damn warehouse."

Kevin and all the college boys looked uncomfortable. Lola was right; there was something not quite right about their operation, and she'd found a weak spot.

"Oh, just tell her everything. We could use the extra person. Maybe it would get them off our back." Brayden shrugged, looking resigned.

"Shut up," Kevin said.

"Tell me what?" Lola pushed. There was a crack and she was going to take advantage of it.

"You don't need any of your own money. When we started, we were betting a little bit here and there, pocket change. But now, money is wired to our accounts every week and we use that to play. But we still get a cut, even though the money isn't ours in the first place."

"Where does the money come from?" Lola asked.

"I don't know. Kevin is the one who set it all up, but he's never told us, if he knows," Brayden said.

The boys looked at Kevin, who glared back at them. There was trouble in paradise.

"You said you enter hundreds of games. How many accounts do you have?"

"Twenty each," Brayden said. "We don't overlap more than a couple of teams per game so we're not taking money from each other, but we need to have the big money games covered by a few iterations of the best lineups from the algorithm."

"You have this down to quite a science," Lola said. "I'm impressed. So you keep a cut and the rest goes back to your mystery investor? What's the problem?"

"Kevin skimmed money from our investors. Now they're pissed at him and want it back." Brayden glared at Kevin. "And they're holding us all accountable."

"Who are these investors?" Lola asked. She looked at Kevin this time.

"The kind who don't like being stolen from," Kevin said.

Brayden and the college boys looked mighty pissed. The skimming clearly wasn't a group decision.

"I've got it under control. I'm going to get the money back," Kevin said.

"That hasn't worked out yet," one of the other guys said.

"It will," Kevin said.

Lola couldn't believe what an amateur hour she was witnessing. These guys couldn't put together a solid plan to bake a pizza.

"So what, that's why you want money from me?" Lola asked. "To pay off some debt I've got nothing to do with? What's the plan to get the money back and make some more? It better be good or I walk."

"It will work. Everything will be fine in two days." Garvey sat back in his chair, his attempt at confidence belied by the sweat on his forehead.

"He's got a daughter with a rich girlfriend," Brayden said. "He thinks he can force her to pay the money."

"Which hasn't worked at all," one of the other helpful guys said.

"He forgot to mention his daughter hates him and hasn't spoken to him in years," Brayden said.

"That's why your email threatened her as well as saying they would kill me," Kevin said. "I wasn't just relying on her love for her father."

"No fucking way," Lola said. Dubs was laughing in the earpiece. "You fools are on your own. No amount of money is worth this shit show. Good luck with getting the money. Brayden, boys, I really do wish you luck. My advice is talk to your investors and tell them you have nothing to do with this moron."

Lola headed to the entrance of the warehouse. Brayden ran after her. He stopped her just before she got to the door.

"You really think we should walk away?"

"About six months ago," Lola said. "Do you really not know who the investors are?" Lola figured they were bad news if they were willing to sink that much money each day into this foolish operation.

"No idea. Kevin found them. Like we said before that, my buddies and I were betting a couple hundred bucks at a time. We were winning, but not on this scale. Now we're the biggest sharks in the game. We're not on the major sites, but we still win big."

"Has anything you've done been illegal?"

"No." Brayden look confused. "Of course not."

"Of course not. Good Lord, kid. Time to walk away. I'm serious. Cut bait. Kevin's on his own. You and the rest are out of this game. Forever. You're just going to have to trust me on this one. And I'd forget you ever knew the address of this place too."

Lola got on her bike and headed home. She needed a few more hours sleep, but Dubs was already informing her the rest of the team was gathering in the conference room for a briefing. *No rest for the wicked.* Sleep would have to wait.

I guess this means the case is over. Do I have to go home? Do I have to leave Quinn? As much as she loved her chosen family, the thought of leaving Quinn made her chest hurt. She wasn't ready to return to Rhode Island and breakfasts alone, learning from a textbook, and no chance of being dazzled by Quinn's gorgeous smile.

CHAPTER THIRTEEN

Despite her case essentially being over, Lola was still in LA. Holt had asked her to stick around a few more days to coordinate with the LAPD, and she'd jumped at the chance. The information about a huge flow of cash into the online daily fantasy sports market had piqued the LAPD's interest and she'd been meeting with representatives from their cyber crime division.

But today was Friday and she had a date with Quinn. She hadn't found a way to tell her yet that she was leaving. Probably because she didn't want to say good-bye. They hadn't made any commitments to each other. Hell, she'd only kissed her once before she even knew her, but Lola liked the direction things were going.

Admit it, you like her.

Lola waved hello to Jessica as she entered the psychology offices. For once Jessica didn't seem interested in teasing her.

"You okay today? You don't look like your usual annoyingly competent, better than all the rest of us, self."

"Just fine," Lola said. Apparently, she needed a better poker face. "Is she in?"

"She's running a little late from a meeting across campus. Go ahead and wait in her office. You look dead on your feet."

Lola hadn't been getting much sleep. She'd kept her custodial job since she was sticking around for a few more days. If she was honest, it was an excuse to stay close to Quinn as much as to keep up her fake identity. She'd also been meeting with LAPD and phoning in to briefings back home, all of which took place during normal business hours.

She slumped down on Quinn's couch. It smelled like Quinn—jasmine, citrus, and a hint of cedar. She fought sleep, but it didn't take long to claim her.

Lola was awakened by a soft caress on her cheek and the touch of soft lips to her own. She opened her eyes slowly and saw Quinn kneeling next to her, her hand resting on Lola's thigh.

"Hi," Quinn said. "I'm sorry to wake you. And for kissing you. You looked so beautiful, I couldn't help it. And if we are going to make it to the scanner, we have to leave. You should feel free to sleep here until I get back if you want. You still look tired."

"I'm not sorry about either," Lola said. She pulled Quinn onto the couch next to her and put her arm around Quinn's shoulders, holding her close, but didn't take her physical affection further. She needed to tell her she was leaving before she did that. It was the only fair thing to Quinn. Then they could both decide what they wanted from the time they had left together.

"So you still want to see what I do?"

Quinn looked shy about sharing her work, and it made Lola's chest ache just a little more. It scared her to react so strongly, but it felt like the kind of fear you face, not run away from. "Of course I do. Lead the way."

This time when Quinn interlocked their fingers, Lola didn't pull away. They walked hand in hand across campus to the neuroimaging lab.

How am I supposed to leave this behind?

Lola tried to concentrate on what Quinn was telling her, from what the scanner looked like, to what the training would entail. She was finding it difficult tonight to focus given the other thoughts weighing on her mind. Once they walked into the lab, however, and Quinn entered her domain, Lola was mesmerized. All other thoughts flittered away as she watched Quinn go to work.

This is Quinn the researcher. God, she's beautiful doing what she loves.

"There are a couple new techs training today and we're working out a modified protocol for one of our studies," Quinn said. "I'm going in the scanner. I like to experience what the participants do at least once for each new protocol. I'll get you set up by the monitors so you can see what's happening in real time. Remember how I told you the brain was beautiful in an fMRI?"

Lola nodded. She already thought Quinn's brain was pretty amazing. All of the high tech equipment surrounding them was astonishing. Max would probably understand it, but she was at a loss. She saw computers and medical devices, and in a sterile room a giant tube with a table in the middle.

"Is that the scanner?" Lola asked.

"Yes. It uses magnetic fields to take a series of two-dimensional pictures of the organ we are imaging, the brain in this case, and when put together, they form the three-dimensional whole."

Lola followed Quinn into the control room where a bank of monitors were set up. They were blank at the moment. She sat in the chair Quinn indicated at the back of the small room.

"And what's an fMRI?"

"Ah, those measure neural activity in real time. That's what you're going to get to see. The scanner picks up changes in blood flow. Think about your muscles when you're working out. You need more blood to lift whatever heavy thing gets you looking like this." Quinn indicated Lola's body. "Same principle. When you are using a specific part of your brain, more blood is needed for those neurons to fire. The fMRI sees that blood flow happening."

"You're amazing, you know that, right?" Lola said.

"Nothing I've said is all that amazing," Quinn said.

"Agree to disagree," Lola said. "Now, everyone looks like they're waiting for you. Go squeeze yourself into that sardine can. I'll be here watching."

The next few hours were technical and filled with neuroimaging procedure, but Lola found it engrossing. When Quinn wasn't in the scanner, she was directing the small group of people working all around her. Even when she was in the machine, she was present in the control room through the microphone allowing communication between the technician and the patient.

After the last scans, Quinn found Lola. She was carrying a large sheet of glossy paper with a series of brain images on it.

"These are for you," Quinn said. "They're from the scans today."

"So they're your brain?" Lola asked. She studied the brain images. Quinn was right; they were incredible. The brain structures were grayscale, but the areas of neural activity, or increased blood flow, were red, orange, and yellow.

"Yes. It sounds a little weird when I think of it like that. I just thought you might like to have some pictures to remember our date."

"You were right," Lola said. "What were you thinking about right here?"

Lola was surprised when Quinn blushed.

"You," she said quietly.

"Well, then, these are definitely going on the wall," Lola said. She puffed out her chest.

That elicited the desired mock exasperated reaction from Quinn.

"What part of the brain is this that's all lit up?" Lola asked.

"You're taking my Intro to Neuroscience class," Quinn said. "You'll have to figure that out on your own."

"I'm a very good student," Lola said. "So you know I will. But not today. I have other more important things to do. Like part two of this date. Are you up for an extension?"

"I don't know. I'm pretty busy. What did you have in mind?" Quinn asked.

Quinn was obviously teasing, but Lola played along.

"Well, Dr. Golden, what I had in mind was a ride on my bike to the beach. Have you ever ridden on a motorcycle?"

Quinn shook her head.

"Well, then, I also had in mind you having to hold on tight the entire ride."

"Hmm. I guess I'd have to hold very tight to something big and strong the entire way to the beach, wouldn't I?" Quinn asked. She traced her finger down Lola's bicep.

"I suppose you would," Lola said. She was doing her best not to pull Quinn into her arms and kiss her, but it was difficult. She had started a game she couldn't win.

"Deal," Quinn said. "But I pick the beach, and we stop when we get close and buy what we need for a picnic."

"You drive a hard bargain. How will I ever accept?" Lola asked. This time she was the one who reached for Quinn's hand and held it. Quinn looked up at her and gave her one of her heart melting smiles. Lola thought she'd be happy to walk all over LA if Quinn just kept looking at her like that.

Not good. You've got to tell her you're leaving. First you've got to get it through your own thick head.

By the time they reached the beach, Lola wasn't thinking all that clearly about anything except Quinn's hands and the meandering paths she'd explored along Lola's stomach, chest, thighs, and sides while they drove. It was distracting enough having her pressed tightly behind her, her entire front molded to Lola's back, but Quinn seemed to have taken the idea of holding on tightly very seriously. Lola didn't actually mind, but now she was turned on and uncomfortable right before they embarked on a hike down to the beach.

"The ride was incredible," Quinn said. "Thanks for suggesting it."

Quinn's eyes were sparkling and her smile was just a little bit mischievous.

She knows exactly what she did to me and she likes it.

They made their way down from the parking lot to the beach a few hundred feet below. The path wasn't particularly dangerous or slippery, but Quinn found plenty of excuses to require Lola's assistance. Lola hardly minded. If she thought Quinn was playing the delicate woman in need of rescue, she would have been annoyed at the game, but Quinn was far from that. Quinn was clearly using every pebble as an excuse to get close to Lola, to touch her, and Lola didn't mind that at all.

When they were on flat ground they kicked off their shoes and walked along the wet sand at the edge of the water holding hands. Lola carried their picnic, Quinn the blanket they'd grabbed from her office before they left. The beach was littered with beautiful rock formations and few other people.

"This is my favorite beach," Quinn said. "The natural beauty and peacefulness make it nearly perfect."

"I can see why you love it," Lola said. She studied the ocean. It had a different feel than the Atlantic. Wilder, untamed. She liked it.

They spread the blanket and their picnic. Lola watched the waves crash against the rocks.

That's how I feel lately, a wild energy constantly crashing against an immovable object. Maybe Holt's right. Maybe it's time for a change.

"Where did you go?" Quinn asked, running a hand through Lola's hair, bringing her out of her wandering thoughts.

"Just thinking about an offer Holt, my sister, made to me recently. She wants me to think about going to college. It feels a little scary."

"I think I've made it pretty clear I think you're made for higher education, so my vote is to do it, if it's what you want. What's scaring you?"

"It's just so different from anything I've ever done before," Lola said. "And I'm old. Certainly compared to the kids I'd have classes with. And there's no way I'm living in a dorm."

She almost added that living next door to Dubs was close enough to dorm life for her, but she couldn't tell Quinn that.

"I don't like the idea of you living in the dorms either. Too many hot young women around."

"Jealous?" Lola wasn't opposed to the idea. Quinn moved to Lola and straddled her lap. Her lips were inches from Lola's. "And if I were?"

"I wouldn't hate the idea," Lola said. She was amazed she could still manage coherent thoughts.

Quinn leaned closer and brought her lips to Lola's. "Me either."

Lola pulled back.

"Quinn, wait. I have to tell you something."

Quinn backed away but didn't move off of Lola's lap. She looked confused, a little hurt, but not angry. Lola was relieved.

"I've noticed all day something's been bugging you," Quinn said. "Hazard of my job is to collect data and make observations. I want you to be able to tell me anything, always. But I also really want to kiss you for a little bit right now, enjoy our picnic, walk on the beach holding your hand, and then take another magic motorcycle ride home before you walk me to my door for a good night kiss. If whatever you want to talk about can wait, can we have tonight?"

Lola hesitated only a moment before she pulled Quinn to her and kissed her. She didn't know if it was the right decision, or fair to Quinn, but Lola wanted tonight too. Quinn fisted her hands in Lola's hair and pulled her close. Lola traced her tongue along Quinn's lower lip, seeking entrance.

She tried to pull Quinn closer, but Quinn put her hands on Lola's chest and forced her down. The sand was cool against Lola's back, even through the blanket. Quinn was hot against her front.

Quinn started kissing her again. It felt like she was everywhere. Lola didn't know what to do with her hands. Quinn had said she only wanted to kiss her, but Lola was so turned on from the ride out to the beach, and Quinn on top of her, she didn't trust herself. That didn't stop her from kissing Quinn back. She wasn't dead. Not yet.

"You can touch me, you know," Quinn said. She ran a finger along Lola's cheek and down her neck.

"Probably not the best idea right now," Lola said. She clenched the blanket with both fists and lay still as Quinn traced farther down. "Your fault."

"I'm not sorry that I can do this to you, but I really did just want to kiss you. In my defense, you're the one who made me wrap my legs around you and find the best thing to hold on to, for safety of course, the whole way out here."

Quinn rolled off of Lola but stayed in the circle of her arms. She rested her head on Lola's chest. Lola wasn't sure if she was relieved or disappointed.

"Well, you certainly explored all your options," Lola said. She kissed the top of Quinn's head. "I almost drove us off the road."

"I'm a scientist. I have to collect all the data before drawing conclusions. It would be irresponsible not to."

"Were you like that as a kid?"

"Yes. But it wasn't so weird in a family of cops. Not at first. They thought I was just showing the skills needed to be a good detective. When I started insisting neuroscience labs and not crime scenes were going to be my workplaces, that's when things got a little tense."

"I can't picture you as a cop, although you would look *very* good in the uniform." Lola wondered if she'd met any of Quinn's family members working with the LAPD.

Quinn swatted at Lola's arm playfully.

"My dad, brother, two aunts, and a cousin are all cops. Family dinners always had minimum one member missing, and even if everyone was there it was shop talk, debriefing from a bad case, or an underlying tension waiting for the next thing to come along. I saw how much my mom and my uncles worried about their spouses. That they might not come home. That wasn't the life for me."

Lola's heart sank. *Quinn would love your job. Probably better you're leaving before this turns into something.* "Are you close to your family now?" she asked.

Quinn got up and started dishing out the food they'd brought. Lola could tell she was uncomfortable. She wished she could take back the question. She wanted Quinn to lie back down in her arms for a little longer.

"Hey, I didn't mean to upset you."

"It's not your fault," Quinn said. "I was just thinking what a perfect day this has been and this," she gestured with the container she was holding, "is the reason I barely speak to my family."

"Macaroni salad?" Lola asked. She reached for Quinn and made sure she knew she was joking. "What happened?"

"Women."

"Fuck them," Lola said.

"That's the general source of the conflict," Quinn said. "My desire to do so, my family's horror at the thought. We already had so much trouble relating to each other after I told them I wasn't going into the family business and was going to be a scientist. I guess it was easier to get the rainbow sheep out of the family."

"Who in their right mind would let you out of their life?" Lola asked. As she said it she almost choked on the words. *What the hell am I going to do?*

Quinn shrugged. She handed Lola a fork and moved back into Lola's personal space on the blanket. They sat together and finished their picnic as the sun set over the water.

Lola drove them home and gave Quinn the promised good night kiss on her doorstep. As she returned to her own apartment Lola couldn't remember enjoying an afternoon more. The case was over, the apartment was hers through the end of the month, she had vacation time owed her, plenty of money in the bank, and she'd promised Holt she'd think about her offer. LA was a great place to do some thinking.

You don't know your ass from your elbow with women. What if you stick around and it blows up in your face again? What if you leave and you regret it forever?

CHAPTER FOURTEEN

Quinn stretched and pushed back from her computer. She'd been up for about an hour but hadn't really gotten much done.

I really should stop sleeping in my office. Not much motivation to go home when I know Lola will tuck my blanket back on here. She's not waiting for me at home.

When she thought of Lola, she got a pleasant thrill in her stomach. She looked forward to their breakfasts more than any other part of her week, and she could barely think about their beach date without blushing. Lola was hotter than sin, but Quinn was just as attracted to how intelligent Lola was. She was surrounded by academics, but none of them seemed to have the intellectual curiosity Lola did. It was invigorating.

Jessica popped her head in. "Need some coffee, Dr. Golden?"

Quinn had given up asking Jessica to call her Quinn in the office. "I can get my own coffee, Jessica."

"Not with that dreamy look. You would probably walk into something. Thinking about janitor hot body?"

Normally, Quinn would have denied it, but what was the point? She was thinking about Lola and the description fit.

"So, have you two sealed the deal yet?" Jessica asked.

"We're moving at a pace that works for both of us," Quinn said. She thought of how close she'd been to losing control at the beach. Lola said she felt the same way. Quinn felt like she needed to go slow with Lola. She'd mentioned a bad breakup. She didn't mind the slow burn either.

"Well, she would be a fool to not be into you," Jessica said. "And anyone with eyes can see she is. Let me get you some coffee so when she comes to pick you up for breakfast you can carry on a conversation."

"Do you mind bringing it to the lab? I think I'm going to take a look at some of the new scans."

"Excuse me," Jessica said. She slapped both hands on her cheeks in mock horror. "Are you bringing liquids into Dr. Golden's research lab?"

"I won't tell her if you won't. I hear she's a real hard-ass."

Quinn made her way down the hall to her lab. She could hear Lola at work a few doors down. She wanted to stick her head in to say hi, but Lola would be all hers in about an hour. It was easier to picture after the beach.

As she approached the lab, Quinn's thoughts turned to work. She had new data to look at that she needed for her final grant application. She keyed open the door and pushed. It resisted about a third of the way open. She pushed harder, thinking a student must have left a chair in the way.

She slid in to remove the obstacle and stopped, frozen at the horror before her. She wanted to scream, but nothing came out. The world seemed to stop, and her mind, which now seemed to be spitting out thoughts in slow motion, reminded her that everyone in the movies screamed in situations like this. She stepped back out of the room, pulled the door handle, slamming the door shut, and started yelling for Lola. She held the door handle, as if the door would spring back open of its own accord.

Lola and Jessica came running. Lola was still carrying the wastebasket she'd been attending to. She dropped it when she got to Quinn.

"What's wrong?" Lola's hands were everywhere on Quinn's body.

Quinn wasn't sure if she was comforting her or, more likely, checking for injuries. Either way, it felt nice. Quinn threw herself into Lola's embrace. She couldn't yet put into words what was behind the door. She knew she was shaking uncontrollably. She started to cry now that she was safely wrapped up. There was a reason she called for Lola. She just knew that Lola would keep her safe, would make this okay. Somehow.

Jessica started to open the door to the lab.

"Don't!" Quinn reached out to stop her.

Jessica jumped back.

"What's in there?" Lola asked. She didn't let go of Quinn even when she held her a little farther away so she could look her in the eye.

"I can't," Quinn said.

"Okay. That's okay," Lola said. "I'm going to take a quick peek. Stay here with Jessica. I'll be right back."

Quinn wanted to tell her not to go in, not to look at what she'd seen, what she could never unsee, but Lola seemed so sure of herself and in control of the situation, Quinn let her go. She shivered as Lola withdrew and handed her off to Jessica, who wrapped her in a hug. Lola didn't stay long. She stepped back out and quietly closed the door.

"Come here, baby," Lola said.

Quinn flew back into Lola's arms.

"Jessica, can you please call the police? Tell them there's a dead body in Quinn's lab. They're going to need their homicide team. Quinn and I are going to stay right here until they get here to make sure no one else goes in there. Can you get the blanket from Quinn's office, please? And if there's a way to keep people off this floor until the police arrive, that would be great."

"Did you just say homicide?" Jessica looked shocked.

"And a few things after that. Did you get the rest of it too?"

"Yes. Police, blanket, lock people out until the police get here," Jessica said.

As soon as Jessica ran off down the hall, Quinn let Lola pull her down to the floor still wrapped in her embrace. She settled between Lola's legs, nearly in the fetal position, with Lola's arms wrapped around her. She rested her head on Lola's chest and listened to the steady beat of her heart.

Lola broke the silence first. "You okay? No, of course you're not. That's not what I mean. Wanna talk about it?"

"How are you so calm?"

"Not my first dead body," Lola said.

"Mine either," Quinn said. "But I've seen them at funerals. I've never seen a man with his throat slit in the middle of my research lab. And I know him. He's the old janitor, Kevin, I think his name is. Why is he there?"

"I don't know," Lola said. "Did you know him well?"

"No, not at all. I couldn't help look at his face," Quinn said. "With his throat. You know. God, I saw that bloody...I don't know. No one's neck should ever look like that. I got out and yelled for you, I guess."

"I'm glad you thought of me. I always want to be there to keep you safe."

"Seriously, how are you so calm?" Quinn was feeling like something was wrong with her for freaking out as much as she was. She was queasy and her heart rate felt unhealthy. Lola didn't seem all that affected by the scene in the lab. "I wish I could be as unaffected as you are right now."

"I'm not calm or unaffected," Lola said. "I'm experienced. You don't want the kind of experiences that makes what we just looked at anything less than horrifying."

Quinn wondered at the riddle. "Will you tell me?"

"Someday, perhaps," Lola said. "But not now. Just know I didn't perpetrate that kind of violence and did everything in my power to stop it from ever happening."

"I know," Quinn said. And somehow she did. She trusted Lola would never do anything like what she had just seen.

When the police arrived, Quinn was still firmly ensconced in Lola's embrace. She didn't much feel like getting up and giving a statement, but Lola promised not to leave her side. She didn't, except for a brief moment when she asked to talk to one of the detectives privately. Quinn wondered about it, but didn't ask Lola.

After the police released them, Lola suggested they get breakfast as usual, but Quinn wasn't hungry.

"Let me take you home then," Lola said.

Quinn thought about her apartment. It didn't feel like home. She hardly spent any time there. Lola must have read her mind.

"Home doesn't have to be your place. Come on. We'll go to my place. But we're bringing food with us."

Lola drove Quinn's car and practically carried her upstairs to her apartment.

"It's not much," Lola said.

"It's not what I would have pictured for you," Quinn said. She took in the furniture and decorations.

"It came furnished."

"That explains it," Quinn said. "The mystery continues then."

"What mystery?"

"What your place looks like." Quinn appreciated the momentary distraction of collecting data about Lola's apartment.

"This is my place," Lola said.

"No, it's not. This is someone else's place that you're renting."

"Well, I'm here. Doesn't that make it mine?"

"It makes it all I need right now," Quinn said. It was true. Since they left the CLA campus, she felt much better. She knew being with Lola was a large part of the reason for that. "I don't think I thanked you for being there with me. I was, am, so scared."

"It was a scary situation. And as I said, I always want to be there to keep you safe, to ease your fears, to make you feel better."

"Can I ask you a question?" Quinn asked. "Well, a couple, actually. The first one is, can we get in bed? I'm suddenly exhausted." Quinn almost laughed at the look of panic on Lola's face. Dead bodies were apparently no problem, but the thought of slipping under the covers with her was sending this brave, strong woman into emotional turmoil. "Just to sleep. You've been up all night, and I'm spent. I can sleep on the couch if you would rather, but I don't really want to leave your arms."

"Of course that's okay," Lola said. "I'll get you something to change into. I've got to send one text message and then I'll be right there. I promised my sister I'd check in this morning about a Facetime date with my nephew, but given the excitement, I think I'd rather reschedule."

Quinn felt bad about keeping Lola from her nephew. She was going to protest and insist Lola Facetime anyway.

Lola seemed to read her mind. "Murder isn't really the greatest mood setter for chatting with a toddler. I'll catch him another day."

As soon as Quinn changed into the clothes Lola provided, she slipped under the covers and waited for Lola. She joined her momentarily. Quinn snuggled against Lola's side and rested her head on Lola's chest.

"Can I ask my real question now?" Quinn asked.

"Of course," Lola said. She sounded half asleep.

"Are you really a custodian? You talked to the cops like you've been around cops, or like you are one. Remember, I come from a whole family of cops. You pick up a few things." Quinn felt Lola stiffen under her.

"I'm not a cop," Lola said.

"Not a janitor either? Criminal? Please not a criminal." Quinn felt her heart breaking, but there didn't seem to be any good reason for Lola to have lied to her. *Who are you, Lola Badger? What were you trying to tell me on the beach?*

"No," Lola said. She pulled Quinn all the way on top of her so they were eye to eye. She looked like she was weighing her options. "Not a criminal. Never a criminal. I'm a bond enforcement agent."

"A bounty hunter?"

"Why does everyone say it like that?" Lola asked. "Yes, a bounty hunter. Although, we do a lot of security and high-risk investigative operations as well."

"So why are you here? Chasing someone who missed court? Wait, is anything you told me true? Do you have a sister? Is your name Lola?" Quinn tried to roll off, but she was held in place.

"Can I explain before you run away from me?"

Quinn didn't answer, but she stopped trying to get away. Truth was, she didn't really want to go anywhere. It felt pretty damned good right where she was, even if Lola, or whatever her name was, hadn't been completely honest.

"Yes, my name is Lola, but it's Walker, not Badger. Holt's not my sister, although she's the closest thing I have and I do consider her family. I'm not here chasing a skip. I'm tracking down someone who's threatening Holt and her family. Or I was. But the case is over now. Or I thought it was. That's why I was undercover. I didn't know who was involved. For a hot second I thought you might be."

"Me?" Quinn was incredulous. "Involved in threatening someone? But you know me. How could you think that?"

"Well, now I know you. I didn't when I first got here. And there was some evidence that pointed your way. It's sorted out now."

"Evidence? What evidence?" Quinn wasn't feeling so scared and sorry for herself anymore. "And hold up a second. If your case is over, does that mean you're going to be leaving? How can you tell me you want to always protect me and keep me safe when you're going to be leaving?"

This time Quinn did roll off of Lola and tried to get out of bed. She made it as far as the edge of the bed before Lola's arm wrapped around her waist. Lola didn't pull her back, just held her there loosely.

"Where are you going?" Lola asked. She kissed Quinn's shoulder lightly.

"Away from you."

Quinn pushed Lola away and got out of bed. She was still on edge from finding a dead body in her lab, and now the person that had broken through the fear and made her feel safe was leaving. It was too much. She knew it wasn't fair to be mad at Lola, she was trying her damndest to get out of LA too, but the stress and overwhelming terror of the morning wasn't coming out all that rationally.

"Please don't go," Lola said. She was so close behind Quinn that she made her jump. "I don't know what the future holds, for either of us. I wanted to talk to you about all of this, but we just didn't have the chance. I was hoping to over breakfast today. Do you think it was easy for me to hear you talk about jobs you were applying to all over the country? To be honest, I'm a little surprised my residence is the part you're most upset about. Most people would be mad about the lying."

Quinn shrugged. "Family full of cops, remember? Undercover work is part of the job. My family might have turned their backs on me, but I understand the job. That part I get. But today, when I felt so scared, and vulnerable, and horrified, you made me feel safe. And you said you always wanted to make me feel that way. And now you tell me you won't actually do that, because you can't. I don't need you to be my savior or my protector, but it felt really nice today to have you there when I needed you. But I refuse to do a long distance thing. I'm not settling for that."

Lola moved so she was standing directly in front of her. She tilted Quinn's head up and kissed her forehead, then her nose, and finally, placed a whisper of a kiss on her lips.

"I said what I said earlier and meant every word. I told Holt I needed some personal time before I came back. I was going to talk to you about that today too. I was hoping we might figure out what this is between us and if it's possible to make it work. When we had breakfast the other morning and you mentioned Providence, that gave me hope. That's where I live."

"So, what, we're supposed to wait and see if I get a job in Providence and then I'll call you?" Quinn thought that sounded like a horrible plan.

"Well, things might be all shot to shit now," Lola said. "Kevin Garvey was part of the reason I was here. Either the threat to Holt is over with him dead and Holt will want me back, or we've got a much larger issue."

The idea of Lola tangling with murderers changed Quinn's mind about a few things. It gave her a new fear to add to her list, but it also showed her they cared about each other, and that, right now, was all that really mattered. They could work the rest out later.

She pulled Lola down and kissed her, fiercely at first and then more tenderly. "Get back in bed."

"Fine, but I'm not sleeping with you just because you think I'm leaving or in danger."

"Is everyone on the East Coast this much of a prude?" Quinn asked.

"Land that job in Providence and come meet a few of us," Lola said.

"I'm only interested in one," Quinn said.

"Better be." Lola pulled Quinn to her and backed them up to the bed. When her knees hit the mattress, they both tumbled back and landed in a tangle of limbs. Quinn emerged on top and pinned Lola.

"I'll agree to your terms, but you're going to kiss me for the next couple of hours. And there's a lot of territory between kissing and sleeping together for us to work with."

CHAPTER FIFTEEN

L ola was awakened by the sound of her front door being kicked in. She was out of bed so fast she barely had time to register the wonder of waking up with Quinn in her arms.

"What was that?" Quinn asked.

She sounded terrified. Lola wished she could take the past twenty-four hours away and spare Quinn all the horror.

This wasn't how Lola had planned on spending her time with Quinn. "Not good," Lola said. She didn't have time to explain anything. Whoever was paying her a visit was heading their way. She pulled Quinn out of bed and pushed her into the closet. "Stay in here and don't make any noise. And no matter what you hear, don't come out. Understand?"

Lola gave her the most stern, "please, this is important" look she could muster. She kissed her quickly when Quinn nodded, and then shut the door silently.

She'd just finished with shorts and a T-shirt and made it across the bedroom threshold to the hallway when two men grabbed her and dragged her to the living room. She didn't fight them until they were as far away from the bedroom as she could get them. Once they were in the living room, she flung them off of her and put some distance between herself and the intruders, but kept herself between Quinn and the men.

"I hope you boys brought coffee," Lola said.

"Our boss would like to talk to you," one of men said.

"Quite the entrance. Show him in."

"He's not here. You're going to him."

"I don't think so," Lola said.

"I was hoping you'd say that," one of the men said.

She lunged for her phone, which was on the coffee table and was able to push the panic button before she felt two pinpricks in her back. She watched the confetti from the Taser flutter to the floor as the painful current contracted her muscles and she hit the floor with a grunt. Her body wasn't her own as she had no muscle control, but the fury these two elicited hadn't been paralyzed.

They must have realized they had limited time to subdue her long-term because they sprang into action, zip-tying her hands and loosely binding her feet. Apparently, she was still expected to walk out of here. *Fat chance.*

When her muscles were no longer contracting painfully, the two men tried to drag her to her feet. She did nothing to help them. She didn't see any reason to offer assistance in her own kidnapping. Besides, she was pretty sure she'd managed to activate the panic button. Sooner or later, the cavalry would arrive. It might be a while, but this is where they would come.

"Walk."

"Tell me why and I'll think about it," Lola said. He punched her in the stomach. She doubled over but made no sound. *Bastard.*

"Walk."

"You didn't say please."

He punched her again.

"Walk."

"No. And your form sucks. You punch like a four-year-old."

He pulled his fist back to punch her a third time, but his buddy stopped him. "Just pick her up and drag her. There will be plenty of time for that if she's this bitchy later. Boss Man wants to talk to her, and she can't talk if she's unconscious or puking up blood."

"How do you suggest I do that? She's bigger than both of us," the first guy said.

He was so whiney Lola was almost enjoying herself. Almost.

They grabbed her and pulled her from the apartment. She resisted as much as she could, but there were two of them and she was still feeling the effects of being Tased. With her hands bound, she was largely at their mercy. They threw her in the backseat of a waiting SUV and sped off. She marveled at the ease of her kidnapping. No one was out walking their dog or wandering the sidewalk to witness the abduction. Quinn was the only one who knew it had even taken place.

She thought of Quinn. Between dead Kevin and kidnapped Lola, she'd be lucky to ever see her again. That thought made her nauseous. She might be facing an unsure and obviously very dangerous situation, but somehow the thought of losing Quinn was the most terrifying outcome to flitter through her mind.

She's probably better off without you. Look at the danger you've brought her. After all the shitty relationships you've been in and now you're the toxic one.

Lola knew she'd promised Quinn she'd stay and they could see what there was between them, but that was before the kidnapping. If bad things happened in threes, just what end did this unholy trinity have in store for her? Quinn shouldn't be anywhere near her when her number three showed itself, assuming she survived number two.

Maybe I should let them kill me. It's gonna hurt when I leave.

Lola was jarred out of her musings by a whack across the head. "Hey, we're taking you to see the boss of the CMC-15s. You would do well to show some respect when we get there, you understand?"

Now Lola knew who her hosts were. The knowledge wasn't comforting, although she didn't have any idea why one of the larger and more violent street gangs in LA would want anything to do with her.

When the urban landscape started to look familiar, Lola's unease grew. She kept her outward demeanor calm, but she had a bad feeling about just why the CMCs were interested in chatting. She'd been uncomfortable with the fact that Kevin Garvey's body had been dumped in Quinn's lab. The connection to Lola seemed too coincidental, but she'd hoped she was wrong.

The SUV pulled up in the front of the warehouse Kevin Garvey had been holing up in and stopped. *So much for coincidence. Fuck.* Her escorts pulled her out and dumped her in the dirt. The whiner kicked her in the ribs. "Get up and walk."

It didn't seem like a great time to provoke him so she complied. She'd also noticed both of her new buddies were strapped. She preferred a boot to the gut to a handgun pointed at her head. Besides, now she needed information from them. That information was waiting inside. *Hopefully, I'll live long enough to relay it.*

Lola took a minute to adjust to the dim lighting of the warehouse. She could see a group of people on the far side, just as there'd been the last time she was there. When her eyes adjusted, she barely stifled a loud, enthusiastic curse. Brayden was there, tied to a chair and looking a little worse for wear. Four other men stood around him, while a fifth, clearly the leader, bent down to talk to him. Brayden flinched away.

"Hello, Lola," the man in charge said. "Welcome. Come. Join us."

Lola was shoved into a chair next to Brayden, the zip tie was removed, and a new restraint was put in place, tying her to the chair. She caused as much resistance and trouble as she could during the process. She hoped that the distraction would allow her to keep her hands loose enough to work free later. It worked to a degree but gained her another shot to the ribs as a trade-off. At least they hadn't bothered to retie her feet or secure them to the chair.

"Who are you? What can I help you with?" Lola asked.

"I'm hurt you don't already know my name. Someone like you not doing your homework? Tsk. My name is Malcolm."

"I dropped out of high school. I didn't do a lot of homework," Lola said. "Are you going to tell me why I'm here?"

"I'll get to that. But first, I'm going to tell you a story," Malcolm said. "Do you know what the CMC-15s are?"

"A dime a dozen street gang," Lola said. This guy was starting to annoy her, but the longer he talked, the more time she had to work on getting her hands free. She wasn't scared yet. There were still possible solutions to this problem and Malcolm only seemed to want to talk.

"That's where you're wrong. We're a business empire."

"That seems a little grandiose, but we can agree to disagree. Potato, delusions of grandeur, etcetera."

Malcolm seemed content to ignore Lola's needling, or was too involved in his self-promotion to notice.

"We had income last year of over ten million dollars. But that isn't something that can go in the bank. You feel me? But that's where real businessmen get creative. That's where your boy Kevin Garvey and Brayden here came in."

"Wait, you used online fantasy football to clean your dirty ass money?" Lola was impressed. Cleaning that much money was no easy task, and Malcolm had found a creative way of doing it.

"Legit winnings come out squeaky clean the other side. And boy genius here already had all I needed to guarantee I made a little more on top too."

"You got in bed with these clowns?" Lola said. She was looking at Brayden. He didn't have to answer. He clearly had no idea where the money had come from or what his algorithm had been used for. How he and his buddies weren't even the slightest bit suspicious when all that money started pouring in, Lola didn't know, but willful or actual idiocy didn't make him a hardened criminal.

"Kevin brought him in, and he brought you in. We're all in this big comfy bed together. Except, Kevin stole from me, thought he could fix it on his own, and ended up bringing more trouble to me and my boss, which was stupid and had to be dealt with. His debt transfers to Brayden. Brayden can't pay. Kevin has a big fucking mouth, so I know all about his daughter and her rich girlfriend back East. Which is what you're here to talk about."

"Except, as I told Brayden here, I'm not any part of this," Lola said. Malcolm's assumption that she and Holt were connected was concerning. He shouldn't know about that. His allusion to dealing with Kevin was also disconcerting. She was pretty sure she'd found Kevin's killer, and the fact that he had been dumped in a place where she was likely to run across him wasn't good, especially if he knew about her connection to Holt and who Holt was. Kevin's death was starting to feel like a message. So was her kidnapping. Hopefully, it didn't have the same outcome.

"You're involved now. The sooner you and Holt realize that and start taking steps to rectify the harm you have done, the better for everyone. Especially you, given your current situation. You became involved when you started snooping around in our business and stirring up trouble with the police," Malcolm said. "We're fully aware of who you are." He pulled a gun and held it to Brayden's head. "Bring out our other guest," he said to one of his soldiers.

Lola's heart rate spiked from anger to genuine fear when Jessica was dragged from a small office in the corner of the warehouse. She didn't look physically injured, but she was clearly scared. She'd planned on trying to get Brayden out if she could manage it, although he had clearly sold her out, but she would do whatever it took to rescue Jessica.

"I wanted to invite your professor friend to join us, but she wasn't home when we stopped by. Luckily, Jessica was a willing conversationalist."

For a moment or two, all Lola could feel was the wave of relief that Quinn had insisted on staying with her. The thought of Quinn scared and alone, being questioned by Malcolm, nearly made her gag. She centered herself like she saw Holt do in the middle of a confrontation. It looked easier when Holt did it. She'd been in plenty of tricky situations, but with a team, or with Holt. She was on her own now.

"And just what is it that you think you know about me? Jessica and I don't know each other that well. Let her go. You've got what you wanted."

"Not just yet. I'll wait and see how cooperative you're feeling," Malcolm said. He seemed to sense the shift in Lola's attitude now that Jessica was on the scene. "Kevin had a plan to get my money back through his daughter. So says Brayden. What do you know, her old lady is rich as fuck. Lucky for her. Lucky for Brayden. You know what's lucky for you?"

"Can't wait to find out," Lola said.

"Jessica told me you have a sister. A sister named Holt. Three guesses who the rich lady who's gonna give me my money back is?"

"Pretty sure this isn't going to work out the way you think, Malcolm."

"Uh-oh. Is that because you don't have a fucking sister?" Malcolm was smiling, but it did things to his face that turned Lola's stomach. "You think I run an operation pulling in the kind of money I do and not have eyes and ears all over the LAPD? You should have left when you found Garvey alive and well, and we could've avoided all of this, but lucky for me, you and Holt decided to stick your noses where they don't belong."

Malcolm waved his hand at his soldier still holding Jessica. She was dragged in front of Lola and shoved to the ground at her feet.

"You kidnapped me to get money from Holt?" Lola asked. Holt never would have paid before because Kevin didn't have anything Holt cared about. Lola wondered how much Holt would pay to save her life. She hoped not a damn penny. She never wanted Holt to be vulnerable to anyone who could get their hands on one of Holt's crew to extort her.

"Money? This isn't about the money. Did you not hear me say we had income in the millions last year? You think I would risk pissing off Holt Lasher over a hundred grand? That money was Garvey's problem, and he's dead now, problem solved." Malcolm didn't look the least bit torn up about Garvey's demise.

"My beef with you and with Holt is your sticking your noses where they don't belong. So now we have to send a message. Back the fuck off and stop talking to the police. I'll start with you. That'll get my message to Holt. I'd deliver it personally, but Rhode Island's too far to travel on short notice. I'll leave my message somewhere she can't miss it."

Now was the time to get Jessica to safety. Lola didn't have time to worry about Malcolm's plan or her own tenuous situation with the CMCs. She thanked whatever higher power had been looking out for her when her captors had used zip ties and not handcuffs to secure her to the chair. She'd been working on loosening them the entire time Malcolm was talking. She torqued her shoulders, jerking hard against the plastic. It cut into her wrists, but she felt the restraints snap under her assault. *Look out, boys.*

She lunged forward and hurdled Jessica. "Run," Lola said as she cleared her prone body. When she landed, she connected a solid hook across the chin of one of her kidnappers, knocking him cold. She fished quickly in his pocket and retrieved the keys. He wasn't armed so she couldn't arm herself, but she knew the two who had dragged her in were. She whistled to Jessica and flung her the keys as two of the other CMCs grabbed her.

"Bring her down," Malcolm yelled from somewhere to Lola's left. "Don't kill her. No gunshots."

As Lola grabbed one off her back and flipped him to the ground, she reached out with a foot and flipped Brayden's chair. As she hoped, the wooden back broke on impact. He was able to work his hands out from between the cross support, and he took off after Jessica out the door. Lola kept fighting until they were clear. All of the CMCs were either too preoccupied with her, or were unconcerned enough with the others to go after them. It was likely she was the real prize anyway.

One of the men landed a punch to the side of her head, a second to her body. A third man grabbed her arms and held them behind her back, while a fourth kicked her behind the legs, buckling her knees. Someone punched her in the face again, and then in the ribs. She spat blood on the floor and tried to stand, but she was still being restrained.

She managed to break free momentarily and landed a few additional punches, but they were on her again before long. There were too many of them. Lola took another body shot and fell to her knees. This time she didn't need to be held down. The pain was overwhelming. She tried to stand but sank down once again. Malcolm appeared in her field of vision. He squatted so he was at her level, grabbed her chin, and forced her to look at him.

"You're stupid, Lola, but one hell of a fighter. I respect that."

"Just kill me already," Lola said. As she said it she thought of Quinn. What she wouldn't give for one more look at her. She hoped the panic button call had gone through and Quinn was safe. *Holt will keep her safe.* At least she would die knowing that.

"I never had any intention of killing you," Malcolm said. "This," he said, indicating her battered body. "This was always going to happen. But this was a surprise." He pointed to his men, a few of whom were still on their backs. Lola could barely see and was having trouble staying conscious, but it looked like she'd landed more than her share of punches.

"Now," Malcolm said. "It's time to end this and move on to round two. Stand her up. I can handle the police, Lola, but when you start snooping around and worrying my colleagues, you make my life difficult. I can't have that. Walk away now and forget everything in LA, or I will keep coming for you."

Lola felt herself being lifted. She saw Malcolm draw his fist back and vaguely felt it connect with her abdomen, but she was beyond feeling. Then she watched his fist come closer and closer to her face and the world faded to black.

CHAPTER SIXTEEN

Quinn sat on the sofa in Lola's apartment and stared at the missed call tally on Lola's cell phone. So far it was up to eleven. Quinn's phone was silent. She desperately wanted, needed, to hear from Lola, but she couldn't will that to happen. It had been six hours and twenty-eight minutes since Lola's apartment had fallen eerily silent, and Quinn had worked up the nerve to emerge from the closet.

She'd called the police and reported the violent abduction. The police had come by, done their jobs, and now she was once again alone in the apartment, the silence only broken by the frequent buzzing of Lola's cell phone. Quinn thought about answering a few of the calls, but she didn't recognize any of the names. Holt hadn't shown up on the caller ID. She didn't know what she would say even if she'd answered. She had no information, nothing that felt relevant, like who took Lola or where she was. She'd told the police what she'd heard, which wasn't a lot.

One of the things she liked about science was the order and control it afforded. You asked a question and worked hard to find an answer. There were no answers to be found in this situation, and she didn't even know what questions to ask. All she was left with was her overwhelming feelings—terror, sadness, anger.

"God, what if I never see her again?" Quinn said to the empty apartment.

Lola's phone rang again. The caller ID said "Moose." It seemed fitting that a giant reindeer was trying to get in touch with Lola. When her phone stopped ringing, a text came through.

"*I'm already on my way. Don't get dead.*"

Quinn wasn't sure if she found that comforting or worrying. But he seemed to be coming to help. Maybe he would have some ideas about how to find her. She thought about calling her father or one of the other cops in her family, but she wasn't sure they would help. She couldn't see her dad dropping everything to help her search for a woman she cared for.

For lack of anything better to do, Quinn tried Jessica's cell for the third time. As with the other times, it went straight to voice mail. Quinn hoped she'd found someone hot to spend the night with and had been enjoying her day cut off from the world. As much as she needed the support of her friend, she liked thinking someone was having a really great day.

As Quinn was contemplating her next move, she heard screeching tires just outside the apartment. She jumped up, her heart pounding, the blood rushing in her ears. Were the men back? Should she hide again? Quinn took a deep breath. It was more likely just a reckless driver.

It took a few seconds, but she worked up the courage to peek out the window. A black SUV was at the curb directly in front of Lola's building. Quinn watched in disbelief as the rear passenger door was flung open and a person was dumped out onto the sidewalk. The SUV drove away with as much screeching of tires as it had arrived.

Quinn focused on the person lying in a crumpled heap on the sidewalk. They weren't moving. Recognition was slow in coming, but when it did, she sprinted for the door. How could she have not immediately seen it was Lola lying there, so obviously hurt? She hoped that was all she was. She thought about what Moose had said, "*Don't get dead.*"

"Don't be dead. Do. Not. Be. Dead. Don't you dare," she said as she skidded to a frantic stop in from of Lola. Now that she was next to her, it was no wonder she didn't recognize her right away. Lola was a bloody, swollen mess. "Oh, God. Baby, what did they do to you?"

"I'm not dead," Lola said. She spoke slowly, as if the words hurt coming out of her mouth. It looked like they did. "And would you believe me if I said the other guys look worse?"

"No. But I'd believe they look just as bad. I'm really, really glad you're not dead. I was so worried about you."

"I know. I'm sorry."

"We have to get you to the hospital."

"I'll go," Lola said. "But I need my phone first. I have to call the bat phone. They're probably going nuts."

"Your phone has been ringing nonstop. I didn't know if I should answer." Quinn helped Lola sit up. The process seemed to be a little more than she could handle, and she faded out in Quinn's arms. Just before she did, she pointed to her phone. Quinn hadn't realized she was still holding it.

"Bat phone."

Although Lola had stated her order of priorities, Quinn didn't agree the hospital should wait. She called nine-one-one first. Once she was satisfied an ambulance was on the way, she used Lola's thumb to unlock her phone and scrolled through her contacts looking for the bat phone. When she went to hand the phone to Lola, she saw she'd passed out, so she called herself and cradled Lola's head in her lap.

"Update." The voice on the other end of the line sounded stressed, but more than a little relieved.

Quinn didn't know how to respond to the unusual greeting. She didn't say anything right away. Apparently, she waited too long for the woman on the other end.

"What the fuck, Lola? You hit the panic button, then go off the radar for hours. I need a report. Do you have any idea what condition H's in? Not even Isabelle could stop her, so they're both on a plane out there. Max was ready to redirect satellites, and this time I was going to help her. You know I can't go back to prison, but for you, anything. But that shit isn't summer camp, you can't pick your roommate, you know what I mean? And the handcuffs there aren't for my kind of fun. Conjugal visits, don't get me started. Lola?"

"Um. This isn't Lola." Quinn didn't quite know how to answer the kinetic force on the other end of the line. "She's with me, but she's hurt. I'm taking her to the hospital. She asked me to call the bat phone, but she's unconscious at the moment."

Now it was Quinn who waited for a response. "Hello? You still there?"

"Unconscious? Jesus, Holt is going to have kittens. Is she going to be okay? You must be Lola's Professor Hotty."

"It looks like she was beaten. She was conscious for a little bit when they threw her out of the car, but she's in and out now. You were kidding about redirecting satellites, right?" For some reason, sitting on the sidewalk, cradling Lola, waiting for an ambulance, and talking to a stranger who didn't want to go back to prison, that seemed vitally important.

"Yeah, sure. If you want. The cavalry is on its way. Keep her phone with you and everyone will find you at the hospital. You don't need to update us. When Moose gets there, tell him Holt is riled. He'll know what that means. Between Moose and Isabelle, they should be able to handle her. Look, keep Lola safe for us for the next couple hours."

Quinn wanted to ask just what the woman on the other end of the phone meant by her warnings regarding Holt, but the ambulance pulled up and interrupted.

The next few hours were a flurry of activity as Lola was poked, prodded, evaluated, scanned, bandaged, stitched, cleaned, and patched. Throughout the process Lola politely refused Quinn's offers to give her privacy or space and the hospital staff's gentle encouragement that Quinn wait elsewhere. Lola held on to her hand whenever possible, and when it wasn't possible she asked Quinn to wait nearby until it became possible again.

Quinn didn't know if it was for her benefit or Lola's, but she didn't care. She sat next to her and held her hand as Lola's body stiffened in pain, and she tried her best to soothe her when Lola turned to her, her eyes filled with unshed tears.

Even if Lola had asked her to leave the room, she wouldn't have gone far. Lola felt safe, even flat on her back and half dead, when nothing else in Quinn's life did right now. She knew she was overly focused on Lola's care, probably to avoid thinking about the horror movie her life had turned into recently, but avoidance was working for her. It sure felt better than falling apart.

By the time Lola was wheeled upstairs to a room for overnight observation, she looked far less like a combination of rare hamburger and roadkill. Remarkably, there was nothing that was going to cause lasting damage.

"Just lie to me and tell me I look like my old self again," Lola said. She cracked half a smile, which looked like it took all the energy she had left.

"Do you know anything about comic books?"

"Holt loves them. I think it's the only thing she reads. So I'm somewhat fluent in nerd," Lola said.

"Do you know who Dr. Manhattan is?"

"Big blue guy?"

"That's like saying Darth Vader is just a dude with a cape, but yes, he's blue. You look a little like the adult love child between you and Dr. Manhattan. I expect that to change as your bruising progresses. Vision, purple android, Gamora, green alien, Lego Batman. You get the idea."

"So I look awesome, and you've got a nerdy side you hadn't really exposed yet. That's what you're trying to tell me?"

"Right. I don't know if I want to know what happened. But not knowing means I'm making things up, which I think is worse. Lola, I'm so scared. Please tell me this isn't normal for you."

"Hey, it's okay to be scared. I was scared too. This isn't normal for anyone. Come up here."

Lola tried to scoot over on the bed to make room for Quinn, but she didn't make it far before she gave up. "Pathetic. Defeated by gravity."

Quinn didn't point out it was more likely the severe beating that was causing her problems. Maybe Lola needed to believe that hadn't slowed her down at all. For some reason Quinn found comfort in that thought. If Lola was avoiding thinking about it too, maybe Quinn wasn't alone in her freak-out. She sat carefully on the edge of the bed, trying not to disturb Lola.

"Holy shit, Lola, you look terrible."

A man stood in the doorway to Lola's room shaking his head. He had a half smile on his face, but his eyes were soft with concern. "How many of them were there? Twenty? Fifty?"

The man came in and plopped down in the seat next to the bed. He grabbed one of the Jell-O cups on Lola's tray and started eating. It looked laughably small in his enormous hands. Quinn hadn't fully appreciated his size from the doorway.

"Hey, hands off my food, you big lump. And get out of the chair. That's Quinn's chair."

"She looks pretty happy where she is. I'm Moose."

Moose extended his hand. Quinn lost hers in his grip, but returned the handshake.

"You can spare a little of this hospital fare. You might have gotten your ass handed to you, but I had to respond to your panic alarm. I'm not even wearing underwear."

"I'll let Jose know," Lola said.

Quinn found it endearing when Moose blushed.

"What is this panic alarm everyone keeps talking about?" Quinn asked. "The woman I talked to on your phone mentioned it too."

"I forgot about that," Lola said. "Which of the Wonder Twins did you get?"

Moose must have read the confusion on her face. "Did you feel like you were talking to a normal, calm human or a lit firecracker?"

"Oh, the firecracker, definitely." Quinn wouldn't have thought of that description herself, but it really was perfect.

"Dubs," both Lola and Moose said.

"She told me to tell you Holt is on her way. With Isabelle, I think. And that she's riled. She said you would know what that meant."

"Fuck," Lola said. She pinched the bridge of her nose between her thumb and index finger and then winced. "Oww, what did they do to my face?"

"Well," Moose said. "What did you expect? This is you we're talking about."

"I know. Another thing I screwed up. She didn't have to get on a plane to deliver that news."

Moose stood up and moved to the side of the bed. "Excuse me for a minute," he said to Quinn as he moved into Lola's direct line of sight. Quinn didn't have a choice but to move off her perch next to Lola on the bed.

"That's not what this is about and you know it. You want to have a pity party because you're lying in a hospital bed, fine, but don't you dare try the pitiful fuckup routine with me. After George, you know perfectly well why she's riled."

Quinn was confused. Had something happened to that cute little boy whose pictures Lola had shown her? She was pretty sure she said he was Holt's son.

"Did something happen to Holt's son?" Quinn felt her adrenaline spike again. She still didn't know why the men had come after Lola, or why there'd been a dead body in her lab yesterday. The idea of an injured child was too much.

"I'm going to get some coffee," Moose said. "Pull yourself together before H gets here."

The room was silent for a few beats after Moose left. Quinn wasn't sure if she should be the first to speak. She was overflowing with questions, but now didn't feel like the time for an interrogation.

"Holt and Isabelle's son, George, is named after George the First, my brother. He was one of Holt's best friends when they were kids. Holt, Moose, and George. I followed them around everywhere and drove them nuts, but Holt always looked out for me, especially after George died."

Quinn saw the same look of raw pain on Lola's face she'd seen the first time she'd asked Lola about George. She'd been asking about Holt's son, but now she knew why Lola had reacted the way she did to the name.

"Sweetie, I'm so sorry. What happened?"

"I'm not sure I can right now, I'm sorry," Lola said.

Quinn understood, but couldn't help feeling slightly hurt that Lola wasn't willing or able to share her brother's death with her. *She doesn't have to relive past trauma; she's got plenty of present trauma to keep her busy. Give the woman a break.*

"I dropped out of high school right after George died, but Holt wouldn't let me come work for her until I got my GED and turned eighteen."

"So that's why you were so skittish when we were talking about what college you attended?" Quinn asked.

"Well, yeah. It was a little intimidating talking to a PhD when I never finished high school. Now that seems like the least of my worries. I get kidnapped too, apparently. Very charming."

"They're just letters," Quinn said.

"With a lot of meaning behind them," Lola said, looking unconvinced.

"True, but your Lola Walker, GED means a lot too. It means you worked hard after something awful happened in your life to finish what you started. You had a goal and you worked to achieve it. That's the same thing my letters mean."

"You're full of it, but I'm weakened so can't argue. Besides, for the first time in hours you don't look shell-shocked and terrified, so I'll take it."

"Do you ever get used to it?" Quinn couldn't imagine a life filled with such danger. She thought having cops in the family was bad.

"Getting kidnapped? If it ever happens again I'll let you know."

"No, all of it. Dead bodies, kidnapping, the violence and horror. Because I've been part of this for a very short time and I've spent the entire time in a constant state of severe anxiety. The scientist in me wants to see a scan of my brain because I bet it looks like Times Square, and the human in me wants to hide in a panic room for the next month."

"I wish telling you that my job is usually not all that exciting would be helpful, but I know all evidence is leading you to a different conclusion. I'm going to keep you safe. I promise you that, and then I will let you lead a normal, non-scary life."

"What's that supposed to mean?" Quinn didn't like what Lola was implying.

They didn't have a chance to talk further. Moose popped back in.

"Holt's inbound. And she doesn't look happy. You prep Quinn?"

"Is there any way to do that?" Lola asked.

"Not really," Moose said.

Lola looked at Quinn. "This is going to get a little loud. Help me get up."

Quinn started to protest Lola's insistence on getting out of bed, but realized it was better if she helped her instead of letting her do it herself. A moment later, a human tank engine and the most beautiful blonde Quinn had ever seen entered the room. Well, the tank engine barreled in, the blonde walked in calmly, like a normal person. Lola was trying to stand tall even though Quinn knew it was agony in her current condition.

Quinn positioned herself between Holt and Lola. "I'm Quinn Golden. You must be Holt."

"I need to talk to Lola," Holt said. "What's she doing out of bed? She looks like shit."

"That's what I told her," Quinn said. "But she insisted on getting up since you were here. Visiting hours can wait." Quinn saw Moose's eyes bug out and a look of surprise and what she hoped was respect cross the other woman's face. That wasn't the look on Holt's face. Quinn couldn't describe it, but explosive was the best she could do. She was briefly scared.

The woman behind Holt put her hand on Holt's shoulder and turned her gently. She looked at Quinn. "I'm Isabelle. Just give me a minute."

Quinn couldn't hear what Isabelle said to Holt. She was speaking quietly in her ear, holding one hand and running her other through Holt's hair. Holt nodded and rested her forehead against Isabelle's. The transformation was incredible. The tension seemed to evaporate from Holt's body as she relaxed.

"She's the only one that can do that to her," Lola said. "It's beautiful the way they love each other."

"I love the way you stood up for me, but I do need to talk to Holt." Lola must have sensed Quinn's misgivings. "I'll be fine. She's all gruff huff and puff."

As if by telepathic understanding, Lola stepped forward and Holt stepped out of Isabelle's embrace. They moved to the back of the small hospital room to talk. Quinn joined Isabelle and Moose. Holt started motioning to the bed. Lola was shaking her head emphatically.

"This should be fun," Moose said. "These two have never been good at talking to each other."

"I think they communicate their feelings through grunts and shrugs. And something's been eating at Lola since before she left," Isabelle said.

Quinn was torn between wanting to interrogate Lola's friends and eavesdrop on her conversation with Holt. The decision was made because Holt's and Lola's voices were now raised loudly enough to be heard clearly.

"Get back in bed," Holt said. She pointed at the bed again as if Lola might have forgotten where it was.

"I'll stand, thanks."

Quinn knew Lola must be close to falling over. She wondered why she wasn't doing as Holt suggested.

"Lola, you stubborn ass, you've always picked the weirdest battles since we were kids. Last chance. Get in bed."

Lola didn't say anything, but made no move to the bed either.

"Fine," Holt said.

Quinn wouldn't have believed it possible if she didn't witness it with her own eyes. Holt moved so quickly Lola didn't have time to defend herself. Holt scooped her into her arms and carried her the few steps to the bed as easily as if she were carrying a child. Although Holt looked angry, she held Lola with tenderness and lay her on the bed gently, obviously mindful of her injuries.

"Can we talk now?" Holt asked.

"Are you going to dump my ass back in bed if I get up again?"

"Yes."

"Then let's talk," Lola said.

"How are you?" Holt asked.

"I'll be fine. A little worse for wear right now, but I could go another couple rounds if I needed to. They admitted me for observation, but I think it's because I didn't look so hot when I arrived and they felt like they had to."

"I'll put all of that through the bullshit filter and assume you are in pain, feel terrible, and are glad I dumped you back in bed. Moose is getting the rest of the team on the line so you can do a full debrief, aren't you, buddy?"

"Sure am," Moose said. He stepped out to place the call.

"But right now, you and I need to talk about what part of 'I'm your first call' you didn't understand."

Quinn started forward to tell Holt she was the one who placed the call, but Isabelle stopped her.

"Let them work this out. I don't know what this is all about, but it's been building for a while."

"You said call. I did. Well, Quinn did," Lola said.

"No, Lola. I said I was your *first* call. You called Dubs. I didn't save George when I had the chance, and that's a debt I'll be paying you for the rest of our lives, but I can't lose you too. Not George and you. I was out of my mind worrying about you. Isabelle came because, well, you know how I get. She's the only one who could save this state from me. I would have torn it apart to get to you if I had to."

"You don't owe any debt to me," Lola said. "You caught the guy who killed my brother."

"Exactly. I caught the guy who *killed* your brother. He shot George the First standing right in front of me. I didn't do anything to stop it. Now's not the time to talk more about the foundation, but I was serious when I said you have the potential for so much more."

"Potential? What potential?" Lola asked. "Look at the mess I've made."

"What mess? There's no mess. There never has been. You don't work alone, Lola. You're part of my team. We rise and fall together. You know that. A year ago you helped me teach Dubs that."

"No," Lola said. She pushed Holt in the chest, shoving her back, away from the bed. "I almost got Dubs killed last year. She was cleaning up my mistake. *My* mistake almost cost you little George. I know why you didn't want me out here, but I'm the one with a debt to pay. I'll keep paying it until the slate is clean. You've been looking after me my whole life. I owe you for that."

Quinn thought Holt looked stunned, but she recovered quickly. Lola was crying.

"I didn't want you out here? You owe me something? What the fuck? And how are you going to wipe that slate clean? By risking more and more until you get yourself killed? You think that will wipe the slate clean? Or make me feel better?"

"No, fuck you." Lola shoved Holt again. They were shouting at each other now.

Isabelle closed the hospital room door after a nurse came around the corner and looked into the room. "Just a family disagreement," she said to Quinn quietly.

"What about Holt?" Quinn asked. She didn't know how to delicately ask if Holt would hit back if Lola escalated the physical confrontation. Even from a prone position, Lola was hitting Holt pretty hard.

"Holt's okay. She won't hit Lola. I don't think she ever would, but especially not in her current condition. I wish she wouldn't always let her friends beat on her to solve these family disputes though."

"This kind of thing happens a lot?"

"Not this exactly, but there are a surprising number of situations Holt has managed to solve by getting punched in the face. Wait until you meet the rest of the crew. Then it won't seem so weird," Isabelle said.

Despite the censure in her words, it was obvious to Quinn how much Isabelle loved Holt and the rest of the crew she was referring to.

"Look," Holt said. "I owe you, you owe me. Doesn't really matter. What matters is I love you and you scared the hell out of me. Seeing you shot in the head was enough. Now this?"

Quinn felt a little queasy when she heard Holt say Lola had been shot in the head. How did a regular person survive something like that? How did that happen to a regular person?

"How about we focus on the case and when it's over we can write each other love poems or arm wrestle or something," Holt said.

"Whatever we decide, Isabelle's the judge, and boxing isn't an option," Lola said.

Quinn saw she was smiling, but she looked like she was trying to hide it. Moose knocked and Isabelle opened the door for him.

"Deal. Moose, do you have everyone?"

"Ready for you, H."

"All right. Anyone who wants to hear the details, come on over. Quinn, you've already lived this once. I understand if you don't want to relive it. We can find a safe place for you while we debrief," Holt said.

Quinn appreciated Holt's thoughtfulness, but she didn't want to be outside this room. Holt looked like the kind of woman to have on your side, and Lola clearly cared for her deeply. The sheer size of all these people was also comforting. If the shit hit the fan, she could always hide behind one of them.

Max and Dubs, both of whom Quinn had spoken to previously, were on speakerphone. Lola gave everyone a full report.

"Near the end of my shift at CLA, Quinn alerted me to a problem in her research lab. She'd entered and found Kevin Garvey, deceased. I confirmed that information. His throat was cut. His body had been left in the lab, but he was obviously killed elsewhere."

Quinn wanted to ask how she knew that, but decided she didn't really want more details about that crime to add to the slideshow she already had playing on repeat every time she had a quiet moment.

"Anything else of note with the body?" Holt asked.

"No. But it felt off to me at the time. The location of the dump felt too convenient. My suspicions were confirmed earlier today during my stay with the CMC-15s. I was supposed to find Garvey's body."

"Max, everything you can get on the CMC-15s, please," Holt said.

"Already working."

Quinn was amazed at how calm everyone was discussing events that still had her fight-or-flight system in overdrive. Everyone here looked and sounded like they were talking about a midseason baseball game.

"Do you know why the CMCs took you?" Dubs asked.

"And why they let you go?" Moose asked.

"I'm a greeting card to Holt," Lola said. "Hallmark doesn't make 'back off or else' cards, so you got me. Their leader is a guy named Malcolm. He had Jessica and used her to get information on me. Oh my God, Jessica."

Lola sat up and looked around frantically. She stopped at Quinn.

"Have you heard from Jessica?"

"No. She had her cell phone off all morning." Quinn's insides felt like ice. She replayed what Lola had said. *They had Jessica.*

Lola grabbed Moose's shoulder. "You have to find Jessica. I got her out of the warehouse, but I don't know what happened after that. I don't think they followed her out, but she took one of their SUVs."

"I'll find her." Moose was already on his way out the door.

Isabelle moved to Quinn's side. "Is Jessica a friend of yours?"

Quinn nodded. She didn't think she could find words right now. She couldn't lose Jessica. Not on top of everything else.

"If she's out there to be found, Moose will get her. And if Lola got her out of the warehouse, there's a good chance she's safe."

Since there wasn't much else she could do, Quinn went back to observing the briefing. She felt numb.

"Is all of this because of Garvey? Because of the money?" Holt asked.

Lola shook her head and then looked like she regretted it. "Malcolm admitted he was part of the online fantasy scheme. They're using the system to launder dirty money, a lot of it, and Garvey skimmed off the top, that's what got him killed, I think. But Malcolm was pissed that I was hanging around the LAPD. He said he had eyes and ears in the department and knew that we were trying to bring heat on his operation, even though we didn't actually know who was behind it. He doesn't care about the money. That was Garvey's problem according to him. He said if we don't walk away from the LAPD and the investigation, he'll keep coming after us."

"Is he the mastermind?" Max asked. "Did he seem like he had the chops to orchestrate something so large?"

"I'm not sure," Lola said. "He seemed intelligent and he was brutal, but he could've killed me and the other two, Jessica and Brayden, but he didn't. He was eager to take credit for everything, but he slipped up and said something about a boss, meaning there's another player in the game."

"Max, start searching for him," Holt said. "We can work out from there. Anything else relevant?"

"Not at the moment. I don't like this guy, but I think he could be useful down the line. I don't think he's in charge, although he wanted me to think he was," Lola said.

"Do you think he'll back off if we head home and end our part in the investigation?" Holt asked. "What was your sense?"

"I don't know," Lola said. "That was the message he was sending, but I really don't know. He went to a lot of trouble to send it, and if we walk away and he still keeps coming, all it does is piss you off. I don't see the logic in that."

"Fine. Briefing over. Dubs, Max, check back in regularly, sooner if you have anything I'd want to know."

Quinn thought Holt looked contemplative as she considered all the information she had been presented. Quinn was glad she wasn't in charge of sorting through all this kind of data and drawing conclusions. The stakes were much higher here than in her research lab.

Once Holt was off the phone, Isabelle suggested they get some coffee and snacks from the cafeteria. Holt had argued she wasn't hungry, but Isabelle told her it wasn't a choice. They were giving Quinn and Lola space.

Now Quinn and Lola were alone and Quinn didn't know what to say. Quinn's whole world, usually so neat, orderly, and understandable was upside down and horribly jumbled. She'd felt repulsion, terror, horror, grief, anger, and panic on a scale she hadn't known existed. Yet here she was with the people who were apparently the epicenter of the trouble and were the only ones who made her feel remotely calm and safe. *Life sure is funny sometimes.*

"I'm sorry you got caught up in all this," Lola said. "I never meant to hurt you or scare you. If I'd known I was putting you in any danger..."

"I know," Quinn said. She did know. She knew Lola well enough to know she wouldn't have deliberately put Quinn in harm's way.

"I can't imagine how you're feeling right now. Isabelle might be a good person to talk to. She hates this stuff and says she'll never get used to it. But I *will* keep you safe."

For some reason that made Quinn angry.

"Really? How can you possibly promise that? You can't even keep yourself safe. Look where we are."

"Yes, I got my ass handed to me. I appreciate everyone reminding me. My safety wasn't my top priority."

Lola was more agitated and testy than Quinn had ever seen her. "What could possibly have been more important than your own safety?" Quinn felt like she was getting to know an entirely new person.

"Getting Jessica out alive," Lola said quietly. "They were going to kill her, right at my feet. I didn't care what happened to me as long as they didn't hurt her."

"I cared what happened to you," Quinn said. Quinn looked for the closest wastepaper basket as she felt nauseous thinking about Lola's complete disregard for her own life. *How can I let myself care so much when she may not come home at the end of the day? And why does she have to be so damned noble about it?*

"I know," Lola said. "I was thinking about you the whole time."

Lola shifted on the bed so she could look more directly at Quinn, but Quinn wasn't sure she wanted the eye contact. She wasn't sure where this anger at Lola was coming from, but anger felt better than the unrelenting powerlessness and fear that had been with her since she found the dead body in her lab. Anger felt strong. "Am I safer with you or as far away from you as I can get?"

"Honestly," Lola said. "I have no idea. But I wouldn't blame you for getting the hell away from me. I actually thought I should probably encourage you to."

Damn it. The anger was really working for me. "Well, now I know I'm more scared of the idea of being away from you than sticking close," Quinn said. "But I felt much better being mad at you than all the other emotions that have come with all the crap we've been through recently. Therapists buy second homes because of stuff like this."

"Hey, sorry to interrupt," Holt said, poking her head into the room. "I don't mean to rush you, but we've got company coming and you don't look in any shape to entertain. Time to move."

Quinn didn't know what any of that meant, but Lola seemed to. She was already getting out of bed, ripping IVs out of her arm, and looking for her clothes.

"Can you put pressure on this while I get my pants on?" she asked. She held out her arm.

"Lola, what's going on?" Quinn held gauze on Lola's forearm. This was scaring the shit out of her. Maybe more than the dead body.

"Unfriendly visitors headed our way. We've gotta leave."

"Do you think it's the CMCs?" Quinn asked. *How many other horrible people are out there that mean you harm?*

"Probably. They must know Holt is here. Not much use coming after me again if they can get straight at her."

"How do they know Holt is here?"

Lola was dressed and heading for the door. She shrugged. Quinn figured it didn't matter. Holt and Lola seemed more in-the-moment women of action. Lola pulled Quinn along behind her, shielding her.

Holt and Isabelle were arguing quietly just outside the door. Quinn couldn't hear what they were discussing, but Isabelle looked pissed and Holt looked resolved. It appeared Holt was trying to convince her of something.

"Time's up," Holt said. "D North is that way. Your point of egress is D West." Holt ducked back into Lola's hospital room and returned a moment later with what looked like part of the portable IV pole. She handed it to Lola. "If you need it."

"I must really look like crap," Lola said. "Since when do I need a chopstick to fight off bad guys?"

Holt gave her a look and Lola stopped arguing. Quinn had the urge to laugh, the kind of out of control hysterical laughter that was inappropriate for any situation, but especially this one.

"I'm not okay with this plan," Isabelle said. "I hate when you switch to work Holt on me mid-crisis."

"I have to keep you safe. George and I need you."

"And George and I need *you* too. Your ass better return in pristine condition."

"There are only four of them," Holt said. "I'll be fine. And one of us has to stay behind to make sure you and Quinn get out safely. I alerted hospital security, but by the time these guys actually did something to prove they were a threat, we'd already be in trouble."

"God, I love you and your sexy over-inflated self-confidence," Isabelle said. "Go do your superhero thing since standing here arguing isn't doing anyone any good. See you soon."

"Love you too," Holt said. She looked at Lola. "D West. Sit rep to the Wonder Twins. Max has a safe house set up. I didn't even ask how she managed that already. You get everyone there in one piece. Yourself included. I'll catch up with you there. Keep the chopstick. Just in case."

"Maybe Isabelle's right, H," Lola said. "They don't want me. Maybe I should stay behind. You take Isabelle and Quinn to the safe house."

Holt was gone before Lola finished her final pitch.

"Let's go," Lola said.

Quinn noticed she used the IV pole as a walking stick, supporting a fair amount of her weight, but she was moving well. They headed quickly in the direction Holt had identified as D West.

"Why didn't Holt let you stay if they aren't interested in you?" Quinn asked.

"Because they most likely would've killed her, because she's of no use to them anymore," Isabelle said quietly. "But they want something from Holt. She's the leader and the only one who can provide it. If they killed her, the investigation would probably intensify."

"She'll be fine, Isabelle," Lola said. "There are only four of them."

"Isn't that a lot?" Quinn couldn't imagine fighting one person, male, female, adult, or child, let alone four angry men. She felt panicky, on the edge of control, but Isabelle, who had just watched Holt walk off to face down four men, was holding it together. She should probably do the same.

Lola shrugged again. She pushed through an exit door, looked carefully around, and signaled them through. "Not for Holt. Especially not in an enclosed space like a hospital hallway. You haven't seen her in action. Four is sort of like a good warm-up."

"That sounds like something out of my comic books. Like Captain America or something."

"She's a huge Cap fan," Isabelle said. "But I think she wore her Wolverine underwear today. You two can talk comics when she gets back."

"The claws will be a nice surprise for our guests," Lola said. "Across the street to the coffee shop, then we check in with Max."

Quinn had always thought being part of the comics she read would be fun. Now she felt like she was and the reality was something else entirely. Lola was the perfect superhero—kind, strong, gorgeous— but the events in this story had lasting, gruesome consequences for the people involved.

How was it that she could still find Lola so attractive? How could she still want to be close to her when so much violence was part of her everyday life? Quinn knew she could never live like this, she didn't know how anyone could. Yet here she was, sprinting across the street while a fight with real life or death consequences took place in the building behind her.

Don't be sick. Don't be sick. Don't be sick.

CHAPTER SEVENTEEN

Holt felt exposed on the street in an unfamiliar city. She didn't know the landscape or the players in Los Angeles. She was desperate to get back to Isabelle, but she had to take care of a couple of things first. Things that would help ensure Isabelle, Lola, and Quinn were safe.

As she walked, she scanned her surroundings. She was almost certain she wasn't being followed. She'd dispatched the CMCs at the hospital without trouble. They hadn't put up much of a fight after they realized who they were dealing with. In close quarters, like the hospital hallway where they'd tried to ambush her, she was close to unstoppable with nothing but her fists. Security had arrived as she was slipping out.

Now she wanted to stay under the radar and connect with the local police. Although it seemed likely that the CMCs had been alerted to her landing by someone at the airport or had somehow flagged her arrival, she couldn't rule out the possibility that her phone had been compromised and her location was being tracked.

She'd removed the battery and SIM card, and the battery was going for a joy ride in the back of pickup truck, while the SIM card had seen better days thanks to the business end of her boot. Being without a phone heightened her feelings of vulnerability. At the first opportunity, she bought a prepaid burner phone, texted Max her identification code, and waited for confirmation.

As soon as she had it, she called. "Talk to me, Max."

"Isabelle and the others are fine. Lola checked in about thirty minutes ago. George is secure, fed, and about to go down for the night. Tuna might request hazard pay after the last diaper change though. Fair warning."

"Remind him which one is the baby," Holt said. She missed her son, even his nuclear diapers.

"Oh, we have been. Constantly. Are you okay? How you doing making friends out there? Why the new phone? I asked you to be nice with my things."

"First, I tried to make new friends four times. It's just none of them were very nice to me, so I guess those relationships aren't going anywhere. And second, I was very nice to your phone. It doesn't have a scratch on it. It just might need a new battery and SIM card. Has Moose checked in?"

"Holt." Max sounded exasperated.

"What? I couldn't take the chance I was being tracked."

"You were. By me. Now I have no idea where you are. No word from Moose yet. We'll hear from him soon, I'm sure."

Holt looked around. She gave Max the landmarks she could see. "Now can you please find me the fastest way to the police chief? I have a few things to discuss with them. And get an update from Moose. Quinn is probably going out of her mind worrying about her friend. And we should probably look for the kid they took as well, Brayden whatever his name was. Lola said she got him out as well."

"Uh, H, you aren't in Rhode Island. The police chief isn't just going to let you walk into her office and have a chat."

"I'm aware, Max. Get me her schedule and then let me talk to Dubs."

Half an hour later, Holt sat in the backseat of the police chief's SUV waiting for her to leave work for the day. According to Max, she had a dinner date in ninety minutes so Holt would keep it succinct. Dubs had been almost giddy at the prospect of helping Holt break into the chief's car. Holt probably could've managed on her own, but if you employ one of the premiere car thieves around, why not use them?

Holt didn't have to wait long for her guest. The police chief climbed into the driver's seat, tossed her work bag onto Holt's lap in the backseat without looking behind her, and was about to start the car when Holt spoke.

"Hello, Chief. I need a moment of your time."

Years of speed bag work had honed Holt's reflexes, but she was impressed with how quickly she found herself staring down the barrel of the chief's service weapon. She put her hands up casually. Although she hated guns and having one in her face was bringing back unpleasant memories, she knew sudden movements and tense body language would be misconstrued.

"My name is Holt Lasher. I'm a bounty hunter out of Providence, where I work closely with the local police force. I've been working long distance with some of your fine officers too. Your weapon isn't necessary. I'm unarmed. No nefarious intent."

"If that's true, why did you break into my car and ambush me?"

"No ambush," Holt said. "I just need to talk."

"Make an appointment."

"I'm on a bit of a tight schedule. Some of your citizens aren't being very nice, and they threatened some people I love. That pisses me off. These people aren't very nice in general, so I think there's an opportunity for you and I to get along."

"Oh really? And just what did you have in mind? Who are these people?" She hadn't lowered the gun a millimeter.

Holt wanted to prove who she was before she laid her cards on the table, but she couldn't do anything with a gun in her face. She didn't have a lot of options except to talk. "I'll start from the beginning. A friend of the CMC-15s wanted to be my new best friend. First, he tried to extort money from me. You'll see that we filed a police report with your department. He ended up dead. A colleague and friend of mine let your guys know about an online money laundering ring, and was providing plenty of information. The CMCs took exception. They kidnapped and beat my friend to send me a message. When I arrived today, they tracked me to the hospital and brought out a welcome party. I have no reason to think they'll stop coming for me, despite them saying if I pack up and go home they'll leave me be. Do you mind lowering your gun? Search me if you want. I'm unarmed."

"That was you at the hospital?"

Holt nodded.

"Then the gun stays up. I got a personal report about that incident. The officers on the scene didn't believe accounts, but there were seven eyewitnesses and security camera footage. You engaged with and subdued four armed gangsters."

"They started it," Holt said. "Like I said, they've been coming after me. Will you verify I am who I say I am? I need your help and I believe I can help you as well, but there's not a lot of time to waste."

"Keep your hands on the headrest. Don't exit the vehicle until I give you instructions. Do you understand?"

"You're the boss," Holt said. She put her hands on the back of the chief's seat and waited for her to get out and come around to the back passenger door. Holt didn't really expect anything else, but the gun stayed trained on her for the entire maneuver.

"Out now. Slowly. Hands on your head."

Holt complied and quickly found herself slammed against the side of the SUV and her hands cuffed behind her back. She wasn't thrilled with the development but didn't fight it. She was still hoping for cooperation. Despite her strong, almost overwhelming desire to get back to Isabelle, right now she needed to be here. She trusted Lola to keep Isabelle and Quinn safe.

"This isn't necessary, Chief Groden. I'm not a danger."

"It's Chief Sam. If you want me to like you, don't even consider calling me Samantha. I'm not taking your word for it that you aren't here to cause trouble," Sam said. "You want my help, this is how you get it."

"If my mother could see me now," Holt said. The thought made her laugh. Her mother would faint seeing her daughter being led into a police station in handcuffs. It was her worst nightmare come true. How it would disgrace the Lasher name.

"Look," Sam said as she pushed open the doors to the precinct and led Holt inside. "If everything checks out and I can verify the things you tell me, I'll get these off. Deal?"

"Deal. And if you find out I've lied to you or I get squirrely, you have my permission to shoot me. Just a word of warning though, my girlfriend really, really hates it when people shoot me, or at me, or even in my general vicinity. So if you do have to go that route, she's going to take exception."

"Jesus, how often do people take shots at you?"

"It's been an eventful couple of years," Holt said. "My line of work isn't usually so exciting, despite the reputation."

Sam pointed Holt to an uncomfortable metal chair in an interrogation room and sat down opposite. She asked her full name, address, the dates of the reports she'd filed with the LAPD, associates, and any other information Holt wanted to give her.

Holt gave her the phone numbers of the commissioner of the Rhode Island State Police and the Providence mayor. She considered the governor too, but thought she would start with those two. She hoped the State Police weren't still smarting about the Dubs operation. It had worked out in the end, but there were a few bumps in the road. When the chief went to make her inquiries, Holt sat thinking about what Lola had told her at the hospital. She considered all the angles of Malcolm's involvement from his being at the top of the food chain to him being a mid level lieutenant punching above his weight class. Malcolm's repeated reference to another player gave her pause. Those that clawed their way to the top of a street gang didn't show weakness by admitting shared leadership with anyone.

So who's pulling your strings, Malcolm? Another gang member? An outside player?

Although Holt wasn't sure it was possible, if she could, she wanted to turn this case over to the LAPD and extract herself and her team. The CMCs seemed to think she was a threat to them, but she'd just as soon let the local authorities handle the heat and go home to her own cases. She was worried about Malcolm's implication that without her involvement he could make a case go away by pressuring dirty cops, but she wasn't willing to risk the safety of her family to bring him down. That's probably why he was so worried when Lola got involved with the case. Holt and her crew were wild cards and outside his sphere of influence. She needed more information.

It seemed like hours before Sam returned. Holt had been watching the clock and was aware the chief was cutting it close to get to her date.

"And will you be shooting me this evening?"

"It doesn't appear I have any reason to," Sam said with a wry smile as she removed Holt's handcuffs.

"That's good, because the paperwork would probably keep you here all night, and you have a date tonight if my information is correct. I'm not going to keep you from that."

"How the hell do you know that?" Sam asked. She didn't look amused.

"My job is to know everything about a person so I can find them. My team is the best there is."

"I hear you are also pretty good at security and investigative jobs as well. How much background have you done on me? Don't lie to me, Holt. Remember our deal."

"Just what I've told you and what you've seen. I needed to find you. You're not my focus. I've told you what I'm interested in. Keeping the CMCs from messing with me or my family, that's my focus. I'm willing to continue helping with the money laundering investigation, but only if it doesn't put my family or my team at undue risk. I'm not sure that's possible, but we can discuss it."

"All right, follow me. We've got our version of the situation room here. We can fill you in on what we have on the CMCs there. And you can tell me how you can help."

"In the interest of full disclosure, a member of the CMCs who claimed he was the leader intimated he had moles in your ranks. I'd like to keep this session small if we can. I almost lost a friend today."

Sam didn't look pleased, but she nodded and led her down the hall. Holt followed Sam to the technology hub of the precinct. She got Max on the phone so she could be part of the briefing.

Holt introduced Max and Dubs to Sam. She subtly warned them to behave themselves. She wasn't sure the message got through.

It took a few minutes for the LAPD techs to pull up the files Sam requested and get everything set up for the briefing. Holt could feel Max getting antsy. When one of the techs ran into a problem, Max clearly couldn't handle it any more.

"Chief, you're going to be late for your date if we don't get started. Can I get us going here?"

"You guys are really worried about my social life," Sam said. "Just how do you plan on getting us up and running from Rhode Island, Max? My guys say they'll have it sorted out soon."

"Tell them to stop typing, H. Give me thirty seconds."

Holt indicated the techs should step away from the keyboards, and as promised, Max had everything they needed up on the screen almost instantaneously. She started running through the LAPD files and filling in the details from Holt's team, briefing everyone before Sam interrupted her.

"Did you just hack the LAPD? In thirty seconds?"

"Don't be ridiculous," Max said. "I invited myself in. Just in case there were any problems we needed to iron out. Good thing too. And it took me a little bit longer than thirty seconds."

"But probably not much," Holt said.

"Since you're asking me to ignore a rather blatant crime, I don't suppose you can use your magic skills to get my reservation changed to an hour later?" Sam said.

"Of course," Max said. "But why aren't you taking her to that new place downtown? Do you not really like her?"

"Listen, pipsqueak," Sam said. "No one can get in there. Doesn't matter if I was asking her to marry me tonight, it's just not possible."

Holt hid her smile. Sam had accurately assessed Max in under five minutes without ever laying eyes on her. She liked her.

"Well, now you've challenged me. Dinner for two, new place, one hour later than originally planned. Can we get to work so you don't blow this one too, please?"

Sam looked stunned. "You've got quite a team here, Holt."

"That I do," Holt said. "None better. But you got off easy with Max. You didn't have to talk to Dubs."

"Discourteous. I'm right here, boss."

"So, Sam, what can you tell us about the CMCs?" Holt asked.

"Are you working this case as a liaison or a concerned citizen?" Sam asked. "We've got an open case with your name on it, but if you came here tonight to tell me I've got dirty cops, a new kind of gang problem, and to get as much information as possible before making me promises and leaving me holding my dick tomorrow…tell your hacker to get out of my computers and I'll show you to the door."

Holt fought the urge to rock on her heels, something she did when she was uncomfortable. She did want information from Sam and didn't know how much she was willing to promise her. Threading that needle without lying was tricky.

"I've told you the conditions of my continued cooperation," Holt said. "Nothing is more important to me than the safety of my family and team."

"I'm a public servant," Sam said. "I can't afford such luxuries. My city is in danger. I need to know if you can help."

Max started to protest Sam's subtle dig, but Holt interrupted her. She was proud of the work she and her crew did. That was all that mattered.

"Let's share what we know, Chief. Hopefully, we can make this work for both of us."

Sam inclined her head for Holt to go first. Holt filled her in on Kevin Garvey and what Lola had learned from her time with Malcolm. There were police reports for everything, but she tried to add details and observations that weren't in the reports. Sam asked good questions. She was a sharp cop.

"What we don't know," Holt said, "is very much about the CMCs, or if there's someone pulling their strings. Someone who might not even be part of the gang."

"We started hearing about them about eighteen months ago," Sam said. "It started as the usual chatter about a new gang flashing their colors. But these boys incorporated and went public at warp speed. They started gobbling up street corners and soldiers from other smaller gangs so rapidly we had trouble keeping up with the changing map."

"How did they convince others to join?" Dubs asked.

"Violence mostly. Intimidation. This isn't a nice group. Sounds like you've seen that firsthand," Sam said.

"Is the violence more than other groups?" Holt asked.

"Almost everything about them is different from other gangs. They're like a tech unicorn. Industry disruptors. It feels like they sprang onto the scene fully formed. We never saw any of the usual growing pains most of these groups go through as they grow. And their expansion seems deliberate, well thought out. I don't know if that's a sign of a new model or a behind-the-scenes player," Sam said.

"Do you know what their revenue source is?" Holt asked. It would be helpful if they could follow the money.

"Another oddity. We have no idea. They're well funded as you know. The usual suspects are all viable options, but their money is hidden much more securely than we're used to. That's one reason this money laundering case is so exciting around here. We're hoping it can help us track back to the source of their funding."

Holt thought about the information Sam had provided. The CMCs could very well be the next iteration of street gang adapting to changing times. But she trusted Sam's gut that they felt like a leap past what should be natural evolution. Coupled with what Malcolm had hinted at to Lola, Holt was becoming more and more convinced there were more players in this deadly game than they'd identified. The question was could she afford to stay in the game?

CHAPTER EIGHTEEN

Since they arrived at the safe house, Quinn felt more secure. Maybe that's why they called it a safe house. For her, it felt familiar, which was comforting. It had a refrigerator, couch, dining room table, recognizable things unaffiliated with violence or chaos. Not yet. If Lola hadn't planted herself at the front door like an angry dragon guarding its gold she could have convinced herself everything was fine.

Isabelle was helping too. Even though Quinn could tell she was worried about Holt and less than thrilled with the situation they were in, she was so calm. It was helping her keep her cool. They were both on the couch. From where she sat Quinn had a view straight down the hall to Lola. She could see how haggard she looked. The pain appeared to be catching up to her, but Lola had rebuffed her suggestion that she lie down earlier.

"Lola said you'd be a good person to talk to about everything that's happened," Quinn said. "She said you'd have a good perspective on wrapping my head around it and figuring out how to make it okay."

Isabelle looked at her quizzically. "If she thinks I'm going to try and convince you of that, she's an idiot," Isabelle said. "Nothing about what's happened to you recently is okay. It's not okay for Lola either, but unfortunately, she has more experience with this sort of thing than I hope you do."

"I don't think that was exactly what she meant. Maybe it's my wishful thinking," Quinn said. "Then I could stop feeling so out of control and terrified. How do you handle being on Holt's team and being with her?" Quinn asked. She didn't know if she could do what Isabelle did.

"I'm not part of her crew, not really. I'm an accountant. I've integrated into her team doing forensic work, but it didn't start out that way. I wait at the office, feeling helpless and out of control most of the time while she and the rest run headlong into danger. It almost kept us apart at the beginning. I couldn't stand the idea of her job."

If Isabelle was an accountant, she wasn't that different from Quinn. She dealt with data and regulations. If she was good at her job, she probably needed organization and didn't like huge surprises. *And she fell in love with Holt.* "How did you get past the fear?" Quinn asked.

"My situation was a little different," Isabelle said. "When Holt and I met, I was in considerable danger, although I didn't know it right away. I might not have liked what Holt did, but she was determined to keep me safe, even if it cost her life. She proved to me, over and over, through her actions, how good she was at her job, how hard she worked to keep everyone safe, how she didn't take unnecessary risks. She broke that rule a few times to keep me safe, but never allowed anyone else to."

"But I wasn't in danger until I met Lola," Quinn said. "I really care about her. I wanted to see if there was some potential there, but this is a lot to deal with. I have grant deadlines I should be working toward, but I'm not sure I can ever go back into my lab again."

Isabelle gave her an understanding smile. "One thing I learned about Holt early on is that she'll do anything for those she cares about. Or for people important to those she cares about. Lola is the same way. I know you're scared. You have every right to be. I know your feelings about Lola are complicated. That makes sense. But Holt and Lola will keep you safe. Moose too. And I can't believe I'm saying this, but Lola's job usually isn't this extreme. Holt tried telling me that when we first met and I didn't believe her."

Quinn didn't know why everyone was trying to convince her she was safe. What data could they point to? "Lola's been shot in the head and beat to hell, and those are just the things I know about," Quinn said. Her voice was rising, Lola would probably overhear, but she was getting angry again. "She can't seem to keep herself safe. How can she make promises to me?"

"Is everything okay?" Lola called out from her perch.

"We'll be fine," Isabelle said, waving Lola back down. Quinn was pretty sure Lola wouldn't leave her post to come down the hall and see what she was yelling about, but she might pace the small hallway for a while. As angry as she was, she was happy to see Lola sit back down. She was in no condition to pace.

"Lola did get grazed by a bullet across her temple," Isabelle said. "She took on two armed intruders, unarmed herself, after a third man broke into my home. She stood her ground to give me time to get to safety."

That sounds like what Lola did for Jessica. Doesn't she have any regard for her own life? "Sounds like what she did for Jessica in the warehouse. Does she have a death wish?"

Isabelle looked down the hall at Lola fondly. Quinn could tell she cared for her deeply.

"No, I don't think so. But she and Holt and a few of the others are so confident in their skills they're always convinced they're going to come out of just about anything. It's infuriating."

Isabelle checked the time quickly, something she'd been doing regularly as they'd talked. Quinn figured she'd been tracking the time since Holt had split from the group.

"Do you think Lola would mind if we joined her?" Quinn asked. Her feelings were still complicated, especially as they related to Lola, but she knew she felt better when she was close to her. With everything else so jumbled, she was willing to hold on to solid data points. That was one.

Isabelle led the way back to the front room. "We're joining you," she said.

"Absolutely not," Lola said. She looked outraged at the thought.

"We outnumber you," Quinn said. "So you're outvoted."

"And I'm pulling rank. I know you all call me 'the Queen' behind my back. I know you don't mean it as an insult, but a royal title should have some perks, right?" Isabelle pulled up a chair.

Lola groaned. "This isn't fair. I think Holt took the bad guys because she knew what I was in for. I'm demanding hazard pay. I knew you two would get along. Now you're using it against me."

"If Holt knows what's good for her, she'll get her butt back here soon. I don't like the idea of her out on the streets alone."

"And until she does, you're going to look after me?" Lola asked.

"I'll let Quinn handle you," Isabelle said. "You tough guys are all the same. You'll run straight through a brick wall without flinching to protect the ones you love. But it's up to us to protect you, even when you don't think you need it."

Quinn remembered the first time she met Lola. Lola must have been thinking about it too. She leaned in close to Quinn and whispered, "I'm pretty good at letting you take the lead."

Heat radiated through her body at Lola's words. It was an unexpected sensation given how she'd been feeling for hours. But Lola was still incredibly hot, terror or no terror.

Lola tried sneaking a quick kiss, but Quinn moved back to her own space. She felt a little bad, but she wasn't ready to pretend everything was back to normal.

Just then, there was a noise at the front door only feet from where Lola had positioned herself. She stood and motioned Quinn and Isabelle farther back into the house. Quinn started to protest. She didn't want to be a bystander in another act of violence, but Isabelle quieted her complaint and led her back to safety.

What the hell were you going to do back there anyway? Let Lola handle the scary stuff.

Although they could have hid in the bedrooms, neither she nor Isabelle made any move to do so. They'd gone over exit plans when they arrived, something Quinn hoped never to do again, but she couldn't remember a word of them now. Quinn hadn't actually seen Lola in action and was fascinated, in a watching-a-train-crash kind of way. Lola moved right up to the door and relaxed her body.

The door started to open. As soon as it was open a crack, Lola grabbed it and yanked it open and pulled the intruder inside. She threw them on the ground and they landed facedown. Lola put a knee in their back and secured the door with the chair under the doorknob.

Quinn recognized the woman pinned under Lola. It was Jessica. She saw Lola cock her fist, ready to strike at the back of Jessica's head.

Does she not know who she has? Is she in a blind rage?

Jessica started sobbing. Quinn could hear banging on the door and shouting. She tried to yell for Lola to stop, but she wasn't sure if anything came out. Her feet felt sunk in the floor.

Miraculously, Lola lowered her fist without striking and eased off of Jessica. She flipped her over and immediately lowered her fist. "Little Chihuahua? My God, are you okay?"

"Lola," Jessica said. "No, I'm not all right. Is Quinn okay?"

Jessica looked small and vulnerable on the floor. Lola pulled her up and they both slowly stood.

"Yes, I'm here. I'm fine," Quinn said, moving closer.

The pounding on the door intensified. Quinn thought it was Moose on the other side.

"Settle down, Moose. Give me a minute. And don't you dare break down this damn door," Lola shouted to him.

"Jessica, I was so worried about you. Lola told me what happened. I thought I might have lost you," Quinn said when she hugged Jessica to her.

Jessica started crying intensely. "You might have, except for Lola. Quinn, what she did for me…What they did to her…I thought they killed her. Look at her. I'm not sure they didn't."

"She's okay," Quinn said. "Are you okay?"

"She got the shit kicked out of her and was still fine enough to dump me on my ass and scare the crap out of me just now. Seriously, I think I might need new underwear. I thought we finally ran into something Mr. Moose couldn't protect me from."

"Oh, you did," Lola said. "Or he did."

She threw the chair out of the way and yanked the door open. Moose was pacing outside.

"Get in here," Lola said. Once Moose was inside and they were once again safely buttoned up, Lola let him have it. "What the fuck is wrong with you? Do you know what I almost did to her? Since when do you sneak up on a safe house?"

"Whoa," Moose said. He had his hands raised in capitulation. "It wasn't ideal, no doubt. But we're dark. Didn't Max tell you?"

"Tell me what?"

"H hasn't ruled out that the CMCs used her phone to find her so quickly. She ditched it. Max got in touch with me and told me to do the same. She said not to call you or use any of your phones. I guess H is bringing us replacements. Look, letting Jessica get through the door before me was sloppy, I own that. But I had no way of warning you."

Lola pulled her phone out of her pocket. Quinn could see it was off.

"Max must have done something to my phone," Lola said. "Can she come through the wires and shut it off?"

"It's a little more complicated than that, but sure," Moose said.

"You could've used a secret knock or a carrier pigeon," Lola said.

"Asshole."

"What else did you get from Max? H better get back soon or Isabelle's gonna kick her ass," Lola said quietly. "She's okay, right?"

"Yeah. She's good, last I heard. She should be here soon. Maybe you could give her the benefit of the doubt and let her in the door? Actually, why don't you let me take door duty? You look like shit," Moose said.

Lola looked like she wanted to argue, she even opened her mouth as if to start, but then she closed it and nodded. Quinn was amazed. *After I make sure Jessica's okay, I'll have to check on Lola. She must be in more pain than I thought.*

"Is there more I need to know about your day?" Lola asked.

"Yeah," Moose said. "But let's wait until Holt gets back. You and I should be able to keep everyone safe until she does. Then we can make a plan to get us all home."

Lola headed to the back of the house where the bedrooms and bathrooms were. Quinn ushered Jessica toward the kitchen.

"I know you're not okay," Quinn said. "But is there anything I can do? Are you all right? At least for right now?"

"I could really use something to drink," Jessica said. "And for you to tell me I'm safe here."

"You are," Quinn said. "Lola won't let anything happen to you."

It felt funny saying that after she'd gotten so angry hearing those words herself. But saying them to Jessica felt different. She believed them. She knew them to be true. Maybe it was her talk with Isabelle. Maybe it was seeing Lola in action. Whatever the reason, she was willing to concede Lola would do whatever it took to keep her safe.

She got Jessica some water and turned to find Lola standing at the door to the kitchen, looking unsure of herself. Quinn waited for her to say something, or come in and join them, but she didn't. Finally, she'd had enough.

"How much longer are you going to stand there?" Quinn asked. "Seems like you're off guard dog duty."

Isabelle asked Jessica something that required they both leave the room.

"I wasn't sure what you'd want from me," Lola said. "Things haven't exactly progressed how I'd hoped with us. I don't know where we stand."

"Come sit with me. Do you even realize you're about to fall over?"

Quinn led her to the couch and instructed, in no uncertain terms, that she was to lie down and not argue. Quinn sat on one end and gently lifted Lola's head onto her lap.

"Isabelle was right. You do need looking after."

"I'm fine," Lola said.

It didn't sound convincing.

"Shh. Don't argue with me. I don't think a bulldozer could get through Moose. I'm safe. Isabelle's safe. You found Jessica, and she's safe."

It looked like it was difficult, but Lola complied. Quinn ran her fingers through Lola's hair, and for the first time since she found Kevin Garvey's body in her lab, she felt something close to peaceful.

"I think I'm supposed to be looking after you," Lola said, her eyes closed.

"Says who? I believe what you promised repeatedly was you would keep me safe. I'm safe. Mission accomplished."

"I hope so," Lola said. "Are you feeling better? I'm sorry you've been so scared."

"I think it's going to take a while to get back to normal," Quinn said. "Talking to Isabelle's been nice. She's like me, data focused. I don't get accounting, but I do understand her. She's been explaining how she lives with Holt. I'm still so scared. I'm a scientist. I work with data and way too much peer review. The last forty-eight hours I've seen the most horrific murder victim, listened to you get kidnapped, then returned beaten, I've run for my life, thought my best friend might have been killed, and I'm in danger too. Cherry on top, you're probably leaving to be sexy and heroic across the country while I look over my shoulder and panic here alone."

"Haven't you been listening?" Lola asked, stilling Quinn's shaking hand and lacing their fingers together. "I'm not leaving you here to look over your shoulder, panicked and alone."

"Eventually you have to go back," Quinn said.

"Sure," Lola said. "But not when you feel like this. And never when you're in danger."

Holt's arrival saved Quinn from going back down the rabbit hole of worry and fear.

"Do you want to sit in on the briefing?" Lola asked. "Isabelle hates them, but she always does it if Holt is going to do something really dangerous. She says the not knowing is worse. I see her point, and I think it probably makes her braver than all of us."

"You guys really don't have training wheels for the new kid, do you? I'm with Isabelle. Not knowing would be worse."

Holt and Isabelle were in the kitchen. Isabelle had her hands, palms flat, against Holt's chest. Holt cupped Isabelle's cheek tenderly. They were kissing. It wasn't a frantic, passionate kiss, although there was plenty of that just below the surface.

Seeing them together made Quinn lonely. She'd finally found a brilliant, thoughtful, kind, beautiful woman, and it seemed like the universe was throwing every obstacle in their path before they even found out if a future was possible.

"So is tall, tattooed, and handsome as off limits as she looks?" Jessica asked.

"Private property, Little Chihuahua," Lola said. "She belongs to the Queen. And even if she didn't, I don't think you could handle her."

"Excuse me," Jessica said.

"Hey, no offense. Holt just needs special care and feeding. Everyone's got to punch in their weight class."

"You're one to talk," Jessica said.

Quinn didn't understand the dynamic between Jessica and Lola. At times they seemed antagonistic and at other times playful. She looked at Lola to see how she would react to Jessica's teasing. Lola looked unconcerned.

"Hey, not so loud. The pretty professor will hear you."

"Are you two done? I'm right here you know," Quinn said. She moved a little closer to Lola. She liked the feel of her.

"Good question," Holt said as she and Isabelle entered the room. "Can I start the briefing? I've been in contact with Max. She and Dubs are up to speed on my end. We'll get them looped back in once we're technologically up and running again."

"Just waiting on you, boss," Lola said.

Holt shot her a look but didn't comment. Quinn noticed Isabelle was staying about as close to Holt as she could without crawling into her skin. Quinn didn't blame her.

"I had a nice chat with the LAPD police chief, Sam," Holt said. "She's up to speed on Lola's new friends. They're a relatively new player on the scene here but have grown in size and influence quickly. They're violent, as we've seen, and not afraid of public displays to get what they want or to send a message. Kevin Garvey, our initial target, is dead. They kidnapped Lola to send me a message, but then let her go. No offense, but that feels out of character. It makes me think either they're serious but they're also still amateurs, or someone else is pulling the strings, and they knew killing Lola wouldn't get them anywhere with me, which is true. I would have torn this state apart to find them, which is the opposite of what they say they want. They took a big risk assuming I wouldn't just for laying their hands on her at all. For now, we need more information before tearing LA asunder."

Quinn saw Holt look to Lola before continuing. There was tenderness and love in her look, and maybe a bit of an apology.

"No arguments here," Lola said. "Retaliating seems like the wrong play. I think it would escalate things with the CMCs and more people would get hurt. Malcolm is scared of you being involved in his business for some reason. At this point, I don't think getting publically involved on that kind of scale is the right move."

Lola and Holt looked at each other for a long moment, neither speaking or blinking from what Quinn could tell. Holt broke the spell with a quick nod and returned to the briefing. Quinn wished she knew what they had just communicated.

"Lola thought Malcolm might have let slip about a boss a few times when he was talking to her, so we can't rule out a silent player we haven't identified yet. I think it's likely. Regardless of who's involved, they're willing to hurt people to get what they want," Holt said.

"I saw that firsthand," Quinn said.

"I know it's hard, but try not to think about what you saw in your lab," Lola said.

"Thanks for the reminder of that horror show," Quinn said. "But I was talking about you." She traced one of the bruises on Lola's face.

"Clearly, we've had a couple of recent examples," Holt said.

Holt took Isabelle's hand before continuing. "Max and Dubs briefed the chief on the email threats and what they've been working on back home. We got the officers involved in the online money laundering case to give a quick briefing too. They don't have a lot right now. I think we know about as much as they do. Lola, you've been working with them pretty closely, which is what put you on their radar. It didn't take much for them to figure out where you fit in."

"What happens if you guys pack up and go home?" Quinn asked. "Does all this trouble end? Do the CMCs stop coming after you?"

"Honestly," Holt said. "I'm not sure. The police investigation is going to continue. If we stay involved or they think we're still involved, there may be consequences. Malcolm threatened as much. More so, I would imagine, if we stay here than if we returned to Rhode Island. Sam has asked for my help. I made it clear I won't continue in any capacity if it increases the risk to my family or crew, but I don't like the idea of bad guys walking free. It seems like the chances of that happening go up significantly if we scurry off home."

"Jessica and I have some relevant information," Moose said. "Both Jessica's and Quinn's places have been tossed. We didn't venture to CLA, but it wouldn't surprise me if her office and lab were given the same treatment."

"Don't forget the artwork," Jessica said.

"Eight-by-ten photo of each of them," Moose said, pointing to Jessica and Quinn in turn. "Right on the front door of each apartment. Each had a bull's-eye on the forehead and a knife driven through the throat holding it to the wall. 'She's next' was written on each picture. Jessica has a front door security camera. The footage is time stamped about an hour after I left the hospital."

"Oh, hell no," Lola said. "They can't stay here. They'll have to come with us when we go."

Moose nodded his agreement. "That's what I thought."

Quinn could feel Lola's body tense. She felt like she had the night they met and Jessica had interrupted them and grabbed Quinn. Even exhausted and at diminished capacity, Lola felt powerful in her anger. *Why did I doubt she would do everything to protect me? Maybe I'm worried it won't be enough.*

"As I told Mr. Moose, I don't want to stick around here waiting to get my head blown off. The threat of that once was enough," Jessica said. "And you guys scare the crap out of me, but you're better than the alternative, so I don't see as I have much choice."

"We're also the reason you're in danger," Isabelle said.

"Yeah, you are. So help me put my fucking life back together. And I'm sending you the bill for my therapy," Jessica said.

"That's it?" Quinn asked. "You're just going to pack up and go?"

"You didn't see my place," Jessica said. "You've been listening to the same crap I have. If they keep poking around, the CMCs keep coming. Did it sound like they're going to stop poking? I take 'she's next' with a knife through my throat seriously. You think I'm happy about this? My whole life got turned on its ass cause she takes out the trash in our building." Jessica pointed angrily at Lola. "But I'm holding my nose and jumping in bed with the devil I know. Or the one you're sleeping with, because I really like being alive."

"We're not sleeping together," Lola and Quinn said, stumbling over each other as they did.

"Do you think I actually fucking care right now?" Jessica asked.

She stomped out of the room. Quinn started to follow her. She felt horrible. She'd been wrapped up in the awfulness of her experiences and hadn't considered the trauma Jessica had experienced. And she'd weathered it alone.

"Let me go," Moose said. "We've found a bit of a rhythm."

Quinn watched him go, thinking of the irony of Jessica wanting to get away from LA and now having a chance to do it under terrible circumstances. But they would stay together, whatever the next move was, which was something. Maybe she could still finish some of her projects.

Oh my God, my lab. My research.

"If they were at the college and got into my office or my lab… my research," Quinn said.

"Is your data secure?" Holt asked.

Quinn was relieved Holt seemed to grasp what she was concerned about without her having to spell it out.

"Yes," Quinn said. "It's on the research servers. I have remote access to my files so my grants can still go in on time, assuming I can finish them and I still have the support of CLA after this mess. Everything should be safe from the CMC's destruction. If I disappear I don't know that I trust my colleagues. But my office. And the lab computers. I have some specialized equipment and a lot of research material stored there. If they haven't already destroyed it, I need to keep it safe."

"Then we'll go and get it," Lola said.

From the look on Lola's face Quinn believed she would fight through a mass of CMCs to get to her lab.

"We will absolutely not," Holt said. "But it will be recovered. I don't know if the computers are still intact, but I'll make sure whatever is salvageable from your office is returned to you, Dr. Golden."

"What's our plan, sweetheart?" Isabelle asked.

"The safety of my family and crew is tantamount. That never changes. If the CMCs visited Jessica's and Quinn's apartments while I was at the police station, they're threatening an additional escalation. Maybe they knew I was meeting with Sam; maybe that was their plan all along. Either way, we're de-escalating. Quinn, you can think about it, but I'd like you to come back to Rhode Island with us. I don't believe you're safe here. If you choose to stay, Lola and I will too, but I'll be honest with you, I don't think that will ratchet down the tension."

Quinn felt like her head was spinning. She couldn't just leave LA. She was in the middle of a semester. Her job, her research, her life, was here. She looked around the room. Everyone was looking at her. She leaned into Lola and looked up at her. Quinn could tell Lola was trying to keep her expression neutral, but she looked worried. That made Quinn nervous.

She knew Lola would stay if Quinn did. But how was that fair? Sure, it wasn't fair that she had to pack up her life and move across the country to avoid threats against her life, either, but it didn't give her the right to be selfish. She didn't have the right to put Lola's and Holt's lives in danger when she could avoid it. *Doesn't mean I have to like it.* "Fine," Quinn said. "Doesn't seem like there's much choice. I have no idea how I'm going to explain this at work."

"Medical leave, sick relative, personal time due to finding a dead body in your lab, you pick," Holt said. "We'll take care of the paperwork."

"Doesn't matter," Quinn said. "Choose the one that's going to screw me and my career the least, long-term."

"I'll let Max sort it out," Holt said. "All right, final order of business. As you know, I ditched my phone and asked you to get rid of all of yours as well. I don't know how sophisticated the CMC's operation is, but I don't like how quickly they knew I was in LA."

Holt dumped a bag of phones on the counter. They were old school flip phones. Quinn hadn't seen one of those in years.

"These are what we've got as replacements for now. Max will get us reequipped when we get home, but for now, no fancy software, no panic button, no GPS."

Quinn noticed only Lola looked happy with the new technology. She'd noticed Lola's discomfort with just about anything with an on/off button. When Holt indicated she grab a phone from the pile, she pulled out her smartphone and realized it was powered down. She tried to boot it back up but was unable. *Guess I really am part of the crew. No turning back now.*

Jessica and Moose returned in time to get their own new, old school phones. Jessica looked less angry than when she'd left.

"Looks like I'm getting you out of here after all," Quinn said. She hoped Jessica was open to a joke.

"Next time I'll be more clear what I'm looking for. Maybe put my specifications in writing," Jessica said.

She was smiling. It didn't reach all the way to her eyes, but Quinn had hope they would be okay.

"It's too risky right now to return to either of your places to pack anything. I'll make sure whatever you want is shipped. Until that happens, you can buy what you need when we arrive. You'll probably need a slightly different wardrobe when we land anyway."

"Why?" Jessica asked. Realization dawned on her, and she looked like she was reconsidering.

"It's February. We're going to Rhode Island. It's probably buried in snow right now. This just keeps getting better and better."

"All right, catch what sleep you can. I'm going to get an exit plan from Max. I'll take first shift on the door. Moose, you're next. Lola, Moose will wake you for your shift if we aren't ready to move. Jessica, you have the couch. Isabelle, there's a bedroom in the back for us. Quinn, Lola, take the second bedroom. Moose, buddy, bunk where you can."

"Don't be ridiculous, Holt. Moose, come and sleep in the room with me until Holt gets you," Isabelle said. "You won't be getting that much sleep as it is. You might as well be comfortable."

Moose looked like he was going to argue, but one look from Isabelle and he swallowed whatever he was going to say.

"Yes, ma'am."

Holt pulled out her flip phone and dialed as the rest of them shuffled off to bed. The last thing Quinn heard as she walked down the hall for some much needed rest was Holt giving instructions to faceless crew members.

"Max, we need an exit plan for six. Assume airports and outgoing flights are being monitored. I don't know if that's true, but I'm not taking chances. Book subsets of us on no fewer than eight flights leaving over the next three days at all the airports in the area. We'll rent a car and head north. I need you to find me a private jet out of one of the airports north of Santa Barbara or west of the California border leaving tomorrow. I don't care how. Just do it."

It sounded like tomorrow was going to pick up right where today was leaving off. Quinn's feelings were still a mess, but she was glad she and Lola were sharing a bed. She thought back to their date at the beach. It seemed like a different life and a different person who had experienced that beautiful day, but that felt like safety, peace, and happiness. Maybe she could find a little bit of it again sleeping next to Lola tonight. If she tried to sleep alone she wasn't sure she'd be able to stop her mind from reanalyzing the data she had collected, been presented, and force-fed since the awful things had started happening in rapid succession. She didn't need any statistical modeling to conclude her life was a living nightmare. Hopefully, Lola could fight away all that haunted her in dreamland as well.

CHAPTER NINETEEN

Lola stepped off the small private plane Holt had chartered for their cross-country flight and onto the tarmac. The frigid air filled her lung and burned.

Home.

Quinn had slept the entire flight, which was a relief. She'd been wound so tight, rightly terrified, that even when she'd caught a few hours of Holt-mandated sleep before the flight, it had been restless. Lola had shushed her back to sleep after she awoke whimpering and crying more than once.

She'd spent the flight chatting with Moose and Holt, playing cards, and debating the pros and cons of staying engaged in the CMC investigation. Isabelle and Jessica had either slept or stayed out of their arguments.

They hadn't solved anything, but Lola knew where Holt stood. She would continue to take Sam's calls, and as long as there was no ongoing threat, she would provide information and assistance, nothing further. Holt had wanted to wash her hands of the entire investigation after she found out about the pictures left for Quinn and Jessica, but Lola and Moose had convinced her that was probably impossible. Sam wasn't going to stop investigating and the CMCs already knew Holt had been working with her. It seemed unlikely the CMCs would believe Holt had cut Sam loose no matter how good their LAPD spies were.

Lola wanted Holt to take a more active role. Even though she'd been most directly impacted by the CMC's violence, she wanted Quinn and Jessica to be able to return home, not that she was in a rush for Quinn to settle back into life in LA without her, but it didn't seem possible until the CMCs were neutralized. Holt had vetoed Lola's plan as too dangerous. Lola understood, but she was still frustrated.

"What happened to my sixty-five degrees and sunny?" Quinn asked. "Do I even want to know how cold it is right now?"

"Here," Lola said. She pulled off the light jacket she was wearing and draped it over Quinn's shoulders. "Max and Dubs will have a warmer jacket for you in the car."

"I can't take your jacket. Now you've only got a T-shirt."

Quinn looked like she appreciated the extra layer despite her protests.

"Don't worry about it. It's not that cold," Lola said. "Not to me. I'm used to this."

She quickly backpedaled when Quinn shot her a look.

"So, how cold is it?"

"I don't know. Probably twenty-five, thirty. No wind though and the sun's out. It's actually a beautiful day."

"See, I knew you were too good to be true," Quinn said. "Turns out you're insane."

"We all have our faults."

"So how is this going to work?" Quinn asked.

"Uh, Max or Dubs is going to have a jacket and warmer clothes for you. They'll be waiting for us in the terminal, I think. We'll get you more clothes as soon as we can."

"That's not what she means, sweetie," Isabelle said. "I don't mean to eavesdrop, but if you're anything like me, you're trying to figure out why this person you care about has been acting like two different people, one the normal version you know and the other Batman, and to top it all off, we just uprooted you and moved you across the country without so much as an extra pair of underwear. And if Lola is anything like Holt, she has no idea why any of that's a problem."

"That about sums it up," Quinn said.

Lola saw how much Quinn liked Isabelle. They'd both been thrust into Holt's crew during a crisis so they had that in common and Isabelle just seemed to know the question underneath the question. Or maybe everyone did and Lola was just a little thickheaded.

"Ask better questions and give better answers, Lola," Isabelle said before moving off to join Holt at the front of their pack.

"Yes, ma'am," Lola said. "Perhaps you could explain what I can clarify for you."

"Where am I going to be staying? I packed up and left without getting any information about logistics. Will I have my own transportation? Can I use my credit cards or is that too risky? Not having information is leaving my scientist brain a little off balance."

"Just your brain?" Lola asked. "My whole world feels turned upside down, and I'm coming home. I don't know the answers to all of your questions. Max and Holt can answer the money one. Transportation too. Dubs can always get you a car if you ask nicely. I was hoping you'd stay with me, but if you want something else, I'll make it happen. This may surprise you, but I love to shop so we'll have you wardrobed in no time. I'm a passable chef, although my apartment doesn't really lend itself to master classes in culinary excellence."

Quinn pulled out her cell phone so she could start making a list of the questions she had and the things she needed. She looked disgusted when the ancient flip phone appeared instead of her shiny smartphone they'd left in LA.

"Do you have a pen and a piece of paper?" Quinn asked Lola.

"Sure. I'll get them for you as soon as we're inside. I always keep them in case I need to take notes on a case." Lola didn't understand how anyone could take notes on a phone.

"I'm going to make a list of things I need. After we do whatever it is Holt has on our travel agenda for the rest of today, can we take care of my list?" Quinn asked.

"If you want to make the list and give it to me, I don't mind getting anything for you. I'll take care of you as long as you're here," Lola said.

"Lola," Quinn said. Her voice was stern and she looked like she meant business. "I don't under any circumstances want you to start looking at me as someone you have to take care of. If that's how you view me, I'll go and stay with some of your other friends until this business is over."

Lola was stunned. Quinn was scared and overwhelmed right now, as she was pretty sure just about anyone would be, and she wanted to care for her. She thought about what Isabelle said.

Ask better questions. "What do you need from me?"

"I don't need you to treat me like I am incapable of enacting any control over my own life. Don't take that control away from me. I can still feed and clothe myself, if you give me directions to the grocery store and a car. I don't want you to do everything for me. I'm still an active player in my own life. I have to be, or this will be too much to bear."

"I never meant to imply that you weren't," Lola said. "You're the most capable woman I know, and I know Holt. Speaking of, she told me Isabelle had to give her a similar dressing down when they first started dating. I guess she and I share well-meaning, but ultimately less than stellar, traits."

"I hope you take that to heart," Quinn said, getting on her tiptoes to whisper in Lola's ear, "because I'd hate to have to share a bed with any of your friends. I'd much rather be in yours."

"Better only be mine," Lola said. She felt a flare of jealousy at the thought of Quinn sleeping with anyone else. Even amidst all the chaos and gruesomeness, it was hard to ignore the spark between them.

They entered the terminal and Lola saw Max and Dubs waiting for them, winter coats in hand for Jessica and Quinn.

"Hey, boss, Isabelle," Max said. "Welcome home. Eventful trip."

Jessica slid next to her and said, "Do you have ugly friends? Where are the normal looking people? Even Moose is gorgeous and it takes a lot to tip my eye in that direction. Too many beautiful women to keep me busy."

"Behave yourself," Quinn said.

"I'm stuck out here," Jessica said. "Might as well make the most of it."

"Let's move," Holt said. "We'll do intros at the office."

Lola told Quinn the drive from the airport to the office wouldn't take more than twenty minutes, but she didn't look like she really believed her. LA traffic and urban sprawl were so different from compact Rhode Island. Fifteen minutes later, they were parked and inside the office. It felt nice to be back even if Lola would have preferred a much different exit plan.

"I expected something different. I think a little more Hall of Justice," Quinn said.

"Rather than League of Accountants?" Lola asked. "We get that a lot. But there are a few magic tricks hidden around here that may surprise you."

"On your feet, everyone," Dubs said. "The boss is back and we've got out of town company. Shall I do the introductions?"

"Could anyone stop you?" Holt asked.

"Absolutely not. Nor should they. Lola's got a new lady friend visiting from the West Coast. Isabelle has met her and, my Queen, thumbs up or down?"

Isabelle gave two thumbs up. Quinn relaxed her shoulders. Lola figured she was nervous about meeting everyone.

"Oh, one second." Dubs came over and asked Quinn, too quietly for anyone but Lola, who was standing right next to her, to hear, "You're not pregnant are you? I know it's kind of a delicate question, but we had a bit of a problem with that in the past."

"What? No," Quinn said.

She looked so confused Lola would have found it funny, except she was pissed. "What the fuck, Dubs?"

Dubs ignored her and carried on in her announcer voice. "So, I present to you all, Dr. Quinn Golden and," Dubs turned her attention to Jessica, "friend. Who do we have here?"

"Jessica Serrano. And just who might you be?"

"I'm Dubs, a car thief and a felon," Dubs said. "And this is my whole world, Max, our very own computer dominatrix. You've met Moose, terrible motorcycle driver and threat to large mammals the world over." She pointed to Holt and Isabelle. "Holt, boss. Isabelle, Queen."

Everyone in the room seemed highly amused by Dubs's introductions. Even Holt was laughing. Dubs motioned Quinn and Jessica to follow her.

"These five are newbies. We know nothing important about them yet. Keep working, newbies; you'll make an impression soon. Tuna and most of the night shift is at home. This is Jose, mechanic."

"And what is that a euphemism for?" Jessica asked.

"Surprisingly, nothing," Jose said. "I work next door at the auto shop. But I heard lug-head was home and had picked up strays. No offense. Beautiful women usually just follow Holt around so I had to come see for myself. I'm not disappointed."

"Oh please, you wanted to welcome Moose back," Max said.

"And now we have Tomato Face Moose. Do I have to do all the work around here?" Dubs asked. She dragged Jose by one hand toward Holt's office. On the way, she grabbed Moose. She kicked the door open and shoved them both in. She pulled the door closed, shouted, "Welcome home from all of us, Moose. Holt keeps condoms in the bottom drawer of her desk. Just a friendly FYI," and returned to the group. "Did I miss anyone?"

"Just Lola," Holt said. "And why do you know what's in my desk drawer?"

"Isn't the better question why you have condoms in your desk?" Dubs asked.

"I have everything I could need to talk to someone on the streets. Sometimes people need condoms and they'll trade information. That drawer also has Starburst, winter gloves, hypodermic needles, and tampons."

"I know. It's like the Mad Hatter's Quickie Mart. Lola hardly needs an introduction. They both already know who she is. My bet is Quinn already knows where Lola's morning breath ranks on a one to ten scale, but Lola is the office Doberman. Loyal, protective, fierce, strong, and just the right amount of scary."

"I would add sexy, kind, and brilliant as well," Quinn whispered to Lola.

Now Lola was pretty sure she was blushing. She liked hearing Quinn's assessment though. She liked it a lot.

"Remind me to never leave Dubs in charge of public relations," Holt said.

"I'd be amazing," Dubs said. "And since you won't let me steal anything anymore, I've got to do something to be useful."

"You want to be useful, go upstairs and pack."

"You're kicking me out of the attic?" Dubs looked crestfallen.

Lola's heart rate kicked up a notch. *If Dubs is getting the boot, what does that mean for me? Where are Quinn and I going to stay?* "No. Well, yes. All of you, actually. Until I'm sure the CMC threat is neutralized, I don't want anyone living in the attic. I don't like the safety risk. We've seen in the past what a target this place is. It would send a message to hit me at my command center. I would be annoyed if I lost my office. I would be devastated if I lost any of you. You have until this time tomorrow. If you need help finding another place, let me know."

Dubs looked like she had something she wanted to say, but Max was trying to get her to stay quiet.

"Yes, Dubs, I'd be devastated to lose you too. I'm pretty sure you know that."

"Looks like you aren't going to get to spend any time at my place after all," Lola said. "The mystery continues."

She thought about the options for housing. She knew Quinn would want to know where they would be staying. Holt had offered her a place in the lofts where she used to live. If that was still an option there wouldn't be any furniture. They could always stay with Jose or Moose. Not ideal, but better than a hotel.

"I'll still get to see it, right?" Quinn asked, pulling her from her thoughts.

"Well, it does sound like I need some help packing," Lola said. "Know anyone who could help?"

"I don't know. I'll have to think about it. Is there compensation?"

"Depends what kind you had in mind," Lola said. She licked her lips.

Quinn looked like she got the message. "I think I'm just the woman for the job."

As they teased each other and flirted, Lola was almost able to forget that she'd been kidnapped and forced Quinn to run for her life across the country. It felt like they should be getting ready to walk across campus to breakfast or like they were back on the beach. She'd missed this feeling of connection and possibility with Quinn and didn't want to do anything to jeopardize it.

They walked up to her apartment and Lola wondered if Quinn would be disappointed now that she was about to finally see Lola's home. She'd read you could tell everything you needed to know about a person by being in their living space for ten seconds or something like that. She hoped Quinn liked what she saw.

When they got inside, Quinn circled the room taking in everything. She ran her hand idly along the back of the old wingback chair in the corner and glanced at the stack of textbooks by the bedside. There were books everywhere.

"This is more like it," Quinn said. "This is the Lola I know." Quinn turned and stared at the print hanging on the wall above Lola's bed. "You have a neuron hanging on your wall."

"I do," Lola said. "I always thought it was both beautiful and captivating."

"Given my career path, I'm not inclined to argue with you," Quinn said.

"Do you think things are meant to be?" Lola asked. She pointed Quinn to the chair, sat on the bed herself, and then got back up immediately. She pulled out a couple of bags from the small closet and started shoving clothes inside.

"Like destiny?"

"Sure. Or like my buying a neuron to hang on my wall and blowing up the life of a beautiful neuroscientist so she'd have to come live with me for a while because she's in danger? And none of it would have been possible if things had worked out the way I thought they would not that long ago. Maybe things really do work out for a reason."

"Do the things that didn't work out have anything to do with Dubs asking me if I was pregnant?"

Lola rubbed her face with both hands and then ran her hands through her hair in frustration. "Ugh, that kid. I do love her, but sometimes I think Holt had the right idea handcuffing her to things. Kept her out of a little trouble."

"Excuse me?"

"I'll explain that too, but it's not really related to the other thing. Come on over here. That's a chair for one," Lola sat down on the bed and made room for Quinn to join her. "This might take a while. My place isn't that big so you've already done the tour."

"You're supposed to be packing," Quinn said.

"I don't plan on bringing most of what's here and it's a studio apartment anyway," Lola said. "Besides, I'm convalescing. I need frequent breaks."

"Well, that's the first you've noticed you're in any way compromised since you ripped those IVs out back at the hospital," Quinn said.

"I'm feeling much better. Close to one hundred percent," Lola said. She flexed to prove her point.

"My God, Isabelle was right about you. She did warn me."

Yesterday, Quinn had reacted angrily when Lola had spoken of keeping her safe and not having her own safety at the top of her mind. At least today she was willing to joke about it. In fact, unless Lola was reading things wrong, Quinn seemed to be finding the idea of Lola's tough guy posturing a little bit appealing.

Lola settled on the bed and opened her arms for Quinn.

"I don't want to hurt you."

"Quinn, sweetie, you could never hurt me. But I'll tell you if I need to shift into a different position, okay?"

She slid between Lola's legs and leaned back against her. She rested her head against Lola's shoulder and relaxed fully into her embrace. As it was back in LA, Quinn fit perfectly and it felt right.

Even though Lola promised a story, she wasn't in a hurry to get to it. She ran her fingers slowly up Quinn's arms, making goose bumps erupt where her fingers passed. Lola kissed Quinn's temple, and then once on her neck, just below her ear, but otherwise just held her. As had been the case on the night they met, Lola was content to let Quinn take the lead. She had no expectations, but after what they'd both been through recently, it felt nice to just hold Quinn for a few minutes, while they were awake and happy.

"You're supposed to be telling me a story," Quinn said.

"You want me to move my hands, just say the word."

"Yes," Quinn said.

Lola didn't know exactly what that meant, but given that Quinn's breathing hitched every time she moved up her arms or kissed her neck, she took a chance. She slid her hands down Quinn's arms and across her stomach. She reached under her shirt and slowly flattened her palms across her abdomen and sides. Lola felt Quinn's muscles contract under her palms.

"Higher."

Lola moved higher but stopped her explorations just below her breasts and didn't move any farther. Quinn must have gotten tired of waiting. She leaned back farther in Lola's arms, reached one arm back over her head, and pulled Lola down to her. Lola didn't protest as their mouths came together. They battled for supremacy for a moment before settling into a give-and-take.

It didn't take long before Quinn pushed Lola's hands away and turned to face her. She straddled her lap, pulled Lola's face to her again, and held it close with both hands as she gently bit Lola's bottom lip. Lola responded by grabbing her ass and pulling her closer still. She sucked her lip into her mouth before releasing it just as quickly and following it with a fierce kiss.

"You are so beautiful," Lola said. "Every part of you. Your mind, your body, this amazing ass."

"Keep talking and we'll both get a chance to forget about the last few days," Quinn said.

Lola moved her hands from Quinn's ass under her shirt and up her back. She unhooked Quinn's bra and started to pull her shirt over her head.

"Lola, do you think Holt expects us to move all of our stuff out of here? Or just enough to get us through—holy shit. I should have knocked. I forgot you have company. I'm used to you being my single neighbor. You should get a sock for your doorknob, or maybe use a lock?"

"Dubs, get out," Lola said.

Lola wanted to get up and chase Dubs from the room since she seemed in no particular hurry to vacate, but she was pinned as Quinn was still straddling her.

"So, maybe this is payback for the time you rolled up on Max and me after we snatched that gorgeous ride downtown? Are we even now?"

"Not even close," Lola said. She was more growling than anything. "And if you don't leave now, there's no car you could steal that would be fast enough for you to run from me."

"Understood. Nice seeing you both. Catch you later."

"I'm starting to understand your handcuff comment," Quinn said.

Both Quinn and Lola dissolved in laughter. Quinn kissed Lola and rolled off her. Lola followed and pinned Quinn to the bed, her arms over her head. She kissed her gently on the lips, then the tip of her nose.

"God, she sure does know how to kill a moment, doesn't she?" Lola rolled onto her back on the bed and let out a frustrated sigh.

Quinn curled on her side and rested her head on Lola's chest. Lola snaked an arm around Quinn and held her.

"You were supposed to be telling me a story about why it's a good thing I'm not pregnant. We'll have to let the anticipation build."

"All right. Well, I have this ex named Tiffany," Lola said.

"Doesn't everyone," Quinn said.

Lola was nervous. This was one hell of a story, and Lola had a few in her past. So far Quinn had heard about her murdered brother, her getting shot in the head, and a pregnant ex-girlfriend. That was quite a list for one woman. At what point was Quinn going to decide she wasn't worth the risk? Why hadn't she already?

"Probably not like this one," Lola said. "She was a pretty lousy girlfriend actually, but at the time I wasn't really willing to see that. We were on and off, and I'm not sure we both agreed on the timing of those intervals. She cheated on me a couple of times I'm sure of, but I don't know how many, or if she would define it that way. Regardless, about a year and a half ago, maybe a little more, she left a positive pregnancy test taped to my door and said the baby was mine if I wanted it, because she didn't."

"That's…life-changing." Quinn looked like she didn't know what to say. "What about the father? I mean the baby couldn't have been yours biologically, so there must have been someone else involved. I'm assuming you didn't plan on having a child with her?"

"No. That was the biggest shock of my life. So I ran straight to Holt and Isabelle and bawled my eyes out on their couch in the middle of the night. Then I decided I'd keep the baby. I couldn't imagine sending an innocent kid off to a home I knew nothing about. I felt responsible for her kid even though I know that's dumb. Logically, I know wherever the kid ended up would likely have been a wonderful home, there are so many people who want to adopt, but I wouldn't have been able to screen them. As soon as I knew this baby existed and she offered him to me, I felt like I had to make sure I did what was best for him."

"Seems like how you move through the world," Quinn said. "You protect the ones you care about."

"Everyone around here does," Lola said. "But as you've probably deduced, no baby here. Dubs and Max were helping me figure out what I'd need for the little guy, and I realized I couldn't do it. So I asked Holt and Isabelle if they would adopt him. They did. That's how George came into their life."

"And you get to be part of his life. That's wonderful," Quinn said.

"Well, it would have been a perfect happy ending except Tiffany and George almost died and Dubs got shot."

Quinn was quiet. She looked shocked.

"Yeah, there's not really anything to say," Lola said. "I didn't know what to say at the time to make it right either. So I haven't said anything. That's one of the things Holt and I were arguing about at the hospital."

"Just because I didn't say anything right away, doesn't mean I don't have anything to say. I just needed a minute because that wasn't where I expected the story to go," Quinn said. "But I guess I can see why there was some concern about the status of my uterus. Why do you feel so much guilt about what happened?"

"Because it's my fault."

"I find that hard to believe."

"It's true. I was so caught up in getting George the best home and having the adoption go through, I didn't pay attention to what was happening in front of me. I was also working this crazy case we had at the time but didn't see that the big bad scary dude had been sitting across from me signing adoption papers and lurking in the shadows keeping an eye on Tiffany every time I met with her. Turns out George's father was also the one behind this car theft ring we were trying to crack. He freaked out when we moved in to take him down. He said Tiffany brought us all down on him and was going to kill her.

Stupid, wonderful Dubs jumped in front of her and got shot instead. Luckily, her ego is too big to be really damaged by something as puny as a bullet. I think that saved her life." Lola ran a hand through her hair, trying to relieve some of the anxiety that always came when she thought about that day.

"I don't know her that well, but I can see it. She's like Supergirl. Impervious to just about anything," Quinn said.

"Except Max. That's her kryptonite. And if they weren't so freakin' cute, it would be annoying as hell."

"I'm still not seeing how Dubs getting shot was your fault. Sounds like all the guilt rests with the man who pulled the trigger, right? And Dubs is part of this team? You just said everyone around here protects those they care about. Doesn't Dubs care about you and Holt and Isabelle?"

"Well, technically all of that's true," Lola said. She felt like she was being outmaneuvered.

"I sense a 'but' in there. Let me recap what you've said, just so I understand. You found out a baby needed a home. You considered turning your whole world upside down to take the baby but decided you wouldn't be the best parent for him, so you found the best parents. You and your team tracked and captured a very mean man and put him in jail. As part of your takedown someone on your team did what you all seem to do, which is look out for each other. Then, once Dubs was injured, someone, or a whole host of someones, provided aid until she could get to the hospital. Does that about cover it?"

"Well, yes," Lola said. "But when you say it like that, there's not as much room for me to fit in the bits where I screwed up."

"Of course not," Quinn said. "Because you didn't, sweetie."

Quinn looked so sure Lola hadn't screwed up, it gave Lola a sense of hope. *Please help me find that much faith that I did nothing wrong.*

"You just might make me believe that," Lola said. "Some protector I am. I'm supposed to be making sure you're safe and don't feel scared and you're the one reassuring me."

Quinn reminded Lola how she felt about being seen as someone who needed protecting and was incapable of being an equal player in her own life. It wasn't easy for Lola to wrap her head around. She'd either been on her own, or been with women who were happy to have someone take care of all their needs and problems.

While she packed, Lola snuck glances of Quinn working on revising her list of logistical needs while curled up on her bed. Her hair was pulled back loosely, but strands had pulled free and were falling down around her face. Lola knew she'd never seen anyone more beautiful. Lola would do anything to make sure she stayed safe.

CHAPTER TWENTY

Quinn felt at loose ends. Lola was engaged in a long meeting with Holt and Moose, and Isabelle and Max were doing something related to money tracking. Jessica had left a while ago to settle in with Jose, her roommate for the foreseeable future. Everyone else around the office looked quite busy. Everyone except Dubs, who Quinn noticed was watching her across the room.

She'd never really been shy so she headed over to Dubs. She wanted to get to know the people in her orbit now.

"How is it being the new kid?" Dubs asked.

"Is that all I am? I seem to recall getting a grander title in my introduction. What was it you said? Lola's 'out of town lady friend'? Or something like that?"

"Not even close," Dubs said. "It took me a little while to understand how protective everyone is of everyone else around here. Especially the boss. But I learned through personal experience. Now I guess I'm just as guilty as anyone else, so I was staring, and it takes a lot for me to admit guilt about anything."

"Part of the felon and a thief thing?"

"Exactly. You don't get out of prison years early by admitting to anything."

"You also don't make new friends by lying your ass off," Quinn said. Lola had told her how Dubs came to be in Holt's employ.

"I knew I was going to like you," Dubs said. "It's execrable trying to break into this group in the middle of a crisis. Do you need anything? Looks like you and I are the only ones with nothing to do."

"Oh, you must be the one with the crazy Scrabble words. Lola warned me about you. Is there a place I can check my email? I'm allowed to do that, right?" Quinn hadn't had a chance to talk to her mentor at CLA or confirm her research was secure since she'd abruptly left LA. She might not be able to really work out here, but she could do some familiar things to help her sense of normality. It was on her list.

Dubs set her up on one of the computers and she spent thirty minutes making herself feel better that her affairs were indeed in order. Lola hadn't oversold Max's abilities to safeguard her research. Even she hadn't been able to access it.

"You know what's been bugging me?" Dubs asked.

She must have noticed Quinn close out of the browser and turn off the computer. Quinn couldn't even begin to guess. "Can you give me a hint on topic area? Are we talking global warming or that it took so long for Marvel to have one of their female characters headline a movie?"

"What? No, nothing like that. Although both are problems worthy of discussion. I'm thinking a little closer to home. Why is it that the CMCs, who according to Lola have a pretty good racket going laundering a shit ton of money, went to so much trouble to wave off some bounty hunter from Rhode Island? I get that they don't really want the cops taking too close a look at their operation, but didn't Lola say Malcolm was bragging about his eyes and ears at LAPD? If his business is as big as he says, he should have been able to let his dirty cops handle the investigation. They should have killed Garvey quietly and been done with it. Why risk pissing in Holt's cheerios? She didn't have any power out there. What's up with that?"

"Are you expecting me to have an answer? This isn't really my area of expertise."

"Purely hypothetical. And sure, you're a scientist, but you're brilliant. And I'm a criminal at heart. We can figure this out."

"You want the two of us to do it? Right now?"

"Why not? You have anything better to do?"

"Not really," Quinn said. She didn't have anything else to do. Although she wasn't sure she wanted to be involved in the crime fighting aspect of her new life, it would feel good to be useful. If only

Dubs would stop talking about murder so she could forget what Kevin Garvey looked like lying in her lab with his throat slashed.

"So, were do we start?" Dubs popped her gum and looked at Quinn expectantly.

"How am I supposed to know? Scientist, remember." Quinn shrugged. She wasn't leading the charge on this one. Dubs was going to have to help her out.

"Isn't science just problem solving? You find a question you want to answer and figure out how to answer it, right? Isn't that the basic idea? That's what I did when I stole cars too. So, how do you answer your questions? I bet our methods weren't that different." Dubs kicked her feet up on the desk and again looked at Quinn, waiting for her to jump in.

"God, I hope that's the last time science and stealing cars are equated. All right, we need somewhere we can write. Do you have a big board or a wall where we can hang a lot of paper?"

"Ooh, Max's fancy screen. I've wanted to use this forever. Come on, she's busy and won't notice." Dubs jumped up like she'd been receiving intravenous energy drinks for the past three years and raced across the room.

Dubs led Quinn into a conference room that had a full wall touch screen display. It was linked to a laptop and tablet which Dubs booted up. She handed the tablet to Quinn.

"You can write on here and it will show up on the screen. We can move things around as needed."

"Fancy. Now it looks more like a superhero headquarters in here. All right, so let's start with the things we know," Quinn said, starting to take notes. "The CMCs are new to town. They operate differently than other street gangs, but we're not sure why. They aren't above violence and intimidation. And they really don't want Holt poking around in their business. Does she only work in Rhode Island?"

"Last year they had income in the millions and funneled a lot of it through online daily fantasy sports to clean it. They made more money on top of that just from the daily games. And their leader is a guy named Malcolm," Dubs said. "And no, Holt goes where investigations lead. We were in the middle of the woods in Michigan when we learned about Kevin Garvey."

"Hang on, do we know those things are true? The millions of dollars in income and the money laundering?" Quinn asked. "Or are you basing that on what Malcolm told Lola?" She didn't know if she wanted to admit it, but Dubs was right. This didn't feel that much different than the early stages of idea and hypothesis generation when she was working on a new project or grant idea.

"Yes to the money laundering, maybe not the exact amount, but we can put it at roughly a shit ton. Malcolm is only self-proclaimed at this point," Dubs said. "I knew you'd be good at this."

Quinn moved closer to the full screen so she could look at her data more closely. She drummed her fingers on the tablet as she pondered.

"I'm naïve when it comes to the workings of criminal enterprises, but assuming Malcolm wasn't lying about millions of dollars in income, where was all the money coming from? And how many people are in the CMCs? Do you have a map of their territory?"

"Nobody seems to know where the money is coming from. Poor Chief Sam seems especially frustrated about that," Dubs said. "And she wasn't clear on how many members they have. They're still kinda new, and they aren't behaving exactly like the other gangs out there. She said they could have a couple hundred members, or closer to a thousand. It's not like they keep membership lists anyway. If someone gets arrested and the cops ask if they're a gang member, only an idiot says yes."

Quinn shook her head. This was all so new to her. "I guess I've never thought of that. You hear these sound bites on TV about gang task forces and creating lists of known gang members, but I never think how those are compiled. I imagine the data aren't very clean. Is it common for the cops to know so little about a group though?"

"The data's a mess," Dubs said. "Here's the map we got from Sam of the CMC territory. They've probably expanded some, but it's more or less accurate. Usually cops know more. The CMCs are unusual in just about every way."

The map Dubs put on the screen showed a vast territory controlled by the CMCs. Quinn thought about the thousands and thousands of people who must live in the constant fear she'd experienced for a short time if the CMCs ruled their neighborhood. She shuddered at the thought.

"I wonder if the crime data for these neighborhoods would give us a clue to what these guys are up to," Dubs said.

"Wouldn't the cops look at that too?" Quinn asked.

"Of course," Dubs said. "But they wouldn't be looking at it with my perspective. Let me pull it up. Can't hurt to take a peek."

"I'm never opposed to collecting data," Quinn said.

Dubs pulled up the crime data.

"Whoa. I'm new to this, but that seems strange," Quinn said.

"I wouldn't have predicted that," Dubs said. "Excuse me. That would not have been my hypothesis."

The crime data showed crime had plummeted in the CMC controlled areas since their hostile takeover, and not just a little bit. Those neighborhoods were now some of the safest in the city, as far as reported crime.

"Are people just too scared to call the police?" Quinn asked.

"No idea," Dubs said. "But that's weird. And it sure as hell doesn't help us figure out what they're up to."

"What revenue streams could the CMCs have? You say you're the criminal, how would you make millions in a year?"

"I wouldn't," Dubs said. "I'm not interested in any of the paths I'd have to go down to make that kind of money. But if I were, hypothetically, I suppose the usual suspects are always in play—guns, drugs, prostitution, people smuggling. Since they're obviously computer savvy, I wouldn't rule out identity theft as well. But all of those are things the cops keep a pretty close eye on. It's hard to smuggle goods, people, weapons, that kind of thing without anyone knowing about it. Sam didn't seem to know where their money was coming from at all. Like no clue. That seems really strange to me."

Quinn felt queasy thinking about the real lives and violence on the other end of Dubs's statement. How could people be so cruel to each other?

"If it helps," Dubs said, "we spend most of our time around here trying to prevent what you're picturing right now."

"How did you know?"

"Being perceptive is just one of my many talents."

"But modesty is not," Max said as she entered the conference room. "And what did I tell you about touching my toys?"

"Pretty Girl, I'm going to contain myself because Quinn is here, but replay what you just said and decide if that's really something you want to insist on. You can let me know before the next time we're having fun alone nak—"

"Dubs!"

Quinn was amused by their interplay and Max's quickly reddening face. Despite her obvious embarrassment, she didn't look all that upset by Dubs's teasing. In fact, it was clear from just a glance how much they adored each other. Unbidden, Quinn wondered how Lola looked at her. *Where did that come from?*

"Was there something you needed? Quinn and I are working here," Dubs said.

"I missed you. Isabelle is checking on George and had a few other phone calls to make so we're taking a break. I came looking for you, but you weren't easy to find. Now I know it's because you were in here sneaking a turn with my babies."

"Come look at what we're doing. Maybe you can help." Dubs quickly filled her in. "So now we're stuck," she concluded.

"I'm not so sure," Quinn said. "If they're dealing drugs, what would they need?"

"Supplier and product," Dubs said.

"That's what I was thinking too. And what about guns? Same thing, right?"

"Absolutely. And if they're involved in human trafficking or smuggling, they're going to need contacts and suppliers of sorts for that too. Probably not so much for prostitution, unless it's tied to one of the others, especially the human trafficking."

"Let's set identity theft aside for a minute," Quinn said. "All the other potential money makers have an outside supplier as a common denominator."

"Even if they aren't involved with one of the traditional moneymakers, they might still have the same business model," Dubs said. She paced around the table while she talked. "Holt thinks someone else is involved, probably calling the shots."

"If they're a silent partner and want to stay hidden it might explain why they were so aggressive trying to get Holt off the case," Max said. "If they have LAPD handled, Holt is a wildcard. There is so much fog on the CMCs it suggests a lot of what Malcolm said is true. The investigations are being stalled. But someone like Holt doesn't get stalled and she isn't part of the LA system. She would have no trouble blowing up their ecosystem. It might explain why they let Lola live as well."

"Holt didn't seem to think that should have happened," Quinn said.

This exercise was much less fun when she remembered the reason for its existence. She sat in one of the conference room chairs and leaned her head back, closing her eyes for a moment. That was a mistake, as she once again saw Kevin Garvey's dead body and Lola being tossed out of the SUV, barely conscious, onto the sidewalk. She tried to refocus on what was being said around her.

"Didn't think what should have happened?" Holt asked.

"Hey, private party here," Dubs said.

"It's my conference room," Holt said.

"Good point. Probably good you're here anyway. Quinn and I have been talking about the CMCs and we have questions."

"Don't we all?" Moose asked as he and Lola followed Holt into the room.

Quinn caught Lola's eye. She smiled at her and Quinn felt like her heart stopped for a few beats. *That woman is dangerous.*

"I know we've had different opinions on how to handle this case," Holt said. "But everyone's safety comes first. We're still working with Sam, and we'll nail these bastards as long as it doesn't endanger anyone here. She called this morning and asked for a favor on part of the case. I'm worried about the risk of getting more actively involved again, but I think our fingerprints are still all over her investigation and so far there hasn't been any additional escalation from the CMCs."

"We've never run away from a fight, H," Moose said.

"We're not running away. I'm weighing the risks. We already discussed the likelihood that we're in this till the end whether we want to be or not. I don't think the CMCs and any silent partner they may have are quitters."

Quinn watched the argument build and the tension grow. Holt looked like she was holding on to her temper by the slimmest of margins. No matter how much she wanted to return to her predictable, stable, not violent life, Quinn would never ask Holt to put her family at risk so she could do so. She was also not going to make Holt say, in front of her crew, that Isabelle's and George's lives were more important to her than Quinn and Jessica returning home, even if it was true.

"Little George, Isabelle, hell, everyone's safety, is more important than my getting home quickly," Quinn said. "You've shown me incredible hospitality. I'll keep taking you up on it so everyone stays safe."

Lola looked like she wanted to argue further, but Quinn shook her head and smiled. She hoped Lola understood. She didn't protest so she must have.

"So what have you two been cooking up in here?" Holt asked, turning to Dubs and Quinn.

Quinn thought everyone was probably glad to turn to work.

"Quinn can explain," Dubs said.

"Thanks, buddy," Quinn said. Although everyone laughed at Dubs's joking implication she was throwing Quinn under the bus in front of Holt, Quinn appreciated Dubs letting her lay out their simple work and conclusions. It meant a lot that Dubs was willing to give the spotlight to her.

"Max, get the rest of the crew," Holt said.

When everyone was jammed into the conference room, Quinn and Dubs shared their thoughts. Quinn had continued working on the theory in her head since the meeting had been called, so she had a few additions.

"Two things of note. First, we compared the map of known CMC territory to the crime data from the city. There's an inverse relationship between crime and areas controlled by the CMCs. Reported crime dropped precipitously. I don't know enough to say if their taking over the territory is causal, but based on timing, they are highly correlated."

"That's just crime reported to the authorities, though," Holt said. "I agree it's strange to see the kind of steep drop you're describing, but do we know if actual crime has truly gone down? Max, can you delve into social media, local news reports, and any other source material you can find to see if you can get some more evidence one way or another to confirm or refute this? What's the second thing?"

Quinn liked the way Holt worked a problem. She was organized in her thinking—logical, thorough, and disciplined. She gave her confidence and she could see the others in the room fed off of Holt's steady leadership as well.

"The CMC money has to be coming from somewhere, even though it's currently a mystery. You said you think there's a player behind the scenes who is either a partner or the one actually in charge. It makes sense that person also controls the money. We were thinking that even if they aren't utilizing traditional bad guy moneymakers, they might still be using a similar business model. They might need suppliers, distributers, etcetera. Somewhere in that line we can probably find a way to the top." Quinn wondered when she started thinking and speaking in terms of "we" when it came to combating the CMCs. *I'm supposed to be finishing a grant, not developing a model for stopping a violent street gang.*

"This is good work, you two," Holt said. "If this theory is true—"

"We're calling it the Sugar Daddy Theorem," Dubs said.

"We absolutely are not," Quinn said.

"Like I was saying," Holt said, ignoring Dubs. "If there's a silent partner pulling the strings and funding the CMCs, they're not only using their power to control the CMCs. They also changed the street gang model. According to Sam, this gang is different from the others in growth and structure. It's speculation, but perhaps not unreasonable to assume whoever is behind the scenes had a hand in creating the CMCs, or were instrumental in their rapid rise. Why? And how does the crime data, assuming it really has gone down, fit in?"

"What else happened in LA around the time the CMCs rose?" Moose asked. "I'd be interested to hear the chief's perspective on our theory."

Max started typing rapidly on her laptop. "Let's see, the NFL looked like it was finally going to get a football team back in LA, the Dodgers were making a playoff run, it was an unusually hot summer, the drought was in full swing, it was a mayoral election year, LAPD busted a smuggling operation coming out of the port."

"I want more information on the port case and the election. Max, did you and Isabelle find anything on the money?" Holt asked.

"We were working from Kevin's skimmed money and back-tracing. Isabelle was able to follow the money back to the accounts set up for Garvey and the college kids, but all the deposits came from an offshore account owned by a series of shell corporations. It would probably take me months to crack them all, if I was ever able," Max said.

"I'm assuming more of the same on the way out the other side?" Holt asked.

Max nodded. She looked glum. Quinn suspected there weren't many computer problems she couldn't solve. Dubs had mentioned Max wanting to redirect satellites to look for Lola when she'd been kidnapped. That kind of skill didn't seem defeated often.

"I'll confirm with Isabelle she is comfortable with the risk," Holt said, "and if you are all okay as well, I'll get in touch with Sam."

Everyone at the table agreed. Quinn felt the fear that felt like it had had a vice grip on her innards for days return. Logically, she understood the need for Holt to help the LAPD, and that the threat hadn't really disappeared despite being across the country, but logic didn't matter when the people who swore to keep her safe were evaluating risk potential and were worried themselves. Playing pretend crime fighter with Dubs had been one thing. This suddenly felt like something else entirely, again.

CHAPTER TWENTY-ONE

E xplain family dinner to me," Quinn said. She and Dubs were driving to Holt's house from the office. Quinn didn't have her own transportation, but Holt had promised that would happen soon. For now, Dubs had offered to be her personal chauffeur whenever Lola wasn't available. "Will I be meeting Holt's mother?"

"Definitely not," Dubs said. "But Isabelle's sister will probably be there. She usually is. Family dinners are awesome. You've already met most everyone who'll be there. It's Holt and Isabelle's chosen family. We have dinner pretty regularly and are absolutely not allowed to talk about work. Isabelle doesn't allow it in the house. Max is usually in charge of the bat phone just in case anything exciting happens, but mostly we just have fun. You'll like it."

"Why was Holt lecturing you about not getting a scratch on her truck? You seem like a pretty good driver," Quinn said. She'd been a little nervous to get in the truck with Dubs after overhearing Holt reading Dubs the riot act, but it seemed she had nothing to worry about.

"I don't know what kind of car thief she thinks I was. You can't damage the merchandise before you chop it to sell it. She's still a little miffed about her last truck getting stolen. I think it embarrasses her."

Dubs seemed miffed that Holt had questioned her former professional skills. She eased into traffic and headed across town toward Holt and Isabelle's house.

"How did you go from car thief to so settled down?" Quinn asked.

"I don't think anyone's ever described me that way," Dubs said. Quinn would have to agree, nothing about Dubs the individual ever seemed settled. Unless she was with Max.

"I mean with Max. You two seem so happy."

"We are," Dubs said. "She's insane for loving me. Don't tell her I said that. She's the best thing that's ever happened to me. When I got shot last year, I thought I was going to die. I didn't mind because I finally did something good in my life that I could be proud of. That felt nice. But I kept thinking how I wouldn't see Max's face first thing in the morning when I woke up if I died and what a bummer that was. That's what I look forward to most. Is that the definition of being settled?"

"I don't know," Quinn said. "Maybe. It's very sweet, whatever it is." Quinn thought about what she most looked forward to when she woke up in the morning. It used to be work. Now she didn't know.

Dubs made a quick lane change and then a hard left turn. Quinn was jerked against her seat belt.

Maybe I was too quick to give her a pass on her driving skills. "Dubs, what's going on?" Quinn asked. The niggling fear was back.

"Fuck trumpets," Dubs said. "Can you please call Max and ask her for a license plate trace for me?" Dubs relayed the plate number as Quinn dialed. She put the phone in the center console on speaker.

"Is someone following us?" Quinn asked. She was trying to remain calm. *What has my life turned into?*

"I don't know," Dubs said. "A car picked us up as soon as we pulled out. They're staying back, but they seemed to be following us. Now I know they are."

Max got back to them with the information they needed. Rental car from the airport. Bogus information given for driver's license and a corporate credit card that was going to take her a while to track.

"Come back to the shop," Max said. "I'll loop Holt in. Looks like family dinner is going to start late."

Dubs didn't wait for an intersection before flipping an abrupt U-turn. Quinn looked out the driver's window as she did and spotted the car Dubs had described. It seemed like slow motion as she watched the driver roll down the window and level a gun at the truck. Panic unlike anything she'd ever felt surged through her body. *Don't throw up. Don't wet yourself. Holy shit, don't die.* "Get down," she said. She pulled Dubs practically into her lap. Bullets peppered the rear quarter panel of the truck. The shots sounded like the firecrackers kids set off in her neighborhood at home, but she could feel the impact of each bullet as it ripped through the metal frame with a metallic tinged pop.

"Fucking, mouse dicked, cock nosed, piss wizards," Dubs said, righting herself and slamming down the gas pedal.

Quinn felt like her heart might beat out of her chest. Her adrenaline was surging and her face felt hot from the rush. She wasn't sure if she felt fear, excitement, or both. Whatever it was, her body was telling her to go, act, survive, in a big way. Trouble was, she was strapped into a car she had no control over. *I didn't need to know it was possible to level up being scared from the shit-show a few days ago. Please let me survive this.*

"Dubs, Quinn, are you okay?" Max was yelling through the phone. She sounded panicked.

"We're here," Dubs said. She looked over at Quinn and did a quick visual inventory. "Okay might be a stretch, but no one is hurt. I'm not bringing these guys back your way. We need a plan to lose them. I'm assuming you called the cops. What do they say?"

"Quinn, baby, where are you?" Lola was on the phone now and she didn't sound good. Quinn could picture exactly how she looked right now, wild with fear, angry, determined to get to her. "I'm coming to get you."

"No. You can't come out here. Lola, listen to me," Quinn said. She wanted this nightmare to end. She wanted to be out of this truck. She wanted to never be shot at again. But she didn't want Lola putting herself in jeopardy to make that happen.

"Quinn, down again," Dubs said. She pushed Quinn's head between her knees as gunfire exploded through the back window.

"Can I get up now?" Quinn asked. She was surprised she hadn't puked. It seemed that all systems were busy pushing the panic button.

Dubs nodded. She made a hard right, nearly on two wheels.

"Fuck that," Lola said. "Dubs, one scratch before I get there and I'm coming after you."

"I'm fine too," Dubs said. "Thanks for your concern. See you soon. Do we have a plan yet? Because I'm good, but at this speed I don't have a large margin for error in tight quarters. I've got to get out of the city. There are too many people around and these fuck buckets are shooting indiscriminately. Where are the cops?"

"You're hitting fifty miles an hour through downtown. They don't want anything to do with that kind of high-speed pursuit. You as well as anyone know the reason for that rule. Get out of town and you'll have more help."

"Sure," Dubs said. "The shitflaps are following the rules because it's me. They're still salty because of that state trooper SUV I stole last year."

Quinn dared look out the window. She expected to see a cruise missile aimed at her head, or a tank with its main gun leveled at them, but she didn't see anything threatening. Relief flooded her. "I don't see them. Do you?"

"No, I think I may have lost the shit nubbins, but I'm not sure. I'm not willing to take a chance—Fuck stick, ass badgers," Dubs said as the pursuing sedan roared into view. "Where did you come from?"

Dubs threw the truck into reverse and slammed on the brakes, turning the wheel while she did. Quinn was terrified as the car grew closer to her window. There was no raised gun this time, and the occupants seemed content to ram them.

"This isn't really fair to ask, but I only have two hands," Dubs said. "Do you mind snapping a picture of those two as we pass? Max should be able to use some facial rec to figure out who's trying to climb into our lap."

Quinn heard Lola explode, followed by Holt cursing, but she tuned it out as she waited for the car to get closer. Having something to do felt much better than sitting helplessly in her seat awaiting her fate, even if what Dubs was asking was insane.

Dubs was executing a rather nifty pirouette to remove her from the direct path of the impact, but she needed them to stay in view just a moment longer. The closer they got the clearer the picture would be.

When she thought they were as close and as directly in front of her as they were going to be, she snapped the picture. "Smile, fuck waffles," Quinn said.

"Nice one," Dubs said.

"Your penchant for very creative swearing has apparently had an effect on me," Quinn said. "Max, picture's on its way."

"Any luck on getting us some backup? What if we head for the state park just up One Forty-six?"

"Already suggested and approved. Do it," Holt said. "They asked for ten minutes to set up. Can you hold out that long?"

"No problem, H. Beautiful day for a drive," Dubs said. As she said it, she jumped three lanes and dodged into an alley. It was a tight squeeze, and a few trash cans and one of Holt's side mirrors were casualties of her decision. The sedan didn't seem inclined to follow, and for the moment they were alone on the road with the normal flow of Providence city traffic.

"It was a game we played in prison. Scrabble and creative swearing. Sometimes I revert to it when I get stressed."

"Jesus Christ, Dubs," Lola said. She sounded ready to come through the phone to strangle Dubs. "That car is too fucking close. Holt, I'm not staying here. There's nothing you can do to keep me from getting to her."

"Lola," Quinn said, trying to break through Lola's worry. "Without Dubs's superhuman driving just now, neither one of us would be talking to you. Take it down a couple pegs."

"She's gone," Max said. "Holt was literally holding her in place to keep her from getting to you before. She might have been sitting on her."

"Did she take company transportation or her own? Does she have comms?" Dubs asked.

"Her own. Unless she calls in, she's on her own. I don't have a comms link."

"Fucking idiot," Dubs said.

Quinn didn't know why Dubs was so angry with Lola, but she could tell she was worried about her.

"What's wrong?"

"Aside from the piss fidgets shooting at us," Dubs said. "Your lady has decided to join a gunfight on a fucking motorcycle."

The pit of Quinn's stomach felt like it fell out. She felt tears roll down her cheeks. Lola had said she put her own safety below those she wanted to protect. In theory that sounded noble; even hearing about the scary reality after the fact was okay. But this was real and Quinn was going to have to watch her die.

"Hey, you guys may not like this very much," Max said. "But any chance you can get close to that car again?"

"Pretty Girl, I thought you liked me without bullet holes."

"I expect you to remain bullet free even if I ask you to hop in the car with those two, understood? But facial rec is back and the shooters are from LA and suspected CMC members," Max said.

Quinn thought she sounded as scared as Lola. Quinn knew Max had been there when Dubs was shot and had nearly bled to death. She didn't know how Max was able to make this ask.

"What do you need from us?"

"I'm going to use your phone to bluesnarf one of theirs, but I need you to be close. I've been working on a little worm. Once it's on one of their devices it will jump to any other device they text, email, or call. If they're part of the CMCs we should be able to follow the trail through their phones. Hopefully, it will lead us to our mystery money suppliers."

"Is a bluesnarf like Mystique with a head cold?" Dubs asked. She slammed on the brakes as a UPS truck double-parked in front of them. Four cars behind them in the left lane honked loudly as she cut them off.

"Can you get close enough or not?" Max asked.

"Of course," Dubs said. "How close do we need to be?"

"Fifteen feet, twenty at the most."

"No," Holt said. "Come back to the office and swap me in for Quinn."

"I can do it," Lola said. Apparently, she did have communication capabilities.

She appeared next to Quinn, alongside the truck on her bike. She looked so exposed. Her only protection was a helmet and a heavy coat, neither of which would stop a bullet.

"Too dangerous," Quinn said, surprising herself. "Dubs and I are going to do it. We'll be fine. Right, Dubs?"

"Absolutely. Now we just need to find them again."

Oh, God. We're going looking for the guys with guns. What did I agree to? "I'll leave that to you," Quinn said. "Lola, please go back. I don't want anything to happen to you."

"Look out, Lola," Dubs said.

She weaved through slower traffic and made a quick right turn. Quinn didn't know the landmarks of Providence, but she thought they'd circled back to where they'd last seen the sedan.

"I'm not leaving, Quinn," Lola said.

"If you're staying, do something useful. Help me find these guys," Dubs said.

"For the record, I don't like you staying, but I realize there's nothing I can do about it. So let's find them so we can be done with this. The longer it takes the more scared I am," Quinn said.

That seemed to motivate Lola. She shot off ahead of them and down a side street.

Dubs eased the truck around a corner and stopped. They both looked cautiously up and down the street. Dubs pulled into traffic. No sign of the sedan.

Dubs circled back toward the shop, retracing their steps, but not getting close enough to put anyone else in danger. Quinn could see Dubs was getting frustrated. She patted her shoulder reassuringly. She didn't know if she actually wanted to find the sedan or not.

"Are you two ready?" Lola asked. She rode into view from a cross street. "I think they're behind—"

"I think we're about to—bitchtits. Thunderfuck, hairy shit house, fuck turnip."

Dubs unbuckled Quinn's seat belt and threw her to the floor. Quinn screamed as bullets flew across the truck cab and through the door, right where she'd been sitting. She heard the hissing through the air above her head.

"Dubs," Quinn yelled. She didn't know how Dubs could have survived that.

"All good," Dubs said from the floorboard next to her. She had one hand on the steering wheel and one mashed on the gas pedal. As soon as the shooting stopped, or more accurately, as soon as the bullets stopped entering the cab, Dubs slid back into the driver's seat.

"Lola, are you okay?" Quinn looked out the truck windows, or what was left of them, trying to catch a glimpse of Lola.

"My bike's been hit, but I'm okay," Lola said. "I thought... Jesus."

In the excitement, the phone had fallen under the seat. She retrieved it before pulling herself back into her seat. It sounded like everyone in the office was yelling simultaneously trying to ascertain their status.

"We're okay," Quinn said. "Thanks once again to Dubs. No-look driving is a new one, even for her I'm guessing. Max, can you do your barfing thing?" Quinn didn't feel scared anymore. She didn't feel anything. Perhaps this was yet another level of terror, one so all-encompassing it short-circuited her whole system.

"No," Max said. "You're not close enough."

"Should I ask them to pull over so we can coordinate the next street for a 'not close enough' shootout? How close do we have to be? And for how long?" Dubs asked.

Max thought she needed about a minute to break into one of the phones and upload her program. That sounded like an eternity in close proximity to gunfire.

"We'll see what we can do," Quinn said. She took the phone off speaker and covered the mouthpiece. "Can we do this without getting killed?"

"I sure as hell hope so," Dubs said. "Our friends are back. This is our chance. You ready, Pretty Girl? Lola, I hate to ask, but can you run interference?"

"All set," Max said. "Be careful."

"Will do." Lola pulled up alongside them. "Watch yourselves."

The sedan approached from behind. Quinn glanced in her side mirror, which remarkably was still attached, and saw one of the two men hanging out the window with his weapon leveled at the truck. She thought about jumping out the window. It seemed safer than what they were about to do.

"Hang on," Dubs said.

Quinn grabbed the handhold above the window and braced herself. Dubs made a rapid lane change and slammed on the brakes. The sedan shot past them. As Dubs was braking, she put the truck into a spin so they were one eighty to where they'd been. As soon as they were facing the opposite direction, she floored the gas again and reversed after the sedan.

Dubs chased the car and accelerated after it until their bumpers hit. Quinn watched through the shot out back window of the truck. The two men in the sedan seemed unsure how to react to this new development. The driver looked like he was trying to disengage Dubs from his back bumper, and the passenger, for the moment, didn't seem to remember that he had a weapon he could be using against them as he stared at them like they were insane.

Their hesitation didn't last long. The passenger hung out his window and took aim once again, spraying bullets at the truck. Quinn and Dubs ducked down to avoid those that sprayed high enough to reach the cab. Lola roared in on the passenger's side. She had her helmet in her hand now, and swung it at the shooter. She got him in the shoulder, which stopped his shooting momentarily. He took aim at Lola, and Quinn was certain her heart stopped as she watched the two tussle over the gun while streaking down the road.

Lola jabbed her helmet at the shooter again, connecting with his nose. Quinn saw blood splatter through the air. He tried to take aim at Lola again, but she pushed the barrel of the gun skyward and his shot flew off target.

"Get out of there, Lola," Dubs said. "He's not going to keep missing."

Dubs had put into words what Quinn had been unable to express. She'd been watching Lola using a motorcycle helmet to fight off an automatic weapon and she'd felt almost nothing, though she couldn't speak. Maybe she'd overloaded her panic circuits. Or maybe it was self-preservation.

"If I can get that gun away from him, we all stand a better chance out here," Lola said.

Unfortunately, the driver didn't seem to like Lola's interference. He pulled out a gun too and trained it on Lola over his buddy's shoulder.

"Shit," Lola said.

The driver lost focus on the road and swerved so erratically Lola had to correct hard to stay upright.

With the swerving, Dubs was having trouble keeping the truck in contact with the sedan.

"How much longer, Max?" Dubs asked.

"Twenty-five seconds," Max said.

"Too long," Dubs said. She depressed the brake again and let the sedan speed away. She stayed close, but out of shooting range. "H, do you still have a baseball bat in this truck?"

"Out of range," Max said.

"Of course," Holt said. "They aren't that good against guns, though."

"You haven't seen me use it," Dubs said. "Quinn can you dig the bat out? Behind the seat, right?"

Quinn didn't like where this was going, but she did as asked. She didn't like getting shot at either, but there didn't seem to be much choice in that particular matter today. Dubs was a lot of things, but she didn't seem reckless. If she had an idea, Quinn was willing to hear her out. It wasn't like she could ask her to pull over and get out anyway.

"What's the plan?"

"Gotta get rid of those semiautomatics," Dubs said. "We've only got one more chance at this, I'm guessing, and I'm going to need your help so I don't get shot. You in?"

"Why not," Quinn said.

"Remember, wait until he comes out of the car to shoot, then ram him," Dubs said. "He'll pop back in if he knows what's good for him. Just don't hit it too hard or they'll bounce too far. Just a love tap. When he pops back out, I'll get him. That'll be one down. As long as the driver learned his lesson from that last multitasking experiment, Max can do her bluefarting thing. Lola, you're on backup with the driver in case he gets frisky, right? Keep him focused on you."

"Got you covered," Lola said. "But I'd rather you gave the bat to me and let me handle this."

"Of course you would," Dubs said. She was chasing after the sedan, which was now driving wildly, looking like it was trying to escape them. "But you've got fuckall for protection. I've got a truck that weighs more than your bike or their sedan and a better plan than yours. Not that helmet whack-a-mole wasn't fun to watch."

"Right, simple, piece of cake," Quinn said.

"I don't like this plan either, Dubs," Holt said. "You're both too exposed."

"And we don't like getting shot at," Dubs said. "But the phone's gotta get the toots and we've gotta get rid of the guns. The cops aren't coming, so it's up to us."

"I should be out there too."

"Then they would be shooting at all of us. How many cars and people are you going to risk today?"

"Quinn is *not* a sacrificial pawn," Holt said. "Neither are you."

"Love you too, Boo," Dubs said.

"Shut up, Dubs," Holt said.

"Here comes our chance," Quinn said. The fear had picked a lousy time to make its return. Her hands were shaking and she felt a little woozy.

"I trust you," Dubs said.

Quinn appreciated that confidence. Dubs had the dangerous job of hanging out the window, but Quinn had to put her in proper position or she would surely die. No pressure.

They came up fast on the sedan and Dubs turned over steering to Quinn. She turned in the driver's seat so she was facing the window. She braced one knee against the back of the seat and kept her other foot on the gas pedal.

"I'm not taking my foot off this pedal, so the speed will stay constant. Just steer us in, nice and steady. The truck will do everything you ask of her. Lola's right on the other side of the sedan, so we've got them flanked."

"You're in range. Doing my thing," Max said.

When they pulled almost even, Quinn watched the passenger in the other car. As expected, when they pulled alongside, he leaned out the window with his weapon drawn. His face was a bloody mess. Quinn jerked the wheel and the truck slammed into the side of the sedan. The shooter tumbled back into the car, almost landing in the driver's lap. The impact was harder than she intended. She held the truck against the sedan a beat, using as much strength as she could muster to counter the force of the bounce back before she eased the truck away enough to give Dubs and the CMC soldier some breathing room.

The two vehicles were side by side now. Dubs had the bat at the ready but not easily visible to their aggressive friends.

"Little closer," Dubs said. "Slowly though, so you don't spook him."

Quinn did as asked. She moved the truck as gently as she could. It was incredibly difficult to make subtle changes when they were moving at nearly sixty miles an hour. *Thank God for back streets.*

As soon as the CMC soldier popped out the window again, exposing his arms, hands, the gun, and his upper body, Dubs made her move. She leaned out the window and swung the bat down hard on the man's arms. Even through the wind whipping by the fast moving cars, Quinn could hear his scream.

Dubs pulled herself and the bat back into the cab and resumed full control of the truck.

"Keep an eye on the driver," Dubs said. "I can't see his gun. I'm going to keep us close enough for the bluesnapper, but hopefully out of his line of fire. Lola, can you see anything?"

Dubs eased the truck back to the rear quarter panel of the sedan and stayed locked there while they waited for Max to give them the all clear.

"I think the driver just wet himself. He's still got his weapon, but not making any move to draw it."

"After this thing is on the phone, they have to contact someone for it to work, right?" Quinn asked. "Does that mean we have to let them go?"

"No," Max said. "I'll get full contacts and email and text messages no matter what. If they use the phone to contact anyone, the worm will jump to that phone. We don't have to let them go, we just have to hope they get in touch. You still have a ten-minute drive to the police roadblock."

"Well, I just shattered one guy's arms," Dubs said. "So hopefully the driver is feeling chatty."

"Are you done yet?" Lola asked. "My buddy has changed his mind about keeping his weapon stowed."

"Done," Max said.

"Get out of there," Holt said. It was a command, not a suggestion.

"Yes, ma'am," Dubs said. She disengaged from the sedan and made an abrupt right turn.

Quinn looked out the back window to check on Lola. She heard gunfire behind them but no corresponding impacts on the truck. She didn't see the bike right away.

No, no, no.

Suddenly, Lola shot past them. Quinn heard tires screeching behind them as their travel buddies tried to follow.

"Okay, Dubs," Lola said. "How fast can we get to the park? That should have been plenty of time for the cops to set up. I think we've done enough to destroy the city today."

Quinn felt like an emotional piñata. The numbness was gone, replaced with overwhelming fear, determination, and triumph, as well as terror and sadness when she'd thought Lola had gone down. Now she was relieved, even though logically she knew there were still armed men chasing them. She was also exhausted. She had no idea how Lola could do this day in and day out. Perhaps worse was the idea that she had no idea how she could live with Lola knowing this was what she faced at work.

CHAPTER TWENTY-TWO

L ola couldn't ever remember feeling the frantic, crawl out of her skin need to get to someone like she had right now. She'd had to slow down once they left the city and the roads were less clear from the most recent snowstorm, which put her a good distance behind Dubs and Quinn. But she wouldn't be good to Quinn if she were dead. Once she made it to the state park, the police didn't immediately let her through their blockade. She considered running it, but she'd had enough guns pointed her direction for one day.

She knew most of the cops, so once she convinced them she was there legitimately, she gunned her bike into the park. She could see flashing lights and lots of activity ahead.

Lola saw the sedan and the two CMC soldiers being arrested. She slowed and surveyed the scene. No truck, no Dubs, no Quinn. An officer tried to flag her. She realized it was the Providence police chief. She didn't care. She flew past them. He could wait for Holt. She could hear through her comms that she was only a minute or two behind with Max.

Twenty feet ahead, she saw the truck. It was littered with bullet holes and dented and bashed. She felt bile rising and had to take a few deep breaths to keep from throwing up. She slowed the bike and dismounted. Quinn was okay, she reminded herself. She said she was okay. Her stomach wasn't getting the message.

Lola ran to the truck. Why wasn't there an ambulance? Were they too late? Had the ambulance already come and taken them away? Was there no need for one? Had they been lying to her? Lola ran around to the driver's side, and there, sitting in the dirt against the front tire were Quinn and Dubs, shoulder to shoulder, holding hands. Quinn was drinking a bottle of water.

"Hey look, a damsel in distress," Dubs said. "Think we should offer assistance?"

"She does look distressed," Quinn said. "Looks like a couple others are on their way over. But this big strong one had better get her butt over here if she knows what's good for her. I'm done playing superhero."

Lola didn't need to be told twice. She was on her knees in front of Quinn instantly. She was vaguely aware that Dubs had gotten up and was walking toward another truck that had pulled up.

"You're hurt," Lola said, touching the blood on Quinn's cheek. "Why isn't there an ambulance here?"

"We're fine," Quinn said. "Just cuts from the flying glass. I'll probably have some bruises from playing bumper cars, but I'm really okay. Physically. Nothing like what you went through."

Lola pulled Quinn to her, crushing her in an embrace she never wanted to end.

"I'm sorry I didn't keep you safe."

"Lola Walker, look at me," Quinn said.

Lola did as she was told and stared into Quinn's clear, beautiful eyes.

"You raced out on a motorcycle to face a bullet storm for me. You fought an armed man with nothing but a motorcycle helmet. No one has ever done anything so brave for me. But you scared me. I thought I was going to have a front row seat to watch you die. Do you know what that would have done to me?"

"But I could have lost you," Lola said. "And we just found each other." Her chest was constricting and it felt hard to breathe. She leaned her forehead against Quinn's and put her hands on her shoulders. Quinn grounded her.

"You didn't though. We still have time to figure all of this out," Quinn said.

"Is that what you want? Even after all I've put you through?" Lola couldn't imagine why Quinn would want anything to do with her, or any of them, from here on out.

"You haven't put me through anything. Some very bad people have. They've put you through a lot too."

"But it's my job," Lola said. Saying that chafed in a way it never had before. "Although I'm not sure if it will be forever. Holt has given me other options."

"Are you saying that because you think I need to hear it to give you a chance?" Quinn asked.

"No," Lola said. "Right now, what you see is what you get. I'm just not sure it will always be this way."

Quinn held out her hand for Lola to help her up. She dusted off her pants and shuddered when she glanced at the truck.

"Maybe we could continue our chat somewhere warmer and out of the shadow of this," Quinn said.

Lola led Quinn toward Holt, Max, and Dubs. Holt had brought one of the SUVs, which Lola was thankful for. She wasn't putting Quinn on the back of her bike, given the weather and road conditions. As they walked, Quinn slipped an arm around Lola's waist. Lola wrapped her arm around Quinn's shoulders and held her close. She could feel Quinn shaking. She didn't know if it was adrenaline or cold. She wanted to take her somewhere safe and warm and stay there for days.

"Quinn, look at this," Dubs said, holding out her hand. It was shaking. "Are you still vibrating too? That was amazingly shitty, but you were so good under pressure. The perfect chaos wingman. We're building a pretty significant special club here. The CMC survivors' consortium, fellowship, guild? There has to be a secret handshake, a specialty cocktail, and matching tiaras."

"You really think you're getting Lola to wear a tiara?" Holt asked. She was leaning against the truck, looking far calmer now that she knew her people were safe.

"You need to spend more late nights up in the attic," Dubs said. "You might be surprised by what you would see."

"Hard pass," Holt said. "But thanks for the invite."

"Speaking of invitations," Max said. "I don't think you're going to be able to put off that one much longer."

She pointed to the police chief, who was waiting impatiently for Holt about fifteen feet from where they were. Lola saw him tapping his foot, checking his watch, and trying to get Holt's attention.

"I'm going to talk to the cops," Holt said. "Dubs, Max, no sneaking away to burn off Dubs's post-adrenaline high. Got it? It's still family dinner night. I think we all need it tonight."

"H, stealing cars gives a smooth high. The kind you can ride and makes you want to celebrate. That shit wasn't the same. Family dinner is about all I'm good for right now. I'm spent."

Lola took Quinn's hand. She was unusually quiet, which worried Lola. She'd just been through an incredible trauma. Dubs would probably talk about it incessantly, but Quinn might need something different. Whatever that was, Lola wanted to provide it. "Are you still up for family dinner?"

"Yes," Quinn said. "I like your friends. It's clear how much you all love each other and after…all of that," she waved her hand back toward the truck, "I would like to be surrounded by love."

As long as I'm around, you always will be. She pushed the thought away. Rushing things was never a good idea. *Still…*

"Sweetheart, you've got applesauce in your hair. The crew's going to be here any minute."

"I know," Holt said. She was swaying with George in her arms even though he was already asleep. "But I missed an entire day of snuggling."

"Get out here, you big softy," Isabelle said. "You're messing up his routine."

"I think that pretty much went out the window about two hours ago," Holt said. "You know you want in on this."

"I do," Isabelle said. "Hand him over."

Holt passed her their sleeping son. He protested softly and then snuggled into Isabelle. Holt had never seen a more beautiful sight.

"Did you expect you'd love him so much?" she asked softly.

"I didn't expect I *could* love him so much," Isabelle said. "Or you. I wonder if Lola knows the gift she gave us."

"Probably not. How could she? But unless you want every last one of those ruffians parading in here and asking for their turn, we should get out of here while we can."

"Oh sure," Isabelle said. "Now you're in a hurry to wrap this up."

Holt mocked innocence and put her hands up. Isabelle settled George in his crib and followed her out of his room, quietly closing the door behind her.

Holt was barely three steps from George's door when Isabelle had her by the waist and spun her against the wall. Isabelle pushed into her, pinning Holt in place.

"You think you're going to get away with that?"

"I hope not," Holt said.

Isabelle bit down on Holt's neck and ran her hands up her sides, flaring her palms over her breasts. Holt felt her nipples respond instantly.

"If I stick my hand in your pants, am I going to find you wet and hard for me?" Isabelle asked.

"Are you going to find out?" Holt asked.

"No, not yet," Isabelle said. She kissed Holt possessively and sauntering off down the hall.

Holt was sure she was swaying her hips a little extra for her benefit.

"But I'll be thinking about you uncomfortable and ready for the rest of the night. And I'll know I'm the reason why."

The doorbell rang before Holt could do anything she'd regret later, like begging or whimpering.

"You coming?" Isabelle asked.

"Apparently not," Holt said. "Just need a minute."

Isabelle looked back up at her from halfway down the stairs and smiled. It was the smile that made her weak in the knees. The effect hadn't lessened in the time they'd been together, and she suspected it would be that way until the day she died.

She reached in her pocket and felt the ring she'd been carrying with her since she bought it. She still hadn't found the perfect moment to ask Isabelle to marry her. Today when Quinn and Dubs had been in so much danger Holt had watched Max and Lola struggle in their own ways to keep the women they cared about safe. She'd done that for Isabelle in the past and felt guilty that today, she'd felt a measure of relief that it wasn't her in the car, in danger. She'd held on to the ring so tightly it had left indentations in her fingers. It felt as if it was already an extension of the two of them. Now she just needed to get it on Isabelle's finger.

❖

Despite the terrible day, family dinner was as advertised, laughter filled, goofy, and full of love. Quinn had expected to feel uncomfortable in the group, especially as part of something that was clearly so important to everyone, but she felt just the opposite. Lola seemed delighted to share this side of her life with her and was present and attentive. Quinn felt cared for but not smothered. Somehow Lola found the perfect balance.

"Jessica, how is it at Jose's?" Dubs asked. "We won't tell if you want a new roommate."

"Are you kidding?" Jessica asked. "It's amazing. It's enough to make me reconsider my plan to follow Quinn wherever she lands next."

Quinn didn't blame her. She'd never seen a group of people live and work the way Holt and her crew did. Teamwork, collaboration, and collegial spirit weren't just corporate buzzwords. On top of that, they loved each other. And trusted one another. Any one of them would probably be scratched from a movie for being too good to be true, but here was a whole room full of them. *And one of them wants you.*

"That's right, Quinn, Lola said you were applying for jobs. Any word yet?" Isabelle asked.

Quinn felt Lola stiffen next to her. They hadn't really talked much lately about what it would mean for them when she got a job. They'd been too busy running from bad guys and dodging bullets. It felt weird to be talking about it now when just hours ago she and Dubs had been in a firefight. But life didn't stop just because you had a shitty day. She'd always thrown herself into work. Why should today be any different? "Nothing yet, which is frustrating. I interviewed for a position in Michigan a couple of weeks ago. I thought I would have heard about that one by now."

"Lola mentioned you applied to UPVD too," Holt said. "Do they know you're in town?"

"I tried to get a message to the department chair," Quinn said. "But I don't know if it will get relayed. If the psychology department there is anything like CLA, things can get lost in any number of filters."

"Wait, is Albert Castellano still chair?" Isabelle asked.

"He is," Quinn said. She didn't know where Isabelle was going with her question.

"I did his taxes for years."

"I'm the only one he trusts to look at his rattletrap old Volvo," Jose said.

"Went to school with his daughter," Dubs said, holding up her hand.

"Holt, babe, hand me my phone," Isabelle said.

"What are you doing?" Quinn asked. She was appalled at the thought of Isabelle trying to influence a former client on her behalf.

"Calling an old acquaintance to let him know you're in town."

Isabelle stepped out of the room while she waited for Dr. Castellano to answer.

"I don't want him to think I'm abusing his friendships with you all," Quinn said.

"He won't," Holt said. "This is Rhode Island. This sort of thing happens all the time. In LA could you sit down to dinner with a group of people and have three of them be connected independently to the person you are trying to give you a job interview?"

"Unlikely," Quinn said.

"And this isn't even that weird an example," Lola said. "Moose used to housesit for his dentist. And the first apartment I ever got I ended up moving in downstairs from my kindergarten teacher's son. When I moved to a new place, her other son lived on the first floor. Total coincidence."

Isabelle returned and everyone looked at her expectantly.

"Bertie was thrilled to hear you're in town. I gave him your number. He said he'd be calling shortly to set something up."

"Just like that?" Quinn asked. Her cell phone rang.

"Guess so," Isabelle said.

She didn't think she was in any shape to answer questions about her professional goals, her research. She'd almost been shot a few hours ago. She was still shaking and her heart rate was probably four times normal. It certainly felt like it.

But she took a deep breath, answered the phone, and stepped out of the room. Luckily, Dr. Castellano didn't ask why the two grants that were supposed to be her ticket to an independent research career were likely not going to be submitted, or what she was doing in Rhode Island unexpectedly. They agreed on an interview time and hung up.

When she returned to the table it was clear everyone had been trying to eavesdrop but were now pretending they hadn't been. Lola looked at her expectantly.

"I have an interview in two days. Will you help me prepare? This one means a lot to me."

"Of course, yeah, sure," everyone at the table answered.

"Oh, did you mean just Lola?" Dubs asked.

"I'd be happy to," Lola said.

She kissed Lola on the cheek and went back to her dinner. Lola slid her hand onto Quinn's knee under the table. It didn't seem to be a gesture of seduction, instead one of comfort and connection.

Quinn liked the feeling. For the first time since she stepped out of the truck earlier, she stopped shaking. Having a focus for the future helped and made her feel a little bit like her old self. She liked the warmth and solid strength of Lola's hand too. That made her feel like the whole world was new and full of possibility.

CHAPTER TWENTY-THREE

"How did the interview go?" Jessica asked.

"God, Jess, it was amazing. Everything about it was exactly what I want. They're interested in me doing the kind of research I want and there isn't pressure to come in already funded. Which is good since these two grants aren't happening. I would have a little time before they'd expect me to support myself. But this job was a long shot when I applied. I'm not fully qualified. I think they're looking for someone more experienced and established. I still felt that way when I left."

"So what does that mean for you?"

"I don't know. But I heard about the Michigan position I interviewed for a couple of weeks ago. They made an official offer. I don't know what to do about it. I like the position at UPVD so much more. It's just better in every way, except actually being mine. That I have to wait and see about."

When she'd first started applying for faculty positions and thought about leaving her postdoc early, she'd imagined joy, excitement, a sense of adventure and challenge. What she was feeling now was closer to the opposite end of that spectrum.

"In all the years I've trained for my career, nothing has gotten in the way of my goals. Now I feel like I'm about to achieve one of the most important ones, and I've actually thought about throwing it all away. Dubs joked that Holt would try to hire me and I should insist on an obscene salary. It's crazy, but there's a part of me…how can I walk away from her?"

"I'm assuming we're talking about Lola here, not Dubs?"

"A safe assumption."

"Why not ask her to go with you? We could be a little trio off on an adventure. Lola and I could be your guard dogs. I'll be your little Chihuahua and she'll be your big strong Doberman."

"I can't ask her to do that, Jess." Quinn said. *Could I? Lola said she wanted a change. How big a change would she consider?*

"You've got to talk to Lola," Jessica said. "Lay it all out."

"Talk to me about what?" Lola asked as she sauntered in.

"That's my cue to be elsewhere," Jessica said. She scampered out of the room faster than Quinn thought was necessary.

"She's in a hurry," Lola said. "This must be serious."

"Sort of. I guess. I got a job offer." Quinn watched the emotions flit across Lola's face. First confusion, excitement, panic, sadness, tenderness.

"And what does that mean for us?" Lola asked.

"I don't know," Quinn said. "Jessica was just telling me to stop being a coward and talk to you."

"Probably good advice," Lola said. "What do you want?"

"I had my interview this morning at UPVD," Quinn said.

"That's a fact," Lola said. "But what do you want?"

"I got a job offer from Michigan. The position is great. I should be happy, but I'm hesitating. I don't want to make any decisions before I hear from Providence." Quinn felt like she was rambling. She was listing the data points she had and hoping to draw some conclusions.

"Is that what you want? To work at UPVD?"

Quinn considered. Of the two jobs, yes, that was the one she wanted. But was it what she *really wanted*? She looked at Lola and what she needed was clear. She walked to Lola, put her arms around her neck, and kissed her. Lola didn't react immediately, but when she did, she lifted Quinn in her arms. Quinn wrapped her legs around Lola's waist and Lola held her tightly as they kissed.

When they separated, Quinn ran her hands through Lola's hair and traced a finger gently down Lola's cheek. "I want you."

Lola spun them both around until they were laughing. "I want that too," she said. "How do we make it happen?"

"Why do I have to have all the answers?" Quinn asked.

Lola set her down and they both sat. Quinn leaned into Lola's chest.

"Is the job in Michigan good for your career? Is it at a good school? Do they know about the grants?"

"It would be great for my career. They have a very strong, well respected research program," Quinn said. She felt like she was having trouble remembering what her career looked like, what research was, what she did. Her life was so different these days, in mostly negative ways, but in a few very important positive ones as well.

"They do a lot of research that's similar to what I've been doing with my mentor now. The grants hadn't gotten derailed when I interviewed, so that wasn't part of their decision-making. I informed them when they made the offer, but they said it still stood. They expect you to have funding quickly though, so there'd be pressure to write again immediately."

"But you don't want to do that kind of work," Lola said.

It meant a lot that Lola understood her work and career goals to know she might have hesitations with the expectations at Michigan.

"Maybe these grants not going in is a blessing," Quinn said. She was so comfortable against Lola's chest, as if this spot was custom made for her. "I've been thinking about what you asked me, about why I can't do the research I want. I don't think I'm going to submit these. I'm going to propose a project I actually want to build a career around."

"That's my girl," Lola said.

"I hope so," Quinn said.

"Once you take a position," Lola asked. "Is that where you'll be for your whole career?"

"Thankfully, no. Especially not once I have my own money. Researchers can move their grants pretty easily. It's a little complicated if you have a special population you're recruiting from a specific site, but people move institutions all the time." Quinn thought about it. Obviously, it wasn't ideal, but perhaps they could make a long distance relationship work for a while and then figure out how to be together down the line. "Were you thinking if I moved to Michigan in a few years I might be able to move back here to be with you?" Her heart ached at the thought of two or three years of only seeing Lola a few weekends at a time.

"Close," Lola said. "I was thinking if we both moved to Michigan, we could move back at some point, but only after I finished my undergraduate degree. How long does that take?"

"Is Holt opening a satellite office?"

"Before all the shit really hit the fan with the CMCs, Holt said she'd pay for me to go to school, full-time or part-time, it's up to me. If I'm still in the area, the director of Holt's charity is looking to retire in five or so years and wants to hand it off to someone who really cares. Holt thought of me, which is incredibly flattering. The charity helps kids who are headed down a bad path straighten out their lives. It hits close to home because of my brother."

"Is this what you were talking about when you implied you might not be a bounty hunter for much longer? How do you feel about it?" Quinn was just starting to get used to the idea that Lola could spring into action at a moment's notice and stop a speeding bullet in her teeth. Somewhere along the line it had become a little bit of a turn-on, despite the scary parts.

"I'm a little nervous, to be honest. I didn't even finish high school, and college seems daunting. But I figure I have one of the most brilliant women in the world right here to help me if I get stuck, so what could go wrong?"

"You better not have one of the most brilliant women in the world," Quinn said. "I'm protective of what's mine and I don't like sharing." To prove her point she kissed Lola, slowly at first, then deepened the kiss until they were both breathing heavily.

"No one but you," Lola said, gasping.

Lola seemed interested in continuing what Quinn had started with the kiss, but Quinn wasn't done talking. Her mind was still churning with all the new information and she needed to process it.

"What happens to Holt's college tuition offer if you leave Rhode Island with me?"

"Doesn't matter where I go," Lola said. "I can choose any college I want. Holt reiterated the offer last night and made that part very clear. She must suspect I was considering following you. She usually knows things are happening three steps before anyone else."

Quinn appreciated the unspoken support from Holt. She knew it meant a lot to Lola. It meant a lot to her too. She'd come to respect Holt, even in the short time they'd known each other. "But what about the charity?"

"What about it?" Lola asked. "It's a great opportunity if I'm here. The charity is amazing and something I would be happy to be associated with. But it, or something like it, will be available if I come back someday. Or I'll find something else I love. No job is more important to me than you. Besides, I don't know what I might be interested in doing once I'm done with my education. All I've ever done is work for Holt. It's all I know, all I've ever known, but there's a big world out there. Maybe I'll be an engineer, or a paleontologist."

"Ugh, then I'll have to follow you all over the world while you dig up dinosaur bones," Quinn said.

"Nah, that wouldn't work for me anyway," Lola said. "I'm a fan of malls and creature comforts. Dirty little secret."

"I won't tell," Quinn said. "Superficial question. Are you keeping these if you change careers?" Quinn ran her fingers along Lola's biceps and up and over her shoulders. "I'm a big fan."

"Seems like we've got some time to make that decision," Lola said. She was laughing but seemed to be enjoying the attention. "But if you like them this much, I think I'm going to be pretty damned motivated to keep them. Before you distract me completely, tell me more about your interview today."

Reluctantly, Quinn stopped massaging Lola's muscles and relaxed back into her arms. She'd never had anyone to share these kinds of important life decisions with. It felt sublime.

"The interview here today seemed to go well too. I loved the department, and the job is a dream. It's everything I told you it was, including out of my reach. So I'm going to ask the Michigan folks for a few weeks to decide and keep my fingers crossed that Jose's mechanical wizardry is enough of a recommendation to set me apart and get me the job here."

"Did Jose really come up in the interview today?"

"He most certainly did. I said he was currently very graciously hosting my best friend as a houseguest. Dr. Castellano is enamored with Jose."

"Everyone is," Lola said. "It's part of his charm. So we have you and Jose on our side for Providence. I like our chances of staying right here."

Quinn hesitated when she thought about what Lola was offering. Could she really leave her whole life, all of her friends, family dinners, to take a chance on her? "Lola, I want you. I want you to come with me if I leave, but I can't ask you to do that," Quinn said.

"You aren't asking, but it wouldn't be out of line if you did. I want to go where you go, wherever that is, as long as that's what you want too. We want this to work, but there's a real chance you are going to move. If you have to take the job in Michigan, that's not negotiable, but my job is."

"But all your friends are here. Your job." *Shut up. Why are you trying to talk her out of this?*

"And they'll still be my friends, even if we live across the country, or the world."

"How can you be so sure that giving up your whole life here to follow me and my career is the right decision? What if I let you down?" *Seriously, what's wrong with you? Shut up.*

"That's easy," Lola said. "You could never let me down. It's just not possible."

Quinn was in Lola's arms before she remembered to be careful of her still healing injuries. She tried to loosen her hold, but Lola just pulled her tighter.

"I know there isn't data to collect or past research to consult saying this is going to work out. We have to trust how we feel, which is a little unscientific. I know that's not your usual style, but I'm not letting go unless you tell me to."

"You know my whole family disowned me when I came out," Quinn said. "You have no idea how much it means that you want to fight for me."

"Anyone who would let you out of their life, especially when they could do something about it, is a fool," Lola said. "I will always fight for you. As long as there's fight in me."

Quinn didn't know what it meant to share her life with someone else, to lean on, love, and support each other. The people who were supposed to do that for her in her early years had cut bait at the first chance. Now she had Lola. Part of her wanted to take the Michigan job so they could start fresh without all of Lola's friends and family, so she could have her all to herself. But she would never do that to her. She was just excited about the possibility of building something she'd always wanted with an amazing woman.

CHAPTER TWENTY-FOUR

Quinn watched the flurry of activity from across the room. Max and Holt were at the center of it, which she assumed meant Max's program had just jumped to a new phone. They'd been tracking the CMCs via cellular communication for three days and were beginning to flush out a picture of their network. Since the bluesnarfing had started paying off, Max had left the financial inquiry to Isabelle and had gone full-time tech. Isabelle, in turn, had teamed up with Dubs and Quinn. They'd formed a power trio analyzing the tremendous amount of data coming in from the phones. The CMCs were a very social group.

They were also chatty and had been emailing Holt or calling the office regularly to threaten Isabelle, George, Quinn, Jessica, and Isabelle's sister, Ellen, and her family. The threats of violence were graphic, and after listening to the first one, Quinn had declined to hear a second. Just knowing they were still coming was enough for her.

Holt said Sam was getting threats now too. Since the attack on Quinn and Dubs, Holt seemed more driven to close this case. She was single-mindedly focused on LA, the CMCs, and a potential mystery player. Lola said Holt and Sam talked multiple times a day. Quinn wasn't sure anything could stop Holt now. Watching her work, she almost felt sorry for the CMCs. They didn't know what they had unleashed.

So far, they hadn't detected any communications that indicated any CMCs, aside from their friends from the sedan, were in Rhode

Island or headed east. That didn't mean they could rule it out. They weren't picking up all of the network chatter.

In addition to background, Lola and Moose were running security for all locations where crew members were congregating, eating, sleeping, or working. Isabelle and Holt's house was locked down tighter than the governor's residence, with security twenty-four hours a day. Lola and Quinn were sleeping at Holt's. So was Moose. Everyone else had been moved to the loft apartments where Max and Dubs were living. The entire crew, newbies included, had rotating guard shifts.

"At least our joy ride wasn't in vain," Dubs said.

"I'm disappointed in you, Dubs," Isabelle said. "That's the best you could do? No fancy word I have to pretend to know and look up later?"

"To be honest, I get a little nervous around Dr. Golden," Dubs said.

Quinn laughed. "That's a complete lie."

"Fine," Dubs said. "We've been working on this data set, as you call it, for so long I couldn't think of nugatory or otiose fast enough. This is what you erudite people reduce me too."

"I'm really feeling for you, Dubs. Not like it was your idea to sort the data by call volume to try and establish a hierarchy, after all."

They'd had been struggling to make sense of the huge volume of data until Dubs had suggested they look for a pattern in who was calling and texting whom. She'd argued in a staff meeting that lowly soldiers would call, text, or email the much smaller number of people higher up the food chain, but the number of return messages would be relatively small. Bosses didn't need to initiate frequent contact unless there was a problem. Especially when the work was illegal and communications might be monitored.

As soon as they had that framework to work with, they'd made real progress. They'd identified an extensive network of lowly foot soldiers and what were probably rather unimportant lower level lieutenants. Sam, from the LAPD, was able to confirm most of what they found, or at least parts of it. They provided batches of names and for those she knew were CMCs and could provide information, what she shared reinforced that their model was working.

Quinn was surprised at how much she was enjoying this work. She got the same thrill working on this data set that she had back in her lab at CLA. It seemed working with data, making sense out of chaos, and finding the hidden meaning in a mass of numbers was something that excited her no matter where the data was coming from.

They were just starting to piece together some of the more interesting and fruitful upper management positions. When new data came in, someone would run the name over to Isabelle, who would add it to her spreadsheet for financial research if necessary. Dubs and Quinn would enter the relevant data points to be added to the model Quinn had built.

"Holy shit," Quinn said.

"Good or bad?" Isabelle asked. "Can go either way around here."

"That new phone," Quinn said. "Max just sent over the data. Take a look."

Isabelle looked over Quinn's shoulder, jockeying for position with Dubs.

"Is that?" Dubs asked.

"Holy shit indeed," Isabelle said. She called to Holt who was by her side in an instant. "It looks like your fishing paid off. You currently have Malcolm on the line. Maybe now we can get some answers about who's pulling his strings."

Quinn knew her posture was stiff and she was grinding her teeth. This was the man who had beaten Lola nearly to death. She wished there was a way to exact some form of revenge instead of looking through his contacts like a switchboard peeping tom.

"Holt, can you and Dubs get started on putting Malcolm's contacts up? I've got to ask Quinn something. We'll be right there."

Holt looked confused but didn't ask questions. As soon as they were out of earshot, Isabelle turned to Quinn. Quinn saw Isabelle looked concerned.

"You okay, Quinn?"

"This is the guy who beat Lola."

"Yes, that's true." Isabelle looked at her kindly. She didn't say anything else. She was clearly waiting for Quinn to explain what had her on edge.

"All I can think about is hurting him. Making him feel what she felt, or what I felt. I've never believed in the eye for an eye philosophy, but I want to hurt him. Do you know what it's like to think the person you love is dead?" *Did I just say love?*

"Yes, actually," Isabelle said. "I watched Holt get shot in the chest from point-blank range. Jose saved her life by insisting she wear a bulletproof tuxedo that night, but as the bullet hit her, I was sure she was dead."

"Bulletproof tuxedo?" Quinn asked. "Who are you people?"

"I'm an accountant, remember?" Isabelle said. "And I keep telling you, you kind of get used to the rest of them."

"Says the woman on the arm of the founder of the Justice League."

"Someone has to be," Isabelle said. "Might as well be me."

"Right, she really settled. Even a blind man could see how crazy she is for you," Quinn said.

"Thank you," Isabelle said. "It would seem you and Lola are pretty solid as well, given that you want to go back to LA to avenge her beating."

"I think I'm in love with her," Quinn said. "I know Lola told you she said she'd move anywhere I go for work. I want her to come with me so badly, but I feel like I should be telling her not to. Her whole life is here, with all of you."

"That's ridiculous," Isabelle said.

That caught Quinn by surprise. Isabelle was usually so calm, but she sounded a little peeved.

"She's choosing to make a life with you. The only reason to tell her not to go with you is if you don't want her with you."

"I want her there," Quinn said quietly.

"Then I'll make a deal with you," Isabelle said. "You don't do anything rash, like going after Malcolm or convincing Max to redirect a missile to his general vicinity, and I'll remind you that none of us, including Lola, think you're stealing her, as often as you need it."

"Before I agree," Quinn said. "Are you angry at the man who tried to kill Holt?"

"Yes," Isabelle said. "But at the time I was also angry at Holt. The man, Decker, was after me, but she goaded him into coming after her instead. To protect me. I know now that she'll do anything to protect me, but at the time, her job and that single-minded focus were sticking points for us."

"Somehow I get the sense it's not Holt who captains the ship around here." Quinn knew everyone called Isabelle "Queen." It didn't take her long to observe why.

"I let her handle the icky things and the things that require doors to be kicked in. But I'd kick in a door to save her ass if I had to," Isabelle said. "That's the beautiful thing about true love and trust. Every once in a while, when you really need it, you can ask the person you love to step outside their comfort zone, to trust you, and they will, because you've never let them down."

"I'd pay good money to see you wielding an automatic rifle to save Holt's buns," Quinn said.

"She should be so lucky," Isabelle said. "But no guns. Holt hates them."

"Seriously? What if you were under siege? Not even in self-defense?"

"I honestly have no idea what would happen if a small army descended on us. My plan would be the same whether Holt was shooting back or not. Duck and cover, let them handle the superhero stuff. So, do you agree to my deal? Trust Lola?"

"Yes," Quinn said. "And thank you."

Isabelle reached out and squeezed Quinn's hand. "Excellent. Let's get back to work."

They made their way to the conference room where Holt and Dubs were staring at Max's fancy touch screen. It was filled with names and numbers. Quinn assumed they were Malcolm's contacts.

"This doesn't make any sense," Dubs said.

"Get Lola in here," Holt said. "See if she recognizes anyone on this list. Maybe she can make sense of it."

"What's the problem?" Isabelle asked.

"Malcolm's contacts. There's only a single connection to the CMCs, but Lola said he was in charge when she encountered them," Holt said.

Quinn thought she looked frustrated.

"Second phone?"

"Always a possibility," Holt said.

Dubs returned to the conference room with Lola, who had been working with Moose in the other room. Lola looked over the list of contacts carefully.

"What's wrong?" Isabelle asked Holt.

"Something isn't right here. I just can't put my finger on it. And it's driving me nuts."

"Just with Malcolm?"

"Nah. There's something more. I'm missing something, like it's just there, in my peripheral."

"Anything jumping out at you, Lola?" Holt asked.

"Kind of. I mean, I wouldn't believe this was Malcolm's phone data if I hadn't met him or we hadn't extracted the information ourselves. What I know of him means this list doesn't make sense."

"Explain," Holt said.

"The people I recognize from my research in LA are city councilmen and women and a few prominent local business owners. That one," Lola pointed to one of the contacts, "is the superintendent of the Los Angeles School District."

"How do you know all this? I've lived in LA most of my life and have no idea who any of these people are," Quinn said. Lola had talked about how much she liked watching Quinn work, but she was enjoying watching Lola work too. She totally got why people found cops attractive. Lola didn't have a uniform, but it turned out the crime fighting thing worked for her. If she could extricate herself from direct involvement, all the better.

"Research when I first arrived," Lola said. "Figured it couldn't hurt to be thorough, that it might come in handy."

"Impressive, my love," Quinn said. Lola didn't seem to notice her affectionate term, but Dubs certainly did. Dubs looked liked a golden retriever puppy who was trying her hardest to contain her excited wiggle, but mostly failing. That was kind of how Lola made Quinn feel on the inside too.

"So, gumshoe," Dubs said. "What does it all mean?"

"I have to do all the work around here?" Lola asked.

"Obviously," Dubs said.

"Fine," Lola said. "Then make yourself useful as my lackey." Lola shooed Dubs toward the screen.

"Oh, I didn't sign up for that," Dubs said. "Why don't you get Quinn to do whatever you're about to ask of me?"

"For your own good, we're all ignoring that. Now get up to the screen." Lola studied the list of names again. "We're going to sort everyone I recognize into groups. Quinn, can you do a basic Google search on the rest and see if anything useful comes up?"

"This is good," Holt said. "Lola, how far along were you and Moose in your compilation of background on LA during the CMC's rise?"

"We were almost done," Lola said. "He's probably just finishing up our report."

"You guys keep working here. I'm going to help Moose. Everyone gives a report in an hour."

Quinn marveled at the speed at which things happened here. She figured when there were life-or-death consequences, speed mattered, but even with a few days of relative calm, everyone had been working quickly and efficiently. It was so different from her research lab which was dependent on participant recruitment and whatever pace those at the top of the hierarchy felt like working.

"We've got it covered, H."

Lola, Quinn, and Dubs searched and sorted through Malcolm's entire contact list until they'd divided everyone into three categories: business, CMC, and "other," probably friends and family. As they'd suspected earlier, there was only one name they'd thus far been able to connect to the CMCs listed in Malcolm's phone. Even that guy was a high-ranking member who also ran a legitimate business. To an outsider, Malcolm would look like an up-and-coming mover and shaker in the LA political and business world, not the leader of a violent street gang.

"This still doesn't make any sense," Dubs said. "What is up with this guy?"

"I think I might have the answer," Holt said. She poked her head back in the conference room. "Give me a minute to get the rest of the group."

Quinn watched as everyone jostled for chairs and fought over the best seats. Quinn didn't care where she sat. Lola pulled out a chair for her and took the seat to her right. Quinn saw Isabelle didn't join the scrum. She took the chair no one else had attempted to claim.

"Lola, can you get us up to speed on what you guys found?" Holt asked. She stood at the front of the room.

"Sure. Malcolm appears, on the surface, like an aspiring businessman or politician. His phone is a who's who of movers and shakers in LA city happenings. The only CMC contact is also a big business guy. If I didn't have personal experience with the guy, I would say he's trying to build something other than a name for the CMCs."

"I think that's because he is," Holt said. "I remembered reading an article about how small businesses are starting to grow in unlikely neighborhoods in LA. It's gotten national attention as a model to replicate. Max, can you pull up the maps from the article?"

Max tapped her tablet and wiped the large screen of the lists Lola and her small team had been working on.

"You better have hit save before you did that, Pretty Girl," Dubs said.

Max rolled her eyes. "This is a map of the areas from Holt's article," she said. "And this," she layered a second map on top, "is data we got from Sam about areas the CMCs have taken control of since they came into existence."

The two maps overlaid almost identically.

"Those crime statistics that were so low were for those areas too," Dubs said.

"What does this mean? Do we like this guy now, if a gang is actually making things better?" Moose asked.

"I don't," Quinn said. "I don't care what his neighborhood maps look like." She put her hand protectively on Lola's leg. The image of Lola being dumped on the sidewalk would always stay with her.

"As with most things," Holt said, "I think it's probably quite complicated. We clearly don't have all the facts, but if I had to speculate, it looks like he's performing hostile takeovers of other gangs' territories, and then trying to bring in businesses and opportunity to previously neglected neighborhoods. It's an interesting model for revitalization. I would be curious how he's viewed by the residents of these neighborhoods."

"So the CMCs aren't a violent street gang after all?" Dubs asked. She threw her hands up in defeat.

"They're incredibly violent," Max said. "They crush their rivals. Especially early in their expansion, they annihilated the competition. Sam said things are starting to settle in terms of the violence. Maybe other gangs are seeing the writing on the wall and choosing to assimilate." Max shrugged.

"And I'm sure the narrative that the CMCs are a vicious and brutal gang willing to do anything to defend their territory is helpful for fending off rivals and border skirmishes," Lola said. "Are we sure that everyone they assimilate stays on as a soldier? Gangsters join up for all kinds of reasons, but having a place to belong, people you can count on, and opportunities in your community are usually high on the list. If these neighborhoods are stabilizing, the appeal of the gangs might lessen." She moved to the front of the room and looked at the map more closely.

"The question becomes, is that a consequence or the desired outcome?" Holt said. "Former soldiers who are getting a second chance in their own neighborhood would be powerful protectors."

"But how does Malcolm convince the power players in the political and business world to invest in his neighborhoods when they're controlled by the CMCs?" Isabelle asked. "If I'm a small business owner and I can open a shop anywhere in the city, a place under the control of a street gang with a violent reputation, no matter the decrease in crime statistics, isn't going to be particularly attractive to me."

"He's got to have help," Holt said. "Someone more powerful who can funnel the types of opportunities he wants for his community in his direction."

"The election," Lola said. She smacked Holt's shoulder in her excitement.

Everyone looked at her. Quinn knew that look on Lola's face. She'd seen it when Lola had figured out a neuroscience concept she'd been explaining to her, or when she found one of Quinn's classes particularly interesting.

"The mayoral election in LA had more money in the campaigns of the candidates than any other before. It was a two-way race for most of the spring, but a dark horse candidate entered in the early summer. He hit hard on law and order and lowering crime in high risk neighborhoods."

"I read some of those articles," Moose said. "LA was pretty desensitized to gang violence, so his message wasn't resonating, but then the CMCs sprang onto the scene a couple months after he entered the race and they really started taking off that fall."

Quinn remembered that campaign. She hadn't bought into the hysteria, but plenty of others had.

"His message was effective," Quinn said.

"But he didn't just promise to crack down on crime," Lola said. "He campaigned on rebuilding the gang-ravaged communities. He harped on it. I watched footage. Over and over, he talked about how he would bring in new businesses, make the streets safe for kids to play in their front yards or walk home from school."

Quinn couldn't believe the mayor could be involved with the CMCs. That he would have anything to do with almost getting her killed.

"Lots of people campaign on those kinds of messages though," Quinn said.

"Sure, of course," Lola said. "This is all speculation for now. But it's rather coincidental. It makes sense, in a twisted way. Tell people there's a major gang problem, and when they ignore you, put a violent gang in place to show them it's true. Then promise to clean up the city and help businesses, and use the gang you've got in place to make it happen. You win your election, neighborhoods get better, and you're in control of the biggest and most violent gang in the city. Perfect political concoction if you're into cynical, horrible, immoral things. He was also accused of misappropriating massive amounts of campaign funds, although he was never charged and there was no formal investigation. The allegations just quietly disappeared."

"Was there ever a number attached to the allegations?" Holt asked. She looked like she was buying Lola's theory.

"About ten million dollars," Lola said.

Moose let out a low whistle. "Well, that can't be a coincidence."

"Is the mayor on Malcolm's contact list?" Holt asked.

"Yes," Dubs said. She looked like the cat who ate the canary, but Dubs, Quinn was learning, often looked that way.

"So is his top aide. And Malcolm calls him a lot."

"I want a secure video chat with Sam, right now," Holt said. "Not another officer on her entire force. Understood?"

Max got up to set up the call. Quinn still had a hard time believing the mayor of LA was responsible, but the data was convincing. The fact that Holt and her crew were pulling on these loose strings was likely what made them such a threat to the CMCs in the first place. They were tenacious investigators, but also smart and resourceful.

Quinn's cell phone rang. Everyone jumped. "Not Malcolm," Quinn said. "But I do need to take it."

UPVD was calling. Quinn's stomach was in knots. *Here we go.*

CHAPTER TWENTY-FIVE

Quinn waited until she was out of the conference room before answering the call. It was from a Rhode Island number, and aside from the people in this building, there was only one other place in Rhode Island that would be calling her. Her hand shook as she answered the call.

"Hello, this is Dr. Golden."

"Quinn, hello, it's Albert Castellano. I hope you are well."

What Quinn wanted to say was, the mayor of LA was corrupt, she felt like throwing up, and her level of wellness depended a lot on what he had to say, but instead she answered, "Fine, thank you. And you?" She needed Jessica's moral support, and she was visiting Jose in the garage. Jose's shop was connected to Holt's office, and she'd only have to be outside for a couple of steps. She looked cautiously out the door and darted out. She was in Jose's shop in three quick bounds.

"Wonderful. I'm sorry it's taken me so long to get back to you about the faculty position. We had a candidate interviewing from overseas, and the time change was a nightmare for scheduling. I don't really enjoy interviews over videoconference, but sometimes it's the only way."

For God's sake, get to the point. She forced out some benign agreeable statements she hoped wouldn't prolong his chatter. No one else was in the garage. Jessica and Jose must have gone out for lunch. She wished Jessica were there to hold her hand.

"I wasn't really calling to talk to you about videoconferencing, obviously. A formal offer will be forthcoming, but I know you probably have people banging down your door. We don't want to lose the opportunity to have a brilliant young scientist like you join our team, Dr. Golden. I'm calling to extend a formal offer to work at the University of Providence. I know the relocation to Providence would be quite an adjustment, but the city has a lot to offer."

Quinn jumped in the air and flipped the antenna on a car Jose had the engine out of. It gave a celebratory "thwap" as it snapped back in response. He'd just offered her a dream job, and it was in Lola's city. *We don't have to move.* She thought about the fact that Providence already felt like home. How could it not when Lola lived here and she'd met such wonderful people? She couldn't wait to tell everyone. Jessica would be thrilled. She leaned against the car while she finished her call.

Despite her excitement, she did the professional thing and told Dr. Castellano how much she appreciated the offer and would look over the formal proposal when it arrived later that afternoon. She promised him she wouldn't accept anything else without talking to him first. It was very nice to be so desired professionally.

She turned around to head back to Holt's side of the building when two men came up behind her. They jostled her out the big rolling door where cars drove in before she was able to fully process what was happening. One of the men tried to grab her arm. The hairs stood up on the back of her neck.

Lola doesn't know where you are. You have to fight this like she would.

She swatted his hand away and swung her arm wildly. It connected with the first man's face. She didn't see where. Then she kicked him in the leg. He groaned. She turned to the second man and kicked out. She was aiming for his shin but missed. She ended up hitting him square in the nuts.

He gurgled something unintelligible and went down. Quinn ran. The first man wasn't incapacitated and pursued. Quinn tried to get to Jose's shop, but she was cut off. He held out his arms to keep her from running past, his smile menacing. Quinn turned and ran down the alley, knowing he was right behind her. She still had her phone in her hand. She tried to unlock it unsuccessfully. Voice recognition didn't work. Apparently, it didn't understand panting panic. She considered throwing her phone at the man chasing her, but then Max wouldn't have any way of tracking her.

The panic button!

Quinn slid her screen and activated the panic button. When Max had gotten everyone equipped with new phones, she'd insisted Quinn and Jessica get the same software upgrades the rest of Holt's crew had.

Quinn saw a fast food restaurant up ahead. If she could make it, there'd be people. Hopefully, diners would take note of a kidnapping if she made a big enough fuss.

But Quinn didn't make it to the restaurant before Lola screeched to the curb on her motorcycle. Lola leapt off and landed in a fighting stance, her body in front of Quinn, protecting her. Quinn peered around Lola and saw the man scurrying off. She noticed he was limping badly, which she wasn't sorry about in the least.

Lola turned back to Quinn. She ran her hands up and down Quinn's arms. She wasn't wearing a helmet so her hair was wild around her face. There was fear in her eyes and she looked over every part of Quinn, probably checking for injuries.

"What happened?" Lola asked.

"I left your office and went to Jose's shop while I took my phone call. I just wanted to see Jessica. When I headed back, two guys tried to force me out the door. I kicked one hard enough in the crotch to bring him down, and then I tried to get back, but I couldn't. The other one was chasing me. Then I remembered the panic button." Quinn pointed to the man moving quickly away.

Lola repeated the information, seemingly to no one, then cocked her head like she was listening. She must have noticed Quinn's puzzlement because she pointed to her ear and mouthed "earpiece."

"I'm getting her out of here. You want us back at the shop?"

Lola handed Quinn a helmet, tied her own hair back in a tight bun, and flicked at her own ear.

"Where's yours?" Quinn asked. She didn't like the idea of Lola riding without a helmet.

"Not required for the driver," Lola said. "I usually wear one, but I left in a hurry. I'll be careful. It's not far."

They straddled the bike and Lola roared from the curb. Quinn expected to return to the office and the rest of Lola's crew, but she hung a left and took them in an entirely different direction, to a part of town Quinn hadn't been.

Lola pulled into the parking lot of what looked like an old warehouse. The neighborhood was a little rough around the edges, but Quinn trusted Lola. She would follow her anywhere she led, even into a weird looking building in a less than gentrified area.

The main entrance wasn't much to look at either, but once they were inside, Quinn was impressed. The industrial roots had been completely renovated. The front desk attendant greeted Lola by name.

Lola took Quinn's hand and led her down the hall. They took the stairs to the third floor. There were numbered doors along the hallway, and Quinn realized it was an apartment building. *A beautiful one.* Lola let them into 3C.

The space was a loft with an open floor plan. The kitchen was updated, and everything was brand new. Quinn walked over to the floor to ceiling windows on one wall and looked up. The ceiling had to be twenty feet high. They were high enough to see downtown Providence and college hill. It was spectacular.

She turned back and examined the rest of the loft more closely. There was one armchair pulled up in front of the gas fireplace and a folding table. Other than that, there was no furniture in the entire space.

"What is this place?"

"Somewhere safe," Lola said. "Holt didn't want us going back to the office until she had a chance to talk to those guys."

"So I didn't overreact?" Quinn felt the fear returning. She also felt foolish for leaving the office and requiring rescue.

"No. God no. That's what the panic button is for. No one should ever lay a hand on you. If they do, you should always feel free to push the panic button or call me. We'll all show up and explain our feelings on how you should be treated."

"I only saw you," Quinn said. "Who else was there?"

"Moose and Holt. But they're ghosts when they want to be. I was on rescue duty so I could be splashy."

"I'm sorry they're in danger now. Those guys were CMCs weren't they? I shouldn't have left the office. I didn't think it would be risky to walk over to see Jessica. That was dumb." Quinn couldn't believe she'd almost been kidnapped and that now Holt and Moose were heading off into danger. She thought of Isabelle and what she must be feeling.

"You didn't do anything wrong," Lola said as if reading her mind. "It's only a couple of steps to Jose's shop."

"Oh my God, are Jessica and Jose okay? What were those two doing over there?"

"They're fine. They were eating lunch in the back office, but the fact that the bad guys were there and we didn't know is concerning. Holt is going to worry herself into an ulcer over that. The office is secure, but Jose argued he needed to run his business without it looking like the New England crime families were having some repair work done. You should've been able to walk over and see the Little Chihuahua. Next time though, let me know where you're going so I can walk with you. Then I won't have to come flying in to the rescue."

"I liked it," Quinn said. She traced a finger down Lola's neck and along her collarbone. "How many ladies can phone for their very own superhero to come to the rescue?"

"Oh, I'm not sure I qualify," Lola said. She stepped forward slowly, forcing Quinn back.

"I think every superhero would say that to protect their secret identity." Quinn took another step back and bumped into the kitchen counter. Lola stepped forward again and pinned her there, their bodies pressed together. Lola felt so good and strong and solid when once again everything else felt so chaotic.

Lola ran her fingers through Quinn's hair and dipped her head to kiss just below her ear. As she did, she whispered, "Only one way to find out."

"Are you implying I might find a spandex suit under this enticing wardrobe?" Quinn said, tugging at Lola's shirt.

Lola lifted Quinn onto the kitchen counter effortlessly and kissed her. Quinn wrapped her legs around Lola's waist, pulling her tight. Lola deepened the kiss and moved her hands to Quinn's ass and squeezed. Quinn moaned and ground her center against Lola's abdomen.

She pulled at Lola's shirt and got it off with minimal interruption to their kissing. She didn't find a super suit, but nearly naked Lola was more than enough.

"Oh my God," Quinn said. "You just keep getting better. Take off your bra, then undress me."

Lola's eyes flared. Quinn could tell she was enjoying the power dynamic. She had the first time they met. Quinn did too. She liked that Lola let her be in control, when Lola was in charge in so many other ways. She was throbbing and Lola hadn't even touched her yet.

Slowly, Lola unclasped her bra and let it fall to the floor. That almost undid Quinn's resolve. Lola's breasts were tight and perfect. She ached to touch them, but Lola was working on her clothes and wouldn't let her hands wander. Maybe the power dynamic wasn't as one-sided as she thought. Quinn liked this too.

Lola lifted Quinn's shirt and discarded it, then did the same for her bra. She feathered kisses along her collarbones and down her chest. Lola circled her nipples but didn't give them any attention. Quinn gripped the countertop to keep her hands still.

Much too quickly for Quinn's liking, Lola moved back up and kissed her again. Then she unbuttoned Quinn's jeans, gently laid her flat on the counter, and finished undressing her. Quinn tried to sit up off the cold granite, but Lola held her gently in place. She pulled her closer to the edge and rested one of Quinn's legs on her shoulders. Lola dipped her head and stroked her tongue along Quinn's clit. Quinn moaned loudly.

That seemed all the encouragement Lola needed. She sucked Quinn's clit into her mouth, nearly sending Quinn over the edge, then let go, stood up, and scooped Quinn off the counter and carried her to the living room.

"Sorry, there isn't a bed," Lola said. "But I have this." Lola flicked on the fireplace and kicked out a blanket in front of it, over the plush rug. She laid Quinn down carefully and was about to join her when Quinn stopped her.

"No pants allowed on my blanket."

"Yes, ma'am," Lola said and made short work of the rest of her clothes.

Quinn enjoyed the view. Lola's body was spectacular. She was muscled and strong, but so beautifully feminine. She looked like she could bench press a car in the morning and walk a catwalk in the evening.

"You're beautiful," Quinn said.

"That's my line," Lola said. "But I'm glad you like what you see. It's all yours."

She kissed her again, and this time Quinn wasn't shy about letting her hands wander. Lola moved on top of her and her leg slid between Quinn's. Lola kept a steady pressure as they kissed, bringing Quinn higher.

Quinn felt drunk with pleasure. Being with Lola, touching her, was intoxicating. She grabbed Lola's ass and demanded more. Lola resisted and rolled off of her, smoothing her hand down Quinn's stomach and making small, teasing circles just above the apex of her thighs. She lowered her mouth to Quinn's chest and traced first one nipple, then the other before sucking one into her mouth.

Pleasure shot through Quinn. She wanted Lola everywhere. How could one woman make her feel so much? She knotted her fingers in Lola's hair and held her tightly to her breast. Lola switched her attentions to the other nipple and moved her hand lower, just teasing her clit. Quinn wasn't sure how much more she could take. She was aching for release, but loving the buildup. Lola had her on razor's edge, touching her just enough to hint at release and then backing away.

"I need you," Quinn said when Lola removed all pressure from her center once more.

Lola moved back up Quinn's body and reclaimed her mouth. Their kiss was fierce and hungry. She rolled them so Quinn was on top, straddling Lola's hips.

"Take what you need," Lola said. She moved her hand lower and slipped two fingers into Quinn, rubbing her clit with her thumb.

Quinn bit down on Lola's neck. Lola groaned in pleasure and started moving her fingers in a steady rhythm. Quinn rode Lola's fingers, her pleasure building rapidly. *So good. Fuck, it's so good.*

She came in a wave of ecstasy.

Lola tried to roll them again, but Quinn stopped her. She eased off of Lola's fingers and slid down Lola's body. She paid brief attention to her breasts, she would be back to those soon, but right now, she wanted Lola to feel what she was feeling.

Quinn slid farther down until she was between Lola's legs. She kissed Lola's inner thighs and carefully parted her. Quinn flicked her tongue along Lola's length. Lola whimpered at the soft touch. That was all Quinn needed.

She stroked with her tongue until she heard Lola's breathing become erratic and she knew she was close. She reached up and took one rock hard nipple between her fingers, teasing it, then the other. Lola arched off the blanket under her, but Quinn pushed her back down.

Quinn moved her hand back down Lola's body and slipped two fingers inside her, matching the rhythm of her mouth. Lola came in her mouth with a cry. She removed her fingers slowly and wriggled up Lola's body so she was draped over her. Lola held her tightly.

"I love you," Quinn said.

Lola had been making lazy circles on Quinn's back, but she stopped abruptly. Quinn hadn't meant to tell Lola how she felt, but it had slipped out. It was also true, and now that she'd said it once, she wanted to tell Lola again and again. Hopefully, Lola wouldn't mind.

Lola flipped Quinn onto her back and pinned her hands above her head. "You love me?"

"I do," Quinn said.

"You, Dr. Quinn Golden, love me, high school dropout?" Lola kissed her nose.

"Yes, I love you," Quinn said. Lola's smile was contagious and Quinn stole kisses every few words.

"The genius neuroscientist loves the unrefined bounty hunter?"

"I'll argue with your labeling, but yes," Quinn said. They were both laughing.

"And how would you describe us?" Lola asked.

"The lab rat loves the gym rat," Quinn said. "Or the science nerd loves the superhero." She ran her hands along the muscles in Lola's back. *My superhero.*

"Whatever I am," Lola said. "I love you too."

"Let's move in here," Quinn said. "We won't have to worry about waking up George."

"There's no furniture here," Lola said.

"But it's your apartment, right?" Quinn had noticed the way the woman at the front desk greeted Lola. And the armchair was a match for the one in Lola's studio apartment in Holt's attic.

"It was going to be," Lola said. She looked sad.

"Tell me."

"When I was going to keep George, I realized I couldn't do it in the attic apartment. So I asked Holt to get me one of these places. After I decided not to keep him and things went sideways with our case, I didn't feel right moving in here. It didn't seem like I should be rewarded for screwing up."

Quinn gave Lola a disapproving look.

"I know, I know. Holt kept the apartment for me in case I changed my mind, but as you can see, I've not really done much to make it a home. I should probably give it up so someone else can really use it." She rolled off Quinn onto her back and stared at the fire. Quinn followed her. Now she was on top.

"Hold on to it a little longer," Quinn said. "If UPVD comes through, it would be nice to not be living with Holt and Isabelle on my first day of work." Although she had a verbal offer, Quinn wanted to see the formal offer in writing before she told Lola. She knew how much it would mean to Lola to be able to stay in Providence, and she didn't want to get her hopes up only to have a quirk in the contract derail the entire thing. It was only until tomorrow morning. Any longer and she would tell her.

Quinn lay awake in Lola's arms long after Lola fell asleep. She looked around the loft and tried to picture making a life in the space. It was remarkably easy. The loft was gorgeous. Unfortunately, she could also see anxiety and stress hiding in the nooks and crannies. She knew staying in Providence and loving Lola meant agreeing to living with worry and fear as well. But she didn't have a choice. Loving Lola wasn't a choice. It was part of her. Whatever Lola decided about her future, Quinn would support her, just as Lola had proven she would support Quinn. Isabelle had made her peace with Holt's job, which meant she was a perfect case study. Quinn would do whatever research was necessary. Lola was worth it.

Chapter Twenty-six

Holt dodged George's sippy cup for what felt like the hundredth time and tried to find a slightly less dangerous position. That mostly involved repositioning George on her lap in the glider so his swings had less access to her face.

"You going to drink any of that, buddy?" she asked him. He looked noncommittal. "Shall we get back to our story? I'm dying to find out what happens to this little truck on his big adventure."

George geared up to throw the sippy, but Holt caught it before he could launch.

"Nice try, little man."

Holt shifted him again, this time so he was in one arm, against her side. She held the book with the other and began the story again.

"Momo," George said, patting her chest.

"That's right, I'm Momo. Where's George?"

He pointed to himself and laughed the big goofy baby laugh that melted her heart every time she heard it.

George had come up with Momo on his own. They were pretty sure it was his baby attempt at saying "mama" and "Holt" that had gotten mashed together. It seemed to have imprinted on Holt and now she was Momo. She loved it.

He snuggled into Holt's side and held onto one of her fingers. She read two more stories, the adventurous truck and one about barn animals, before she settled him in his crib and kissed him good night. He was close to sleep but would probably spend a little time amusing himself before finally drifting off. He usually needed some time to process the day. Holt was thankful he was able to almost always do it on his own.

How long until he's old enough to be scared by the danger I bring to his life? What happens if I'm not enough someday to keep him safe?

Holt pulled the door closed to George's room and saw the light on in the master bedroom. That meant Isabelle was home early, which was a welcome surprise.

"Hi, sweetheart," Holt said when she saw Isabelle. She walked over, helped her unzip her dress, and pulled it over her head. She wrapped her arms around Isabelle's waist from behind and pulled her close. She nuzzled her neck. Isabelle held all the cards in their relationship, but Holt didn't mind. She was the keeper of all of Holt's innermost gooey, emotional bits, and all she had to do was give a little squeeze and all of Holt's messy feelings would come spilling out. But Holt trusted she never would. She cared for her so gently when she needed it. Her thoughts at the moment strayed in a different direction the moment Isabelle's dress hit the floor.

"Even your considerable charms and good looks aren't getting you out of cooking me dinner," Isabelle said, batting Holt away playfully. "Now go stand a safe distance over there while I change."

"What fun is that?"

"None at all," Isabelle said. "But I'm hungry and I want to hear about your afternoon. It won't kill you to wait."

"Hmph. George is down. Changing his diaper is starting to become my workout for the day. The kid is full of wiggle."

"He is your son. It would be weird if he weren't active and strong."

"It's true. I don't like having my diaper changed either," Holt said. "How was your meeting tonight? Who were you meeting, again?"

Holt followed Isabelle downstairs and into the kitchen. She pulled things out of the fridge and set them on the counter. It was her night to cook and she had half a plan. She surveyed what she'd pulled out. *Sure. I can do this.*

"I met one of my former colleagues for coffee," Isabelle said. There was something in Isabelle's voice that gave Holt pause. Isabelle was nervous about something.

"Oh, shit, you're leaving me," Holt said.

"What?" Isabelle looked horrified. "Don't be ridiculous. I'm not going anywhere. I love you."

"That's not what I meant," Holt said. She didn't question Isabelle's love for her. "You're leaving the crew. Are you not happy there anymore? God, how did I not see that?"

"Baby, slow down a minute." Isabelle came over and took the knife out of Holt's hand. She set it on the counter and took Holt's face in her hands. "I love working with you and the rest of the crew. More than I thought I would. That's why I've stayed so long. But we both knew it probably wasn't forever. The guy I met with tonight is a forensic accountant. I wanted to get more information from him about what he does. I'm not interested in going back to being a CPA. But talking to Quinn has reminded me that I was on a different career path when we got together, and like Quinn, I really liked what I did. So I'm just rethinking where I want to go with it."

"I've ruined you," Holt said. She felt better. She hadn't missed Isabelle hiding professional misery from her.

"Completely," Isabelle said. She pulled Holt down and kissed her. Holt let her deepen the kiss before pulling away.

"Hey, you had your chance. I'm cooking here."

Isabelle swatted her on the ass as she wandered back to her side of the kitchen island.

"So, how was the meeting?"

"Pretty great. He does cases involving money laundering, tax, and securities fraud. He's hoping to expand into forensic analytics and some higher stakes cases. It sounds like a lot of what we do now, just not restricted to your cases."

"So we could still work together," Holt said. "Except I'd have to pay you."

"When you put it that way it sounds weird," Isabelle said. "But I could see a scenario where you were an important client, yes."

"Well, as long as I was an *important* client. I guess that wouldn't be so bad."

Holt thought about Isabelle setting off on her own. She hated the idea personally, since she would see less of her. She loved driving to work together every day, but professionally, this seemed like a great thing for Isabelle. She didn't think there was anything Isabelle couldn't do.

"Wait a minute," Holt said. She replayed something Isabelle had said. "You said forensic analytics. You can't take Max."

Isabelle tried what Holt was sure she thought was an innocent expression. "I wasn't even thinking about it. But now that you brought it up, she would be really helpful. Joint custody?"

"No. And you can't poach anyone else either."

"Can we ask her and she can decide?" Isabelle was needling her and clearly enjoying it.

Holt was happy to play along. "Absolutely not. Everyone in that building would choose you over me. I would end up with stacks of paperwork and, if I was lucky, one of the new kids." She shuddered at the thought. They were good, but still raw.

"Okay, we can talk about Max later. If it happens. I'm still thinking about it. I wanted to talk to you first, but I should have known you would figure out something was up. I forget what a good detective you are."

"I know you. It has nothing to do with detective work," Holt said. "Whatever you decide, I support you. I'll help any way I can. If you want to stay and I can make changes to give you your dream job, tell me. If you want to set up your own shop, tell me how I can help you make that happen and we'll do it."

"Thank you. Don't go buying any buildings for me unless I ask you to," Isabelle said.

She gave a warning look. Holt knew that look. It could make army generals fall in line.

"I know you like to help, but if I set up shop, it's going to take some time. Now tell me why you, Moose, and Lola flew out of the office so fast earlier and didn't come back for hours."

"Ugh. It appears the CMCs are the gift that keeps on giving. Quinn hit her panic button. Two guys tried to snatch her out of Jose's shop. She actually did a pretty good job of fighting them off herself. Lola went and picked her up and Moose and I tailed the guys back to a hotel room downtown. They were the sloppiest...whatever the hell they were...I've ever seen. Anyway, we knocked on their door and had a little chat. I think Moose made one of them wet himself."

"Is Quinn okay? Isabelle asked. "Were they CMC guys? I don't mean to tell you how to do your job, but isn't it time for you to find these bastards already and stop all this nonsense?"

Holt knew Isabelle didn't really think she was slacking off, but not being able to stop these attacks on her family and crew was frustrating. More than that. They made her furious. "I'm trying, babe. These guys swore they weren't CMCs and they aren't in our known network, but that doesn't prove anything. They said they were here on a business trip," Holt said. "We didn't get a lot out of them, to be honest. They gave us their names, said they were in Jose's shop because their rental car was making a funny noise and they wanted him to take a look. Moose leaned on them pretty hard. We turned them over to the cops even though I'm sure they're already out. It looks like attempted kidnapping from our end, but they could explain it away with a half decent lie."

"That's awful," Isabelle said. "You didn't get anything useful?"

"Max helped herself to their phone data when I paired mine with theirs. They're chatty with the mayor's guy, the same one Malcolm talks to. We spent the rest of the afternoon retracing their steps since they arrived. One of them had an app on his phone that tracked all their mileage by GPS. It was like he was going to put in for reimbursement."

"Please tell me they were here from Cleveland sightseeing."

Isabelle's voice was calm, but her face was tense. Holt knew this case was wearing on her as well.

"LA. And the only sights they visited were the loft, our house, Amy's place, the office, and Ellen's house. There were pictures of everything on their phones too. I'll spare you the details of how the next fifteen minutes of that conversation went since I know you don't like hearing about it. Moose kept me from crossing any lines. I haven't lost my cool like that in a while." Holt clenched her fists thinking about finding pictures of her house in those men's possession.

"I can understand why," Isabelle said. "The thought scares me and I didn't see it without warning."

"They're collecting data. Learning more about us, looking for a weakness in our network. I don't know. But I know the extra man hours I've had everyone putting in to keep our family safe is looking pretty damned good. I'm tempted to double the crew keeping an eye on everyone."

"That will just wear everyone out," Isabelle said. "I didn't see Lola's bike when I got home. Are they still here? Quinn must have been terrified being in that situation. I'm glad you three got to her so quickly."

"Don't think they ever came here," Holt said. "Pretty sure they went to Lola's loft."

"All she has is an armchair." Isabelle said. "Not exactly homey." Isabelle looked like she thought Lola should know better.

Holt thought it adorable how outraged Isabelle was that Lola would even consider bringing Quinn to the loft in its current state. She understood Lola's reasoning. It was a secure location, and even without much furniture, it was comfortable. Besides, Holt was sure they wouldn't mind sharing the chair.

"What happens if we're attacked?" Isabelle asked. "Quinn asked and I didn't know."

"I protect you," Holt said. That would always be true. The thought of an attack left her in a cold sweat, but she would walk into a hail of bullets to keep Isabelle safe.

"As comforting as that is," Isabelle said, "you're not bulletproof, despite your insistence that you are. What if the guys that attacked your truck had come to the office instead? What if they had friends?"

"Do you trust me?" Holt asked. She thought about all the safety plans, defense strategies, and contingencies they had for the office, her house, the loft, and every other building she or her crew lived or worked in.

"Of course I do, love."

"Then trust I have plans A to Z to keep everyone safe. Some I like more than others, but I'll use any or all if I need to. If it makes you feel better, I'll spell them all out for you. But let me finish dinner. We'll probably need a full stomach."

"I know the plans for our house, and I knew about the loft. I'm never alone in the office. Your crew all knows A to Z, right?"

"Everyone," Holt said. She hoped they never needed to use any of them.

"Then I don't know that hearing how you've planned for an invasion will actually make me feel better," Isabelle said. "But I'm glad you have."

"Hazard of the job."

As they fell into a comfortable silence, Holt finished cooking and thought about plans A to Z. It was plan Z she worried about. Any scenario that required that response would be close to a personal hell. She thought about the hidden gun safe in her office. Only a few of her employees even knew it was there, although everyone knew the general outline to Plan Z even if they didn't know it involved weapons. She'd installed and loaded it as an extreme backup to a worst-case scenario. That was why only a few knew it existed. She didn't want anyone who worked for her thinking they should reach for a weapon to solve any problem. She'd had bombs delivered to her doorstep and been shot, attacked, and threatened multiple times. Not once had she considered opening the safe. She hoped the resolution to the current tension wouldn't break that streak.

CHAPTER TWENTY-SEVEN

Lola stood next to Holt, arms crossed, as they both stared at Max's screen in the conference room. Lola found Quinn's method of listing information they knew helpful, so she'd written it all down on paper. Holt had transferred it to the computer. Lola didn't know how to operate the damn thing.

As they'd worked, they'd begun to speculate and hypothesize. The mayor was involved, they were pretty certain of that, even without iron-clad proof, but they still needed a way to tie him up and deliver him to Sam.

"Is there anything in his financials we can use?" Lola asked. She pointed at the tablet Holt was holding. She knew it held the information she was asking about even if she didn't understand how to retrieve it.

"Nothing jumped out," Holt said. "Max said she was being extra careful given that he's a sitting mayor. His campaign funds are locked up tighter than she expected. But if she invites herself in, even if we find something, it's no use to Sam. She needs something she can use to get a warrant."

Holt looked frustrated. Lola understood.

"I prefer detective work to skulking around the Internets anyway," Lola said.

"To recap, we know the mayor won the election by pounding the law and order drum. The CMCs rose to prominence and scared people enough to be susceptible to that message. He also promised to revitalize downtrodden neighborhoods. Now that he's in office, violence is down and businesses are moving into previously ignored areas. There was also an allegation of campaign financial misdeeds," Holt said. She ticked things off on her fingers as she listed them.

"What was the ten million used for?" Lola asked. "The CMCs said they had it. Are they paying for new businesses to come in?"

"Maybe," Holt said. "But it doesn't seem like Malcolm has the clout to be that kind of power player. He'd have to really be making that money work for him, and it seems like someone would have talked. I doubt many of these new businesses are dirty. More likely the mayor is encouraging them in some small ways to set up shop in CMC territory. Tax breaks maybe, or small business loans. The promise of added police presence." She walked over and leaned against the conference table, looking tired.

"So he bought a private army for ten million dollars and let them invest it to keep paying themselves? Where's he getting money for those other improvements you're talking about? Is he still stealing from his campaign?" Lola asked.

"That's a good question. The campaign funds are still there. Max checked. Let's call Sam. I have a question for her."

While Lola waited for Sam to answer she poked her head out of the conference room and looked for Quinn. She'd always thought it was a little funny how often Holt made transparent excuses to seek out Isabelle during the day, but she would stop teasing her. It had been a couple of hours and she missed Quinn.

"She went with Isabelle and Jessica back to the house," Dubs said from her desk. "They have their guard dogs with them."

"Why didn't she come say good-bye?" Lola was disappointed she didn't get at least a quick kiss.

"Turns out, I'm not the doorman here," Dubs said. "But did you check your phone? I think I heard her say something about texting you."

Lola pulled out her phone. There were two texts from Quinn.

"You and Holt looked hard at work. We didn't want to interrupt. Going to Isabelle's with a full entourage so I'm safe. I love you."

The second one let her know they made it safely. Lola wrote back that she loved her. It was all she could manage to hunt and peck on the tiny screen before Holt called her back to the conference room.

Sam was larger than life projected on the wall on Skype. Holt and Sam were already talking shop.

"Just the woman I wanted to talk to," Sam said. "I've been digging into the mayor like you suggested, but I've had to be careful. He's a slimy bastard. I didn't like him before all this. If what you said about my department having unfriendly eyes and ears is true, I'm feeling a little exposed. The threatening phone calls and emails are giving me the impression I should wrap this up too."

"Jesus, Sam. Be careful. The CMCs are insane and won't hesitate to come after you. Do you want me to come out to LA?" Holt asked, dead serious.

Sam laughed. "And just what would you do out here, kid? I'm the police chief of the Los Angeles Police Department. You're a preschool badass who would what, be my bodyguard? You've got enough on your plate out there. But thank you for the offer."

Lola looked at Holt, expecting her to explode. She didn't think anyone had ever spoken to her that way, not that she'd seen. Instead, Holt threw her head back and laughed along with Sam.

"How about I handle my business, you take care of yours, and no one gets dead?" Holt asked.

"Did you call me for a reason, or just to imply that I'm too geriatric to watch my own back?"

"We've got a couple of questions about the mayor," Holt said.

She indicated Lola should go ahead. Lola thought Holt was going to run this call so she was caught off guard, but she repeated the questions she'd asked Holt earlier.

"Where's the mayor getting his money? We think he gave the CMCs his campaign money, but he needs influence to manipulate the city the way he is. Influence requires money."

Sam looked like she was considering. There was a map of the city on the wall behind her. She turned in her chair and looked at it. She abruptly spun back to them.

"Son of a bitch. How could I have missed that? The fucking port."

"Excuse me?" Lola asked. Even though she didn't know what Sam was alluding to, she felt excitement building.

"There's been rumors of a smuggling operation out of the port that we just can't get in front of. Every time we get a hot tip, everyone's cleared out before we arrive. The mayor has a task force so information is flowing through his office, which is convenient for him. Care to guess where the first CMC activity popped up on our radar?" Sam asked.

Lola recognized the look in Sam's eyes. It was the same look Holt had when she was on a hunt and had her prey in sight.

"Max, Dubs, get in here," Holt hollered into the other room.

Max and Dubs skidded to a stop just outside the door. "What's up?

"I need you to find a smuggling operation at the Port of LA," Holt said. "It might be the key to bringing down the mayor."

"That sounds fun," Max said. "I'll start doing a little poking around at the Port."

"You make it sound like you're going for a stroll on a container ship," Dubs said.

"Have you ever stolen a boat before?" Max asked.

"You're picturing me as a pirate, aren't you?"

"Don't answer that," Holt said. "Role-play and dress Dubs in sexy pirate gear on your own time."

"Now you're picturing it too, aren't you, boss?" Dubs winked at Holt.

"You two never disappoint," Sam said.

Lola felt her phone vibrate. She pulled it out and checked the text. Quinn, Isabelle, and Jessica were on their way back. Her belly did the now familiar and quite welcome flip it did when she thought about seeing Quinn. She considered standing in the parking lot waiting for her, but that seemed like too much. She'd be here in ten minutes.

Lola was pulled from happy thoughts of Quinn by a loud bang on the video call with Sam. Another one followed. Sam was on her feet and moving. She'd called them on her tablet, so they were still with her.

"Someone's gained entry to my house. I'm calling it in."

They all listened as Sam made the call. Lola didn't need to hear the other end of the call to get the gist of what Sam was told.

"I'm on my own. Seems I found one of my dirty cops," Sam said. "Unfortunately, he just answered my fucking call for help. Pretty clear that dispatch isn't going out. I'm going to try to get in touch with someone backchannel, but I don't know who to trust."

"How long can you hold out?" Holt asked.

"Not long enough for you to fly out here," Sam said. Although she looked resolved to her fate, she looked pissed as hell. "I've got to tell you where my files are and then I'm signing off. You're not watching me die."

"I'm not letting you die. Just hold on a minute and give me a chance to think," Holt said. She was pacing around the conference table.

"This is probably the CMCs, right?" Lola said. "Why don't we call Malcolm? The mayor's going down, but maybe he doesn't have to. Or maybe his neighborhoods can survive. If he kills the police chief, nothing's going to save him."

Holt looked like she was considering. Sam stopped her breakneck motion and stared directly into the camera for a moment as well.

"Do it," Holt said. "Get him on the line. Hold on for me, Sam."

"No problem," Sam said. "Just going to look for a bigger gun."

Lola's phone buzzed again.

"*Just pulling in,*" the text message read.

She hoped Quinn wouldn't find her right away and could avoid experiencing Sam's peril live. Hopefully, it would have a positive resolution and Lola could give her an abbreviated version later. Lola turned back to the screen when three rapid pops that sounded like extremely loud firecrackers, followed immediately by a loud scream filled the air. Lola was out of the conference room at a sprint, but before she'd made it far, the large picture window facing the lot exploded directly in front of her. She hit the floor as bullets whizzed overhead. Those working at computers in the main room were already on the ground, moving along the ground like overgrown bugs, toward designated rally points and safety zones.

All Lola could think as she army-crawled under the onslaught was of Isabelle, Quinn, and Jessica exposed in the parking lot. Had they really arrived? Had they been hit? She felt her throat starting to close and her breathing become difficult at the thought of Quinn shot and bleeding. *Focus. Get to her and then worry.* She let the anger rise. That she could work with, if she could control it.

As she moved past one of the desks, she reached up and grabbed an earpiece and shoved it in her ear. She flicked it on.

"You there, H?"

"Right behind you."

Lola glanced behind her. Holt was indeed a few feet behind, crawling along the ground as she was, covering ground rapidly.

"What's going on?" Dubs asked. She sounded way too serious, and that made Lola feel worse about the situation.

"Trying to find out. Max, get Malcolm to back off Sam. Dubs, get a head count, care for any wounded. Try to get in touch with Jose. He's exposed in the shop out front. I need someone on the roof. Get me information. Keep people safe and stay down."

Holt nodded at Lola and they started to move. Lola reached the front door first. She got to her feet at the main entrance, shielding herself as best she could with the doorjamb. She chanced a peek outside. Isabelle, Quinn, and Jessica were huddled against one of the SUVs, trying to remain out of sight. Isabelle looked like she was evaluating exit strategies. For the moment, the shooters weren't directly aiming at them. Lola wasn't going to take a chance the situation would change.

It was fifty feet of open ground to where the three women hid. She had a better chance of getting to them alive if she approached from around the other side, through the alleyway that ran the length of the building, but she wasn't willing to crawl all the way back and work her way around. It would take too long.

She needed something that would make the shooters stop long enough for her to get to Quinn. She scanned the office and saw a can of spray paint Tuna had confiscated from a teenager looking to redecorate the office a few weeks ago.

She quickly tied a rag tightly around the can and wedged a few pushpins in the rag facing the can. Her plan was to light the rag and fling it at the shooters before running like hell. Aerosol cans were remarkably easy to puncture, and the contents of the spray can were flammable. Even if the can didn't puncture, Lola hoped a flaming object hurling their way would give the shooters pause. Holt was by her side and nodded at her improvised work.

"I hope you two morons aren't thinking of running out there under cover of that," Dubs said. She was in the door to Holt's office holding an assault rifle.

"What the hell are you doing?" Holt said.

"Keeping everyone safe. That includes your dumb asses. Plan Z is in effect. They have guns and there's nothing stopping them from walking in here and picking us all off. Wait for me to get to the roof. I'll cover you while you collect the ladies."

Lola knew Holt hated guns. She didn't like them either, but right now bringing a can of flammable spray paint to a gunfight was foolish. Dubs was right. Plan Z was in effect.

It was nearly impossible for Lola to wait for Dubs to get up to the roof and into position. All she could see was Quinn out there, exposed. Holt was clearly feeling the same way with Isabelle in harm's way as she was crawling up Lola's back.

Lola's anxiety wasn't helped by the overwhelming chatter over the comms. It seemed everyone was on and giving updates, checking in, and implementing Plan Z.

Finally, Dubs checked in. "Okay, I'm in position. I'm going to lay down cover. If you are interested in the fireball, go ahead and fling that can out and I'll light it up."

Lola figured it couldn't hurt. She heaved the can as far as she could and took off for Quinn. Dubs's aim was true and the can exploded in a fiery sphere. Lola shielded her eyes but didn't slow. She could feel Holt right behind her.

The sounds of gunfire hadn't diminished any, but the pace of fire being sent toward them had slowed since Dubs began firing back. Lola and Holt made it to the SUV unharmed.

Quinn and Jessica threw themselves into Lola's arms and she held them tight.

"So which of your plans involved Dubs on a rooftop with a gun?" Isabelle asked.

"Z," Holt said.

"If you've put her in a position to kill someone…" Isabelle said.

Lola felt a little sorry for Holt. She was clearly terrified about the danger Isabelle and the rest of the crew were in, and now Isabelle was pissed at her.

"Of course not," Holt said. "Dubs knows the Batman rules apply. Right, Dubs?" Holt held out her earpiece to Isabelle so she could hear Dubs's reply. Isabelle seemed satisfied.

"How are you so calm?" Quinn asked. She was looking at Jessica.

"They just blew up a hand grenade and ran through a hail of bullets. All things considered, I'm feeling pretty safe," Jessica said. "But I already got kidnapped and watched Lola get creamed, so I'm totally signed up for a lifetime of therapy."

"Where are Moose and Tuna?" Holt asked. "Weren't they supposed to be with you?"

"I let them out at Jose's shop," Isabelle said. "It's not their fault, Holt. I said I'd park and go right in. I figured how much trouble could we get in ten steps from the door?"

"Max, can you get everyone to shut up long enough to give me a coherent update?" Holt said.

The gunfire had resumed and bullets pinged off the car, spraying metal and glass everywhere. Lola knew they couldn't keep the ladies here much longer. Even with Dubs laying down return fire it wouldn't be long until the gunman moved in on them.

"Dubs is on the roof as you know. She said there are ten shooters she can see. All with assault rifles and body armor. I called for backup, but given what we're up against, they're activating SWAT. It's going to take a couple extra minutes."

"We don't have that, Max. We've got to get everyone back inside."

Lola released Quinn and Jessica, and both let her go reluctantly. She scooted to the edge of the SUV and peered around the bumper. She could see four of the ten shooters. She thought she saw another pair of boots, and if so, Dubs had taken one shooter down.

She looked at their options for retreat. Going back the way she and Holt had come wasn't a good option. It was stupid when they'd done it, but with five of them, the odds weren't good that they would all make it. She had to figure out a way to keep all of them alive, and it wasn't looking good. *We need weapons too.*

She scooted to the driver's door and reached up to the door handle. Her hand strayed a little too high as she blindly reached and a bullet careened off the hood of the SUV, sending shrapnel piercing into her knuckles. Lola yanked her hand back and looked at her newly pierced skin. She glanced at Quinn, who almost looked exasperated. It was better than panicked.

"I know, I know, I need to be more careful." She tried again. This time she got the door opened and quickly removed the emergency kit from under the driver's seat. She rooted around until she found the flare gun and three flares.

"Even your emergency kits are mini Batcaves," Quinn said.

"I knew a flare gun would come in handy eventually," Holt said.

"Whoever's at the front of the shop, I'm sending Isabelle, Quinn, and Jessica your way," Lola said. "We need more cover for them. Is anyone else armed on the ground level?"

"Yes, I'm coordinating from up here," Dubs said. "I've got a couple of our guys covering the back, but they can be repositioned. Say the word."

"Get them in position," Lola said. "Tell them not to shoot me in the ass though. I'm going to be covering them from out here."

"The hell you are," Holt said. She pointed at the flare gun. "It's *my* flare gun."

"It's *my* plan," Lola said. "You can escort them back." She waved toward the shop.

"Fuck that," Holt said. "I'm more likely to get them shot. Everyone seems to point their guns at me."

"When this is over, we need to talk about that," Isabelle said.

"Prep them to get to cover," Lola said. She turned and loaded the first flare.

Quinn was quiet next to her.

"I'm sorry you're in danger again," Lola said. "I'm going to make sure you're safe."

"That's not enough," Quinn said. "My life without you isn't enough." Quinn grabbed Lola's T-shirt in her fists and pulled her close. "You better come back to me. I love you."

"I love you too," Lola said. She kissed her. A kiss of promise.

Holt tapped Lola on the shoulder.

"Now, Dubs," Lola said.

Gunfire erupted from the shop. Lola shot out from behind the SUV and leveled the flare gun at the first shooter she saw. She fired. The man dove out of the way. Another man behind him, standing at a higher vantage point, didn't see the flare in time. It hit him square in the knee. He screamed in pain.

Lola kept running. While she ran she loaded another flare. She aimed and fired again.

A bullet hit the pavement six inches from her. It kicked up chunks of asphalt and debris that lodged painfully in her shin. The impact was enough to throw her off stride and trip her. She went down.

Pain ripped through her as she landed. At first, she thought she'd been shot, but it was just her still healing ribs protesting the hard landing. *Get up. Keep moving. If you stay down you're dead.*

She tried to stand up, and when she'd barely managed, something hit her from behind and she was flying through the air. She landed in an uncomfortable heap behind a rock a few feet from where she'd fallen. She took inventory. No major damage and she still had the flare gun.

She caught her breath and refit the comms unit in her ear. "Dubs, what can you see?"

"Holt's down. Fuck, Lola. Holt's down."

Lola's insides felt cold. Dubs must have misspoke. "Where? Did everyone else get in okay?"

"All three got in okay," Dubs said. "Holt's about five feet from you. She threw you behind that rock and then went down. I don't have a full view, but she hasn't moved."

"How far away is the SWAT team?" Lola asked. She loaded her last flare and prepared to move. She wasn't leaving Holt out there exposed. She refused to think what Holt being down could mean. Holt had been the stable foundation that allowed Lola to build a life after her brother died. If Holt was pulled away, she didn't know what it would do to her.

"Ninety seconds out, so they say," Dubs said.

"I'm going to get Holt," Lola said. She looked around the rock. "Think you can take care of the two closest to us?"

"You got it," Dubs said.

Lola heard a scream. *One down.*

She took off from her rock and headed for Holt. She slid to a stop on her knees next to her. She wasn't moving and was bleeding from her temple. *Fuck, fuck, fuck. Don't be dead. Don't you fucking be dead.* Another shot hit the dirt next to her, and Lola took aim at the second guy and fired. Another scream. *Two down.*

Lola didn't think she could safely get Holt all the way back to the shop so she grabbed her by the arms and started to drag her. It was faster and Holt would be less exposed than a fireman's carry.

"This is embarrassing," Holt said. But she didn't try to stand on her own.

"Fuck," Lola said, looking down at her. "I thought you were dead. I should leave you out here for scaring me like that." She pulled Holt the final few feet until they were both behind the rock.

"That's the thanks I get for flinging you behind this lovely rock?"

"This rock's shit," Lola said. She was looking Holt over, making sure there weren't any injuries that needed immediate attention. The cut on her face looked superficial. "What happened to you?"

"I got knocked on my ass after tossing you. I think some debris or something hit me. I stayed down for a second to evaluate and a funny thing happened. They stopped shooting at me."

"I wasted my last flare on you playing possum?" Lola was a little angry but also giddy with relief.

"We could have avoided all of this if you'd let me handle the flares."

"Oh sure, and then you get all the glory and I look like a punk in front of my lady. So what's the plan?" Lola asked.

"I'm sitting on my ass in the middle of a parking lot, hiding behind a rock," Holt said. "What makes you think I have a plan?"

"Because you're the one who keeps flare guns in your SUVs. When were those ever going to come in handy? Signaling aircraft?"

"No, shooting at these fucknuts. Max, do you have an update on Sam?" Holt looked worried.

"I'm here, boss. My connection was lost a few minutes ago, so I haven't gotten confirmation she's safe, but I got in touch with Malcolm like we talked about. It's not his guys at Sam's house. I think

I convinced him helping Sam was in his best interest. As was flipping on the mayor. He said he was sending soldiers to her house."

"How the hell did you do that?" Holt asked.

"I finally cracked one of the offshore shell corporations," Max said. "It was registered to Malcolm. I'm willing to bet the others are too. It looks like the mayor transferred all the money to himself, laundered it, and then got away squeaky clean on the other side. Malcolm didn't know anything about it though. The mayor set him up to take the fall if things went south. You can imagine how Malcolm felt about that."

No honor among thieves. Lola ducked as debris showered the air around them.

"Let me know when you confirm Sam's okay. Did I hear SWAT is almost here? I don't want to be out here when they roll up. I don't get the feeling these guys will go down without a fight and this rock doesn't feel like enough cover," Holt said.

Lola looked carefully around the rock to evaluate their situation. There was no sign of SWAT yet. The intensity of the shooting had lessened although there were still bullets careening off the back of their rock with sickening regularity.

"I think this is our chance, you two," Dubs said. "You and Lola need to stick close and keep low. Lola, are you okay to run? Boss dumped you on your ass pretty good, and no offense, but you still look rough."

"I'll be fine," Lola said. She hurt like hell, but she would fight through it since the alternative was being stuck out here when SWAT arrived and things had the potential to get really deadly.

"Move to your right on my mark."

Dubs fired off three more shots and then gave the go signal. Holt grabbed Lola and the two of them sprang from behind the rock and ran crouched low to the ground for the next measure of cover they could find, in this case another car. The intensity of fire picked up again, shattering the concrete behind them as they ran.

"Moose is on ground level providing cover now too," Dubs said. "He promised not to strafe you. Hold there for a minute. Our guests are moving."

Holt and Lola held their position. Lola tried to keep her breathing even and steady, but adrenaline was threatening to overwhelm her system.

"They're trying to outflank you," Dubs said. "I can hold them off long enough to get you inside, but if SWAT doesn't show up soon, you're going to need more than Moose on the ground down there. Tuna's reporting it's the same around back."

"Just get me inside," Holt said.

"You got it. When I give you the go, you two run like hell." Dubs fired again and another shooter went down. The rehabilitation from the shot to the kneecap would be unpleasant, but he would live.

When Dubs told them to go, they ran full-out for the office. They had to go between two parked trucks in single file. As they did the windshields and side windows burst into tiny shards as bullets flew through the glass. Lola could feel the glass hitting her face and arms, but she didn't dare slow. Her damaged ribs were aching, making it hard to breathe. Once they were out from between the trucks it was less than ten feet to the door. Moose and one of the newbies were waiting with the door open, Moose holding an assault rifle, returning fire.

Holt burst into the office with Lola right behind her. They landed tangled together on the floor and Moose slammed the door shut behind them. Lola's immediate concern was Quinn. She felt like she couldn't see or hear clearly in the chaos. She knew people were shouting and the gunshots were still overwhelmingly loud, but it all seemed like background noise, muffled as she tried to pick out the one voice that mattered most.

"Finally," she heard someone shout. She was aware of sirens, but even that couldn't fully penetrate. She needed to get to Quinn.

"Where's Quinn?" she asked Moose.

"Max has everyone barricaded in the conference room. She's safe," Moose said.

That was all Lola needed to hear for the time being. She wanted to see Quinn and confirm that for herself, but right now, the best thing she could do was fight.

❖

"SWAT is on scene," Dubs said. "I'm coming down from the roof now. I don't want to get shot off of here for looking too much like an unfriendly sniper."

After a very short gunfight, the shooters were subdued. The SWAT team swarmed the office and cleared the building. Everyone was led outside, checked for hostile intent, and then released. Holt felt disoriented standing back in the parking lot she'd run through just a short time ago desperately trying not to die.

She scanned the crowd as the last of her people were led out of the building. Quinn came first, then Jessica, and finally, Isabelle. Isabelle saw her and launched into her arms. Holt always found words lacking at times like this.

The feelings of fear, disorientation, anger, and terror melted away as she held Isabelle. *Thank God.* No matter what else was happening in the world, this was her home. This woman, who grounded her, calmed her, loved her, the mother of her child, was all she needed in the world.

"I love you," Holt said.

"I love you too," Isabelle said. "I thought I was going to lose you."

She set Isabelle down and took a step back. She reached into her pocket and pulled out the ring she'd been carrying around for weeks. She dropped to one knee on the snow-covered ground, with shards of glass embedded in her jeans and stuck in her skin, and blood still dripping down her face. But life was precious, and sometimes tenuous. She wouldn't wait another second.

"You can't lose me," Holt said. "Because I'm yours forever. I've been yours since the day I met you. Every day with you is the best day of my life, and I want those best days to continue for the rest of my life. Isabelle Rochat, will you marry me? Will you raise George with me as my wife?"

"You sure know how to pick your moments, Holt Lasher, but we met in a hail of gunfire, so I guess this is appropriate," Isabelle said. She had tears in her eyes. She took Holt's hand and pulled her to her feet. "Yes. I say yes. Of course I say yes." Isabelle pulled Holt in for a kiss, but Holt held back.

"You'll get blood on you." She slipped the ring on Isabelle's hand instead.

"Hey, you're the one who picked the proposal time and didn't wash your face. I get the ring, you get a kiss."

"That, I can definitely live with."

Despite having been under siege and in deadly peril, this was the best day of Holt's life. She'd never understood how she'd gotten lucky enough to share a life with Isabelle, and now they would promise each other forever. Her heart already knew it was true; standing in front of family and friends to declare it to the world was something of a formality, but one she couldn't wait to undertake.

CHAPTER TWENTY-EIGHT

I can't believe you proposed surrounded by the SWAT team," Lola said. She and Holt were out for drinks, crammed into a booth at a local dive bar down the street from the loft.

"Hey, it did the job," Holt said. "I think she understood the romance of the moment."

Lola laughed. "You're lucky you've found the one woman on this planet who understands you enough to put up with your bullshit. There was absolutely no romance to anything that happened that day."

Holt scrubbed her face with her hands. "You've worked with me almost from the beginning. Am I getting older and settled, or was that the craziest case we've ever worked?"

"Sheer insanity. If another case comes along like that in my lifetime it will be too soon."

Holt looked uncertain, something Lola almost never saw from her.

"Hey," Lola said. "She agreed to marry you immediately after a gunfight. She wouldn't have agreed to forever if she thought that kind of danger was going to be a regular thing."

"Oh, so you're a mind reader now?" Holt looked amused.

Lola shrugged. "It's what I would be worried about. Look at the danger I brought to Quinn. I still have no idea why she stuck with me."

"I can think of a few reasons," Holt said. She took a pull on her beer and they were silent for a while, both staring at the TV in the corner of the bar playing sports highlights.

"You think I finally got this one right?" Lola asked. She cared deeply what Holt thought about Quinn.

"Doesn't much matter what I think," Holt said. "Can't find out if you love someone from a third party, even one who cares as much as I do. But for what it's worth, I think Quinn's wonderful. You two light up when the other is around."

"Oh, I'm not asking if I love her," Lola said. "I'm crazy about her. But if she tells me she's going to Michigan, I'm going to pack my bags and follow her. Away from you. Away from Jose, and Moose, and everyone here. It sounds like the sort of stupid shit I've always done, but it feels different this time. You'd tell me if you thought I was making the same mistake again, right? Because I've let her all the way in. She could destroy me."

"Do you trust her not to?"

Lola answered without hesitation. "Absolutely." The truth of the statement was liberating. She realized she'd always held back part of herself in previous relationships, just waiting to get screwed over. Even though she'd tried to hold back with Quinn, it had been impossible. She'd given more of herself than she thought she had to give.

"Guess you have your answer," Holt said. "But I'm going to miss you like hell if you end up in the Midwest. Who's going to keep Jose in line for me?"

"I'm not giving that up no matter how far I move. Although Jessica said she's staying here even if Quinn moves, so she'll fill in when I'm unavailable," Lola said. She thought about the other things she would miss if she left, like watching George grow. All she had to do was think about Quinn's smile, her touch, and the life they wanted to build together, however, and everything else faded away. "Michigan's not a sure thing yet," Lola said. "She's still waiting to hear back from UPVD. I've had everything crossed for so long, I feel like a pretzel."

Holt made a funny face and then laughed. "I'm trying to picture it, but the best I can do is reliving you riding in the backseat of that tiny car Dubs stole to get us back from our run through the woods. Seems like you have a thing for Michigan."

"I love Dubs, I do," Lola said. She was laughing too. "But that car was almost enough for me to kill her."

"She's moving in with Max. Even if you stay, I'm assuming you and Quinn wouldn't be staying in the attic. Mind if I offer your place to one of the newbies?"

Lola didn't mind at all. The apartment she had occupied for so long was one of the things she loved most about Holt, or what it symbolized. If you were part of Holt's family, she took care of you.

"Max and Dubs offered to host Sam when she comes out to recuperate, but the wise woman turned them down. She's going to stay with us until she's back on her feet," Holt said.

It was a minor miracle that Sam had made it out of her house alive. Once the shooting had started at the shop, Lola had forgotten all about Sam in her single-minded drive to get to Quinn, but Holt and Max had multitasked.

"I still can't believe Max convinced Malcolm to rescue Sam," Lola said. She pushed aside her beer.

"I'm not sure Max believes it either. Showing him proof that the mayor intended him to be the fall guy for the entire scheme if things went sideways was key. She played masterfully to his ego and sense of self-preservation."

"Who were the guys at Sam's house?"

"Guns for hire," Holt said. She looked disgusted. "They were paid to get the hard copy files Sam had hidden there and kill her. The mayor hired them to clean up. He was the one that was so scared of my involvement. I'm politically connected, even if it's across the country. He had national aspirations, and my friends were people he would need to know. He didn't want me digging deep and finding out about his involvement. His hired guns were wearing CMC colors and I think supposed to look like part of the gang, but they weren't members. Same for the guys that came after us."

"Thank God I'm good with a flare gun," Lola said. "Someone could've gotten hurt."

Holt glared at her. "Another round?" she asked.

Lola thought about it, and for the first time in her life was eager to get home. "If it's all the same to you, I think I'd like to call it a night."

"No complaints," Holt said. "I've got a fiancé and baby waiting for me."

Lola used to be jealous of the look that flittered across Holt's face anytime she thought of Isabelle. It was like a billboard advertising how damned happy and in love they were, and it used to annoy her. Now she was pretty sure it was another thing she and Holt had in common. They were probably sitting in their tiny booth dreamily staring off into space thinking about their ladies, looking like complete fools. Fools in love. Which was exactly what she was.

CHAPTER TWENTY-NINE

Quinn waited on the bed for Lola to finish her shower. She was nervous, even though she didn't think she had any reason to be. Lola had said she would go anywhere Quinn needed to for her next job, no matter the destination. Tonight was the big reveal.

"So," Lola said. "Are you not wearing any clothes because you're worried I'll be upset, or are we going to be celebrating?"

"You're only wearing a towel," Quinn said. "I didn't want to feel left out."

"We'll just have to be quiet," Lola said. "Because George is still next door and Holt and Isabelle are still down the hall."

Quinn dropped her head dramatically on the pillow. "We really need our own place. Remind me why we couldn't move back into the attic after the LA business was over?"

"Because it's the size of a closet."

"And the loft?"

"No bed."

"Wasn't a problem that I recall," Quinn said. Quinn found it endearing that Lola blushed. "But that is still your place, right? You didn't give it away without telling me?"

"The loft? No, you asked me not to. But I'm sure Holt will find someone else to take over the lease once we move."

"But it's yours now? So you could have a say in the next tenants?"

"I'm sure Holt would be happy to turn that job over to me," Lola said. "Did you have someone in mind? Does Jessica want it? I thought she was moving in with Jose? They're oddly perfect roommates."

Quinn pulled Lola down on the bed and rolled on top of her. They were face-to-face. She could still see the faintest signs of Lola's beating at the hands of the CMCs if she looked closely, and now she had new cuts, bruises, and scratches from her adventures with the hit squad.

"Is it always so insane around you? Am I going to be worried about every bump in the night for the rest of my life?" Quinn asked.

"Me?" Lola asked. "I had nothing to do with any of that. Innocent bystander. Go talk to Holt. She's the one who causes all the trouble around here."

"I'm serious. Even if you go back to school, I don't see you giving up working with Holt completely. Not for a while." Quinn needed a real answer.

Lola nodded and looked like she was taking the question seriously. "No, it's not nearly this crazy all the time. I think even Holt was contemplating a career change with this case. Most of what we do is boring and very tame. Is there danger, yes, but it almost never spills over into our personal lives. There have been some recent and very graphic examples, but those are unusual. You've met all of us, seen the way we work. We look out for each other and we're good at what we do. We don't take stupid risks."

Quinn had heard Lola say all of that, or a version of all of that before, but she needed to hear it again. Especially after she'd been in her second shootout. Gun battles weren't part of the daily lives of neuroscientists. It helped knowing that the mayor of LA had been indicted; Sam, remarkably, was okay; and despite Max's promise on the phone, Malcolm wasn't going to walk away a free man, but the last few weeks had been an action movie. She preferred something with far fewer explosions and bullets, especially if she and Lola were going to have a starring role.

"That's good. What good are those beautiful windows in the loft if I'm too scared to take advantage of the view, or if they're destined to get blown away?"

Lola sat up so quickly she knocked Quinn off of her into an unceremonious jumble on the bed.

"Does this mean…"

"Looks like you just solved your last big case. Good detective work."

Lola pounced on Quinn and pinned her down. Lola's weight pressing into her made Quinn instantly wet. She wrapped her lower leg around Lola's calf.

"How long have you known?" Lola asked.

"I was on the phone with Dr. Castellano when you had to rescue me and whisk me off to the loft," Quinn said. "I wanted to wait for the official offer in writing so I could look it over and make sure there wasn't any poison pill in the contract. Then everything else happened and I wanted to wait for a good moment, when we could really talk. Are you happy?"

"I should be asking you that," Lola said. "I was going to be happy no matter what. Being with you makes me happy."

Quinn wanted more from her and her disapproval of Lola's answer must have shown on her face.

"Fine," Lola said. "I'm thrilled. I really would have been happy anywhere, but I'm not going to lie and say being close to my family isn't perfect. What better way for them to really get to know you? Actually…" Lola hopped off the bed and started putting clothes on.

"What are you doing?" This wasn't what Quinn had in mind for the rest of their evening. "Get naked and get back here."

"We have to tell Holt and Isabelle," Lola said. "And then we have to go see our new home."

"There's no furniture there," Quinn said. She got up and started dressing too. Lola was clearly not to be deterred. "Tomorrow we're buying a bed."

"There's a chair," Lola said. "Besides, we're celebrating. I don't think there will be much reason for sleep."

"I like that chair," Quinn said. "I think I'm going to steal it from you."

"I told you the first time I met you I was saving you a seat," Lola said. "It felt that way at the time, even if I didn't know what I meant. Now I know."

"An armchair in an empty apartment?" Quinn was teasing, and she loved how excited Lola was. Her heart felt like it could burst with the beauty and possibility her future held.

"Obviously. But also the seat in the uncluttered, quiet place in my heart where no one else goes because only you're allowed in."

Quinn moved into Lola's arms and draped her arms around Lola's neck. "I know you want to tell Holt and Isabelle our news," Quinn said. "But dance with me first? Just like the night we met?"

Lola pulled her close and pulled up a slow song from her phone. They danced together around the bedroom. This was her place in the world, right here in Lola's arms. She had never felt more loved.

"I want to dance with you forever," Lola said. "I love you."

"I love you too." Quinn listened to Lola's heartbeat as she leaned against her chest. A heart that beat for her. She usually found comfort in data and scientific theories and conclusions, but she couldn't quantify or qualify or analyze what was between the two of them. It just was. Magnificent, beautiful, and theirs. And that was enough.

About the Author

Jesse Thoma is a project manager in a clinical research lab and spends a good amount of time in methadone clinics and prisons collecting data and talking to people.

Jesse grew up in Northern California but headed east for college. She never looked back, although her baseball allegiance is still loyally with the San Francisco Giants. She has lived in New England for over a decade and has finally learned to leave extra time in the morning to scrape snow off the car. Jesse is blissfully married and is happiest when she is out for a walk with her family and their dog, pretending she still has the soccer skills she had as an eighteen-year-old; eating anything her wife bakes; or sitting at the computer to write a few lines.

Data Capture is Jesse's fourth novel and the third following the adventures of Holt and her crew. *Seneca Falls* was a finalist for a Lambda Literary Award in romance.

Books Available from Bold Strokes Books

Between Sand and Stardust by Tina Michele. Are the lifelong bonds of love strong enough to conquer time, distance, and heartache when Haven Thorne and Willa Bennette are given another chance at forever? (978-1-62639-940-2)

Charming the Vicar by Jenny Frame. When magician and atheist Finn Kane seeks refuge in an English village after a spiritual crisis, can local vicar Bridget Claremont restore her faith in life and love? (978-1-63555-029-0)

Data Capture by Jesse J. Thoma. Lola Walker is undercover on the hunt for cybercriminals while trying not to notice the woman who might be perfectly wrong for her for all the right reasons. (978-1-62639-985-3)

Epicurean Delights by Renee Roman. Ariana Marks had no idea a leisure swim would lead to being rescued, in more ways than one, by the charismatic Hudson Frost. (978-1-63555-100-6)

Heart of the Devil by Ali Vali. We know most of Cain and Emma Casey's story, but *Heart of the Devil* will take you back to where it began one fateful night with a tray loaded with beer. (978-1-63555-045-0)

Known Threat by Kara A. McLeod. When Special Agent Ryan O'Connor reluctantly questions who protects the Secret Service, she learns courage truly is found in unlikely places. Agent O'Connor Series #3. (978-1-63555-132-7)

Seer and the Shield by D. Jackson Leigh. Time is running out for the Dragon Horse Army while two unlikely heroines struggle to put aside their attraction and find a way to stop a deadly cult. Dragon Horse War, Book Three. (978-1-63555-170-9)

Sinister Justice by Steve Pickens. When a vigilante targets citizens of Jake Finnigan's hometown, Jake and his partner Sam fall under suspicion themselves as they investigate the murders. (978-1-63555-094-8)

The Universe Between Us by Jane C. Esther. Ana Mitchell must make the hardest choice of her life: the promise of new love Jolie Dann on Earth, or a humanity-saving mission to colonize Mars. (978-1-63555-106-8)

Touch by Kris Bryant. Can one touch heal a heart? (978-1-63555-084-9)

Change in Time by Robyn Nyx. Working in the past is hell on your future. The Extractor series: Book Two. (978-1-62639-880-1)

Love After Hours by Radclyffe. When Gina Antonelli agrees to renovate Carrie Longmire's new house, she doesn't welcome Carrie's overtures at friendship or her own unexpected attraction. A Rivers Community Novel. (978-1-63555-090-0)

Nantucket Rose by CF Frizzell. Maggie Jordan can't wait to convert an historic Nantucket home into a B&B, but doesn't expect to fall for mariner Ellis Chilton, who has more claim to the house than Maggie realizes. (978-1-63555-056-6)

Picture Perfect by Lisa Moreau. Falling in love wasn't supposed to be part of the stakes for Olive and Gabby, rival photographers in the competition of a lifetime. (978-1-62639-975-4)

Set the Stage by Karis Walsh. Actress Emilie Danvers takes the stage again in Ashland, Oregon, little realizing that landscaper Arden Philips is about to offer her a very personal romantic lead role. (978-1-63555-087-0)

Strike a Match by Fiona Riley. When their attempts at matchmaking fizzle out, firefighter Sasha and reluctant millionairess Abby find themselves turning to each other to strike a perfect match. (978-1-62639-999-0)

The Price of Cash by Ashley Bartlett. Cash Braddock is doing her best to keep her business afloat, stay out of jail, and avoid Detective Kallen. It's not working. (978-1-62639-708-8)

Under Her Wing by Ronica Black. At Angel's Wings Rescue, dogs are usually the ones saved, but when quiet Kassandra Haden meets outspoken owner Jayden Beaumont, the two stubborn women just might end up saving each other. (978-1-63555-077-1)

Underwater Vibes by Mickey Brent. When Hélène, a translator in Brussels, Belgium, meets Sylvie, a young Greek photographer and swim coach, unsettling feelings hijack Hélène's mind and body—even her poems. (978-1-63555-002-3)

A More Perfect Union by Carsen Taite. Major Zoey Granger and DC fixer Rook Daniels risk their reputations for a chance at true love while dealing with a scandal that threatens to rock the military. (978-1-62639-754-5)

Arrival by Gun Brooke. The spaceship *Pathfinder* reaches its passengers' new homeworld where danger lurks in the shadows while Pamas Seclan disembarks and finds unexpected love in young science genius Darmiya Do Voy. (978-1-62639-859-7)

Captain's Choice by VK Powell. Architect Kerstin Anthony's life is going to plan until Bennett Carlyle, the first girl she ever kissed, is assigned to her latest and most important project, a police district substation. (978-1-62639-997-6)

Falling Into Her by Erin Zak. Pam Phillips, widow at the age of forty, meets Kathryn Hawthorne, local Chicago celebrity, and it changes her life forever—in ways she hadn't even considered possible. (978-1-63555-092-4)

Hookin' Up by MJ Williamz. Will Leah get what she needs from casual hookups or will she see the love she desires right in front of her? (978-1-63555-051-1)

King of Thieves by Shea Godfrey. When art thief Casey Marinos meets bounty hunter Finnegan Starkweather, the crimes of the past just might set the stage for a payoff worth more than she ever dreamed possible. (978-1-63555-007-8)

Lucy's Chance by Jackie D. As a serial killer haunts the streets, Lucy tries to stitch up old wounds with her first love in the wake of a small town's rapid descent into chaos. (978-1-63555-027-6)

Right Here, Right Now by Georgia Beers. When Alicia Wright moves into the office next door to Lacey Chamberlain's accounting firm, Lacey is about to find out that sometimes the last person you want is exactly the person you need. (978-1-63555-154-9)

Strictly Need to Know by MB Austin. Covert operator Maji Rios will do whatever she must to complete her mission, but saving a gorgeous stranger from Russian mobsters was not in her plans. (978-1-63555-114-3)

Tailor-Made by Yolanda Wallace. Tailor Grace Henderson doesn't date clients, but when she meets gender-bending model Dakota Lane, she's tempted to throw all the rules out the window. (978-1-63555-081-8)

Time Will Tell by M. Ullrich. With the ability to time travel, Eva Caldwell will have to decide between having it all and erasing it all. (978-1-63555-088-7)

A Date to Die by Anne Laughlin. Someone is killing people close to Detective Kay Adler, who must look to her own troubled past for a suspect. There she finds more than one person seeking revenge against her. (978-1-63555-023-8)

Captured Soul by Laydin Michaels. Can Kadence Munroe save the woman she loves from a twisted killer, or will she lose her to a collector of souls? (978-1-62639-915-0)

Dawn's New Day by TJ Thomas. Can Dawn Oliver and Cam Cooper, two women who have loved and lost, open their hearts to love again? (978-1-63555-072-6)

Definite Possibility by Maggie Cummings. Sam Miller is just out for good times, but Lucy Weston makes her realize happily ever after is a definite possibility. (978-1-62639-909-9)

Eyes Like Those by Melissa Brayden. Isabel Chase and Taylor Andrews struggle between love and ambition from the writers' room on one of Hollywood's hottest TV shows. (978-1-63555-012-2)

Heart's Orders by Jaycie Morrison. Helen Tucker and Tee Owens escape hardscrabble lives to careers in the Women's Army Corps, but more than their hearts are at risk as friendship blossoms into love. (978-1-63555-073-3)

Hiding Out by Kay Bigelow. Treat Dandridge is unaware that her life is in danger from the murderer who is hunting the woman she's falling in love with, Mickey Heiden. (978-1-62639-983-9)

Omnipotence Enough by Sophia Kell Hagin. Can the tiny tool that abducted war veteran Jamie Gwynmorgan accidentally acquires help her escape an unknown enemy to reclaim her stolen life and the woman she deeply loves? (978-1-63555-037-5)

Summer's Cove by Aurora Rey. Emerson Lange moved to Provincetown to live in the moment, but when she meets Darcy Belo and her son Liam, her quest for summer romance becomes a family affair. (978-1-62639-971-6)

The Road to Wings by Julie Tizard. Lieutenant Casey Tompkins, Air Force student pilot, has to fly with the toughest instructor, Captain Kathryn "Hard Ass" Hardesty, fly a supersonic jet, and deal with a growing forbidden attraction. (978-1-62639-988-4)

Beauty and the Boss by Ali Vali. Ellis Renois is at the top of the fashion world, but she never expects her summer assistant Charlotte Hamner to tear her heart and her business apart like sharp scissors through cheap material. (978-1-62639-919-8)

Fury's Choice by Brey Willows. When gods walk amongst humans, can two women find a balance between love and faith? (978-1-62639-869-6)

Lessons in Desire by MJ Williamz. Can a summer love stand a four-month hiatus and still burn hot? (978-1-63555-019-1)

Lightning Chasers by Cass Sellars. For Sydney and Parker, being a couple was never what they had planned. Now they have to fight corruption, murder, and enemies hiding in plain sight just to hold on to each other. Lightning Series, Book Two. (978-1-62639-965-5)

Summer Fling by Jean Copeland. Still jaded from a breakup years earlier, Kate struggles to trust falling in love again when a summer fling with sexy young singer Jordan rocks her off her feet. (978-1-62639-981-5)

Take Me There by Julie Cannon. Adrienne and Sloan know it would be career suicide to mix business with pleasure, however tempting it is. But what's the harm? They're both consenting adults. Who would know? (978-1-62639-917-4)

The Girl Who Wasn't Dead by Samantha Boyette. A year ago, someone tried to kill Jenny Lewis. Tonight she's ready to find out who it was. (978-1-62639-950-1)

Unchained Memories by Dena Blake. Can a woman give herself completely when she's left a piece of herself behind? (978-1-62639-993-8)

Walking Through Shadows by Sheri Lewis Wohl. All Molly wanted to do was go backpacking…in her own century. (978-1-62639-968-6)